IN LEAH'S WAKE

By

Terri Giuliano Long

ISBN 0-9754533-9-4

Printed in the United States of America

This is a work of fiction. Names, characters, places, and
incidents either are the product of the author's imagination or
are used fictitiously. Any resemblance to actual events or
locales or persons, living or dead, is entirely coincidental.

Published August 2011

For my husband, Dave, and our daughters,
Jen, Lib, Nat and Kim

Acknowledgements

To all—family, friends, colleagues and students—
who have blessed my life with your kindness and grace,
my heartfelt thanks.

Special thanks to my LIW—Virginia Smith, Holly Robinson and Elisabeth Brink—for your friendship and invaluable insight; Stacey Miller, for your kindness and generous gifts of time and expertise; Emlyn Chand, book marketing goddess and amazing friend, for your guidance and encouragement; Jacqueline Druga-Johnston, for editorial advice; The Reverend James A. Woods, S.J., for believing in me, giving me hope; my sister, Audrey LeBourdais, CRNA, for your love and medical expertise; my parents, Audrey and Jerry Giuliano, for cheering me on, teaching me to persist. A million thanks and hugs to my wonderful family, Dave Lucchese and Chris Kanner, treasured sons by marriage, our beloved daughters, Jen, Lib, Natalie and KK, our little princes, Sam, Matthew and Griffin, and princess, Alexandra, for your love, friendship, inspiration, and, above all, for being yourselves—you are the light of my life.

And my husband, Dave—for all and for everything.

". . . little heart of mine, believe me, everyone is really responsible to all men for all men and for everything. I don't know how to explain it to you, but I feel it is so, painfully even. And how is it we went on living, getting angry and not knowing?"

Fyodor Dostoevsky
The Grand Inquisitor

Prologue

March

Justine strikes a pose before the full-length mirror hanging on her closet door. Chin up, hands by her sides. She draws a breath. "My dear. . ." she begins, and stops mid-sentence. Wrinkles her nose. She's got it all wrong. She's too—Too *stiff*. Too grownup. Too *some*thing.

She rakes her fingers over her short dark hair, sweeping the bangs out of her eyes, tugs at the hem of her pink baby-doll pajamas. She's scheduled to deliver the candidates' address at her Confirmation Mass this afternoon. When she learned, six months ago, that she had been selected speaker, Justine was ecstatic. Now, the very idea of standing in front of the whole congregation, telling hundreds, maybe thousands, of people how she's learned from her own family what it means to be part of God's larger family makes her sick to her stomach.

She has no choice. She made a commitment.

She folds her hands primly, setting them at chest height on her imaginary podium, glances at her cheat sheet, rolls her lower face into a smile, and begins again. "My fellow Confirmation candidates," she says this time. Justine crumples the paper, tosses it onto her bed. *My fellow Confirmation candidates.* What a *dork*. She sounds about twenty, instead of thirteen.

She screws up her face. "I can't do this," she says, wagging a finger at the girl watching her from the mirror. She would feel like a hypocrite.

Justine plods to the bathroom, pees, pads back to her bedroom. The forecasters are predicting snow, starting later today. A dismal gray stratus hangs over her skylight. Her room is dark, the air raw. Her sister's blue and gold Cortland High sweatshirt lies in a heap at the foot of her bed. Justine pulls the sweatshirt over her head, retrieves the balled-up paper. With the back of her hand, she flattens it out, and returns to the mirror to practice.

As always, on first glance, the girl in the mirror takes Justine by surprise. She's grown two inches since Christmas, isn't chubby anymore, her belly flat, the clavicle bones visible now at the base of her throat. She pushes her bangs out of her pale, darkly fringed eyes. With her fingertips, she touches her cheeks. Her features have matured, her nose long and straight, like her mother's, her cheekbones defined. She curls and uncurls her toes. She wears a size six shoe, a size and a half smaller than Leah. Her toes are long and slim, the nails painted blue.

Justine crushes the sheet of paper, tosses it in the trash, strolls to her window, raises the honeycomb shade. Spring feels a long way away, the yard empty, the trees bare. A rush of cold air streams in, under the sash. The air smells of snow. Justine presses her hand against the cool glass, the way she and her sister used to do on the windshield of their father's car, when they were small. *Stop,* their father would scold. *You're making a mess.* She smiles, remembering how Leah loved egging him on. She pulls her hand away from the glass, watches her prints disappear.

Justine wishes, sometimes, that she could disappear, too. *Poof,* just like the handprint.

Poof, just like her sister.

PART ONE

JUST DO IT

One

Just Do It

September

Zoe and Will Tyler sat at the dining room table, playing poker. The table, a nineteenth-century, hand-carved mahogany, faced the bay window overlooking their sprawling front yard. Husband and wife sat facing one another, a bowl of Tostitos and a half-empty bottle of port positioned between them. Their favorite Van Morrison disc—*Tupelo Honey*—spun on the player in the family room, the music drifting out of speakers built into the dining room walls.

Dog, their old yellow Lab, lay on a ratty pink baby blanket, under the window.

Zoe plucked the Queen of Hearts from the outside of her hand, and tucked it center. She was holding a straight. If she laid it down, she would win the hand, third in a row, and her husband would quit. If she didn't, she would be cheating herself.

The moon was full tonight, its light casting a ghostly shadow across the yard. The full moon made Zoe anxious. For one of her internships in grad school, she'd worked on the psych ward at City Hospital, in Boston. On nights when the moon was full, the floor erupted, the patients noisy, agitated. Zoe's superiors had pooh-poohed the lunar effect, chalked it up to irrationality, superstition. But Zoe had witnessed the flaring tempers, seen the commotion with her own two eyes, and found the effect impossible to deny—and nearly all the nurses concurred.

"Full moon," she said. "I hadn't noticed. No wonder I had trouble sleeping last night."

Will set his empty glass on the table. With his fingers, he drummed an impatient tattoo. "You planning to take your turn any time soon? Be nice if we ended this game before midnight."

"For Pete's sake, Will." Her husband had the attention span of a titmouse. He reminded her of Mick, a six year-old ADD patient she counseled—sweet kid, when he wasn't ransacking her office, tossing the sand out of the turtle-shaped box, tweaking her African violets.

"What's so funny?" he asked, sulking.

She shook her head—nothing, *Mick*—and forced a straight face.

"You're laughing at me."

"Don't be silly. Why would I be laughing at you?"

He peered at his reflection in the window. Smirking, he finger-combed his baby-fine hair, pale, graying at the temples, carving a mini-pyramid at his crown.

"Nice do. Could use a little more gel," she said, feeling mean-spirited the instant the words slipped out of her mouth. The poor guy was exhausted. He'd spent the week in California, on business, had flown into Logan this morning, on the red-eye. Though he had yet to fill her in on the details, it was obvious to her that his trip had not gone well. "Sorry," she said. "Just kidding." She fanned out her cards, hesitated for an instant, and laid down the straight.

"Congratulations." Scowling, he pushed away from the table. "You win again."

"Way to go, grumpy. Quit."

"I'm getting water," he said, tamping his hair. "Want some?"

Dog lifted her head, her gaze following Will to the door, yawned, and settled back down.

Her husband stomped across the kitchen, his footfall moving in the direction of the family room. The music stopped abruptly, and the opening chords of a Robbie Robertson tune belted out of the speakers. Zoe loved Robbie Robertson, "Showdown at Big Sky" one of her favorite songs. That didn't mean that the entire state of Massachusetts wanted to hear it.

"Will," she said, gesturing from the kitchen. "Turn it down. You'll wake Justine."

She waited a few seconds, caught his eye, gestured again. The third time was the charm.

Exasperated, she returned to the dining room, bundled the cards, put them away in the sideboard, and gathered the dishes. The toilet flushed in the half-bath off the back hall. Seconds later, she heard her husband rattling around the kitchen, slamming the cabinet doors. Last spring, Will had won a major contract for his company, North

American Construction. Since then, he'd been back and forth nonstop to the West Coast, spending two weeks a month in San Francisco, servicing the client. Zoe hadn't minded his traveling, at first. Over the past two years, with the glut of office and manufacturing space in the northeast, construction starts had dropped, and his sales had taken a serious hit, his commissions steadily dwindling. To compensate, initially they'd relied on their savings. In January, they'd remortgaged the house. When the California job arose, Will had jumped on the opportunity. He had no choice, especially with Leah headed to college next year. But the situation, lately, was brutal. Will hated traveling, hated flying, hated living out of a suitcase. And he resented missing Leah's soccer games. Last November, as a sophomore, their daughter had been named Player of the Year on the *Boston Globe* All-Scholastic team. A week later, in his year-end summary, the sports reporter from the *Cortland Gazette* had called Leah the "best soccer player in the state." The head coaches from the top colleges in the area—Harvard, Dartmouth, Boston College, BU—had sent congratulatory letters, expressing their interest. Will wanted to be home to guide her, meet the prospective coaches, help her sort through her options. Zoe didn't blame her husband a bit. But it didn't seem to occur to Will that his traveling disrupted her life, too. Last year, she'd developed a motivational seminar, called "Success Skills for Women on the Move." Now that the girls were practically grown, the workshops were her babies. The extra workload at home, added to the demands of her fulltime job at the counseling center, left her with no time for marketing or promotion, and the workshops had stagnated. Zoe understood her husband's frustration. It irked her when he minimized hers.

Will appeared in the doorway, a few minutes later, empty-handed. Will was tall, a hair shy of six-one. He'd played football in college, and, at forty-five, still had the broad shoulders and narrow waist of an athlete. Amazing, really: after eighteen years of marriage, she still found him achingly sexy. Crow's feet creased the corners of his intelligent blue eyes and fine lines etched his cheekbones, giving his boyish features a look of intensity and purpose, qualities Zoe had recognized from the start but that only now, as he was aging, showed on his face.

After work, he'd changed into a pair of stonewashed jeans and a gray sweatshirt, worn soft, the words "Harvard Soccer Camp" screened in maroon lettering across the chest. Absently, he pushed up his sleeves, and peered around the room as though looking for something. "Zoe—" Normally, he called her Honey or Zo.

"I put the cards away." She thumbed the sideboard. "You quit, remember?"

"Do you have any idea what time it is?"

She glanced at the cuckoo clock on the far wall. "Ten past eleven. So?"

"Where's Leah?"

At the football game, with Cissy. "They've been going every week. Did you forget?"

"She ought to be home by now."

"She's only ten minutes late." Their daughter was a junior in high school. They'd agreed, before school started this year, to extend her weekend curfew to eleven. "She'll be here soon."

Will stalked to the window, grumbling. Dog rose, and pressed her nose to the glass.

Their driveway, half the length of a soccer field, sloped down from the cul-de-sac, arced around the lawn, and straightened, ending in a turnaround at the foot of their three-car garage. In summer, the oak and birch trees bordering the property obscured their view. Now that most of the leaves had fallen, the headlights were visible as vehicles entered the circle.

"She has a game in the morning." Will stretched his neck . His upper back had been bothering him lately, residual pain from an old football injury he'd suffered in college.

Zoe came up behind him, pushing Dog's blanket aside with her foot, and squeezed his shoulders. "You're tight."

He dropped his chin. "From sleeping on the plane. Got to get one of those donut pillows."

"You know Leah. She has no sense of time. I'll bet they stopped for something to eat."

"I can't see why Hillary won't set a curfew. Every other coach has one."

"Relax, Will. It's not that late. You're blowing this out of proportion. Don't you think?"

A flash of headlights caught their attention. An SUV entered the cul-de-sac, rounded the circle, its lights sweeping over the drive and across their lawn, and headed down the street.

Bending, Will ruffled Dog's ears. "Reardon's coming tomorrow, specifically to watch her. She plays like crap when she's tired."

The Harvard coach. She should have known. "So she doesn't go to Harvard," she said, a tired remark, fully aware of the comeback her words would elicit, "she'll go someplace else."

"There *is* no place else."

8

No place that would give her the opportunities, the connections... *blah, blah, blah.* They'd been over this a million times. If their daughter had the slightest aspiration of going to Harvard, Zoe would do everything in her power to support her. As far as she could tell, the name Harvard had never graced Leah's wish-list. It was a moot point, anyway. For the last two terms, Leah's grades had been dropping. If she did apply for admission, she would probably be denied.

"Reardon has pull," he offered, a weak rebuttal in Zoe's opinion. "He's been talking to Hillary about her. She can't afford to blow this opportunity."

Opportunity? *What* opportunity? "Face it, Will. She doesn't want to go to Harvard."

"If she plays her cards right, she can probably get a boat."

Zoe opened her mouth, ready to blast him. He'd received a full football scholarship from Penn State, and dropped out of college. Was that what he wanted? A college drop-out in a couple years? Noticing the purple rings under his eyes, she held back. "You're exhausted." His plane had barely touched ground at Logan Airport when he was ordered to NAC's corporate office in Waltham, for a marketing meeting. He hadn't had time to stop home to change his clothes, never mind take a short nap. "Why don't you go to bed? I'll wait up."

The look he returned implied that she'd lost it. "You think I could sleep?"

"For all we know, they had a flat."

"She would have called."

"So call her." *Duh.*

"I did. I got voice mail."

Shoot. "You know Leah. Her battery probably died." She was grasping at straws. Leah was sixteen years old. That phone was her lifeline. Still, it could be true. It was possible. Right?

Leah had totally lost track of time. She and Todd had been hanging out at the water tower for hours, perched on the hood of Todd's Jeep, drinking Vodka and OJ, admiring the beautiful night. This place was perfect, the most perfect place in the universe, maybe. Big sky, lots of trees. From here, they could see the whole town, just about—the river, the railroad tracks. An orchard. In the valley, lights began to blink out. Leaning back on her elbows, she gazed up at the heavens. "Look," she said, mesmerized by the inky black sky, the billions and billions of stars. "The Big Dipper." As she stared into space, time fell away, the past merging seamlessly with the future, this moment, up here, with Todd, the only reality there ever was or ever could be.

Todd took her hand, drawing her close, so close she could smell the spicy deodorant under his armpits. Just being with Todd Corbett made her feel dizzy all over. Todd was, by far, the most beautiful boy she had ever laid eyes on. His hair was long on top, short on the sides. He had full lips, and the most fabulous blue eyes, like, like crystals or something. A Romanesque nose, the exact nose she'd once told Cissy she'd die for, only now that she'd seen it on Todd, she realized that that particular nose was meant for a boy. Best of all, he had this incredible aura, all purple and blue, like James Dean or Kurt Cobain.

She curled her legs under her, laid her head on Todd's chest.

They met at a party, the Friday before school started. Todd had been on tour for the past two years, working as a roadie for a heavy metal band called "Cobra." Leah knew he was back—that was all anybody was talking about—had recognized him instantly, from all the descriptions.

She couldn't believe her luck. Todd Corbett! And alone! She'd heard he was hot. He was even better looking in person. Looking back, she couldn't believe she'd been so brazen. She left Cissy in the lurch, sashayed right over to him, took a seat beside him, on the living room floor.

The movie he was watching was stupid. People clopping across a field like zombies, their arms outstretched. They reminded her of herself and Justine when they were little, playing blind. Even the makeup looked phony.

"What are you watching?" she asked.

"*Night of the Living Dead.* Flick's a classic. Hey, haven't I seen you someplace before?"

Maybe, though she couldn't imagine where. Todd couldn't possibly have remembered her from high school. She was only a freshman when he dropped out.

"Leah Tyler, right? You're that soccer chick."

The wind swished through the trees. Leah shivered and Todd shrugged out of his worn leather bomber, draped his jacket over her shoulders. He reached into the pocket of his jeans, retrieved a small plastic bag half-full of weed, began rolling a joint. He licked the edge of the paper, lit the joint, inhaling deeply, and handed it to her, the smell rich and exotic and sweet.

Leah had never smoked marijuana until she met Todd. She used to be scared, which was dumb: weed was totally harmless. (The first few times she smoked, she had to admit, she'd been disappointed.) She pulled, her chest searing, struggled to hold the ice-hot smoke in her lungs.

Suddenly, she was coughing, waving her arms.

"You OK, babe?" Todd rescued the joint. With the other hand, he patted her back.

Once she was breathing easily again, he laughed, a sweet laugh that left her feeling dignified, rather than cheesy or stupid. He pinched the joint between his index finger and thumb, took a hit to demonstrate, and brought it to her lips, holding it for her. "That's it, babe. Good."

They smoked the joint to its stub, and he showed her how to fashion a roach clip from twigs. Afterward, he offered to drive her home. "Don't want you getting in trouble or nothing."

"That's OK," Leah said dreamily. "I don't have to go yet."

Todd hopped off the hood of the Jeep, pulled a flannel blanket from the back of the truck, and spread the blanket on the grass, under a giant oak tree. Leah watched him smooth it out, his hands dancing, the whole world intensely colored, brilliantly alive. She heard the lonely trill of a cricket, calling from deep in the valley, smelled the damp autumn earth, felt the cool blue breeze on her face. Todd was gliding toward her now, floating on air. He scooped her into his arms, lifting her from the hood of his Jeep, and laid her on the blanket. And kissed her.

At eleven thirty, Zoe dialed Leah's cell phone again. When Leah didn't pick up, she tried Cissy, both times reaching voice mail. "I don't believe those two," Zoe said, infuriated. "I'll bet they changed their ringers. The little devils probably know it's us."

"That's your daughter for you," Will huffed.

"She's *my* daughter now?"

By eleven forty-five, Zoe was chewing her cuticles. And Will was pacing.

"This is it," Will announced. "I'm calling the cops."

"You can't be serious. What do you plan to tell them?"

He opened his cell phone. "I can't sit here, doing nothing." He glared at the screen.

"You can't call the cops. She's forty-five minutes late. They'll think we're crazy."

He clicked his cell shut, dug his keys out of his pocket. "Fine. I'll find her myself."

Find her? Where on earth did he plan to look?

"I'll start at the high school."

"The game was over hours ago."

"I'll drive by the Hanson's." He headed for the garage, Dog at his heels.

"And do what?" Cissy's mom, a nurse, worked the early shift at St. John's. Judi was probably in bed by now. He would frighten her if he knocked on the door. "Will? Answer me."

He swiveled to face her. "Look for the car," he snapped, and ushered Dog out the door.

Zoe stood in the mudroom, at a loss, staring blankly at the door her husband had closed. The house, she realized when she came to, was an icebox. She rooted through the hall closet, found a fleece jacket of Will's, and pulled it on, kicked off her shoes, the ceramic tile cool under her bare feet, went to the bathroom, crossed the hall to the laundry, tossed a load of clean clothes into the dryer, and wandered back to the kitchen. She poured a glass of water, gathered the dishes they'd left on the dining room table, and emptied the uneaten chips into the compactor. She loaded the dishwasher. After she finished washing the counter, she flung the rag into the sink, and grabbed the cordless phone, so she would have a phone handy if Will or Leah tried to call.

A family portrait, commissioned last year, hung over the stone fireplace in the family room. For the photograph, the four of them had dressed in blue; their blue period, they'd joked when the photographer showed them the proofs. In the photo, Zoe is sitting on a stool, leaning toward the camera, Will standing behind her, flanked by the girls. Looking at the portrait, you'd never guess how hard it had been for the photographer to capture the shot, the kids squabbling, Will impatient, Zoe frustrated, both parents clenching their teeth. Restless, Zoe stepped down into the family room, sank into the oversized chair next to the fireplace, and curled her legs under her, clutching the phone.

Waiting, she tried to think positive thoughts. *Leah's responsible. She can handle herself.* If the girls had been in a car accident, the police would have contacted them by now. As usual, her effort to avoid negative thoughts conjured them up. Something wasn't right. Leah had been late a few times before, never like this. A half hour was one thing. Zoe often lost track of time herself. She would be at her office, transcribing her notes, look up, notice the clock, and realize she was supposed to have picked up one of the girls—at school, at the mall, at a friend's—fifteen, twenty minutes before. She would rush around her office in a tizzy, collecting her folders and purse, cursing herself for being a neglectful mother, and drive like a madwoman to her destination. But an hour? She checked her watch. And fifteen minutes? This wasn't like Leah.

She wondered if she had missed something. A signal. A hint. This morning, Leah, out of bed by seven, had moseyed into the kitchen, rubbing her eyes. Spotting the sauce pan on the front burner, she'd whined about having to eat oatmeal again. But she always whined when Zoe made oatmeal, which on certain days she found "revolting," on others "disgusting" or "gross." Zoe set the bowl in front of her. "Quit bellyaching," she said. "Oatmeal is good for you."

They were running late. So the girls wouldn't have to rush to catch the bus, Zoe offered to drive them to school. Justine rode shotgun, while Leah dozed in the backseat. At two, Leah called Zoe at work to remind her that she and Cissy planned to go to the game. She was headed directly home after practice, Leah had said; she would fix dinner. At six thirty, when Zoe opened the back door, she smelled Leah's spicy, cumin-laced chili. On the island counter, Zoe found place settings for her, for Will, for Justine, three glasses filled with ice water and lemon. Justine was upstairs in her room, doing her geometry homework. Leah had already left for the game.

Zoe closed her eyes, breathing deeply, attempting to center herself, and, counting backward from ten. . . eight, seven, six. . . summoned an image of her daughter. Leah's face materialized, and her body slowly came into focus. Directing her energy outward, Zoe enclosed her daughter in a protective circle of light. *Be safe, baby,* she whispered. *Be safe.*

Will drove along country roads canopied by the boughs of towering oak trees, the winding streets bordered by stone walls erected in the late 1700's, by the farmers who'd settled the town. In those days, the stone walls served as boundary markers, the average farm occupying fifty acres of land, most of it orchards. It was a hard life, Will thought, working eighteen hours a day, building walls, cultivating the land. He reached for Dog, on the passenger seat, ruffled her ears. "What do you say, Girl?" Dog cocked her head. "Was life harder then? Or harder today?"

The Hansons lived a mile outside the center, on a corner lot in a modest sub-division, built in the late-eighties, a neighborhood of center-entry colonials, garrisons, expanded Capes, set on cramped one-acre lots. Will slowed as they approached the Hanson's newly remodeled Salt Box, he and Dog rubber-necking together. Onion lamps flanked the entrance and the garage doors; matching pole lights lined the drive. The house was dark, the driveway empty. Will turned left, onto the adjacent street, hoping to find a light on in the back of the house, in which case he would knock on the door. Nothing, not even a porch lamp. Frustrated, he rounded the block, passed by the front of the property again, in case he had somehow managed to miss Cissy's car the first time, and headed for the high school, on the off-chance that the girls were still there.

The parking lot was dark when Will pulled in, the lights extinguished hours ago. He pulled down the sloping driveway behind the school, passing the rubberized track, where the soccer players practiced their sprints. He swung by the service entrance, then by the gym, doubled back, and circled the deserted lot, scanning the playing fields. At the ticket booth by football stadium, he parked, and just sat, thinking, Dog curled beside him on the passenger seat.

They'd had no idea, he and Zoe, how easy they'd had it when the girls were young. In their eyes, every little thing seemed like a crisis. They would glance at the window, catch three- year-old Leah zooming down the drive on her Big-Wheel, her legs outstretched, little hands reaching for the sky. In a panic, they would tear out of the house, always an instant too late, too far from their daughter to do anything except cross their fingers and watch. "Leah—" Will would holler, his stomach churning, "hold on." And Zoe would cover her eyes, both parents envisioning the worst, the Big-Wheel rocketing off course, crashing into a tree. Later, the rope swing he'd hung by their deck replaced the Big-Wheel as the most obvious threat. They'd worried about random accidents, obsessed over tragedies they watched on *News Center 5* or read about in the *Globe*: that the girls would fall into the hidden shaft of a well or drown in a neighbor's backyard pool, that a stranger would kidnap one of their daughters when she was outside playing or taking a walk. It was tough being a parent, the welfare of their children utterly dependent on them, yet as long as they were vigilant, as long as they did their job, kept a trained eye on their daughters, their children would be safe. Now that she was older, they had no way of keeping tabs on their daughter. Once the car she was riding in rolled out of the drive, her fate was out of their hands. She could be anywhere, doing anything, with anyone. They had no way to protect her.

"What do you say, girl?" he said finally. "Doesn't look like she's here, does it?"

In a last ditch effort, he took another run by the Hanson's place.

Zoe had fallen asleep clutching the portable phone, her head resting on the wing of her chair. He brushed a curl out of her face, touched her shoulder gently, so he wouldn't startle her.

His wife blinked up at him. "Did you find her?"

He shook his head, dejected.

Dog nuzzled Zoe's leg. Yawning, she scratched the dog's head. "What time is it?"

"Close to one."

"My God." She pulled herself to an upright position. "What do you think is going on?"

Hard to say at this point, he told her. "She didn't call, did she?"

Zoe shook her head in alarm. "You don't think anything's happened, do you?"

"We'd have heard by now."

"I'm worried, Will. This isn't like her."

Will rubbed his neck, squeezing the trapezius muscles, hoping to release some of the tension. "I don't know where else to look. Figured it'd be stupid to keep driving in circles."

His wife attempted to stifle a yawn.

"You look beat," he said. "Why don't you go to bed? I'll wait up."

"You're as tired as I am."

"Go. I can sleep in. You've got to get up in the morning."

"Maybe I should," she said, shifting position. "Have to be up at six. Had to—" She paused, her glazed eyes fixed on the palladium window at the far end of the room. "Sorry." She blinked. "I had to shift my schedule around. Workshop Sunday. Wake me when she comes in? You won't forget?"

"I won't forget."

Will helped his wife out of her chair, walked her to the front staircase, kissed her, and told her to sleep well. From the foot of the staircase, he watched her climb the stairs and wander down the hall to their bedroom. When she closed the door, he went to the kitchen, filled a glass with spring water, brought the glass to the living room, sat on his leather recliner by the window, adjusted the back, and put up his feet. Dog lay on the floor, next to his chair. In ten minutes, she was snoring. He plucked an old issue of *Sports Illustrated* out of the pleated leather pocket on the side of his chair, flipped through. Unable to focus, he tossed it on the floor.

On the windowsill, in front of an eight-by-ten studio portrait of the girls, taken when Justine was a toddler, sat a framed snapshot of Leah. He picked up the photo. They'd been in Cortland for about a year when he snapped the shot. Leah was not quite seven, the youngest child on the under-ten team. Her uniform was two sizes too big, her baggie blue T-shirt skimming the hem of her shorts. The team was in the midst of a game, Leah racing to the net, blond ponytail flying, the ball jouncing in front of her, her tiny face focused, intense.

His daughter was an exceptional player, fast, agile, fiercely competitive, the best player from Massachusetts *ever,* some coaches said. Since she was a child, Will had been grooming her, encouraging her, fostering her talent. Youth soccer, traveling teams. Scholarship to Harvard—that was their plan. They'd practiced, strategized, prepared. Through the rain, the snow, he'd been right there with her. All in service to the crimson uniform she would one day wear. That was her dream, wasn't it? She hoped to play pro. But Harvard first. Time and again, they'd discussed the importance of a good education, the one thing in life that can never be taken away.

Will pushed her, he knew. He wanted the best for his kids. He would do whatever it took to help them succeed, prevent them from repeating the mistakes he'd made. In the spring of his junior year, he'd left Penn State, surrendering a full scholarship, trading his education for a long shot at a music career. In one hour, the time it took to inform his dean he was quitting, walk to the registrar's office and sign a couple of forms, he'd managed to screw up his life. Look at him: forty-five-years-old, stuck in a dead-end job, kissing the asses of people who ought to be working for him. He refused to sit back, watch Leah throw her life away. Kids needed guidance, a motivational coach to push them, keep them focused, drive them when they didn't feel like practicing, pump them up when they lost confidence, spur them on when they wanted to quit.

Will closed his eyes. *God help him.* Tell him he hadn't pushed her away.

Two

Just Do It II

Will sat in his recliner, listening to a Tom Petty recording he'd bought in '89, the day the record came out, the volume low. The clock ticked past one, one thirty, two. Dog lay by his chair, snoring. He considered pouring a bourbon, to help him relax, and immediately thought better about it. Needed to stay alert. Leah had been late for her curfew once or twice before. Never like this. He got up, sat. Got up, paced, went to the kitchen, poured another glass of water. He imagined her lost. Imagined a car wreck, his daughter's body lying on the road, under a tarp.

The seconds ticked. Unable to bear the wait for one more second, he headed upstairs to her room, hoping to find something, a phone number, a name, some clue as to where she was.

Her room was a pigsty, dirty clothes lying on the floor, wherever she'd taken them off, her cleats, shin guards, random shoes scattered over her bed. Her bureau drawers were open, several off track. He stuffed her panties and bras back in the top drawer, pushed it shut, thumbed through the notebook on her nightstand. He lifted her bedskirt, patting the floor under the bed. A Nike poster was taped to the wall over the bed, the top right corner curling into itself. Just Do It, the poster commanded. *Just Do It*. Will shook his head, and looked away. He cleared his daughter's bed, brushing the cereal crumbs from her sheets, and neatened her blanket.

He was set to call the cops, report her missing, when he heard a vehicle rumble down the drive. He raced downstairs, heart hammering, figuring at this hour the news could only be bad.

17

At the foot of the staircase, he stopped to collect himself, and reluctantly opened the door.

A black Jeep Wrangler, its top down, was parked in the drive, next to the light post. And there she was, sneaking toward the garage, the arm of a boy he had never seen before draped over her shoulder. *Thank God*, he thought. Then, *Goddamn, all this time I've been waiting.*

"Leah," he called, choking a shout. "Get in here."

Leah froze, her eyes narrowed, glaring at Will. She tugged on the boy's wrist and the kid, a head taller, bent toward her. His daughter whispered into the kid's ear, the punk taking hold of her hand. He appeared to be six, six-one, Will's height, more or less. Weighed a buck-fifty, tops. Took every ounce of determination he was able to muster not to bolt out of the house, pound the piss out of the kid. Will watched with mounting impatience as they slunk through the shadows under the eaves, past the garage, and up the stairs to the brick walkway that led to the house.

"Get in here," he ordered, as his daughter climbed the three granite stairs, to the stoop.

Leah looked up at him, loopy grin plastered in place. "Dad," she said brightly, her bloodshot eyes darting from Will to the kid. "This is Todd."

Todd. Give him a break. Blond hair, pretty boy lashes. Dressed in ghetto shorts, a black T-shirt. A diamond stud in his right ear. Kid had to be twenty, twenty-one. Too old for Leah.

Will fixed the punk in his sights. Cocky bastard stared him right back.

Leah fidgeted, shouldering away from the boy, and gazed up at her father again, wheedling. "Well, Daddy? Aren't you gonna say hello?"

This time, when she opened her mouth, he caught a whiff of alcohol on her breath. *Christ.* She'd been drinking. "Get in here, Leah." He pushed the screen door open, the hinges creaking. He grabbed his daughter's arm. "Beat it," he said, chinning the Jeep. "Get lost."

For an instant, the three of them stood there, dumbfounded, Will clutching Leah's wrist, congratulating himself for holding his temper. (His old man would have walloped the kid.)

All at once, his daughter exploded, writhing.

"Let *go* of me," she hissed, and jerked her arm free.

Get her inside. That's it—just get her inside. Opening the screen wider, he lunged, and seized his daughter's arm. *Asshole*, she

18

shrieked, batting him away. *Don't touch me.* In a flash, she was five or six, tiny feet planted, fists clenched, sassing him about something, because she wanted to go outside, she didn't want to pick up her toys. He was losing her. His daughter was spinning out of control. In one swift motion, his mind numb, he yanked her inside. Pivoting, he swung left, pulling her clear of the door, so she couldn't get out, couldn't escape. "*Stay* there," he barked. Turning his attention back to the kid, he let his daughter go. In his peripheral vision, he saw her slam into the wall and—*God, no*—slump to the floor.

The kid glowered at Will, his lanky body strung as tight as a bow.

Seething, Will grabbed for the kid, but the boy, too quick, bolted down the steps, and darted across the lawn. Will looked right, left, for a stick, a bat, something to throw. In a rage, he raced toward the Jeep, its engine turning. Screamed at the kid. . . *something, something, something.* . . the words ripping through the hurricane in his head.

Will?

"Will, please."

Turning, he peered blankly at Zoe, and turned back to the truck, its engine roaring, the Jeep squealing out of the drive.

"Come in here. Please." She stood on the stoop, holding the screen. A breeze blew across the lawn, catching the hem of her nightgown, the filmy fabric swirling over her bare feet.

"What's the matter with you?" she demanded, when he went in.

With his palms, he rubbed his eyes. "Don't know. I lost it."

He heard movement, glanced up at the landing at the head of the stairs. Their younger daughter, tiny, dark-haired Justine, stood behind the balustrade, dressed in her pink baby-doll pajamas, peering down at them, Dog at her side. She met his gaze, her expression inscrutable, and retreated to her bedroom, trailed by the dog.

Leah was nowhere in sight.

"She's in bed," Zoe said. "I sent her up."

"What did she say?"

Zoe hedged. "Nothing."

"She said something."

"Let's talk about it in the morning, all right? When everyone's calm."

"I want to know what she said."

His wife shrugged. "That you're crazy. Okay? She said you're psycho. Look, I'm going up. We can talk about this tomorrow. All right? Are you coming?"

He'd be up in a while, he told her. He was too worked up to sleep.

For a good hour, he sat in his recliner, with his eyes closed, replaying the events of the night, *John Barleycorn Must Die*, an old Traffic recording he had listened to religiously in his younger days, in the background. Images flashed through his mind, Will in a rage, seizing his daughter, watching her fall. Over and over the vision played, like a horror movie on an endless reel, the nightmare waking him with a jolt, starting all over again each time he fell back to sleep. He longed to wake her, sit on the edge of her bed, the way he used to when she was a child, tell her a story. *Once upon a time, in a land far, far away.*

He never intended to hurt her.

It was nearly dawn when he turned off the lights. At the entry to Leah's room, he paused, tiptoed inside, stood over her bed. Leah was a fitful sleeper. Her blankets lay in a tangle at her feet. He pulled the sheets and blankets over her, tucking her in, and kissed her forehead. As he was leaving the room, he caught sight of the poster, lit by a slim shaft of early morning light. Just Do It. How many times over the years had he repeated that slogan? To himself? To Leah? No guts, no glory. Put up or shut up. Do what needs to be done. Do it. Just do it.

Just do it.

Three

A Girl Who Knows What She Wants

Leah woke the next morning, her head as big as a beach ball. She'd stay here all day, if she could, in her warm bed, cocooned in the blankets and sheets, but she had to pee. She dragged herself up, shivering as she threw off the covers, swung her feet over the side of the bed. Her head hurt, her stomach, her legs, even her arms. She'd never been this sick in her life. She probably had cancer. *Oh God*, she was going to barf. She dropped her head between her knees, staying put until her stomach had settled enough to move, and plodded to the bathroom.

She could hear her father in the kitchen, fixing breakfast. The odor of maple bacon drifted upstairs, making her gag. In a minute, he would be up here, ordering her downstairs to eat. Her team had a game this morning, at ten, which meant she had to be on the field— she checked her alarm clock—in an hour. She flopped back onto her bed, pulled the covers over her head. No way was she playing soccer today. Not after last night, after her father tweaked out.

She turned on her side, burying her face in her pillow, closing her eyes. Around midnight last night, Todd retrieved a blanket from the truck, spread it over a pillow of pine needles and leaves. She pictured him up on his elbows, staring down at her, the planes of his face accentuated by the shadows. The wind swished through the trees. He pulled her close, pushing her hair away from her face, winding the stray hairs around his finger. His hand slid from her shoulder to her hips. And he kissed her. She made a kissing noise on the pillow. The extra pillow had slipped to her feet. Eyes closed, she wriggled lower, tucking the pillow between her knees.

21

Todd, she whispered. *Todd.*

Her shades snapped up all of a sudden, startling her. In the harsh morning light, Todd's face vanished. Digging lower, she squeezed her eyes tighter, willing him back. She heard her name again, *yes*, pushed the covers down. *Todd.* And rolled onto her back.

When she looked up, her father was standing over her bed.

"Time to get up, Leah. The Harvard coach is coming today."

Her father plunked on her bed. The *nerve* of that man. She curled into a ball, drawing the covers over her head, and wriggled sideways, toward the wall, so his butt wouldn't touch her. Her father's slimy hand slithered under the covers. Now he was wiggling her big toe, the way he used to when she was little. She yanked her foot back.

"Come on, kiddo," he coaxed. "You have to get up." He'd made blueberry pancakes. As if his stupid pancakes made up for last night.

"Go a*way*," she spat, her words garbled by the mountain of blankets and sheets.

"Leah, your team is—"

Who cares *if you're tired?* she heard. *The competition is practicing, even when you're not. . .* "depending on you, Leah" . . . *dedication is what counts. . .* "talk to you, honey". . . *suck it up. . .. get up, get up. . . do it. . . time to get up. . . time for soccer. . . time . . .practice. . . do it. . . just do it. . . Just do it.*

Leah clapped her hands over her ears. "Go away," she cried. "Get out. Get away from me." Why did her father do this to her all the time? Why couldn't he let her be?

"I'd like to talk to you, Leah. Please."

"No," she cried. "I'm not going. You can't make me."

The toilet flushed in the bathroom between her room and Justine's, the faucet sputtered, and water splashed into the sink. Leah's sister was washing her hands. Now she was brushing her teeth. Perfect little angel, never in trouble. Perfect little *dork*. Leah hated her sister. She hated them all—her mother, her father, Justine. Her parents didn't care one iota about her. They cared about controlling her, was all. They expected perfection, wanted perfect robots for kids. Well, guess what? She wasn't a robot. They would have to be satisfied with just one.

"Fine." Her father sighed. "Stay home, if that's what you want."

She pulled the covers down slightly, exposing only her eyes.

He leaned forward, dropping his hands between his knees. "I'm sorry, baby." Her father shook his head. "I blew it," he said, and sat there, staring at the floor, waiting for a response.

22

In Leah's Wake

Good. Leah dug down under the covers. She had him right where she wanted him. She would forgive her father, eventually. First, she planned to make him suffer. She pulled the covers over her head, her elbows angling upward, creating an air tunnel so she could breath.

Her father's weight shifted, and she felt the spring of the mattress.

Wait. Leah shot out of bed. He couldn't leave. They hadn't talked. They hadn't worked things out. At the landing, she leaned over the rail. "Dad," she called. "Daddy?"

After the game, Leah scrambled out of the car, leaving her father alone in the garage, rifling through the contents of his glove compartment, hunting for the stupid inhaler he'd insisted was in there. They'd won the game, two to one, but Leah wasn't her usual self. "What's that supposed to mean? You couldn't breathe?" her father demanded, the instant they got in the car. She. Couldn't. Breathe. Which word did he not understand? "Where's your inhaler?" Look in the glove compartment, he told her. Wasn't in there. *Look.* She twisted the knob, let the door bounce down. One-by-one, she removed the maps—Massachusetts, Ohio, Vermont—laid them on the seat, along with a wrench, the BMW manual, a pile of receipts, and stuffed it all back in. "See," she said, screwing her face into an I-told-you-so-smirk. "It's not in there."

What did he expect from her, anyhow? She'd scored the winning goal.

"You looked like crap," her father said. She would be lucky if Reardon wanted her, after today. She wasn't hustling, he told her, and proceeded to tick off all the reasons why the Harvard coach had probably lost interest.

Leah turned to the window and, chewing her thumbnail, stared at the empty cornfields, the hills that rolled off to nowhere, the crumbling stone walls. So she hadn't played her best today. Who cared? Harvard was her father's dream, not hers. She'd been to the college plenty of times. She'd visited Harvard for the first time when she was eleven (her father had arranged for a tour); she'd attended their soccer camp; she'd been to the stadium to watch their women's team play. She was not impressed, the buildings old, the dorms run-down. The kids all clumped through the Yard, their shoulders stooped, burdened by the weight of their backpacks, looking frazzled and harried. Why would she want to go to a school where she would be miserable all of her life? College was supposed to be fun. She'd taken tons of virtual tours on the Web, found plenty of schools she did like—UCLA, for example. But why bring them up? Her father would never send her to UCLA. No matter which college she chose, unless it was Harvard, her father would be disappointed. She couldn't please him, so why bother trying?

Her father was still blathering on about Harvard.

"Coach Thomas says Wake Forest wants to recruit me," Leah announced, surprising them both. "Maybe I'll go there. Or maybe I won't go to college at all. You don't have a degree. And you did all right."

"Wake Forest?" her father said incredulously. "You want to go to *Wake Forest?*"

Now she was lounging on her futon, her long legs crossed at the ankles, the cordless phone lying, face down, on her thighs. Her sister, in the adjoining bedroom, was pounding on her heavy bag, probably pretending she was Buffy The Vampire Slayer again, the bag whacking into their adjoining wall. Leah banged on the wall. "Cool it, Justine," she hollered. "I can't hear myself think." The sound died down and she picked up her phone, and dialed Todd's number. She got a busy signal again. Why didn't his mother spring for call-waiting? This was so annoying. She'd been trying his line every ten minutes since she got home.

Leah went to her desk, booted her computer, opened her AOL Messenger. No one online. Checked her e-mail, all junk. Bored, she clicked on the icon for the program her parents had ordered from The Princeton Review, when she was a freshman, to help her study for the SAT test. While she was waiting for the file to load, she paged through the workbook.

The math questions were easy. When she looked at a problem, she saw the logic pattern that led inevitably to the answer, the same way she recognized the conflation of angles, saw play patterns taking shape on the soccer field, and knew, better than the coach waving at her from the sidelines, exactly where she needed to be. English had always been tougher.

The first question was easy. Apple is to fruit as asparagus is to____. *Vegetable.*

The next made her think. Hillary is to mountaineer as Columbus is to____. The answer was supposed to be explorer, but imperialist could have fit, too. After all, didn't America really belong to the natives? Her teachers all acted as if Columbus were some kind of hero, and the entire country celebrated a day in his honor, when in fact his so-called discovery had led to the death of thousands of indigenous people, the disruption of a way of life that was every bit as significant as the lives of the Fifteenth Century Europeans. Where did people get off, insisting one lifestyle was intrinsically better than another? Who had the right to make that judgment?

Leah closed the program. Shut down her computer. Why was she taking this test? If she had no idea what she wanted to study, what she wanted to be, what was the point in going to college? The truth was, she knew hardly anyone her age who had a clear idea of what they wanted to do when they were older. Oh, the kids all pretended to know, but it was obvious to her that they were only repeating the dreams their parents laid out.

Just last week, in social studies class, the discussion had turned to careers. (Mr. Mulvany, her social studies teacher, was constantly going off on a tangent.) They'd been talking about the war in Iraq and somebody said something about enlisting in the military; next thing she knew, they were talking about the US social and economic outlook for the future, then their careers.

Leah hadn't minded the shift in direction. She was tired of talking about Iraq. Everybody had an opinion about the invasion, whether the US had a right to be there, but the talk was always distanced, impersonal, as if, regardless of the outcome, the speaker would not be affected. How could people discuss something so important, yet not really care?

The discussion in social studies carried that same dispassionate tone. Mr. Mulvany went around the room, asking each student what course of study he or she planned to pursue. Their answers were shockingly vague. Law, one student replied; business, said somebody else. Not a single person named anything specific. What *branch* of law? Leah wanted to shout. What *sort* of business? Yet Mr. Mulvany was not at all fazed. Each time one of Leah's classmates named a lofty profession, he would nod appreciatively, as if to say, *See? Cortland High is doing its job.*

When her turn came, Leah mumbled her answer. A professional soccer player, she said, the choice they all expected to hear. Since she was a little girl, she'd dreamed of playing in the Olympics, the first step toward a professional soccer career. Lately, she'd begun to wonder if playing pro soccer was something she really wanted to do. The adults in her life all pushed her in that direction, told her she'd be a fool not to play; maybe she'd simply adopted their dream.

An article she'd read in *Sports Illustrated* about Mia Hamm had got her to thinking. Mia's first marriage, to her college boyfriend, had fallen apart because she put soccer first. Now she was married to Nomar Garciaparra, the former shortstop for the Red Sox. All summer long, while she trained for the Olympics and he played ball, they'd lived on opposite coasts, Mia in California, Nomar in Boston. For all Leah knew, Mia was perfectly happy. But that wasn't the life Leah wanted to lead. She couldn't imagine being married and living apart. It was hard enough for her mom, with her father traveling all the time. She didn't want that life for herself.

But if she didn't play soccer, what would she do? She had no interest in anything else. And if she didn't have a clear idea of what she wanted to study, why go to college at all? It was a waste of time and money, going to college just to bide time. She didn't understand why her parents pushed her so hard. It was their money that she would be wasting. It didn't make sense.

Someone tapped on the door. Leah was about to tell her dad to buzz off, when Cissy Hanson strutted into the room, glossy black hair cascading over her shoulders, looking—in a red cashmere wraparound sweater and Levis 501 jeans—as if she'd just stepped out of *Glamour*.

"What do *you* want?" Leah turned back to her computer, logged onto AOL.

Except for soccer, where they had no other choice, Leah hadn't spoken to Cissy in weeks. The girl was a tool, spreading those vicious rumors about Todd. According to Cissy, when Todd was in El Paso with the band, he'd been arrested—for dealing coke. Cissy's mom worked with Todd's mom, in the emergency room at St. John's. Supposedly, his mom told her mom the story. After his arrest, the band dumped him, she claimed. The girl was a liar. When Leah heard the rumors (Cissy didn't have the guts to tell Leah directly), she confronted Todd herself, demanded to know what had happened. The arrest wasn't even his fault. The roadies framed him.

Cissy waved a pair of Leah's old jeans. "I thought you might want these."

Leah shot Cissy a narrow look, told her to put the jeans on the bed. She didn't honestly expect Leah to believe she'd come to return a pair of jeans? Cissy never returned Leah's clothes without being haunted. Besides, she borrowed the jeans a month ago. Why return them today?

Cissy folded the jeans in half, and laid them at the foot of Leah's bed, the light glinting off a small silver charm at the base of her throat. The other half of Leah's Best Friends necklace! She and Cissy bought the necklaces when they were in the eighth grade. Leah had been wearing hers for so long that the necklace had become a part of her, like a birthmark or a mole. When she looked in the mirror, she didn't see it anymore. Horrified, Leah stuffed her charm under the neckline of her sweatshirt.

Hard to believe she'd ever been friends with Cissy at all, never mind best friends. They met when they were ten, the year Leah's dad coached their traveling team. Cissy's father had walked out on the family the summer before, and her mom had trouble getting Cissy to practice. To help her out, the Tylers volunteered to drive. Cissy looked like a geek, with her pixie haircut and plastic-rimmed glasses. She didn't talk much, either. And she wouldn't look at you when she did. Leah had put up with Cissy, but she didn't think all that much of her. She didn't dislike Cissy. She never poked fun at her, as all the other kids did. Cissy was just sort of *there*; she had nothing to recommend her as a friend. In time, Cissy had grown on her, weirdness and all. By the end of the year, they were inseparable. Last year, when Leah's mother started her workshops, Leah had practically lived at the Hanson's. Cissy's mom was engaged to one of the doctors at work and she let the girls help with the wedding arrangements, so there was always plenty to do.

"So what's up?" Leah asked, a cue for Cissy to either speak up or leave.

Cissy sat on the floor, raking her fingers over the rug. "You played awesome today."

Leah rolled her eyes. "I played like crap."

"My step-dad knows the Harvard coach, you know. They went to college together."

As if Leah cared.

"Mr. Reardon wants to recruit you."

Leah perked up at the word "recruit," out of curiosity more than anything else.

"He kept telling my dad what an amazing athlete you are," Cissy said, then she gave Leah a blow-by-blow account of Coach Reardon's reaction to each of the plays Leah had made.

"Seriously?" Leah asked, her anger softening. "You really think he likes me?"

"Likes you?" Cissy shook her head vehemently. "He thinks you're *great*."

Maybe Leah had been too hard on Cissy, refusing to return her messages, ignoring her calls. She thought about all the fun she and Cissy used to have, riding their bikes across town to Sullivan Farms

Ice Cream, splitting double-fudge sundaes; their sleepover parties, she and Cissy talking and giggling until the sun came up in the morning. Leah missed having a best friend, a girl she could talk to, someone to share her secrets. She and Cissy had been best friends for far too long to let a boy stand between them—any boy, even Todd Corbett. Cissy didn't know Todd. Once they were better acquainted, Cissy would realize she had misjudged him, and they could all be friends. Maybe the three of them could hang out one day soon, go to lunch or a movie. It didn't have to be either-or, Leah suddenly saw. She had plenty of love to share with them both.

Leah was about to suggest a date, when Cissy spoke up. "I talked to your dad."

That was weird. "When?"

"After the game."

"What did he say?"

Cissy stared at the rug. "He told me what happened last night."

"My father told you *what*?"

She shrugged, biting her lower lip, her nose twitching.

"Let's go, Cissy. Spit it out."

"The kid's bad news, Lee."

How dare she! Leah got up and opened the door. "Get out," she said. "Now."

"It's for your own good, Lee. The kid's a drug deal—"

Leah scooped the jeans off her bed, hurled them at the wall. "I said, 'get out.' Get *OUT*."

Leah slammed the door and threw herself on her bed, sobbing. What an idiot she was! What possessed her to think she could trust Cissy Hanson, to think they could ever really be friends? Cissy wasn't her friend. Cissy had never been Leah's friend. She'd used Leah, was all. To weasel her way into the popular crowd. Leah hated that girl. She wished Cissy would die. Well, maybe not die, but go away. Someplace far, like maybe Alaska.

Someone touched Leah's shoulder.

"Go away," she said, flinching, and pulled the pillow over her head.

"Leah?"

Leah sniffed, and rolled onto her side. It was only her sister.

"You OK, Lee? Did you and Cissy get in a fight?"

With the back of her hand, Leah wiped her eyes. "I'm fine," she said, sitting.

Leah's sister was not much bigger than the life-sized dolls the girls had played with when they were younger, her tiny hands and feet two-thirds the size of Leah's. She had drop-dead eyes, pale aqua-green, like the Caribbean Sea. Her bone structure was exotic, like their mother's, but her features had not yet developed, the planes of her face less defined than their mom's, her cheeks fleshy and round. In a couple of years, once Justine grew a few inches and thinned out a little, Leah would have to guard her boyfriend. Now, her sister looked like a chubby little pixie.

Justine's bangs were damp. And she was wearing that ridiculous Buffy the Vampire Slayer getup. (Why she thought she looked like Buffy in a hot pink T-shirt and skimpy white shorts was a mystery.) Under the shorts she'd donned electric blue tights. Justine was twelve years-old, way to old to be dressing this way. Too bad for Justine that their parents had listened to the principal of her school, and allowed her to skip second grade. If they'd let her stay in her own grade, with friends her own age, she might have had half a chance to be cool. Leah sniffed. She was about to set her sister straight about those idiotic clothes, when she caught sight of Justine's squinched little face, and felt bad. "What is it, Jus? Did you want something?"

Justine fingered the gold cross hanging from a thin chain around her neck. As if she were not a big enough geek already, Leah's sister was like a religious fanatic—a total contradiction, in Leah's opinion, considering her sister's obsession with science. To Justine, CCD was an actual class, rather than the obligatory hour of boredom each week that normal kids considered it to be. Leah would not be surprised if, someday, her sister joined a cult, like Hare Krishna or Opus Dei.

"Justine," Leah said, again. "What do you want?"

"Sorry." Justine blinked, and handed Leah an envelope. "This came for you."

Leah glanced at the postmark—Cornell—folded the envelope into an airplane, and sent it sailing toward her nightstand. The plane, missing its target by an inch, drifted lazily to the floor.

Confused, Justine scooped the envelope up.

"Keep it," Leah said. It was just another recruiting letter. Coaches weren't even supposed to be contacting her yet. According to MIAA rules, college coaches were not allowed to talk to a potential recruit until the summer before senior year. Rules, evidently, didn't apply to adults. She got at least one letter a week. "I don't want it."

Her sister looked shocked. "How come?"

Leah mulled the question over. Whatever she said would fly directly from her sister's lips to their parents' ears. Maybe that would be good. Their parents trusted Justine. Maybe if they heard Leah's plans from her, they would listen. "I'm not going to college," Leah explained, her fledgling confidence finding its wings. "I might travel around for awhile."

"But you have to go, Lee. What would you do for a job?"

Good question. She hadn't thought that far ahead. Miraculously, a plan materialized: She would be a famous rock star! She didn't say that, of course. Her sister would laugh. Leah played no instruments, after all, had never written a song. She could sing a little, though, and she could certainly dance. "I might try out for one of those reality shows," Leah said, inspired, picturing herself on *The Real World* or *Survivor*. "Lots of famous people got their start that way."

Justine nodded uncertainly, picked up the Paddington Bear Leah had been sleeping with lately, and stroked its head. If Leah kept her mouth shut, didn't engage in conversation, maybe her sister would leave. Go to her own room. Work on her science project or something. You'd think the dumb fair was next week, instead of next year. It was all the little dork talked about.

"So how's your project coming?" Leah asked sweetly, a nasty hint dusted with sugar.

"Great," Justine said, her eyes lighting up. She had this idea. She'd love an opinion. Did Leah mind? Leah flipped through the red vinyl CD case on her nightstand. Most of her CDs were old, recordings she'd bought before she met Todd: Michele Branch, Justin Timberlake. Leah winced. *Britney Spears*. Nothing she would ever listen to now. Leah plucked her new Ani DiFranco CD out of its plastic sleeve, went to her bureau, and slid the CD into the changer.

Justine's idea had something to do with the Milky Way, some new discovery she'd read about in *Science*. Something about planetary movement. Leah heard a few words here and there, nodded now and again, so her sister would think she was listening. She couldn't get Todd out of her head. Todd was cool, and good-looking, but there was a lot more to him than that. He was mature. He didn't get caught up in appearances. He didn't expect her to measure up to some arbitrary standard. He didn't judge her, didn't expect her to pretend she was someone she wasn't. He couldn't care less whether her picture was in the newspaper or if, until recently, she had been the most popular girl at Cortland High. When Leah complained about practice, when she said she hated soccer and told him she didn't want to play anymore, he advised her to do whatever felt right. Never mind what people thought or what anyone said. If she wasn't happy playing soccer, she should quit. With Todd, she felt freer, more like *herself* than she did with anyone else.

". . .orbit." Justine stopped talking and looked over at Leah. "So what do you think?"

"Yeah," Leah said. "Awesome."

"No, I mean what do you *think*? Is it a good idea?"

"I don't know, Justine." Leah was an idiot in science. She'd gotten a C- on her last biology test. Their parents had gone ballistic. Had Justine forgotten already?

"Never mind," Justine said. She'd figure it out. "So what happened last night? I heard you crying."

"Nothing, really," Leah said, and told her sister the story.

"Who's Todd?"

"This boy I'm seeing."

Justine's eyes widened. She wanted to know exactly what Todd looked like, how tall, what color eyes, where Leah had met him, how long they'd been dating. "Not too long," Leah said. "Six weeks and one day." But she expected it to last. "This is it, Jus. He's the one."

"Really? You think so?"

"Yeah," Leah said. "I do."

"That's cool."

Maybe her little sister wasn't such a geek after all. A ceramic cast of Justine's hand sat on her nightstand. Leah wondered what Justine would say if she knew Leah had been using the hand as an ashtray. Maybe Leah should tell her. Make it a test, to see if her sister was trustworthy or not. Before she had a chance to broach the subject, Justine said, "bye," and got up.

"Where are you going? You just got here. I thought you wanted to hang out."

To Holly's, Justine informed her. She and Holly had to plan their costumes. Halloween, Justine reminded her, was only one month away. "Hey? Want to come with us?"

Trick-or-treating? "I don't know, Jus." Sixteen was way too old for trick-or-treating. Leah would feel like a dope. She pictured the three of them, prancing around the neighborhood, making total fools of themselves. Come to think of it, it might be a hoot to see the scandalized look on their neighbors' faces when they saw a sixteen-year-old at their door.

Justine was still waiting. Just Do It, said the poster on the wall above Leah's bed. *Just do it*. Leah shrugged. "Maybe." If she wasn't grounded. She'd think about it, Leah promised. She'd see.

Four

Women on the Move

On Sunday, Zoe invited Leah to her workshop. "Success Skills for Women on the Move," Zoe called it. She held her seminars in the basement of the Unitarian church in the center. Although she marketed her program to a general audience (the wording on her brochure was clearly inclusive), the majority of her students were middle-aged women, hoping to make a major change in their lives: empty-nesters eager to resume their career, battered wives desperate to leave abusive husbands, women battling weight or alcohol problems, or, occasionally, drugs.

The seminars began as a fluke. Zoe had read so many self-help books, listened to so many tapes, she felt qualified, she used to joke, to give a workshop herself. "So, do it," her husband had pressed. She had the credentials. With Will's encouragement, she'd put together a program, based on the advice she gave the moms of her patients: *Believe in yourself. Focus on the joy in your life. Never give up.* In addition to the quarter-page ad she placed in the *Cortland Gazette*, she'd circulated brochures; she'd posted flyers on the bulletin boards in the back of the Natural Grocer, in the churches and synagogue in the center of town, in the front window at the dry cleaner, the post office, the video store. She'd expected a small turnout that first time, maybe four or five people. But when the day arrived, a dozen women were lined up outside the door, and the workshop was such a success that she'd felt obliged to continue.

Early on, Zoe offered her workshops on weeknights. Once the initial excitement died down, the numbers had dwindled. In response to suggestions written on the evaluation sheets she passed out at the

33

end of each class, she'd switched the workshops to Sunday. Zoe hated giving workshops on Sunday: Sunday was a family day, she believed, a day to rest, a day to catch up. These days, the workshops were her saving grace, the one place where she felt relaxed, where she wasn't constantly anxious or stressed. She looked forward to Sundays, the solitary hours she spent at her office at the counseling center reviewing her notes, the drive through town on her way to the church, the quiet ride home, Zoe both elated and spent, to Lily Farm Road.

If she could convince Leah to join her today, if they had a chance to spend time together in a relaxed, neutral atmosphere, Zoe might have a chance of reaching her daughter. She'd done some investigating yesterday, while she was at work. This Corbett character had dropped out of high school, she'd learned. After high school, he'd bounced around for two years, working on and off as a roadie for a rock band. She'd also heard a disturbing rumor concerning Corbett and drugs. Zoe was less inclined to believe that part of the story. Leah was a sensible kid. She didn't smoke cigarettes, for heaven's sake. Zoe couldn't imagine her being involved with a drug dealer.

After work, she discussed the information with Will. It was important, they agreed, to present a unified front. "It'll be hard," Zoe said, with both of them as upset as they were, "but we need talk this through rationally." Be as nonjudgmental as possible. Ask honest questions; listen to her responses. The objective was for Leah to realize they were on her side. If they could help her see how dangerous this Todd character was, maybe she would get rid of him on her own.

When they finished strategizing, they called Leah into the living room, and closed the French doors. The conversation began on a reasonable note, Zoe asking Leah nicely why she'd been late. Didn't she know they would worry? Their daughter answered their questions, less fully than they'd hoped, but at least she didn't shut them out. She and Todd were at the water tower; she'd lost track of time; they hadn't done anything wrong. For ten minutes, Zoe and Will listened patiently. Just as it seemed they were about to break through, Will called Todd a loser, and the accusations and counter-accusations began to fly. The battle escalated, their voices rising, Zoe begging them to calm down. Will brought up the underage drinking, mentioned the cops, and Leah fled the room, sobbing, scrambled up to her bedroom, and slammed the door.

Zoe expected a moderate turnout today. She checked her list. Fifteen pre-registered. Even if a few women brought friends, the gathering would be intimate, a perfect setting in which to introduce

Leah. Justine sometimes accompanied Zoe to the seminars; at twelve, Zoe's younger daughter could still be persuaded to tag along with her mother. Whenever Zoe had invited Leah, her elder daughter had always declined. Normally, Zoe took the rejection in stride. At Leah's age, Zoe would not have walked to the mailbox with her mother. Today, she was more persistent.

"So, what do you say?" Zoe set a plate of blueberry pancakes in front of her daughter.

Leah poured a glass of orange juice, and set the glass on the counter at the center island. "Why don't you ask Justine?" She plunked herself on a barstool. "I bet she'd go with you."

Justine was at church, Zoe reminded her. "With your dad. She has that introductory Mass for the Confirmation candidates today, remember?" After Mass, they planned to attend the reception in the church hall.

"I'd go," Leah said, staring into her juice. "But I've got a ton of homework to do."

She's lying, Zoe thought. After their blowout yesterday afternoon, she didn't blame Leah for turning her down. But they needed to talk. "Please," she wheedled. "It'll be fun."

"Success Skills, Ma? That's not exactly my speed."

"My back has been bothering me," Zoe said, rubbing the base of her spine. (She wasn't lying, exactly; it was more like stretching the truth.) "I could use some help setting up."

"Well." Leah looked doubtful. "If you *really* need the help."

On the way to the seminar, her mom gave Leah a crash course on Success Skills.

"Understanding *how* to achieve your goal is crucial to success," her mother explained. "First, I teach the women to develop a plan. . ."

Earlier, when she first saw her mother, Leah had been angry with her for taking part in that so-called "discussion" yesterday afternoon. Leah understood why her parents were pissed. If her daughter had stayed out until three in the morning, she would have been worried, too. Still, her father had no right blaming Todd. Calling him a loser. How could her father say that? He didn't even *know* the boy. Besides, it wasn't Todd's fault they were late. Leah was the one who'd pushed to stay out. Still, her mom hadn't really done anything wrong. She wasn't the one trash-talking Todd. She hadn't defended him, either. That ticked Leah off. Even so, it was no more fair for Leah to blame her mother for her father's behavior than for her father to blame Todd for hers.

Leah tuned the radio to the soft rock station her mother listened to when she was alone, and fastened her seatbelt. Her mother had a soothing voice. Leah loved listening to her talk, her mom's voice rising and falling, like waves at the ocean. It was hard not to daydream. She said "uh-huh" when it seemed appropriate, nodded now and again to show she hadn't lost interest.

Her mother, Leah suddenly noticed, had stopped talking.

"So," Leah asked. "How do you get them started?"

She advised them to find a mentor, her mother replied, someone whose skills they could emulate. "Say you want to be a pianist, for example." Her mom's eyes slid sideways. *A pianist?* Leah detested piano. When she was a little girl, her parents had forced her to take lessons. She would sit in front of the keyboard for hours, banging the keys, pretending to practice, until her mother, exasperated, would finally let her get up. "Hypothetically," Leah's mom said. Leah nodded, relieved that her mother hadn't completely forgotten her childhood years. "Anyway, you look for the best pianist, someone who plays music you're interested in, and copy her routine."

"Like Ani?"

"Ani?"

"You know, Ani DiFranco? The CD I played after breakfast."

"OK, say Ani practices scales for an hour a day."

"I don't know, Ma. I don't think Ani practices. She's just naturally good."

"Right," her mother said, her dubious sideways glance implying exactly the opposite.

The light turned red as they approached the intersection. Across the street, a heavy-set girl in overalls and a navy-blue sweatshirt emerged from Dunkin' Donuts, toting a bag in one hand, a coffee cup in the other. Her face was long and slim, narrow for someone so pudgy. She had a pug nose, stringy blond hair that drooped past her shoulders. Hope, her name was. Todd had introduced the girls, the weekend before last, at a bonfire by the high-tension wires, across town. Leah and Hope had talked for five minutes, and Hope said she had to jet, she was meeting Lupo, her boyfriend—Todd's best friend, it turned out—and took off. Hope opened the front door on the passenger side of a dilapidated black Cadillac, with an "I Heart Jesus" sticker affixed to its trunk. The Cadillac's left taillight was missing. Leah reached across her mother's lap, tooted the horn, and tooted again, waving both arms this time, so that Hope wouldn't miss her.

Hope made a sour face, and climbed into the car.

"Who was that?" her mom asked. "Did you know her?"

"Nobody." Leah slid low in her seat, chewing the cuticle on her pinky. "Just some girl."

The light turned green, and the car pitched into the crossroad. "I've got an idea," her mother exclaimed. They could be a team. Leah would handle administrative duties at first, circulating flyers, placing ads. Once they both felt comfortable, she'd teach Leah how to present.

Leah rolled her eyes. Her mother conjured up some nutty ideas, but this one, *this* one was the looniest yet. "I'm still in school, Ma. Remember?"

"No problem, sweetie." They couldn't let simple logistics derail them. Leah's mom leaned closer to the wheel, smiling broadly. Programs like theirs took time to catch on. By the time they developed a steady following, Leah would be finished high school, and college would be much more conducive to their routine. Her mom painted scenes of herself and Leah, crisscrossing the country, conducting their workshops. They would be much more than business partners, she said. They would be friends. "Who knows? Maybe we'll be on Oprah one day."

As whacky as the idea sounded, Leah was tempted. She liked the idea of traveling, seeing new places. Plus, it would be nice to do something for other people, for a change. The workshops had clearly had a positive effect on her mom. Since she started presenting the seminars, her mother's confidence had soared. Though Leah hadn't given any real thought to it before, she had noticed. Her mother had lost ten pounds. Since losing the weight, she wore brighter, more fashionable clothes. She seemed happier now, less frustrated, less moody. But Leah wasn't her mother. She lacked her mom's drive. Except for soccer, she had never been a success. She couldn't imagine standing before an audience, dispensing advice. Leah pictured the two of them, lying side-by-side on a lumpy bed in some motel room in Paducah, boning up on material. Never in a million years. Besides, even if she were somewhat intrigued, Leah would never leave Todd.

"There are weeds in every garden." On her grease-board, Leah's mother drew weeds, invading a patch of roughly sketched flowers. "We have to learn to deal with disappointment."

Florescent lights hung from the ceiling in the church basement, magnifying the natural light streaming through the small rectangular windows to the left and right of the room. The hall, with its speckled linoleum floor and muted green walls, reminded Leah of the emergency room at St. John's, where she'd worked last summer, running errands for Cissy's mom. In place of the hospital odors of rubbing alcohol, medication, disease, the hall smelled of incense and candles. A wooden cross hung on the wall behind the podium, an impression of a crucifixion, not at all like the life-sized suffering Jesus in St. Theresa's, the Catholic church where Leah's family belonged.

A woman in the front row raised her hand. As soon as Leah's mom completed her sentence, she called on her. The woman's polyester slacks made a crinkling noise when she stood. "Deal with disappointment?" The woman sighed. "It sounds easy. But how do you *do* it?"

"Look," Leah's mother replied, a sweep of her hand indicating that what she was about to say included them all. "We're here. That's the first step."

The woman grinned and took her seat.

Leah's mother looked so professional, standing beside the podium, a grease-board and flip-chart beside her. She wore patent-leather pumps, a black pencil skirt and flowing silk blouse, the shimmering jade fabric intensifying her aqua-green eyes. As she talked, she drew diagrams and wrote bullets with a red magic marker, her audience scribbling furiously on their notepads.

Leah sat on a metal folding chair, next to the podium. It was weird, sitting in front of an audience, listening to her mother speak. Weeds in every garden? The advice was so cheesy, so unoriginal, and yet, maybe because of the way her mother projected so much of herself into her words, she sounded totally convincing. Leah wondered who these women were, what they were about. She searched their faces for clues, tried to devise stories for the women sitting in these three rows of metal folding chairs in a church basement on a Sunday, when they might have been out doing a million other things: shopping, cooking a roast beef dinner, raking their lawns. These women didn't look at all as she had expected. They seemed, well, normal, Leah supposed. Most were dressed in cotton or wool slacks, with matching sweater sets or button-down blouses. A woman in back wore a plaid suit jacket and skirt. They didn't look wounded, or desperate, as she had imagined, didn't appear to be the sort of people who'd need Leah's mother to pull them along. Yet here they were, on the edge of their chairs, hanging onto her words.

During the break, the participants milled around the room, napkins in hand, chatting with one another, taking turns stopping by the podium to ask Leah's mother a question. They were seated now, attentive again, their chairs arranged in a semi-circle for this part of the program.

"As I was saying." Leah's mom scanned the audience. "We can't be afraid to break self-destructive patterns."

The obese woman sitting beside Leah offered Leah her chips. Leah took the bag, thanked her, and set the chips on the floor, under her chair.

"We have to stand up for ourselves. Eliminate the negativity in our lives. We've got to be strong." Zoe paused, to give the message a chance to sink in. "Have to avoid toxic relationships. Get rid of the people who bring us down," she added, directing a meaning-filled smile at Leah.

Leah squirmed. Her mom was right. If she were ever to fly, be her own person, she had to stop allowing the adults in her life to control her. She had to live her own way. Had to break free. Since she met Todd, she'd become stronger, more independent. But she had a long way to go.

As the afternoon wore on, people began opening up. They talked about their lives, their long-term goals, what they planned to do when they left the workshop. "Tell me," Leah's mother said, and gestured for them to speak out. "Be specific. The more specific we are, the better our chances of accomplishing our goals." The heavy-set woman next to Leah leapt out of her seat. "I'm cleaning out the refrigerator," she announced. "The instant I get home." Her neighbor pumped her fist and everyone cheered. "I'm ordering flyers for my business," shouted somebody else. *Going back to school. Traveling to Italy. Getting my realtor's license. Designing a website.*

I'll stop biting my nails, Leah thought. I'll be my own person.

In the car, on the way home, Leah said, "I'm impressed, Ma."

"Thank you, honey. I appreciate your vote of confidence."

"I mean it," Leah said, turning the radio up. "You're great with them."

The light changed. Zoe stepped on the gas, and the car jerked into the intersection.

Leah grabbed the handhold over her door, let out a yelp.

"Sorry." Zoe grinned sheepishly. "Think there's a Success Skills workshop for driving?"

"Can I ask you a question?" Leah asked, once they'd stopped giggling.

"Certainly, sweetheart. Anything."

"What made you do it? The seminars, I mean."

"That's a tough question." She'd been unhappy. No, unhappy was the wrong word. Frustrated. Discontented, maybe. Something, Zoe said quietly, was missing. She signaled their turn onto Main Street. Don't get her wrong: she loved her family. She squeezed Leah's forearm. Most days, she enjoyed her job. It was just—"How can I explain it?" She needed something more. Something to give her life meaning. She wanted to do something positive, give back. She wanted to feel as though she was accomplishing something, making a difference. "I thought if I could help people make important changes in their lives, I'd be doing something worthwhile."

"Was it hard?" Leah reminded her of the long hours she'd spent developing, organizing, marketing her workshops. She reminded Zoe of her so-called friends, who'd discouraged her, who tried to convince her that in a tiny suburb like theirs she'd never attract enough attendees to make the venture worthwhile, her colleagues, who'd warned her that she was wasting her time. With all that work, didn't she get tired? Leah asked. "Did you ever think about quitting?"

"At times," Zoe admitted. "When I got frustrated, I'd remind myself of what I was trying to accomplish. That would always get me going again." Zoe told Leah about the cards and letters she received after the workshops, thanking her, telling her—she laughed—she was an angel. But it was the confidence in the women's eyes at the end of the day that made it all worthwhile.

After that, Leah grew quiet.

They passed an alfalfa field, the parcel among the fifty acres of conservation land the town had bought or been gifted over the last fifteen years. The farmer was working today, his tractor towing a flail mower across the meadow, cutting hay. Zoe recognized his orange panama hat, the brim shielding his eyes from the sun. They drove by a cornfield, the harvested stalks lying in the furrows, waiting to be shredded for compost. Soon, the fields gave way to forest.

Leah yawned, and stretched out, her head on Zoe's lap. Within minutes, she was asleep.

Zoe switched from the radio to the CD of Liszt piano solos that she always listened to after her workshops. The CD was a gift from one of her attendees. "You'll like the freethinking music," the woman had said, and she had been right.

Zoe stroked Leah's temples, pushing the hair out of her daughter's eyes. Zoe felt sick about yesterday's fight. The business with Todd was as much her fault as Leah's. If she'd paid closer attention to her daughter, instead of allowing herself to be driven by the demands of work, had not been so caught up in her own problems, Leah would not have needed affirmation from a person like Corbett. But that was all in the past, Zoe vowed. From now on, if one of her children needed her, she planned to be available. She would rearrange her patient schedule so she was free to pick up Leah after practice, would attend every game. She would set aside at least four hours of individual, quality time, per week, for each of the girls. She would pack their lunches. Bake cookies. Sew Halloween outfits. She'd be the perfect mother. *Better than perfect*, she thought, her ideas spinning, and brought herself up short. *Let's take this a step at a time.*

On Old Orchard Road, a mile from home, Leah opened her eyes.

"Can't believe I fell asleep," she said, yawning. "I was having this crazy dream."

"What were you dreaming about?"

Leah sat, rubbing her eyes. "I don't know. I forgot already. What's this music?"

"Liszt. *Hungarian Rhapsodies*, it's called. One of my students gave it to me. Like it?"

"It's cool," Leah said, fingering her belly ring. Kind of— Wild, or something."

"It's gypsy music. Did it hurt?" Zoe eyed the ring. "Having it pierced, I mean."

"Not too much. You mad I got it?"

Zoe squeezed Leah's thigh. "No, sweets. But I do wish you'd talked to me, first."

"You're weren't home," Leah said, the hint of an accusation in her voice.

"I'm sorry, honey. I'd like to have been there for you. That's all I meant."

"Dad was pissed." Leah scraped her thumbnail, chipping the garish blue polish.

Yes, Zoe remembered. He'd been angry with her, too. In the Tyler house, by order of both parents, belly rings were expressly forbidden. If the site became infected, the infection could lead to peritonitis. *If you'd stay on top of things, she might not have done this*, he'd charged, once the girls were in bed. "So it's my fault?" Zoe had countered. "Like you're ever around?" As usual, the argument ended in a stalemate. "Dad doesn't mean to be so hard on you, honey," she said. "He just worries."

Leah slid her hands under her thighs. "He doesn't need to." She wasn't a baby.

"I know, hon." Zoe signaled their turn on to Lily Farm Road. "It's just, it's scary being a parent. The decisions you make now—"

"Will affect the rest of my life. God, Mom. Can't you say something different for once?"

"We're your parents, sweetie. It's our job to provide guidance."

Leah bolted upright. "You are such a hypocrite. All day long you tell those women to make their own decisions. And you tell your own daughter she's supposed to listen to you?"

Zoe edged uncomfortably toward her door. True, she had advised the women to take control of their lives. But that advice was geared toward adults. "You'll be an adult soon enough, Leah. Then you can make all your own decisions. For now—"

"I already am an adult."

"You're sixteen, honey. I know you feel like an adult—"

"Well, guess what, Mom?" Leah lifted her butt, shifted aggressively to her right. "In November, I'll be seventeen. And you and Dad won't be able to control me anymore."

"A legal adult," Zoe snapped. She was a child therapist. She was well aware of the state laws governing the legal age of adulthood. Her jaw tightened. "Until you're a responsible, grown adult—living on your own—your father and I are responsible for you."

"So I'm irresponsible now?"

Zoe caught herself, before she went on a rant about Corbett. They'd spent a perfect day together. She'd felt closer to Leah today than she had in ages. She refused to end the day with a fight. She reached for Leah's arm. "Honey, listen. I'm not trying to control you. All I said—"

Leah jerked her arm away. "Is I'm a baby."

Be patient, she told herself. *Take a deep breath.* Zoe eased the Volvo alongside the mailbox, retrieved the mail, folding the smaller items into a magazine, and tucked it in the accessory pocket on her door. "Honey." She cleared her throat, forcing a smile. "Think about it, for one minute. How would you feel if your daughter came in at three—"

"Oh my God," Leah cried. "That's why you were so big on me coming." Leah scooped her team jacket from the floor. "So you could get me alone. Try to get me to dump him. I hate to be the one to break it to you, *Mom*, but you wasted your time. It's up to me who I go out with."

"Leah, please." Zoe eased the car down the drive. "I said nothing about your boyfriend."

"Don't lie to me now."

Zoe hedged. "Well, you have to admit, he isn't exactly the type of person any parent—"

Leah covered her ears.

"wants to see their child—"

"La, la, la, la, la," Leah sang, her hands clapped over her ears.

Zoe pried Leah's hands from her head. "He's not good for you, honey. He'll hurt you—"

"La, la, la, la, la," Leah trilled, her voice drowning Zoe's.

"He worked as a roadie for a rock band. Listen to me. He's not a nice kid."

"I don't need this." Leah rolled her coat in a ball, and flipped the lock on her door.

Zoe caught hold of Leah's wrist. "For God's sake. The kid sells drugs."

"You tricked me," Leah spat. "I'm never going with you again. Anywhere. Ever."

"Don't worry," Zoe shot back. She was sorry she'd convinced the little brat to join her today. Why, for one second, she'd thought she might be able to get through to Leah confounded her. She should have known this would happen. "Believe me, I have no intention of asking."

"I hate you," Leah cried. "I hate you. And I'm not pretending I don't anymore."

Leah slammed the door, then she was hurtling into the house.

The song changed, the histrionic gypsy music ringing in Zoe's ears. She slapped the dash, not really thinking, her fingers fumbling with the dial, and cut the CD off.

She'd lost her cool, said all the wrong things. Leah was lashing out, spewing words, trying to hurt Zoe as much as Zoe had hurt her. Leah wanted reassurance. She wanted to be told she was capable and smart. She wanted to know Zoe was proud of her, that she trusted her to make her own decisions. Zoe had let her down. She'd seen the ache in her daughter's eyes, the disappointment. Maybe this was what people meant by the term "growing pains," not the pain children experienced in their joints as their limbs grew, but the ache they felt in their hearts.

Leah's dollhouse stood on a shelf at the back of the garage, next to some paint cans. She and Will had bought the dollhouses at a yard sale, one for each of the girls, when Leah was six. At night, when the kids were asleep, she and her husband had refurbished the houses, painted the shingles, papered the walls. She cut squares from old scatter rugs to carpet the floors, sewed tiny Cape Cod curtains for the

43

miniature windows. For years, Leah's dollhouse stood on the wooden table next to her bed. One day last summer, she decided she was too old for a dollhouse, and brought it down here. Leah wasn't a baby. Zoe knew that. She wanted to protect her daughter. Prevent her from hurting herself, making an irrevocable mistake. Zoe stared straight ahead, Leah's dollhouse, her tricycle, her wooden blocks dissolving in a watery blur. *If only you knew how hard it is to watch you stumble, to see you in pain.* Pull yourself together, Zoe said to herself. *Don't let your failures defeat you.* Yet here she was, her failures like anchors, sucking her under the sea.

Five

Blue Ribbon Day

Looking back, this is the day Zoe sees: In May, she turned thirty. Will is away, in California, she thinks, though she may have California in mind, because her husband is headed to California this week. They live in Hudson, in a red, Cape Cod-style house they bought two years earlier, when Will's commission finally outpaced his draw. At night, terrified to be alone with her children in this secluded house, she has trouble falling asleep. After she tucks the girls in bed, she blocks all the doors, sits in the living room, with the dog at her feet, paging through magazines, the TV and radio off, listening for intruders. At dawn, she falls asleep.

It's late morning, the end of October—her father's birthday. Today is the seven week anniversary of Zoe's abortion. Exhausted, not yet recovered from the procedure, Zoe is dozing, dreaming about the baby she lost. Her head aches when she comes to.

She rubs the sleep from her eyes. Leah stands at her elbow, cuddling her filthy pink blanket, a bright yellow tutu stretched over her playsuit. The elastic legs of the tutu pinch her legs; her shorts bunch at the thighs. Her bangs are caught unevenly by blue and yellow plastic barrettes. Leah plugs her thumb in her mouth, brings the blanket's satin edge to her nose.

The child is four years old, too old for a blanket.

For the past eight months, since the birth of her sister, Leah's behavior has steadily regressed. Zoe was alarmed, at first, when her four-year-old suddenly began wetting her pants, mangling her once clearly articulated words. The pediatrician assured her that this is

45

normal. "A new sibling is stressful," he said. "She feels displaced. You'll be surprised, how fast she adjusts."

"Take your thumb out of your mouth, honey. You're not a baby anymore. Here—" Zoe curls her fingers. "Give Mommy the blanket."

"I wanna play wif Hammy," Leah says, thumb garbling her words.

"Take your thumb out of your mouth." Zoe extends her hand. "And give me the blanket."

Leah shakes her head furiously.

Zoe's neck aches. She grimaces, rolling her head, left and right. "Fine," she says, too tired to argue. "Have it your way."

The door of the cuckoo clock on the wall in front of the staircase swings open and a bright red rooster springs out. Cuckoo, the bird sings. Cuckoo, cuckoo. *Noon.* She's expecting her parents for lunch in an hour. She's serving tuna salad and chips. She needs to make a dessert.

"How about if you go outside for a while? Play on your swings? Dog's out there."

"Don't wanna go outside," Leah says, unplugging her mouth. Leah turns the blanket over in her hands, twists until the blanket looks like a filthy pink beach ball. "I wanna play wif Hammy. Hammy likes me, Daddy says."

The hamster reminds Zoe of a rat. Will brought it home last month, after one of his trips. In a flash, Zoe sees Leah clinging to her father's legs, begging him not to go. Their daughter asked for her father over and over, at least a dozen times a day, the entire time he was gone. *Where my Daddy? Why he leave?* In a time zone three hours earlier than theirs, he phoned them at night, after she'd fallen asleep. Zoe sees him standing in the doorway, two weeks later, hands behind his back, a guilty grin on his face. Peering over his shoulder, she sees the aquarium, a Habitrail, a month's supply of wood chips. A giant bag of pellets leans against his luggage.

"Where's my girl?" With a flourish, he produces his gift. "Where's Leah?"

"For God's sake, Will. She doesn't need another *pet.*" Zoe had her hands full already, with that puppy he brought home six months ago. The Lab wasn't even housebroken yet. Poor thing—they still called her Dog.

Will pretended Zoe was kidding. *This isn't a joke,* she told him. *You've been gone three weeks this month. Your daughter is starting to forget what you look like.* He turned away. He had no choice, he told her. Problem on one of the jobs. A Marriott, she thinks. Something about the union, the plumbers threatening to strike. His responsibility. He'd negotiated the contract. He'd much rather be home. Didn't she know that? She shook her head, listening, not quite believing.

Leah refuses to budge.

This child is her father's daughter. She's inherited his dazzling blue eyes, his height—at four, she reaches her mother's waist—Will's sturdy athlete's build and silky blond hair. This stubborn streak, too, comes directly from him.

"I wanna play wif Hammy." Leah paws Zoe's arm, climbs onto her knee.

Zoe lifts her daughter, sets her back down. "Later, OK? We'll get him out after lunch."

Leah huffs. This is almost comical, the way she stands, feet apart, legs braced as though ready to fight, eyes flashing, tiny fists pressed to her hips. A miniature Will, Zoe thinks, picturing her husband in nearly that same stance, the night before he left.

"California?" Zoe said. "And you're not taking us?"

She and Will lived in California, before they were married. They met in Berkeley. He was a folk artist then, in his other life, as he calls it. He was playing a gig and she was in the audience, with a group of friends, at a table at the back of the room. Her friends were noisy, rude. Enraged, he'd ended the show early. She looked for him afterward to apologize. They talked for hours that night, and he'd driven her home. Within three months, they were living together. She misses those days, California, the loving, spontaneous couple she and Will used to be.

He would be on site all day. He laid a starched white shirt in his suitcase. "You and the kids would have nothing to do."

Sure they would. They could go to the beach, for example, and she ticked off a list.

"That's ridiculous. I have to work. Besides, we don't have the money."

Damn it, she said. *Why don't we have the money? Where does it go?* Look around. Where it always goes. *Where it always goes?* Toward your three-piece suits, she wanted to say, your nights on the town. *Not here*, she did say, *into the house, as you promised.* They'd made all sorts of plans when they bought the house. They talked about renovating the kitchen. Will promised to raise the ceiling in their bedroom, finish the basement, build a playroom for the kids, none of which he'd done. Here he was, palms upturned, as if he had no idea what she was talking about.

"Will—please?"

47

"Jesus Christ, Zoe." He looked at her hard, and turned away. What? Tell her. Damn it. She wanted to know. *Fine. Look at her. How many more days did she plan on wearing those sweat pants?* She'd gained fifteen pounds over the summer. Her jeans were too tight. Turning, she felt his eyes on her back. *And when, by the way, did she plan to wash her hair?* Zoe raked her fingers over her head. "Listen—" He lowered his voice, took hold of her hand, spun her around. "I know it takes time. But for God's sake, Zoe." *Would she rather she'd died?* The IUD her doctor had inserted after Justine was born was still intact when she discovered she was pregnant again. Her doctor attempted to remove it without surgery and couldn't. One chance in a thousand, he'd told them. It was possible to continue the pregnancy—the choice was hers—but he did not recommend it. With the IUD in situ, he warned, she was at risk for septicemia. And septic shock could kill her. "Think of the kids," Will said. "It's time to pull yourself together."

Leah clambers onto her mother's lap, asks to play the kissing game. Her daughter places both hands at the base of Zoe's neck, and yanks.

"Not now, sweetie." Zoe pries Leah's hands from her neck. "Mommy has a headache."

Leah squinches her eyes. For an instant, Zoe thinks she might hate this child, so like her father.

Yes, it takes time. Of course it takes time.

Her husband, Zoe suddenly realizes, is having an affair. Though she has no tangible proof, she knows. The thought has been winding forward for weeks. She hasn't wanted to see.

Zoe is trembling. Leah says something and Zoe blinks back.

Leah gazes up at her. Zoe sees the confusion in her daughter's eyes and feels bad. "Mommy doesn't feel good," Zoe explains. "Check on Justine, sweetie? Make sure she's OK?"

"I wanna play wif Hammy."

"Please, Leah. Mommy has lots to do. You can play with Dog, for a little. We'll get Hammy out of his cage as soon as I'm done. Right now—"

Before Zoe finishes the sentence, Leah scoots off. Zoe pulls herself up, heads to the playroom, to check on the baby.

The shells are cooling on an aluminum cookie tray, on top of the stove. Zoe's headache is worse. She took a Percocet tablet fifteen minutes ago, and feels woozy. Doctor Marquette prescribed the medication after the surgery, to ease the pain. Two weeks later, Zoe was still having cramps and he refilled the prescription. She's been back a dozen times since, always finagling, working his guilt. Dizzy, she grabs the back of a chair. When she regains her balance, she carries the tray to the counter. The kitchen is warm from the heat of the oven. She pushes the sleeves of her sweater to her elbows, opens the shells, pulls the warm doughy centers, places the bottom halves of the pastries on the sheet. When the shells are cool, she spoons whipped cream into the cavity, replaces the tops, dusts them with sugar.

Zoe put the baby down twenty minutes ago, for her nap. Leah drags a chair from the table to the counter, scrambles up. Zoe left the beaters and empty mixing bowl in the sink. Leah steals one of the beaters. Holding it like a lollipop, she licks off the cream.

Zoe is shaking powdered sugar over the cream puffs when the telephone rings. "Get that, honey?" Her hands are coated with sugar. She wipes her dusty hands on her apron, rinses them under the faucet, dries them on the seat of her sweats.

"It's Grandpa," Leah says, handing the phone to her mother.

Don't, Zoe thinks, as she takes the phone. *Don't you dare tell me you're not coming.*

Zoe slams the phone on the hook, dropping the dishtowel she'd been using to hold the sticky receiver. He's sorry, her father said. Didn't realize she invited them for lunch. Her mother was out all morning . . . running errands. Just this minute returned. Zoe closed her eyes. This very minute, he repeated, as though reading her mind. Her mother has plans for this afternoon, tickets to a concert in Boston. He's terribly sorry. Zoe's throat aches. This is just an excuse. Her mother could have changed her plans. Turned the tickets in, exchanged them for a different show. She doesn't feel like driving to Hudson today. She wants to spend the day with Zoe's father—alone.

Zoe slumps into a chair, head in her hands. Fingers splayed, she massages her neck, the tender spots in front and back of her ears. She shouldn't have quit drinking, Zoe thinks—irrationally, she knows. At least when her mother drank, she'd felt too guilty not to be nice. She thought about her family once in a while.

Leah tugs at her leg.

"I'm sorry, sweetie. Mommy wasn't paying attention. What did you say?" Zoe pushes the chair back, spreading her knees, draws her daughter into the empty space between her legs.

"What Grandpa say?"

Zoe takes her daughter's face in her hands, tips her head back. "Grandpa says they'll come another day. He says tell you he loves you. They'll see you real soon."

"Oh," Leah says, nodding.

With her fingers, Zoe combs the hair out of her daughter's eyes. Leah had been looking forward to her grandparents' visit. Zoe wonders if she's disappointed. She gathers her daughter into her arms, lifts Leah onto her lap. "My sweet baby," Zoe murmurs, holding her daughter close. "Momma's precious little girl."

Leah pulls away before Zoe is ready. "Do trot, trot?" Leah pleads.

Trot, trot is a baby game, but Zoe goes along anyway. She turns Leah around, so they're facing one another, slides her daughter backward, takes hold of her hands. "Trot, trot to Boston," Zoe chants, bouncing Leah on her knees. *Trot, trot to Lynn. Better watch out or you're gonna*— Holding Leah's hands tightly, Zoe opens her legs, dips her daughter down, close to the floor. *Fall in.* Breathless, Leah begs Zoe to do it again. "Again, Mommy. Gain." Trot, trot to Boston, Zoe repeats. Again, again. Finally, Leah has had enough.

"Sweetie," Zoe says, out of breath herself. "Check on your sister? See if she's asleep?"

Leah shakes her head and hops down.

When Leah returns, Zoe makes her daughter a peanut butter and jelly sandwich. Zoe is due for her period. She winces, her uterus contracting, the pain intense, like the phantom pain people feel in an arm or leg after an amputation. When she opens the cabinet to fetch a glass for Leah's milk, she eyes the bottle of Percocet, wedged in the corner. Her breathing is labored. She blinks against the sudden shooting pain in her womb. Just one more, she thinks. Or two. Two would help a lot. She pours a glass of water to wash down the pills, rinses the glass, fills it with milk, hands it to Leah, takes a seat at the table, across from her daughter, and watches her eat.

When Leah finishes eating her lunch, she climbs back into Zoe's lap, twiddles a lock of her mother's hair. "Your hair is pretty. I wished I had pretty hair like you," Leah says.

"Your hair *is* pretty, honey. You have Daddy's hair. Very pretty."

Leah grins, pleased to be told she resembles her father, yawns, dropping her head, nuzzles Zoe's chest. Zoe strokes her daughter's hair. Leah smells of the outdoors, as Zoe imagines a baby robin might smell—of the trees, of the grass, of the air.

In Leah's Wake

Leah falls asleep in her mother's arms. Zoe stands, cradling her child, carries Leah to the den, lays her on one end of the sofa, tucks a pillow under her head. Then she settles on the couch, opposite Leah, her daughter's bare feet tucked between her shins.

Within minutes, Zoe's asleep.

In the dream, Zoe is rowing a canoe, in the middle of the ocean. The canoe bobs in the waves. A swell washes over her, tipping the boat, and Zoe is treading water. She tries to swim, but the current is too strong. The tide carries her downstream, through a narrow passageway, to a saltwater river. A party boat passes, so close she can almost reach out and touch it. People in Twenties-style clothing— mustachioed men in crisp white suits, women in short frilly dresses— are crowded on the deck, two or three of the men leaning precariously over the rail. The women are laughing, sipping martinis. A band, playing on the upper deck, launches into a song; people are singing, dancing. Zoe cries out, but no one hears. Suddenly, she spots Leah, floating toward her. Zoe kicks her feet, harder, harder, propelling her body forward. Leah reaches, grabs onto her neck. *No, Leah. We'll both drown. Take my hand, baby. My hand.*

He's dead, Momma. He's dead. Leah tugs Zoe's hand.

"What?" Zoe says, somewhere between waking and sleep. "Baby, what's wrong?"

Leah is shrieking, her face blotchy, contorted. Zoe raises herself to her elbows. Her tongue is cotton, her ears full of liquid.

A haze has fallen over the house. She searches for the clock.

The room blurs. Zoe thinks she might vomit. Leah tugs harder. She is trying to pull Zoe—Where? Reaching backward, using the arm of the sofa for leverage, Zoe drags herself up. Rubs her eyes, her skull expanding, her mind numb.

"Mommy, listen," Leah cries. "You're not listening, Mommy."

Zoe floats toward the stairs, Leah zooming ahead. Her joints ache, the soles of her feet burning as she presses, one foot then the other, to the hardwood floor, sheer will propelling her forward. She wishes she could go back to sleep. To sleep. She could sleep forever, she thinks.

Sleep forever.

"Mommy," Leah calls, from the top of the stairs. "*Hurry.*"

"I'm coming, Leah. I am."

Zoe holds onto the banister, the stairs moaning under her weight. Leah has drawn stick figures with black magic marker on the walls inside the stairwell. She'll clean it later. Her temples throb, blood draining from her head into her chest. *Mommy. Come, Momma. Hurry.*

What has she done? *My God,* Zoe thinks. What have *I* done?

"I did it, Mommy," Leah cries. "I killed him."

Zoe's breath catches. "Who, Leah?" For one horrific moment, the world goes still. Then Zoe is shaking her daughter—"Who, Leah? *Who did you kill?*"—terrified of the answer.

Suddenly, the baby is wailing.

"I wanted to make him pretty, Mommy. I hadda hold him. I holded him nice. I did. I tied the ribbon around him and he stopped breaving."

She sees the hamster now, in Leah's open palm, a pale blue ribbon cinching its waist.

Zoe blinks, catches her breath. Holding Leah's free hand, she guides her daughter back to the bedroom, removes a shoebox from Leah's closet, lays the hamster to rest. Taking Leah by the hand, she goes to Justine. After she changes the baby's diaper, the three of them will take the hamster outside, bury him in the backyard. They'll say a prayer, sing a song. Afterward, Zoe will read the Genesis story, from Leah's *Bible For Children.* She will take her daughter into her arms, tell her she mustn't blame herself. All creatures die. Death is part of God's plan. Don't be afraid, baby, she'll say. Dying doesn't hurt. Death, she thinks, afflicts only the living. When Leah looks up, Zoe will read in her daughter's eyes the faint stirring of comprehension. And she will hold her tightly, Leah's powdery, baby-soft cheek pressed to her heart, protecting her child while she still can, from the long blue ribbon of earthly disappointment.

Six

Sisters I, *Goblins and Ghosts*

Justine was sitting on the vanity braiding her hair, when the first of the trick-or-treaters arrived. Her father had rigged the doorbell to play Beethoven's Fifth. *Dat, dat, dat, da. . .* The music was annoying. Justine couldn't understand why her family always had to be different, why they couldn't have a normal doorbell, one that buzzed, like everyone else.

"You getting that, Leah?" she hollered. Their parents had gone to dinner, then to a party in Boston, and wouldn't be home until late. Leah was grounded again, for doing poorly on her progress report. Since she had to be home anyway, she'd promised to give out the candy.

Justine was wearing the Pippi Longstockings costume she'd worn the previous year—a plaid farmer's shirt and navy blue overalls. When she finished braiding her hair, she opened the wings of the mirror, turned her head left and right, examining the path in the back, to be sure it was straight. She leaned forward, showing her hairdo to Dog. "What do you think, Puppy?" The braids stuck straight out, from the sides of her head. *Nice*, she said, scratching Dog's head, *sweet*. Exactly like Pippi's. Then she set to work on her eyes. She closed the right eye first, stretching the lid smooth. Holding her mother's copper-colored pencil at a right angle, she drew a thick line from the corner to the outside of one lid, lined the other eye, applied a thick coat of mascara to her lashes. With her mother's Burnt Maple lip liner, she gave herself freckles.

The doorbell rang again, more insistent this time. Now they were knocking. Justine hopped off the vanity, dashed downstairs, Dog at her heels, to answer the door.

A black plastic cauldron sat on the floor, beside the front door. The cauldron was brimming with candy. Their mom had bought the right kind of treats this year: miniature *Reese's Cups, Mallo Bars, Milk Duds*. Their mother didn't eat candy: Carbohydrates made her gain weight. She seemed to forget that, for kids, popcorn wasn't a treat. Year after year, the treats at the Tyler house were the worst on the block. Popcorn, oranges, peanuts. Once, Justine's mother had given out raisins. On the bus, the following morning, the Tyler raisins had been the topic of discussion. Justine had wanted to crawl into her backpack. This year, the kids would be happy.

She scooped a *Mallo Bar* out of the cauldron, tucked it into her pocket, and opened the door. The three trick-or-treaters standing on the doorstep gazed up at her, expectantly. Justine couldn't bring herself to hand out singles, as most people did. Instead, she offered the cauldron, let the kids pick what they liked. The first child, a little girl dressed in a blue and gold uniform (the Cortland school colors), chose a *Mallo bar*, thanked her politely, and took a step back.

"Here you go." Justine handed her a *Reese's Cup* and a box of *Milk Duds*. "Take a few."

The next child—Justine couldn't tell what he was supposed to be, a Goth, she supposed—helped himself to three *Mallo Bars*, taking the candy bars one at a time, glancing at Justine each time for approval. Justine waited patiently. Smiling, she offered the cauldron to the last child, a pint-sized ghost. The ghost peered up at her brazenly. A hand darted out from under the sheet, plunged into the cauldron, and surfaced with a fistful of candy.

"Hey," Justine said, pulling the cauldron back. "I said a few. Not all those."

The ghost tossed the loot into his pillowcase and bolted, signaling the others to follow.

Too bad Leah hadn't answered the door. She would have said something. Leah complained all the time about the kids in the neighborhood, how spoiled they were, how disrespectful. "But they're only little," Justine would say, whenever one of them did something—threw leaves at her sister, for instance—that set Leah off. Now Justine saw how naïve she had been. She couldn't wait to tell Leah.

"Leah," Justine called. "Leah?"

Justine ran to the kitchen, Dog trailing behind her. Her sister was nowhere in sight. Leah wasn't in the family room, either. Justine glanced into the living room, on her way upstairs. She poked her head in the bedrooms, checked in each of the baths, hers and Leah's, the master suite on the other side of the house.

"Leah," she called again. *Leah?*

Finally, she found her—outside on the deck, smoking a cigarette.

Justine's heart sank. She'd noticed the ashes in the ceramic hand on Leah's bureau, but she'd refused to believe they were Leah's. The ashes, she'd told herself, belonged to a friend.

Justine pulled open the slider, Dog settling inside by the door.

A beam, from the floodlights attached to the corner boards of the house, lit the short hill at the far end of the deck. Leah stood in the corner, in the shadow cast by the porch light, leaning back against the rail, the cigarette dangling between her index and middle fingers, like the sticks the girls used to hold when they were little, pretending to smoke. Leah brought the cigarette to her lips, took a long drag, let the smoke filter out through her nose. She was wearing jeans, an olive V-neck T-shirt, her Birkenstock sandals. She had to be freezing.

The oak and birch trees in the backyard had lost most of their leaves, their bare, gnarled branches curling skyward like witches' fingers. Justine stood in the doorway, shivering, hugging herself. When she was younger, she'd been afraid of the dark, of the tickle lady who swooped down from the ceiling, landed beside her in bed. Justine was still frightened, but of other things now. She was afraid of murderers and thieves, of the coyotes lurking in the woods, of the mating cats outside her window, their howl like babies crying at night. She was afraid of the way the full moon turned the water in the pool below their deck this eerie shade of purple. And she was afraid of the way her sister was standing here now, alone, her eyes closed, smoking a cigarette.

"Leah?" Justine said, stepping outside onto the porch.

Leah pulled on the cigarette. "Gonna tell?"

Justine dropped her eyes. How could her sister ask such a question? Imply that Justine couldn't be trusted? At times, Leah hurt Justine's feelings more than Justine could ever explain. Her sister would look at her a certain way, talk to her in a particular tone of voice, and Justine would feel useless—no, worse than useless—*dumb, stupid, invisible even.* Other times, just being around her sister made Justine feel special. Take last month, for example, the week after school started, when Matt Mattiveo called her a monkey. Justine refused to cry. The whole way home, sitting on the bus, she'd choked back the tears. Once she got off the bus, there'd been no holding back. Tears clogged her throat and nose, spilled out of her eyes. Justine's parents, home from work early that day, were sitting in the breakfast nook, drinking coffee. Justine slinked by, covering her face, too embarrassed to let anyone see her. But Leah had seen. Leah was lounging in the family room watching TV (practice, she'd said, was called off for the day), had followed Justine to her room, lain beside her, forever, it seemed, rubbing Justine's back, her shoulders, her arms, Leah's silence, her warm breath on Justine's neck, comforting, until Justine was ready to talk. Leah had listened, eyes narrowed in concentration, until Justine had finished her story. *Matt Mattiveo, the boy Justine had loved since the second grade. . .* Justine had no idea how he'd found out. Maybe he'd caught her staring, Leah suggested. It was possible, Justine said, but she didn't think so. That very afternoon, on the bus, he'd sat beside her. He likes me, she thought. *He likes me.* But exactly the opposite, it turned out, was true. "Look at that hair," he'd said, pointing at Justine's arm. "You look like a monkey." *A monkey.* "What's wrong with me, Leah?" Did she really look like a monkey? "Nothing's wrong with you, Jus," Leah had answered. "He likes you. Don't you see? That's how boys your age act when they like a girl. Immature. Don't you think?" Her response so different from any Justine's mother might have offered. *Ignore him, Justine,* her mom might have said, something Justine could never, ever have done. Or, *it doesn't matter, sweetie, you're beautiful just the way you are. He doesn't see yet, is all. But he will.* Or worst of all, *Matt's a jerk, Justine, forget about him,* her mother's words more devastating even than Matt's. But Leah had known what to say. Leah understood.

Now Justine's feelings were hurt, though she tried not to show it. "No," she said, shaking her head, as she crossed the porch. "You know I don't tell."

Leah shrugged, an offhanded gesture that Justine interpreted as "thanks," and cupped her hand around the cigarette, turning the filtered edge to Justine. "Want to try?"

Justine looked at the cigarette, cast her eyes toward the floorboards. Justine would never smoke. Not after what happened to Grandma Chandler. "No thanks," she said, shaking her head.

"I won't rat you out." Leah crossed her index finger over her lips. "Sister's promise."

"That's OK. Thanks anyhow."

Leah's eyes looked glazed, as if she were coming down with a fever. The flu was going around. Justine hoped she wasn't getting sick. "You OK?" she asked. "Want me to stay here?"

"Nah," Leah said, in that voice that made Justine feel like a pest. "Go."

"Are you sure? Because I—"

Leah ran her hand over her head, twirling her hair. "Told you. I'm fine."

Justine watched her sister take another long drag from the cigarette. "Leah?"

Her sister peered at her, twiddling her shirt.

Justine crossed and uncrossed her feet. She'd been practicing the runaway arm earlier, a trick she'd made up for her sister, to make Leah laugh. Justine lifted her right knee, pulling it into her chest, and wound her left arm. "Look," she cried, winding, winding, her left arm spinning, spinning, spinning out of control, wheeling her forward. "The runaway aaaarrmmm."

When Leah stopped laughing, Justine said, "Can I ask you something?"

Leah brought the cigarette to her lips, her eyes squeezed into slits. "You want," she said, through a mouthful of smoke. "Can't promise I'll do it."

Stop smoking, Justine wanted to say. "It's not anything big. I don't want you to take me anywhere or lend me anything or anything. I just want you to—" Justine felt like a six year-old, talking too fast, tripping over her words. "Want you to—"

"Spit it out." *Shpit*, it came out.

"Stop smoking," Justine blurted. "Cancer runs in the family. I'm scared you're gonna get cancer, like Grandma." And die, she thought. *I don't want you to die.*

"Don't get liver cancer." Leah rolled her eyes. "From smoking."

Of course you don't get liver cancer from smoking. Justine was not a moron. It was the predisposition to cancer she worried about. Her honors science class was doing a section on genes. Their grandmother dying of liver cancer, she'd learned, put them at risk. Justine didn't say that, of course. She would feel like a geek. Instead, she said, stupidly, "You sure you're all right?"

"Uh-huh." Leah took the last drag from her cigarette, flicked the butt onto the grass, then spread her arms wide, both hands on the rail, and tipped her head back. Making an "O" with her lips, she blew rings of smoke into the air.

Justine watched the smoke rings spiral upward. A cricket chirped and the wind blew, a low whistling sound that made her uneasy. Justine located the North Star, the first star of the night. *I wish I may, I wish I might . . .* Please, Justine wished, make my sister stop smoking.

Justine traced an imaginary path from the point of Polaris to Cepheus to Cassiopeia.

"Pipster," Leah said, after a couple of minutes. Her hips swayed, as though she were dancing. "Sleeping at Holly's, right?"

"I could stay home," Justine offered again. "If you want to go to bed. Or go out, I mean. With your friends or something."

"S'OK. By the way, Teenie," she said, using the nickname she'd made up when Justine was a baby. "Cool costume you got there. Zactly like Pippi."

"Honest?"

"Yep." Leah said, massaging her arms. "Fun," she called, as Justine was turning away.

Ten minutes after Justine left, a station wagon teeming with kids pulled into the drive: a ghost, superheroes sporting red and black capes, Dora the Explorer, a set of Sponge Bob twins. Leah invited the trick-or-treaters to help themselves, tossing extra candy into the bags of the shy ones, who took only two or three pieces. When they left, the cauldron was just about empty.

Leah switched off the porch lights and all the lights in the front of the house, and skipped upstairs to change into her clothes for the party—a gold lamé sweater and black leather skirt.

Hope was hosting a Halloween bash, tonight. Everybody who was anybody would be there. Hope had totally outdone herself, this time. She'd even hired a band, a three-piece, punk-hip-hop group that a friend of Lupo had started. The band wasn't signed yet, but they'd recorded a CD, and they'd sold over a hundred copies already, on this cool file-sharing Internet site.

To bide time while she was waiting for Todd to arrive, Leah slid the CD she'd borrowed from Hope into her father's changer. The music reminded her of a John Travolta movie she had watched on cable TV, the lively dance beat transporting her to the seventies, when the world was full of wonder and possibility, when life was open and free. "Love, love, love," Leah chanted, sweat dribbling down her back, gluing her shirt to her skin, her hips and shoulders rolling with the music, the rhythm flowing through her bloodstream and into her bones.

In Leah's Wake

At eight on the dot, the doorbell rang. She scooped the lollipops from the island counter, and pulled on a sweatshirt, in case the temperature dropped while she was out.

"Hey, dude." Todd peered around Leah, scouting the hallway behind her. "Coast clear?"

"Everything's cool," Leah said. Her sister had left a while ago. She waved to Lupo, who was sitting in the driveway, at the wheel of his '94 Lincoln, and followed Todd out the door.

Justine stopped at Holly's house, two doors down from her own, and the girls slogged through the neighborhood, stopping at each of the six houses on their street, dropping the candy they collected into their brown paper lunch bags. Younger kids passed, scratch, scratch, scratch, in their costumes, toting pillowcases, carrying flashlights, waving glow-in-the-dark sticks. Their parents, in clusters, straggled behind. Justine tried to act upbeat, but her face felt like plastic. "What's wrong?" Holly kept asking, but even if she had wanted to, Justine couldn't have said.

They were turning onto Old Orchard Road, on their way to the next block, when a dented black jalopy careened past, a Marilyn Manson decal stuck to its bumper, the driver honking as he swerved around them. *Jerk.* Justine poked her middle finger at the car. "Slow down."

Within an hour, the girls were all petered out. "This stinks," Holly said. "Want to go to my house?"

Justine followed Holly to her room, and the girls chatted online with their friends.

At ten thirty, worried that her sister was sick and needed her, Justine decided to leave.

Wind rustled the branches of the gigantic pine trees in Holly's yard. Justine stood on the stoop, outside the back door, staring at the long, dark driveway. She was a moron, saying "no" when Holly's mother offered to escort her home. "I'm OK," she had lied, too embarrassed to admit she was scared. "It's just up the block." *I'm OK,* she said now, deriding herself. *It's just up the block.* The street was deserted. Some ax-murderer was probably hiding in the woods.

At last, she worked up the courage to leave, and took off at a gallop.

Halfway down the drive, a low skittering noise stopped her in her tracks. She planted her feet, centering herself. Let him try to attack her. She'd land a karate blow he wouldn't forget.

59

She heard rustling under the pine trees. And a raccoon toddled across the drive.

A coon. Scared of a little raccoon. No wonder her sister was always teasing her. *Baby, baby, baby*, Leah sneered. *Time to grow up.* Her sister was right. Justine *was* a baby. She inhaled deeply, and skipped to the end of the drive.

In the circle, she stopped short again. A strange car was parked next to their mailbox. A dented black Lincoln, the paint scraped off the driver's side door. Justine's knees went soft.

A thief! This had to be his getaway car! She had to call the police. She looked around, frantic, trying to decide where to go. Maybe she should run back to Holly's house. She swung around. But what if the car didn't belong to a robber? What if there was no robber? If the police arrived and it turned out that the car was perfectly innocent? If the car belonged to somebody's guest? She would look like a fool. Really, she ought to investigate first.

Justine concentrated on her evidence. Rays from the street lamp fell over the hood, onto the windshield. She edged closer, blinking as she entered the circle of light. The car appeared to be empty. Cupping her eyes, she peered through the driver's window.

A leather jacket lay in a ball on the seat. Empty cups littered the floor. Soda cans. Crushed papers. A lamb's wool sheath covered the steering wheel. She tried the door—locked—and headed for the rear of the car, intending to try the door on the passenger side. As she was passing the trunk, she caught sight of the sticker on the rear bumper. *Marilyn Manson.*

The guy from Old Orchard Road. And he'd been here all along. The whole time she was at Holly's. The guy was a maniac. What if he was doing something awful to Leah?

Justine tore down their driveway, across the lawn, and up the front steps.

The house was dark. Leah hated being alone in the house. She would never turn off all the lights. Something terrible had happened. Justine felt it in her bones. Holding onto the pilaster, she wriggled out of her shoe. Shook her sneaker. The key? Where was her key?

Heart pounding, she rushed down the steps and across the grass, to the garage. The side door was unlocked. She patted the wall next to the door, flicked on the light, and sprinted across the garage, crashing head-on into the dog. The poor thing yelped. Justine had stepped on her paw. *I'm sorry. I'm sorry.* She scratched Dog's head. "It's OK, girl. OK," she said, and tripped up the steps to the mudroom. On the top step, her overalls caught on a nail jutting out of the riser. She ripped her overalls free, the hem tearing.

She barely touched the knob, and the door swung open. She lurched forward, stumbling over the threshold, onto the tiled floor. Picked herself up.

"Leah," she called, her eyes not yet adjusted to the dark. "Where are you?"

She checked the half-bath, the laundry, peered out at the deck. "Leah?" *Please, God*, she prayed. *Don't let him be here.*

Justine scrambled through the shadows to the kitchen, tore open the drawers, one after the other, open, open, open—a knife, she needed a knife—ran her hand over the counter, located the knife block, snatched the one from the top slit, a long, thin carving knife with a razor-like edge.

Footsteps. Upstairs.

She skidded down the hall, around the corner, to the stairs. The lights. She swiped the wall on her way up, missing the switch. Up the steps, two at a time, her heart pounding. *Oh my God I am heartily sorry*, Justine prayed, her fingers gripping the knife's hard wooden shank, *for having offended Thee*, the first prayer that came to her mind.

At the top of the stairs, a hand reached for her, out of the dark.

Duck. She held the carving knife over her shoulder, poised to strike. With the opposite hand, she made a fist, protecting her face. *Tight. Left hook. KIA-HA. Out and back. Quick.*

"What the hell are you *doing*?"

A hulking figure loomed over her.

She waved the knife. "Get away from me," she cried. "Or I'll kill you."

The monster edged closer.

"Get away from me," Justine shouted again, kicking. Left foot. In and out. Connected. Thwap. Heard a thud. All at once, he was falling.

"What the *fuck*."

The lights went on, the sharp beam blinding her for an instant.

"Hey. Dude." Out of nowhere, a blond-haired boy materialized. "It's me. Todd."

"Get back." She pulled the knife over her shoulder, ready to strike.

The boy flashed a smile. Blond curls cascaded over his forehead. The other boy, bigger, darker, was slumped on the floor near the bathroom, his back to the wall, his thick legs spread in front of him.

The kid's head was shaved. A Band-Aid partially covered a menacing cut over his right eye. He looked like a pirate, she thought, with silver hoops running the length of his left brow.

Justine stood her ground.

The bald boy glared at her. "*Bitch.*" He rubbed his head. "Who the *fuck* is that?"

"Her sister, dude. Shut up."

Justine waved the knife at the kid on the floor, swung the blade, pointed at the boy who'd claimed he was Todd. The liar. What would Todd be doing here? Their father would ground her and Leah for life if either of them allowed boys in the house when their parents were gone.

She didn't trust these two for a minute. If they'd hurt her sister, she would kill them. Plunge the knife right into their hearts, drain every drop of blood from their bodies. The kid on the floor pushed himself up. "Get back," she ordered. Before she sliced his ugly face into pieces.

"Come on, dude," Todd urged. "Put the knife down."

"Where is she?" Justine demanded.

Todd pointed his chin at the knife. "Put it down first."

Justine glowered, tightening her grip. "I *said,* where is she? Where's my sister?"

Silence.

Reluctantly, she dropped her hands to her sides.

"In there," he said, and thumbed Leah's room. "She's fine."

"What are you kissing her ass for? That bitch tried to kill us."

The boy who'd claimed he was Todd turned to face his accomplice. "Shut up, Lupo."

Without warning, the big kid hurled himself forward, his puny black eyes driving her backward. Kid was bigger than her father, and burly. Todd yelled something at Lupo and Justine backed up again. Todd reached for her. She batted him away, her windmill arms whipping in circles, the knife swinging this way and that, Todd dodging the blows. . . *get away, get away.*

Todd pitched forward. Justine pulled back, overstepping, her feet slipping out from under her. Her left foot slid off the landing. The wall. Where was the wall? Saw the foyer. The floor.

Todd latched onto her hand, and yanked.

Justine yanked back. "Let me alone," she screamed, kicking her feet.

With a jerk, Todd pulled her onto the landing, catching her in a stronghold.

"Leah," she called, struggling, desperate. "What did you do to her?"

He squeezed her wrist, until the knife dropped out of her hand. Lupo, seizing his opportunity, lunged at the knife.

Todd elbowed the other kid's chest, ordered him to stay where he was. "What's with you?" he asked, turning back to Justine, gripping her upper arms. "Somebody's gonna get hurt."

"Let go of me."

Todd dropped his hands, his flinty blue eyes focused on hers. "What's wrong with you?" he asked again, quietly now. "You trying to kill somebody, or what?"

Justine swallowed. *Baby. Don't cry.* The other boy, Lupo, hands thrust in the pockets of his oversized chinos, was blocking the door to Leah's room. "What did you *do* to my sister?"

Lupo laughed, a deep hawking guffaw, like a hyena.

Justine glared at him.

"We came to help," Todd said. "Your sister's doing good." He led Justine to her sister's room. "Go ahead," Todd said. "See for yourself."

The other boy shot them a contemptuous look, and stepped aside.

From the doorway, her sister appeared to be sleeping. Maybe they were telling the truth. Maybe they really had stopped by to help. Leah had been acting strangely earlier, when they were out on the deck. Justine knew her sister was sick. Leah probably hadn't realized it, yet. Sometimes you don't, until it's too late. She'd probably gotten worse—Justine cringed—probably threw up, called the boys, so there would be somebody here to give out the candy. Justine felt like a fool, jumping to conclusions again. "Does she have a fever?"

"I don't think so," Todd said. "Check, if you want."

Justine's eyes passed over the familiar forms: the piles of clothes on the floor, the revolving black light on Leah's desk, the Paddington Bear at the foot of her bed, the net filled with stuffed animals, hanging from the ceiling in the corner of the room. Justine tiptoed inside. Her sister's head was propped on a pillow. Justine laid her hand on Leah's forehead. Leah must have taken some aspirin. She didn't feel hot. Leah moaned and rolled on her side. Justine squeezed Leah's shoulder, to reassure her, and backed out of the room.

"See?" Todd said, once she had reached the hallway. "What did I tell you?"

Lupo was standing at the front door now, fiddling with the knob. "Let's get out of here," he called. "Before their old man gets home."

Todd held up a finger.

"I'm sorry," Justine said, for accusing him. She hoped he'd forgive her.

"Forget it." Todd wrapped his arm around her shoulder, drew her into a brotherly hug. He was being nice, really nice, considering how badly she'd treated him. She'd lost her mood ring. Blue, for love, it might have turned, if she had been wearing it. He tipped his head, shaking the curls out of his brilliant crystalline eyes. When he smiled again, Justine noticed an adorable space between his front teeth. She saw exactly why her sister was hooked.

Lupo made a show of opening the door. Todd told him, adamantly this time, to hang on.

Yeah. Hang on. She had a million questions she wanted to ask. When Todd turned his attention back to her, she asked him again what had happened.

Before he had a chance to answer, Lupo cut in. "She took some bad shit, man," he called up, from downstairs. "What d'ya think?"

Bad shit? Like drugs? That Lupo was nuts. Her sister got in trouble from time to time, for dumb things—sassing their mother, coming home late—and, yes, her sister smoked cigarettes. But Leah would never do drugs. Justine shifted her attention to Todd, relying on him for support.

"Asshole." Todd turned an apologetic face to Justine. "Sorry," he said, "big mouth down there don't know when to keep his trap shut."

His response confused her, at first. Suddenly, it hit her. *Lupo was telling the truth.* Justine's pulse throbbed, her brain reeling, fighting to keep pace with the thoughts churning in her head. There had to be a logical explanation. In a made-for-TV movie Justine had seen, a teenage girl had been drugged. She was at a party. When she turned her back, a boy slipped a Rohypnol tablet into her soft drink. That had to be what happened to Leah, this afternoon probably, before she came home. "Where did she get it?" Did they know what she took?

"Beats me," Todd said, descending the staircase. "But I'm gonna find out."

Justine closed the door behind them, sat on the bottom step, the cauldron on her lap. Without thinking, she ate the last three *Reese's Cups*, barely tasting the peanut butter or chocolate. Last year, an eighth grade boy at her school was arrested. The principal, acting on a rumor that a student had brought marijuana onto the premises, called the police. The police spent the entire morning searching lockers.

That afternoon, they led a boy out in cuffs. Justine felt bad for the boy. Only kids from the worst of families used drugs. Certainly not someone like Leah.

Seven

Eyes Open Wide

When Leah opened her eyes, it was morning, a sliver of gray-blue light visible under her shades. Her head throbbed. She had no clue how she'd gotten to bed. She squeezed her eyes shut, pulling the covers to her neck. She remembered being at Hope's, dancing, recalled swallowing a second hit of E. Within twenty minutes, her heart was racing and she was sweating profusely, her hair drenched, her clothes soaked, her shirt sticking to her chest and her back. She saw a blurred image of herself running in circles waving her arms, crying, shouting. Something about being attacked by an army of spiders. She vaguely recalled Todd chasing her, picking her up, carrying her over his shoulder out to the Jeep, her arms and legs dangling.

After that, she drew a blank.

Leah would never hear the end of this. Once the goody-two-shoes at her school, tools like Cicely Hanson, caught wind of her behavior last night, Leah was doomed. Last year, at a party, one of the freshman girls downed an entire pint of vodka, climbed unsteadily onto a table, started flashing her boobs. On the way out, she barfed, leaving a trail of Pepto-Bismol pink puke from the doorstep, down the stairs, and onto the lawn. For months, when she walked down the halls, the boys pointed, leering, and the girls made vile hawking noises and laughed. The stunt Leah pulled last night blew that girl's sideshow away. Leah rolled onto her belly, pulled the pillow over her head. With a little luck, maybe she would die in her sleep.

When she opened her eyes again, her sister was sitting on her bed, stroking her hair.

"Hey, sleepy-head."

"What's up?" Leah asked, her voice froggy. She was having trouble adjusting to being awake. A blade of light shot through the slit between the windowsill and the bottom rail of her shade. She rubbed her eyes. "What time is it?" It had to be close to noon.

Justine looked at her Mickey Mouse watch. "Five after one," she said, and got up, switched on the lights. "You OK, Lee? You were crying."

"One?" Normally, Leah had trouble sleeping past seven. She pushed herself to her elbows. "Fine, yeah. Must've been dreaming." She felt better than she had earlier. Her head ached, but the throbbing was gone. "Why are you here? How come you're not at Holly's?"

Justine picked up Leah's rag doll, finger-combed her bright orange hair.

"What's up, Jus? What's going on?" No way her parents could know what happened last night. They weren't due home until late. By the time they got here, Todd would have been gone. "Dad's not in one of his asshole moods again, is he?"

Justine shook her head. "Lee? I need to ask you something."

"Where's Dad? Did they have fun at their party? What did he say?" If she was in trouble, she might as well know now. No point in spending the whole day all caught up in knots, wondering if she was in trouble.

"Dad's at the hardware store. Lee? What happened last night?"

"The hardware store?"

"Come on, Lee. I was worried about you."

Leah swept the stringy bangs off her face. She was wearing a baggy gray T-shirt she'd filched from her father's bureau drawer one day, when she ran out of clean shirts of her own. Someone had changed her out of her clothes. Hopefully, Todd. She threw off the covers, a putrid odor wafting out of her bed. She sniffed her left armpit, winced. She smelled as though she'd been working out for three days without bathing. "What's he doing at the hardware store?"

"Mom asked him to fix that shelf in their closet. The one that fell down?"

"Oh, yeah." Leah rooted through her laundry pile, squeezing the clothes, hunting for her flip-flops, gave up, grabbed a pair of cheap leather thongs she had owned since the eighth grade, and pulled them on, the stiff leather chafing her toes. Turning her back to her sister, she stripped off the T-shirt, tossed it in the general direction of her laundry pile, plucked a cotton camisole off her floor, held it up, checking to be sure it wasn't too dirty, sniffed for B.O., and pulled it over her head, smoothing the fabric over her boobs. She shut her closet door, and examined herself in the mirror. She looked like crap, her skin flaky, mascara smudged ghoulishly under her eyes.

"Lee?" Her sister crawled to the foot of Leah's bed.

"Huh?" Squinting, Leah brought her face closer to the mirror, picked at a zit.

"You can tell me. I'm not gonna rat you out."

"What are you talking about?"

"You know."

Leah spun to face her sister. "No, Jus. I don't know."

Justine stared at her feet. "I came home early," she said.

"What time?"

"Ten thirty. You were asleep."

"Really?" Leah wasn't sure how to handle this. "Must have fallen asleep, waiting for you."

"The boys were here."

"Oh." Leah took a seat on the bed, next to her sister. "What did they tell you?"

Justine shrugged. That Lupo kid claimed Leah had been doing drugs. But she didn't believe him, she said, and rubbed Leah's arm. "He's a big loser. What really happened, Lee?"

"You're right," Leah said. "He is a jerk. Don't listen to him."

"Did you get roophed?"

Roophed? Justine thought someone had drugged her? Leah's sister was naïve, but she wasn't *that* naïve, was she? She stared at Leah, her face hopeful, those big, earnest brown eyes open wide. Leah considered fessing up. Justine had come home early last night because she was worried. She was sitting here now because she cared about Leah. Leah owed it to her sister to tell her the truth. Only Leah would be indicting herself. And who knew how Justine would react?

"Yeah." Leah stared at her hands, unable to meet her sister's gaze. "I'm so stupid." She'd left her new running shoes in her locker, asked some random boy to hold her Gatorade bottle while she ran to the gym to retrieve them. "I was gone for like a minute. It must have been him."

Justine threw her arms around Leah. "I *knew* it," she cried, and hugged Leah tighter. Leah felt odious, a tsunami-sized wave of shame washing away any speck of relief. *Was she scared?* Justine wanted to know. *Did she know the kid's name?* Leah forced herself not to stiffen. She should have been psyched. She'd done something supremely stupid and gotten away with it for once. But the more Justine sympathized, the worse Leah felt. Finally, she told her sister the truth. Well, almost the truth. She omitted the Ecstasy part. She claimed it was weed, in pill form.

For an instant, the light in Justine's eyes dimmed. Then her face brightened, and it occurred to Leah that her sister had made a conscious decision to trust her, to take Leah's word. "I won't tell," Justine assured her, on one condition: that Leah promised, *swear to God, Lee*—"cross your heart and hope to die"—she would never, ever do that again.

Eight

Another Bad Day

"Who gave you that shit?" Todd demanded. The E, on Hallow-een night, Todd meant.

It was a dazzling fall day, hot for November, the sun radiant, the sky a rich, azure blue.

Leah ran her fingers through her spiky blond hair. She couldn't believe she'd actually cut it. Last week, as a joke, she showed her mother a picture, in *Star,* of some British model with this hideous, gelled-up hair. "My new do," she said, assuming her mother would laugh. "Nice. You'll look like a punk," her mother had snapped, leaving Leah no choice except to go through with it.

"I want to know where you got it," Todd pressed.

With her heel, Leah scuffed the sand under her feet. She and Todd were hanging out at the elementary school, on the playground swings. The place was deserted. A young, male teacher exited the building, briefcase in hand, and cut across the tarmac, with barely a glance in their direction. On the playing field at the far side of the school grounds, Pop Warner practice was in full-tilt, the little boys smashing into tackling dummies, their squeals echoing across the field.

Todd had surprised her, showing up at the high school. She'd been huddled with her teammates, psyching the girls up for a five-mile training run, when she spotted the Wrangler. Her boyfriend worked in Ayer, at this hole-in-the-wall used CD shop called Music Head. On Tuesdays, he worked until six. She'd practically choked on her spit when she saw him. He hadn't called her since Halloween—three days ago. Clutching her stomach, she told the girls to go on

70

without her, *emergency*; she would catch up in a minute. She watched her teammates jog to the top of the drive. The instant the dawdlers rounded the corner, she'd sprinted to the truck.

A bee circled drunkenly in front of her nose. Leah fanned the air, chasing it away. This interrogation annoyed her. Eating the E was stupid. Agreed. She had no intention of doing E again. She had no intention of doing any drug again, *ever*. So why fight about it?

"Come on, babe. Fess up. Tell me where you got it."

As if. He would go ape shit if he knew Hope hooked her up. Leah examined her right hand. Her nails needed paint. Blue, she thought, possibly black.

"You can't be doing that shit." He veered toward her, twisting the chains on his swing. What did she think would happen if her coach found out? He'd been a wide receiver in high school, Todd reminded her. His coach had banned athletes for drug use.

"So—" Leah paused, letting the word hang, to achieve maximum dramatic effect. "What did your *boss* say when you left work this afternoon?" She emphasized the word "boss" to taunt him. She meant Jamie, the owner. Leah knew that if Todd asked his permission to leave, for any decent reason, Jamie would grant it. On the nights Todd worked, she and Hope often visited him at the store. Usually, she and Jamie wound up talking, while Todd waited on customers and Hope examined the rolling papers or thumbed through the CDs. Jamie had scared her, at first. He reminded her of an aging rock star, with his craggy face and sour expression. Once she'd gotten to know him, she'd found him interesting and surprisingly easy to talk to. "What did he say?"

"He said, 'tell your girlfriend that shit's bad news.'"

"Liar." She gave him the stink-eye. He wouldn't *dare* talk smack about her to Jamie.

"Ask him," he said, his words punctuated by that annoying downward turn of his lips.

He did tell Jamie. What a *loser.* She could never face Jamie again. She had a mind to leave. If it were any later, she would force him to drive her home. (She couldn't go home now. If her mother showed up from work early, she would know Leah had ditched practice.)

On impulse, Leah swept sideways, torquing her body as if she were swinging a bat—

And swatted.

"Hey." Todd lunged left, his right arm shielding his head. "What are you doing?"

See if you can figure it out, she told him, telepathically—and swatted again.

This time, her chop landed smack between his shoulder blades. He grappled with the chains, his toe catching on a partially concealed rock under his swing. He toppled off, yelping.

She covered her mouth, trying to hide the fact she was giggling.

Sulking, he brushed himself off. "Bitch," he said irritably. "What'd you do that for?"

Bitch? Screw him. She hopped off her swing, and stormed off, pumping her arms.

Feeling him behind her, she pumped harder, her feet moving faster, faster, until she was practically running. Wide receiver—right. Four years ago, buddy. Let him try to catch her.

He was gaining ground. Furious, she broke into a sprint.

He shot past her, breathing hard, and circled back, parked himself in front of her face.

"With. You?" he asked, between hiccupping breaths. "Didn't. Say. Nothing. To Jamie."

"And I'm supposed to believe that?" She was sorely tempted to hit him again.

With his forearm, he swabbed his sweaty face. "I'm telling you, I didn't say nothing."

Leah abhorred lying, especially by people who were supposed to be trustworthy. "Then how come you said you did?"

He sidled up to her, draping his arm over her shoulder. He smelled like a sweat hog.

Stiffening, she pushed a lungful of air out her nose. If he thought she intended to say one more word to him today, the kid was sadly mistaken.

Todd dropped his arm, scowling. "Come on, babe. Lighten up. What if me and Lupo weren't around?" They'd given her a couple of Valium pills to calm her down. (He'd swiped the bottle of pills from his mother's medicine cabinet. Luckily, he'd stashed them in the glove compartment in his truck.) The Valium put her to sleep. "Why'd you do it? Talk to me, babe."

"None of your business," she said, her foot slicing through the overgrown grass. How was she supposed to know that shit would bug her out? She'd never tried Ecstasy before.

The Pop Warner coach was directing position drills now, the boys, no older than seven or eight, darting, willy-nilly, around the field. "Do your job," one of the kids shouted, the pitch of his voice wavering. "Do your job," the squad echoed.

Leah envied the boys. It was hard to recall the last time she played a game, the last time she'd had any fun. Soccer wasn't a game anymore; it was a job. She wished she could turn back the clock, be a kid again, young enough so she didn't have to think all the time, didn't have to apologize, didn't always feel bad. Young enough so she could just *be*.

"This is serious, babe. You coulda got hurt."

"Yeah, well. Let's get out of here." She spun on her heels, made a beeline for the Jeep. "I shouldn't be here, anyway," she said petulantly. "I'm not allowed to see you, you know."

"Huh?" He reached for her wrist. "What are you talking about?"

Leah evaded his grasp. "My father hates you. I'm not supposed to go near you."

"Me?" He stopped short, shaking his head in disbelief. "What did I do?"

You quit high school? You used to deal drugs? "Who knows? He just does."

She climbed into the truck, shoving her backpack out of the way with her foot, and pulled the visor down to shield her eyes from the glare of the sun. Earlier, Todd had played a recording he'd borrowed from the shop by a band called Rage Against the Machine. Todd knew more about music than anyone Leah had ever met, including her father. His father, Todd had told her, was one of the original jazz producers for Rounder Records, an independent label based in Cambridge. Todd didn't know his father all that well. His father had abandoned Todd and his mom when Todd was a baby. Fortunately for him, Todd had inherited his father's musical gene.

"Could you play that Rage CD again?" Leah asked. She thought it was awesome.

Todd pushed *Play*, the angry music instantly diffusing her fury.

"That's bullshit, babe." Todd rapped the wheel, in time with the music. "He just *does*?"

"Yeah, well. He's nuts. What can I say?"

Todd turned the music down, cursing himself under his breath. "It's your sister, isn't it?"

"Keep my sister out of this."

"If it's not because of her, what is it?" He looked wounded. "What did I do?"

Leah had been itching to win this fight since it started. Though she was glad she'd gained the upper hand, hurting him in the process made her feel mean. She massaged his arm, to console him. "You didn't do anything wrong," Leah said. Her sister was cool. She hadn't breathed a word about Halloween night to their parents. This wasn't even about Todd, really. Her father hated all Leah's boyfriends, at first. Once he gets to know you, "he'll love you," she promised. (How her father would ever get to know her boyfriend, when he'd forbidden Todd from stepping within a hundred yards of their house, was a mystery. But she didn't say that, of course.)

Will was perched on a barstool at Marcus's, a brass and mahogany watering hole near his hotel, nursing a spicy October lager, wishing he were back east. He missed Zoe. With Will gone so often, it was hard for them to connect. Time was a commodity when he was home. They were pulled in a million directions, trying to do everything, make up for lost time. The stress made her anxious and him surly, and they fought constantly. He missed his kids, too. Last month, Justine received an award for a research paper she'd written on Mars. The night of the award ceremony, she'd presented the paper to the junior high teachers from all the schools in their district—and Will had missed it. And Leah's soccer season was winding down, sectionals around the corner. After playing all season, her left hamstring tended to tighten. The high school trainers knew about RICE—rest, ice, compression, elevation. They could wrap a bum knee. Will was the only one who stretched her legs properly, lifting until she felt a slight pull, holding for thirty seconds, then stretching farther, just far enough to increase her flexibility without injuring the tissue.

When he was younger, Will hadn't minded the traveling nearly as much. He missed his family, but if he'd realized that if he hoped to succeed, to launch himself into middle America, to achieve some degree of financial success, if they wanted to own a nice house, decent cars, afford a luxury now and again, he had to be on the road, making sales; that was the trade-off. Now that he was older, his values had changed. He wanted more than money, a pat on the back, a plaque to hang on his wall. His kids were growing up. In a few years, they would be gone. He wanted to be home, spending time with them, attending their functions, wanted to be involved in their lives.

Will had flown into San Francisco on Sunday, this trip a last-ditch effort to pump some life back into the Micronics project. The VP Will had sold the job to had left in August, replaced by a mid-level project manager, a tight-ass MBA-type in his thirties, named Cushing. He should have arranged to meet Cushing here, where they could've discussed the project over a few beers.

His leather jacket was folded over the back of his chair. He rooted through the inside pocket, dug out his cell, dialed Cushing's number, reached voice service, left a purposely vague message— "I've got an idea to blow by you," he said—and asked Cushing to give him a ring.

After winning a contract of this magnitude, a six hundred million dollar project for his faltering firm, Will should have felt like a hero. Instead, he felt like the company schmuck. It was the first time NAC had built any structure, never mind a 150,000 square foot facility, in an earthquake zone. When they were bidding the job, to cover unanticipated costs, he'd advised his analysts to build an extra fifteen percent into their proposal. He and Givens, the VP, were tight. If they came in a few points higher than the next bidder, he'd felt confident he could swing the deal their way. If they lost the contact— he couldn't afford to lose: he needed the commission—at least NAC wouldn't go belly-up on the job. Jackman, the owner, overrode him. Go in low, Jackman insisted; they'd make their margin on extras. Brilliant strategy. Too bad it backfired.

At this point, NAC couldn't afford to walk. They were two mil over budget, just on the site work. The reinforced cement concrete (RCC) walls in Phase 2, due to start in three weeks, could put his company under. The construction required expensive rental equipment. The work was also extremely labor-intensive. To do the job right, they needed to hire a specialized crew. If he could convince Micronics to accept an alternative, NAC had a shot at breaking even on this phase. Will had spent the past week researching earthquake-resistant walls, found a shear wall system, in use throughout Asia, that some engineers claimed was better than the RCC walls. In a seismic event, the flexibility of the shear walls slowed their collapse, giving personnel inside the building several extra minutes to leave. The shear walls were also faster and far less costly to build. A good idea was one thing. Selling Micronics on a design that deviated significantly from a plan both companies agreed upon and everyone but the janitors had signed off on was another.

Will downed the dregs of his beer and peered down the bar, attempting to catch the eye of one of the bartenders. The two guys on duty were setting up for the late-afternoon crowd, the tall one checking inventory, the shorter, heftier one replenishing the wine rack under the counter.

This was Will's first visit to Marcus's. Normally, exhausted after a long day on the job, he ordered room service or ate in the bar at his hotel. Occasionally, he'd take in a movie. He'd finished early today, didn't feel like hanging out in his room, asked the concierge at the Marriott for a recommendation. The food was decent, the concierge had told him, and they served a long list of microbrews, which caught Will's attention. The ambiance played to a professional crowd in their thirties and forties: paneled walls, Tiffany chandeliers, mahogany cabinetry, gleaming marble bar, the bottles of top-shelf liquor behind the bar reflected in the bar's mirrored glass. From Thursday to Sunday, they brought in jazz bands. A Brazilian trio called Bossa Rio was playing this month. When he lived on the West Coast, in the 70's, the Latin scene was in its heyday. Too bad it was Tuesday. Would have been interesting to hear how the sound evolved.

Frustrated by the slow service, Will fished for his wallet, planning to cash out. He'd no sooner laid his credit card on the bar, when a third bartender, a perky redhead, strolled out of the kitchen, and he put his card and wallet away. All three bartenders wore the same uniform: tuxedo trousers, black satin vest, starched white shirt, a thin red, white and blue tie. She made eye contact, acknowledging Will's presence, and said something to one of her coworkers. She shook her head, laughing, and pulled the top menu from a pile pushed loosely against the cash register.

She was young—in her mid-twenties, he figured. Her biceps said she was a regular at the gym. She had an upturned nose, dainty chin, congenial green eyes. She wore her wavy red hair in a braid. She reminded him of somebody. Nicole Kidman's less regal, sexier little sister, maybe.

"Hi," she said, extending a small freckled hand. "I'm Kyra. And you are?"

"Will." He pumped her hand, curious why so many women today insisted on shaking.

"So, Will. Another beer? Or try something different?" She turned the menu on its back, pointed to a long list of classic and flavored martinis. "We're known for our martinis."

"Sure. Martini sounds good. Let's see." He scanned the menu. "This 'Gold.'" Stirred, the menu said, extra-dry, with a choice of premium vodka. "With Kettle One, if you have it."

"Dirty?"

He smirked at the innuendo. "Any chance I could get three olives?"

"Sure." She laughed easily. "With blue cheese? They go great with the vodka."

After she left, Will watched the busboy, setting tables in the dining area, his lips moving, the silent words accompanied by grand gesticulations that nobody but an aspiring actor would be caught dead doing in public. Within minutes, Will grew bored. He doodled on a napkin, drawing a rough sketch of the bar, hoping to stir his creative juices, devise a plan to sell his proposal.

Leah stared glumly at her watch. It was close to five. Dusk had fallen twenty minutes ago, the flickering TV providing the only light in Hope's dismal little ranch. This place was a hoot. The three of them, Hope, Lupo, Todd, were all smoking weed, watching a rerun of *Dawson's Creek*, on cable. Just watching. They'd turned the sound off.

Leah pressed the volume button on the clicker, holding it until the TV was blaring.

"Cut it *out*," Hope griped, "turn it back down."

"Yeah," Todd agreed. His eyes were all red-rimmed, rheumy. "Turn it down."

"There was no sound," Leah pointed out, quite reasonably, she felt. "I couldn't hear it."

"Cool, dude," Lupo chimed in. "A silent movie."

Leah couldn't believe her boyfriend had brought her here today. The kid was obtuse. He didn't actually think she enjoyed sitting here, watching him and his friends getting high? When he asked what she wanted to do, she'd told him *whatever*. Any nitwit should have realized that "whatever" did not translate into "take me to Hope's." She hadn't seen her boyfriend in days. You'd think he'd want to do something romantic, for once. Go for a picnic, drive up to the water tower, walk around the lake. He could have taken her for an ice cream. Anything except *this*.

The house reeked. Hope's mom, Mindy, gave their cat the run of the house. The sofa was covered in hairballs. Leah wondered if anybody cleaned the place, *ever*. If you swiped your finger over the end table, you'd probably catch hepatitis or AIDS or some other vile disease. That wasn't very generous, Leah supposed, especially since Hope's mom was so cool about having the kids over, letting them smoke. (On occasion, she smoked along with them.) Leah's mom would go ballistic if she ever caught kids smoking weed in their house.

Leah scooped a handful of barbecue chips from the bowl on the coffee table. The first time she was here, she'd found the atmosphere exhilarating, the rumbling rock music pounding out of speakers standing like mini towers in all four corners of the room— quadraphonic sound, Todd called it—kids everywhere, draped over

77

chairs, lying on the floor. Kids were dancing; still others sat in a circle on the living room floor, passing a joint, the entire scene enveloped in a cloud of marijuana, its smell intoxicating and sweet. Somewhere along the line, the house had lost its luster. She felt lonely sitting here, watching the others smoke weed and act stupid.

Hope excused herself, and she and Lupo left the room. Hope's bedroom door clicked shut, then Hope was giggling. Leah slouched lower, crossing her feet on the coffee table.

"Hey, babe," Todd said, pulling her close. He pressed her into a reclining position, and thrust his tongue in her mouth. French kissing was nasty. For his sake, Leah put up with it.

Slobber dribbled onto her chin. Repulsed, she worked his tongue to the front of her mouth, and, turning sideways, stretching her legs, allowed his hands free reign over her breasts.

Within minutes, he was approaching dangerous territory.

"Don't," she whispered, lifting his hand off her abdomen. "I don't want to."

Lately, whenever the opportunity arose, her boyfriend pressured her to have sex. "Why not?" he pleaded. He loved her. Didn't she love him? In a weak moment, Leah had confided in Hope. Seriously? You don't? Hope laughed, long and hard, until tears rolled down her cheeks, and she finally realized she was the only one laughing. Once the initial shock had worn off, she'd been surprisingly supportive. "Make him wait," Hope advised. "Don't do it until you're ready."

I'm not ready, Leah thought, wiggling out from under him. She might never be ready.

"What's wrong, babe? Come back here."

Leah sat, and moved to the far end of the sofa, crossing her arms. "I'm not in the mood."

"Come on, babe," he whined. "Why not?"

"I told you, I'm not in the mood."

"The mood," he repeated, and grabbed the clicker, started flipping through the channels.

His sulking pissed her off. In fact, everything about her so-called boyfriend irked her today. His greedy hands, his meandering fingers. That ridiculous goatee, with like ten microscopic blond hairs. Even his voice struck her as tinny and grating.

Leah had a sinking feeling that one of her teammates had seen her in Todd's Jeep. As they were leaving the high school, she'd asked Todd to turn right, in the direction opposite of her team's running route. Of course, he'd said no. That part of the road was under construction. With all the detours, he'd informed her, it would take forever to get anywhere. So what if her teammates spotted her? So what if she and Todd had no time schedule, nowhere specific to go?

Coach Thomas was a stickler about practice. Leah rarely skipped. Last week, she'd gotten her period at lunch. In the five minutes it had taken her to reach the girls' room, blood had soaked through her chinos. From the restroom, crouched in one of the stalls, she'd called her mother at work, told her mom what had happened. Thankfully, she'd worn a sweatshirt to school. She tied the sleeves of the sweatshirt around her waist, opened the bathroom door, looked both ways to be sure no one was around, and bolted down the hall to the front office, where she'd waited impatiently for her mom to dismiss her. That night, Leah had called Coach Thomas to explain. At practice the following day, despite having had a good excuse, because she'd broken a team rule, missing practice without asking permission, her coach had forced her to run two extra laps around the track and do twenty-five pushups. Leah had no idea how Coach Thomas would punish her this time, if the girls ratted her out. Whatever, it wouldn't be good.

Nine

Stormy

A week passed in their normal bustling confusion, which for Zoe meant a period of relative peace. Both daughters seemed to be moving in the right direction: no rude outbursts, no undone chores, no "courtesy calls" from the high school, informing her that Leah's grades were dropping or that she was falling behind in her work. Of course, with teenagers you never *really* knew what was happening inside their heads. Just when you thought that you understood your child, the instant you decided that you'd figured her out, the moment you convinced yourself that you appreciated her peculiar tendencies, as soon as you began to believe that you knew what to expect, she would change. Or be kidnapped by Martian invaders. Zoe's daughters had been replaced, this past Monday, by two sullen teenagers who looked exactly like Justine and Leah.

This afternoon, Zoe's five o'clock patient called at three thirty, left a message with the receptionist, canceling her appointment. Every therapist Zoe knew required a twenty-four hour notice of cancellation; if a patient failed to show, the therapist charged for the hour. Zoe posted a similar policy in her office, but she rarely enforced it. Many of the families she counseled lived barely above sustenance level; she didn't have the heart to charge them for missed appointments, last-minute cancellations. (It was a source of contention between her and Will, particularly since their own family needed the money.) Most patients appreciated Zoe's generosity and respected her for it. Every so often, someone took advantage, the rudeness jolting her, ruining her day.

80

In Leah's Wake

Turning out of the lot behind her office, she fastened her seat belt and switched the radio on, adjusting the dial to ZLX, a classic rock station that helped her relax. She was glad for the chance to leave early, today. Leah had given her grief this morning, *again*, about going to school. "It's a waste of time," Leah whined. She could not care less who'd fought which war or where the battle lines had been drawn. She saw no point in reading novels by Joseph Conrad or Thomas Hardy or D. H. Lawrence, authors who'd died before her grandmother was born.

Zoe was sick of Leah's baloney. Until last winter, both girls had been straight-A students. In the spring of her sophomore year, Leah's grades had slipped; this semester, she was barely squeezing by, her progress report littered with Cs. Zoe tried nagging, cajoling, tried rationalizing with Leah. Two weeks ago, she'd logged onto the website for the US Bureau of Labor, printed statistics comparing the income of college graduates to that of people with high school degrees, a difference of nearly a million dollars over a lifetime. "Look at this—" She'd handed her daughter the printout. "—the average salary for a high school graduate is twenty-eight thousand dollars a year." On that salary, a single person couldn't afford to pay the rent on a decent apartment in Boston. *Seriously?* Leah exclaimed. *Twenty-eight thousand? A year? I could easily live on that.* By some minor miracle, Zoe had managed to keep her tongue in check.

A half-mile out of the town center, she passed the Cortland Exchange, a converted mill that housed the Post Office, a Thai restaurant, called "The Lemon Tree," a florist, a yoga studio, a hair salon, and La Mode, the day spa where Zoe occasionally treated herself to a manicure or pedicure. She considered stopping at the spa, asking if they had time to squeeze in a manicure, decided to go home instead, relax, take a warm bath.

She turned into the Exxon Station down the street from the mill. Filling her tank, she remembered that she'd run out of face cream. She paid for her gas, and doubled back to the spa.

It was a perfect afternoon. The limestone pebbles embedded in the asphalt glittered in the late-afternoon sun. The shops were bustling. Women emerged cheerfully from the rear doors of the building, toting brightly decorated gift bags, carrying bouquets of black-eyed Susan and thistle, pots of red and orange mums. Zoe walked briskly across the lot, her purse tucked under her arm, high heels clicking, loose cotton skirt swishing around her legs, all the while humming the Billy Joel tune she'd been listening to on the radio. "We Didn't Start the Fire," it was called.

81

The day spa occupied a quarter of the space on the first floor of the two-story brick building, its back windows overlooking the parking lot. Last time she was here, Zoe had been with the girls. It was a Friday afternoon, the end of August. She'd taken the day off; they'd spent the morning at the Burlington Mall, shopping for school clothes, had eaten a late lunch at Chili's. Afterward, Zoe brought the girls to the spa, for haircuts. As a treat, she'd paid for manicures and pedicures for the girls. It was Justine's first pedicure, and Zoe was still not convinced that her younger daughter had enjoyed it. She'd asked a hundred questions. Why use pumice rather than some other stone to smooth the calluses? Was it hard, learning to do nails? Did it take long? Why not paint the white tip on her toenails *after* they applied "Petal," the pale pink overcoat? Leah, meanwhile, adjusted the leather chair to recline, switched on the vibrator, and closed her eyes.

Through the spa's French door, Zoe saw Nora, the manager, at the reception desk, scowling at her computer screen, her left shoulder cradling the phone. She ran a thin hand over her spiky, green-tinted hair. Two women stood by the desk, waiting impatiently, one studying her bill, the other watching Nora, rolling her eyes. A pretty, light-haired woman Zoe had never seen before stood by a table to the right of the reception desk, selling jewelry, it appeared.

Nora waved as Zoe entered, mouthed a "hello." The clients nodded, sizing Zoe up.

Zoe's stomach churned. As always, she found the spa's affected atmosphere unnerving—the hushed voices, the cascading fountain by the archway leading to the back rooms, the upscale décor (marble walls accented by rich shades of gold, orange, green), the New Age music, synthesized sounds of wind and rain. She felt as if she'd invaded a private club, its cultured clientele more refined than she. Gradually, she settled into the rhythm.

The metal racks lining the walls displayed a dizzying array of skin care products: night creams, day creams, eye creams, lip balms, astringents, exfoliating masks, bath beads, pre- and post-shower lotions, and dozens of soaps, some bars wrapped, others unwrapped. A large block of soap, marbled with flecks of yellow and green, sat on one of the higher shelves on the back wall, a carving knife lying by its side. Another rack was devoted entirely to candles—rosewood, sandalwood, lavender, vanilla. Zoe wondered how Nora could tolerate these warring smells.

In Leah's Wake

They'd moved the anti-aging lotions to a round, triple-tiered display case at the center of the floor. With the weather turning cooler, Zoe was spending more time indoors and needed a cream with a stronger moisturizer than the one she'd been using. She selected the jar with the most enticing label, studied the ingredient list. She'd read an article in *Vogue* recently, touting some new wonder ingredient. Beta hydroxy? Vitamin C? She returned the jar to its designated spot, picked up a lime-green tube, the length of her middle finger. Glycolic acid? She glanced at the reception desk, hoping to catch Nora's eye, ask her for advice. Nora was still on the phone.

"Can I help you with anything? I'm not an esthetician, but I can tell you what I like."

"Hi," Zoe said, turning to face the woman she'd seen in the alcove. From a distance, the woman was pretty; up close, she was gorgeous: deeply set eyes, Mediterranean nose, lustrous skin. She wore a stylish scoop-necked tank and black chiffon skirt, a thick emerald-green belt cinching her tiny waist, black ballet shoes on her feet. *I could never pull that off,* Zoe thought, embarrassed of her dowdy outfit. *Even if I tried.* "Thanks. I'm just waiting for Nora. I love your bracelet, by the way." The woman turned her wrist, the shimmering translucent beads the color of sea glass. Zoe had never seen a bracelet quite like that one before. "It's striking."

"It's called Greta Garbo. All of my bracelets have an identity. Here, let me show you." Zoe followed the woman to her table, set in an alcove. "They're made with vintage buttons, dating between 1890 and 1960. I find the buttons at antique stores, flea markets sometimes. It's a ball. I'm Dorothy Klein, by the way." She extended her hand. "It's nice to meet you."

A small, calligraphic sign in front of the display tree said, "Ruby Slippers Design."

"They're gorgeous." Zoe ran her finger over a deep blue bracelet. "Like pieces of art."

The blue would look great on Leah. And her birthday was just a few weeks away.

"Here—" Dorothy slid three bracelets off the wooden bar, handed the blue one to Zoe. "That one's made of bakelite. I call it 'Stormy.' It's part of my mood collection. Try it on?"

"Stormy,'" Zoe mused, and slipped the bracelet over her wrist.

"I'd go with this one," Nora said, peering over Zoe's shoulder. "It's great, isn't it?"

Zoe returned the blue bracelet, pushed the second one Dorothy offered over her hand, rotating her wrist. The rich yellow undertone in the alabaster buttons brought out the gold in her skin. "Liz Taylor," she read, on the note card that came with the bracelet. On the lower right corner of the card, she noticed the price, written in pencil. A hundred twenty dollars. "Thank you." She handed the bracelet back. "It's exquisite." If money were not tight, she would buy it.

At the register, Zoe handed Nora the jar of mid-priced vitamin E cream she had selected.

On impulse, while Nora was waiting for authorization from Visa, Zoe bought both bracelets, the dark blue, "Stormy," for Leah, "Liz Taylor" for herself, paying Dorothy by check.

Zoe opened her car door, set her bags on the passenger's seat. She was pleased to have found such a unique birthday gift for her daughter. When she unwrapped the bracelet, Leah would know immediately that Zoe had put thought into choosing her gift. She had not simply run into the Gap, plucked a pair of jeans and a sweater from the rack closest to the door, figuring she could always return whatever her daughter didn't care for. Zoe had chosen this gift specifically for Leah. Maybe I'll give it to her this afternoon, she thought, an olive leaf, to make up for this morning. She knew that she shouldn't bribe the girls with presents. One time, though—what could it hurt?

Jerry Johnson had been on duty for an hour. He parked the cruiser in the vacant lot at the corner of Blanchard and Old Orchard Roads, switched off the engine, hoping to sneak in a ten-minute nap. He hadn't slept a full night in three months, since his wife gave birth to the twins.

Asked six months ago to name the one thing he wanted most in the world, Jerry would have said kids. It had taken Maura five years to get pregnant. Early on, they'd blamed their inability to conceive on stress. They'd recently bought their first house, and money was tight. To make ends meet, Jerry volunteered for details whenever the opportunity arose, and Maura had taken a second job behind the bar at an Italian bistro, called Gino's, down the street from the fitness center where she worked fulltime, as a personal trainer. It was tough, both of them working sixty, seventy hours a week, but they could handle anything temporarily, they'd agreed.

Maura miscarried two months after they moved into their house. Though she'd been disappointed, she had handled the loss reasonably well. The timing, she conceded, would have been bad. A year later, she miscarried again. He and Maura started dating when they were sophomores in high school. In eighteen years, he'd never seen Maura so despondent. Night after night, he lay beside his sobbing wife, rubbing her back until she fell asleep. "I'm thirty-five years-old," she would cry. "What if I never get pregnant?" *We'll adopt, honey,* Jerry would murmur, his attempt to reassure her prompting a new fit of tears. He'd been opposed to fertility treatments. It was a turnoff, collecting his sperm in a sterile jar, delivering it to a clinic. Because he didn't know what else to do, he'd agreed. He would have done anything to please her.

Maura lost the first two embryos the doctor implanted. At her doctor's urging, Maura left her job at the restaurant. When the third attempt failed, she sold her fledgling personal training business, took a job in a video store. Jerry's heart broke. He found himself avoiding her eyes. If he didn't love his wife as much as he did, he never would have agreed to try a fourth time.

For seven months, the pregnancy progressed like a dream. He painted the nursery, hung a silly lamb border Maura picked out. They bought diapers and T-shirts and dressing gowns for the babies, ordered a crib. At night, he and Maura took childbirth classes. At week thirty, she began having contractions, and her doctor confined her to bed rest. Over the next six weeks, Jerry had driven her to the hospital four times. Terrified, he begged the doctors to admit her; each time, the obstetrician on call sent her home. At thirty-six weeks, the fertility specialist finally scheduled a C-section, and her mother moved in to their tiny house, to care for her daughter. His mother-in-law had stayed with them until a month after the babies were born. Jerry wanted to help out. He'd offered to feed the boys, rock them, change their diapers. Both women pushed him away.

Jerry took deep diaphragmatic breaths, as his wife had been trained to do in Lamaze. He was all but asleep when he heard the squeal of tires, and saw a powder blue Volvo 940 wagon, license plate SLFHLP, whiz by. He shook out the cobwebs, and switched on the siren and lights.

Zoe never heard the siren, her mind still engaged in the battle she'd had with Leah this morning. At seven thirty, long after the bus had come and gone, around the time her first period class was due to start, Leah dragged herself out of bed. Zoe had a mind to make the kid walk. Maybe next time Leah would get out of bed on time. The problem was, Zoe wanted Leah to go.

From the minute they left their driveway until they arrived at the high school, Leah pestered her for a note. "Come on, Ma. It's no big deal. Just say I was sick." Without a note, she would get a detention.

"Well, then," Zoe had snapped. "A detention it is." Now she felt bad. This was her cycle: She would take a stand on an issue, refusing on principle to budge. Afterward, she always felt guilty. She should have written the note. Was telling a white lie really such a big deal? Worth this miserable day? Worth alienating her daughter?

Zoe recognized the opening chords of a song from *Evita*, and turned the radio up, singing along with Madonna. When the girls were little, they used to beg Zoe to sing. She had a dreadful singing voice, totally tone deaf. Her daughters, if they'd noticed, didn't seem to mind. She would sing their favorite songs: "Over the Rainbow," "A Spoonful of Sugar," "Edelweiss." After the first verse, the girls would join in, their exuberant songs rocking the car. If Zoe dared to sing now, Leah would probably pull her coat over her head.

What troubled Zoe most were the mood swings. For a day or two, Leah would be the ideal daughter, sweet, helpful, attentive. And Zoe would drop her guard, convinced that Leah's recent conduct was a fluke, a glitch, a temporary stage. At last, her *real* daughter was back. One day, out of nowhere, Leah would explode, putting them right back in the war zone, her daughter's outbursts followed by periods of glowering silence that frightened Zoe more than the fits. It would be easier if her daughter acted out all the time. If she and Will knew what to expect, they could plan an effective response. As it was, Zoe tiptoed around Leah, constantly afraid of setting her off. All this tiptoeing, never knowing what was in store frazzled Zoe's nerves. Though it shamed her to admit it, there were days when, if she knew her daughter was there, she would do almost anything—paperwork, errands that could easily wait—to avoid going home.

The Volvo's speed kept increasing. Forty-five, fifty, fifty-five.

Jerry accelerated, until he was right on her tail. The woman's head was bobbing. Nut cake. He flashed his lights. Why wasn't she stopping? He flipped on the PA.

Finally, the woman woke up, and eased the Volvo onto the shoulder.

He climbed out of the truck, wincing, shook out his leg. His sciatica was bothering him again. Had to schedule an appointment with the physical therapist, when he had time to spare.

He walked along the shoulder, his eyes trained on the wagon as he approached.

The woman had lowered her head. All he could see was a shock of dark curly hair, the hood of a black coat, maybe a cape. Probably a witch. He'd heard there was—What did they call them?—a *coven*, operating in Groton. Goddesses, they called themselves. Wiccans. Weirdo nature freaks, held services in the woods. They sacrificed animals—dogs, cats, small birds—some of these people. *Good grief.* He was in for a long night.

As he neared her car, he noticed her rifling through her purse.

He tapped on the glass, gesturing for her to roll down the window.

She pressed the button for the automatic window, raised a finger. While he stood there, waiting, she dug a comb out of her bag. A tampon. She laid a notepad over the tampon, dropped a handful of roller-ball pens on the passenger seat, and removed her wallet, rooted through the credit card pockets, the billfold. Finally, she located the license, wrapped in a wad of tissue.

"Sorry." She offered an apologetic half-smile, handed him the license and registration, which she retrieved from the Volvo's warranty manual. "I thought I'd lost it, there for a minute."

Some people. "Any idea why I pulled you over?"

The woman shook her head, her eyes fixed on the dash. "Speeding, I guess."

"You were doing fifty-five, in a thirty-five-mile-an-hour zone."

A car whizzed by, the teenage passenger eyeing Zoe, gloating. Zoe flinched, and looked away. It mortified her, sitting here like a criminal on display, the cruiser's blue light blinking.

In her rearview, she watched the cop stroll back to the cruiser. His height and compact muscular structure suggested a military background, as did the buzz cut. He favored his left leg. An accident, she mused, during a pursuit: he was a chaser, this one, all righteousness and gusto.

The cop gave her the creeps. He reminded her of a policeman in Boxborough, the rural town north of Cortland where she had grown up. Zoe's mother, once she had reached a certain state of inebriation, had an ugly habit of cutting herself. One particular cop, Officer Regan, seemed to respond to every 9-1-1 call Zoe or her father placed. The cop bandaged her mother's wrists with the efficiency and detachment of a military medic. Though he never looked at her, maybe because she'd felt he'd pointedly ignored her, Zoe always felt judged, as if her mother's drinking were somehow her fault. She pushed the thought away, and flipped open her cell phone.

She let the phone ring, tapping her thigh, wondering why no one picked up. Justine was probably online. Zoe and Will ought to set a rule for using the computer. Limit her to an hour after school, an hour at night. Justine was twelve-years-old. She ought to be outdoors, riding her bike, getting some exercise, instead of sitting all day, staring at a computer screen. When Leah was that age, she was constantly on the go. She'd played on town softball and basketball teams, in addition to playing soccer all year. Justine had zero interest in sports. She'd taken karate lessons when she was younger, quit after earning her first-degree black belt. If not for that silly heavy bag in her room, she would get no exercise at all. No wonder the child was on Zantac. All that nervous energy and nowhere for it to go.

Zoe turned to check on the cruiser, see if she could tell what was taking so long.

His computer was down. They'd been having problems with the network feed. He called Millie, asked her to run the license and registration from the station. *Zoe Tyler.* The name sounded vaguely familiar. Of course—the woman who ran the workshops Maura nattered about, Success Skills, if he remembered correctly. Jerry had discouraged his wife from attending. *Only oddballs go to those things,* he told her. Oddballs and losers. Reminded him of the infomercials he watched when he couldn't sleep, for those empowerment seminars. Bunch of misfits gathered on a beach on some exotic island, Fiji or Bali, extolling the virtues of the seminar, referring to the motivational guru as if he were God. Maura didn't need any workshop. Mild depression was normal after a woman gave birth. His wife would be back to her old self in no time. He hoped.

As he expected, the license and registration checked out.

The Tyler woman was watching him in her rearview, the tipped mirror revealing a partial reflection. Nice eyes. She turned her head, lifting her hair off her neck.

He handed her the slip of paper, along with her license.

"Sorry," she said, tucking her license into her purse. "I didn't realize I was speeding."

Right. If he had a nickel for every speeding driver who said she was sorry, he would be rich. Tempted him to double the cost of the ticket, for lying. Oddly, the Tyler woman didn't appear to want anything from him. If she were finagling for a warning, she would be smiling, flirting, trying to soften him up. That she wasn't impressed him. Instead, she stared straight into space, as if she were apologizing to herself, for screwing up, instead of to him.

He lowered himself to get a better view of her face. She looked younger than forty-two, the age on her license. At thirty-five, both he and Maura looked older. Certain features were striking: her full lips

88

and high cheekbones, her flawless gold skin. Her eyes, a luminous sea-foam green, were arresting. But her nose was a tad long, and her mouth too wide. So, then, why was he standing here, feeling all dizzy and awkward, as if he were in middle school all over again?

"Keep it down," he said, a gruffness he didn't feel invading his tone. He tore the top sheet from the ticket pad and handed it to her. "Before you hurt somebody."

Zoe replied with a dispirited nod.

Before she drove off, she looked at the ticket, hoping she'd gotten lucky for once, thinking maybe he'd cut her a break, charged her a hundred dollars rather than two. As the cop's Explorer pulled away from the shoulder, she rechecked the ticket. A warning. That the cop might have issued a warning had never crossed her mind. Maybe this was a sign. She took in the vibrant blue gift bag on the passenger seat, sparkling white ribbon curling from its handles. Maybe her luck was finally turning around.

Ten

The Rules Are The Rules

The following Friday, Leah stood by the gym door at the back of the school, waiting for Todd to pick her up. Bored, she toyed with the button bracelet her mother gave her last week. The bracelet was supposed to have been a birthday gift, her mom too impatient to wait. "Don't tell your sister," her mom said. "I haven't had a chance to buy anything for her. But I will."

Figures, her mom would buy her a bracelet called *Stormy*, though, Leah had to admit, she sort of liked being thought of as stormy. She rotated her wrist, a fiery blue button catching the light. Stormy, she mused. *Tempestuous. Wild. Raging. Intense.*

The gym door swung open, startling her, and the soccer team marched out, Cissy leading the pack, her callow brown eyes focused straight ahead, as if Leah weren't even there. *The bitch.*

"One, two, three, four," Cissy chanted. "Who we gonna win for?"

"Cortland. Cortland," the team responded, in unison.

Six, seven, eight, Leah mimicked. *Who you gonna annihilate? Yourselves. Yourselves.*

Today's was the final game of the regular season. Cortland was fourteen and one, a game ahead of Westford, the next best team in the Hillside Division. A win would clinch the league title. And Leah wasn't playing. Coach Thomas had dropped her name from the roster. Her coach didn't even have the decency to tell Leah herself. Leah had to hear the news from a freshman, of all people, the sister of one of the seniors. Leah hadn't believed her. Why would Coach Thomas bench her best player? Leah had scored more goals this season than

90

the rest of the team put together. According to the reporter from the *Gazette*, she *was* the team. Infuriated, she skipped her last class, stomped to the gym, into Coach Thomas's office, demanding an explanation.

"I'm sorry," Coach Thomas informed her. "But I've got no choice."

No choice? Leah rocked on her heels. Didn't they resolve their problems last week? Last Friday, after the bell rang, while the girls were changing into their sweats, Coach Thomas called Leah into her office. "You're either part of this team or you're not," Coach Thomas had said.

"I was sick," Leah replied. "My mom picked me up."

"In a black Wrangler?" Coach Thomas demanded, and launched into a long, boring dissertation about responsibility, commitments, teaching the younger kids by example. Leah *was* a good example. An example of how to behave like an adult, how to take control of your life, instead being led around by the nose like one of the sheep. But it was in her best interests to keep her mouth shut. So she'd stood in Coach Thomas's office for the next forty-five minutes, shuffling from foot to foot so her legs didn't fall asleep, while the coach reamed her butt.

Afterward, they'd made up and Coach Thomas had given Leah a hug.

Since then, Leah had been the model player. Running five miles a day. Motivating the younger players. Doing extra drills. What could she possibly have done to deserve this?

Coach Thomas, it emerged, had heard about the party at Hope's, last Saturday night. Hope threw parties every weekend. Last weekend, for no good reason (the kids were not particularly loud) the cops busted it up. Leah, the only sober one there, for a change, answered the door. "What can I do for you, officers?" she asked sweetly. The younger one, grunting, pushed her aside, and barged in. The cops rummaged through every room, slamming doors, searching closets, hunting for drugs, evidently. When they realized they were wasting their time, they'd taken the names of everyone at the party, sent the kids on their way. By Tuesday, when her parents still hadn't confronted her, Leah had figured she was in the clear. Turned out, instead of calling parents, the cops, just this morning, passed the names they'd collected on to the school.

"Nothing I can do," Coach Thomas informed her. "You have to sit out two games."

Two games? That was totally unfair, Leah complained. Missing two games would ruin her stats. This would kill her chances of making the *Globe* All-Scholastic team. "I didn't even drink." She was the only sober kid at the entire party when the cops arrived. Didn't that count?

"You know the rules, Leah."

But what about the girls? Her teammates depended on her. If their team won today, they'd win their division. She couldn't sit out. She had to play. She had to help the team win.

Coach Thomas appeared to be thinking, and, for an instant, Leah thought she might reconsider. Then she opened the filing drawer in her desk, and thumbed through the folders. Leah knew exactly what her coach was looking for: the pact she'd signed at the pre-season captain's practice, promising to avoid being in the presence of alcohol and drugs.

Coach Thomas produced the paper, held it out for Leah to see. "This *is* your signature?"

Leah could have argued, could have claimed she was coerced. After all, Coach had not exactly given the players a choice. But why fight a battle she couldn't win? Instead, she'd issued an ultimatum. "If I can't play today," she announced, "I'm quitting the team."

She'd been stunned when Coach Thomas agreed.

A bus pulled alongside the soccer field. Fuming, Leah watched the opposing team disembark. This was a travesty, Leah's not playing today. For an entire week, she'd been on her best behavior. Twice, she'd made dinner. She helped Justine with her geometry homework. Offered to wash and wax her father's car. (He hadn't let her. But still.) She did her homework every night, whether she felt like it or not, had even turned in several old assignments, ones she'd ignored or neglected to finish. She'd received the only A in her entire class on the biology exam. At the party last weekend, even though she wanted to drink, even though she wanted to smoke, she'd been the model kid, resisting every temptation. When that young cop began taking names, and all the other kids gave fake IDs, Leah had given her real name. She hadn't done anything wrong, so why not? If anything, they should respect her. Instead, they reported her to the school.

Thankfully, her father was in California. Otherwise, he would already be here. He insisted on arriving twenty minutes early for games. The warm-ups, he said, gave him an opportunity to observe the opposing players, size up the competition. Leah wondered if Coach Thomas had called her mom yet, or if she would wait until after the game. If she'd called, Leah was done: Her mom would have immediately called Leah's father, out on the job site. If there was anything worse than her father's hearing bad news, it was hearing it when he was at work. Once, when Leah was ten, she'd broken a metatarsal bone, an injury that had sidelined her for the rest of the season. Her dad was in Chicago. Her mom called from the hospital, interrupting a meeting; her father had caught the first plane home. He hadn't yelled at her exactly, but he had not been pleased. With her luck, he was probably already in the air, on his way home.

Leah kicked her foot backward, hitting the steel door with the sole of her Doc Martin shoe. Leah had to pinch herself to prove she was here, hanging out with all the other losers, outside the gym, waiting for a ride. Her father was going to kill her. He talked incessantly about that dumb All-Scholastic award. If she made Player of the Year, she *might* have a shot at redeeming herself with the Harvard coach. Now, she would be lucky if the coaches in her league voted for her for the All-Star team. She could hear her father, when she broke the big news: This is the last straw, Leah Marie. Quitters never win. Which meant she was a loser. Wouldn't surprise her if he kicked her out of the house. To hear him, he had plenty of reasons. She was disrespectful. A liar. A lousy example for Justine. He and her mother were sick of her antics. Shape up or ship out. Well, she hadn't shaped up. This was it: Time to ship out.

Leah wondered where she would go. To Todd's probably. Or Hope's. Hope was cool; she didn't strike Leah as the type who would mind. Leah would have to find a job, of course. She would probably waitress. (She'd never waited tables, didn't know the first thing about food service. But, really, how tough could it be?) Maybe Hope would allow her to crash on their couch temporarily, until she'd saved enough money to move to a place where she actually wanted to live. If she had to choose right now, she would probably pick New York. She'd been to the city with her parents a few times, when she was a kid, to visit one of her father's uncles. Her great uncle lived on the Upper East Side, in a co-op overlooking the Park. His neighborhood was way too ritzy for Leah. A decent one-bedroom apartment probably cost four or five hundred dollars a month. And she was not about to rent a place with cockroaches or rats. Maybe her uncle would help her find an affordable place in the Village. She pictured herself, in a sidewalk café, serving seeded organic bread, wearing flowery secondhand clothes. Or maybe she would move to southern California, where the weather was always sunny and warm. She had never been to the West Coast, but she knew from all the movies she had seen that she would feel right at home.

By the time her boyfriend arrived, the game was in progress. Cortland was winning: one-zip. But it was early. Still plenty of time to lose.

"Where were you?" Leah snapped. She hoisted herself into the truck, tossing her backpack on the floor. "I've been waiting forever."

"Work," he barked back. "Want me to get fired?"

"Like Jamie would fire you."

"You think he likes it when I cut out early?"

"He wouldn't fire you for that."

Grunting, Todd stepped on the gas. The Wrangler jerked forward. "He accused me of stealing fifty bucks from him this morning."

Leah shot an accusatory look in his direction. "Did you?"

"Steal money out of the register? Hell no."

"Good," she said, relieved. She would be mortified if she thought she were dating a thief. Never mind a thief who stole from his friends. "That's not like him. Why did he say that?"

"I don't know." He lowered his voice. "I told him I was gonna pay it back."

Leah bolted upright, instantly on alert. "So you did steal the money?"

"I said I planned to pay it back. Could we get off this? I don't want to talk about it."

Fine, she muttered. Would he play that Rage whatever it was again? She needed a lift.

He slid the CD into the changer. "Didn't you have a game today?'

Leah shrugged. She didn't feel like talking about it.

"So, what's up? I got worried when you called."

What's up? Where was she to begin? She'd lost her sense of direction. Her boyfriend, she'd just learned, had stolen fifty dollars from his employer. She'd quit playing soccer, the only thing in the whole world she was good at or truly knew how to do. The kids at school gossiped about her constantly. Her parents were on the verge of disowning her. Did that count? Being disowned by your parents? She was about to be thrown out of her house, with no place to go. Life as she'd known it for sixteen years had ended, and she had no idea what would come next. "Nothing," she lied. "I missed you." Since her answer seemed to satisfy him, she left it at that.

Leah laid her head on the rest, closing her eyes, and tried to imagine her future. She conjured a fuzzy image of herself, wearing a funky outfit she couldn't quite see, doing something she liked, though she couldn't tell what. When it came to specifics—what her parents would say to her the day she moved out, what it would feel like to be on her own—she drew a blank. Oh, well. She was resilient. She would manage somehow. What other choice did she have?

Will polished off his martini, and ordered a second. The Micronics deal was unraveling fast. Last week, the project manager blew him off. Late Tuesday afternoon, Cushing's secretary called Will, apologized and told Will that Cushing would like to meet with him on Wednesday morning. Refusing to accommodate the jerk wasn't an option. The meeting, which Cushing, in typical fashion, had set for ten thirty, giving Will barely enough time to deplane, rent a car, and—driving eighty, hitting zero traffic—get from San Francisco International into the city (his anxiety rocketing into the stratosphere every time he encountered a stoplight), lasted exactly six minutes. Cushing had presented Will's proposal at their project meeting on Tuesday, he said. On Friday, at noon, Will was to meet the architects at their downtown office, to go over the details.

By Wednesday night, a friend in NAC's marketing department had produced and posted, by Federal Express, an audio-visual presentation detailing Will's shear wall proposal. For the visuals, he'd created a split-screen demo simulating the Micronics facility after an earthquake, the building on the left side of the screen constructed with RCC walls, the one on the right with shear walls. For the score, he used Wagner's *Ride of the Valkyries* (rather melodramatically, Will felt), the piece reaching its chilling crescendo as the RCC walls collapsed. At the meeting today, about two minutes after he'd dimmed the lights, Will caught the lead architect with his eyes closed. When the video ended, Will quizzed the architects, asking each, in turn, what he or she thought about the possibility of switching to shear walls. RCC walls were standard. End of story. Wouldn't surprise him if, before he was out of the building, they'd called Cushing, advised him to bring in one of NAC's competitors to re-bid the rest of the job. Will had no proof, since Cushing had gone into hiding, neither taking nor returning his calls. But that didn't mean squat.

His first inclination after the fiasco was to drive to the construction site, pay a visit to the trailer. He wanted to confront Cushing head-on, force the pussy to deliver the bad news, if that's what it was,

95

to his face. A mile from the site, he changed his mind—an impromptu visit could kill the project outright, an outcome he could not afford. He tried calling the airlines to rebook his ten p.m. flight, struck out, and headed to Marcus, to get shit-faced instead.

It was after one thirty, the tail end of the lunch shift. The restaurant had begun emptying out, the wait staff comparing notes on their weekend plans as they cleared the vacated tables, the support staff ferrying plastic tubs of dirty dishes back to the kitchen, replacing the tablecloths.

Toward the end of the bar, a kid not much older than Leah, his blond hair tied in a stubby ponytail at the nape of his neck, was talking with the bar manager, discussing the Brazilian jazz trio playing later tonight. The band, Will gathered, was popular with the local crowd.

"Band sounds pretty good," Will said.

"Yeah," Kyra said absently. She was shaking his second martini. "They are."

She poured his martini into a glass, speared two blue cheese olives, laid the swizzle stick over the rim, dropped three extra olives into a shot glass, and set both glasses in front of him.

"Thanks." Will raised the shot glass. "You're taking good care of me, Kyra."

"You sure you're OK? You look kind of down in the mouth."

Business, he told her. He'd met with some architects this afternoon. Bum meeting. Nothing earth shattering, he lied. More a matter of regrouping. "Excellent martini, by the way."

"It's cold enough, I hope. I like to keep the vodka in the freezer. But Joe down there—" Winking, she tipped her head toward the bar manager, who was making his way toward them now, washing the counter, his rag moving in neatly executed circles. "—insists on putting it out."

"So the customers can see it." Joe tamped his forehead with the back of his hand, and tossed the rag in the sink. "Folks don't order—"

"What they can't see." She rolled her eyes, laughing. "I know, Jo-Jo. I know."

Joe untied his apron, draped it over one arm. "You're good, K, right? Ray ought to be here shortly, to help you get ready for happy hour. It's my day with my girl."

"Single dad," Kyra said, after he'd left. "He adores that little girl. She's sweet. Too bad more guys aren't like him."

Last week, Kyra mentioned a daughter. Will interpreted her remark as a dig at her ex, and wondered if she was expecting him to ask questions. Before he had a chance to frame a respectable question, the young kid at the end of the bar signaled to settle his bill.

On his way out of the bar, the boy held the door for three attractive women in their early thirties, active types with deep tans, dressed in designer sweat suits, carrying expensive oversized bags. The women wandered inside, gabbing, distracted. Kyra took their orders: a Coors Light, two glasses of Merlot. She poured the drinks, set them on the bar, and opened their tab, pushing the register drawer closed with her hip, switched the station playing on the plasma TVs at both ends of the bar, tuning in to classic baseball, and disappeared into the kitchen.

On TV, the Sox were playing the Cincinnati Reds—1975, Game 6 in the Series, the most competitive World Series in history. Will had gone to the game with dad. Until he retired, Will's father managed the janitorial services at the Philadelphia City Hall. The tickets were a reward from Mayor Rizzo, for outstanding performance. From the time he was old enough to understand the game, the Sox had been Will's favorite American League team. The night his father showed him the tickets, he did not slept a wink. Early the next morning, Will and his father boarded a train to Boston. They sat behind the Sox dugout, close enough to hear Yaz psyching his teammates up between innings, to smell the cigarettes the players were smoking. That game, those three days in Boston with his dad, had been the highlight of Will's youth.

Half an inning passed before Kyra returned. With the rag her boss had left in the sink, she cleaned the puddle of beer she'd spilled under the tap.

"Baseball fan?" Will asked, gesturing to the TV.

"Oh, yeah." She pushed a curl out of her eyes. She'd cut her hair since last week. Normally, Will preferred longer hair on women. On Kyra, the cropped style looked stunning, soft auburn curls framing her face, revealing a subtle complexity he hadn't noticed before. "I love baseball," she said. "That was an amazing game. Boston against the 'Big Red Machine.'"

"I was there."

"You live in Boston, right? Did you grow up there?"

"Philly. Outside the city. I went to the game with my dad."

"Hold a sec—" She held up a finger, interrupting. "Sorry. I've got to watch this."

The outside door opened, the sunlight pouring into the bar creating a glare on the screen.

Will shook his head, and squinted at the TV. Bottom of the eleventh, Joe Morgan at bat. Will is right there, behind the dugout, in Fenway Park. He's fourteen-years-old. *The pitch.* His father catches his arm. Will's forehead breaks out in a sweat. Now, they're on their feet. Morgan slams a line drive into deep right. Evans sprints back, back, crossing the warning track—

"Yes!" Kyra pumped her fist. "I've seen that catch a dozen times. It still gets me."

"Same here." Will released a breath he hadn't realized he'd been holding.

"You believe the Sox lost the Series after that catch? And Fisk's twelfth-inning homer?"

A guy at the end of the bar lifted a finger to get Kyra's attention. When she didn't immediately jump, the guy snapped.

"Asshole," Will groused, thumbing the offender. "Pardon the language."

"It's OK." She shrugged, pushing a curl behind her ears. "You get used to it." Kyra signaled to the guy to let him know she was on her way. "I've got to get that. Be right back."

After she left, Will turned his attention back to the TV. The girl in a Nike shoe ad reminded him of Leah. *Damn.* She had a game today. He checked his watch. Two o'clock, five at home. With this Micronics crap, the game had slipped his mind. If Cortland won, they would capture the league title. If Leah played well, she would be a shoo-in for league MVP. He couldn't believe he'd forgotten to call, to wish her luck.

On the fourth ring, he reached her recording, left a message, told her he was sorry he couldn't be with her. "But I'm thinking about you, honey."

He clicked off, dialed Cushing again, reached an automated voice, and tried Zoe.

Last night, when they spoke, he'd asked Zoe to videotape the game so he could watch it at home, over the weekend. With a little luck, he would catch her as she was leaving her office. If she'd forgotten the camera, she would have time before the opening kick-off to drive home and get it. Another recording. He left a message, saying he loved her, asked her to wish Leah luck for him. "Tell the girls I miss them," he said, and turned his phone off, and put it away.

On her way home, Zoe had stopped at the supermarket for a few staples: butter, napkins, toilet paper, a package of string cheese for Justine, a bag of Macintosh apples. She'd also run in to the cleaners.

She set the plastic sack of groceries on the island counter, laid the dry cleaning bags over a chair. When Will called last night, he'd asked her to do something important. For the life of her, she couldn't say what. Because her notepad was not in the secretary, where she normally kept it, she'd neglected to write it down. Ah, well, eventually she would remember.

Justine was upstairs in her bedroom. Zoe could hear the shush of Justine's feet as she skated across the hardwood floor, the thwap, thwap, thwap of her punches, connecting with the regulation-sized punching bag that hung in the corner of her room. Zoe used to tease the girls, when they were younger, tell them she would not allow them to grow up. "You're gonna stay six," she would say, "like Christopher Robin—forever and ever." Wouldn't it be nice, she mused, if it were possible to keep your children innocent forever? Prevent them from turning into surly teenagers who frustrated you half the time, scared you out of your wits? *Oh stop,* Zoe scolded herself. *Don't be a drama queen.*

When she finished putting the groceries away, she set a kettle of water on the stove, and lit the burner. From the dishwasher, she retrieved her favorite blue mug, the one with Van Gogh's "Irises" on the face, rinsed the mug, and fetched an herbal teabag from the pantry.

An entire week had passed with not a single outburst from Leah. If anything, Leah's behavior was almost too good, Stepford daughter good. Could this polite, helpful teenager really be Leah? With an A on her biology exam? Zoe had been waiting all week for the bomb to drop, for one of Leah's foul moods to erupt, for her daughter to say or do something to shake her back to reality. This time, as naïve as it sounded, she thought things might actually be turning around.

For the first time in a long time, Zoe felt hopeful. She couldn't wait to talk with Will tonight, when he called. She'd considered phoning him on her way home from work, to see how he'd made out with the architects this afternoon, to share her good mood, but the battery in her cell phone had died and she'd lost the power cord. This business in California was not going well. Will had been to the West Coast four times since September. Every time he seemed close to a resolution, some new problem cropped up. When he called last night, he had evaded her questions, but the frustration was evident in his voice. When they talked tonight, she would remind him of the warning the cop had given her last week. Suggest that, if Leah's team made nationals, as nearly everyone believed they would, the whole family go to Phoenix for the game. If they added the two hundred

99

dollars the warning had saved to her earnings from the last seminar, they would have over a thousand dollars, enough to buy three plane tickets. (They were responsible for Leah's fare whether they went or not.) After the game, they could spend a few days exploring the city; maybe they'd drive to the Grand Canyon one day. They hadn't taken a family vacation since Disney World, when Justine was eight. It would be good to get away, to spend time together in a new place, in neutral territory, with nobody angry or fighting.

The phone rang. Justine answered before Zoe had a chance to pick up.

Zoe finished fixing her tea, waited a few seconds to see if the call was for her, and headed to the family room to relax for a few minutes before starting dinner. As she was setting her mug on the coffee table, she happened to catch sight of the window on the far wall, noticed it was getting dark. She checked her watch. Ten after five. Strange, Leah wasn't home yet. Practice was normally over by four. Zoe didn't recall her daughter having asked for a ride. She hoped Leah hadn't been trying to reach her on her cell phone. Maybe Leah tried calling here.

Zoe was poised at the bottom of the staircase, ready to holler up, ask Justine if she'd heard from her sister. As if on cue, Justine's bedroom door swung open, and her younger daughter appeared on the landing.

"Hey, Mom." Justine leaned over the banister, one foot poking between the balusters. She'd changed out of her school clothes into denim overalls and a white, short-sleeved T-shirt. She'd pulled her short dark hair into a ponytail, the bedraggled ends falling in her face. Her socks, Zoe noticed, were filthy. "I didn't hear you," she said. "I was talking to Holly."

"That's nice, honey."

"Did you have a good day?"

"It was fine. Do you know where your sister is, sweetie? It's awful late."

Justine's face clouded. "She's not home yet."

What was wrong with Zoe? She wasn't thinking. She hadn't meant to shortchange Justine, imply she wasn't important, but that was precisely the message she'd sent. "Would you like something to eat, sweetheart?" she asked, scrambling to rectify the slight. "Hot chocolate?"

"Doesn't she have a game today?"

In Leah's Wake

Oh, shoot. The last game of the regular the season. Will had asked her to tape it. By now, it would be just about over. "Come on, honey. We've got to go *now*. I can't believe I forgot."

Hope and Lupo were in the kitchen, rolling around the floor, crashing into the cabinets, making disgusting animal noises. They were repulsive, those two. If they had to do it, couldn't they use the bedroom? The Lansdown place was worse than depressing, with its dingy Goodwill furniture and battered hardwood floors. The music Todd was listening to, some immature, nineteen-eighties head-banger band, had given Leah a headache. If only she could go home, climb in her bed, snuggle under her comforter, and fall asleep. Forget this day ever happened.

Todd cut a line of coke on the empty plate Hope had left on the coffee table. He rolled a dollar bill and, bending, brought his face close to the glass, snorted, and offered the bill to her.

If she'd told him once, she'd told him a hundred times: she had no interest in coke.

He snorted another line, and tucked the bill in his pocket. "What's with you?" He rolled on his side, patting the sofa, hunting for the clicker.

"What are you talking about?"

"What're you being such a bitch for?"

"Screw you," she said, struggling to stay calm.

"Fuck you, too, if that's how you want to be." His head bobbing, he switched on the TV.

"You *too*," she mumbled, fighting back tears.

She should have been happy. This was what she wanted, wasn't it? She hated soccer. She was tired of carrying the whole stupid team on her back. If she were not such a coward, she would have quit ages ago. Only, she'd wanted to quit on her own terms. In her fantasies, when she announced her decision to quit, she was standing on a bench in the locker room, towering over her teammates. The sobbing girls begged her to reconsider. They couldn't function without her, they cried. Coach Thomas implored to say. *What can we do to change your mind? Anything, Leah. You're in charge now. You don't have to practice anymore! No more drills!* She'd never dreamed Coach Thomas would accept her resignation without a fight. Her coach was supposed to question herself, ask where she'd gone wrong. The team was supposed to stand in allegiance; her teammates were supposed to quit if she wouldn't play. It wasn't supposed to happen like *this*.

Todd flipped through the stations, watched two MTV videos, and switched the television off. "What's up, dude?" he asked, politely this time. "Talk to me. I hate seeing you like this."

"Noth—" Leah burst into tears. "Coach. Thom—"

Todd moved closer, using the back of the sofa to pull himself up, and pressed her head to his chest. "Babe," he whispered, stroking her hair. "What happened? Coach T say something?"

Leah shook her head. "Not," she said, gulping back tears. "Team. Any. More."

"She kicked you off the team?"

Sobbing, Leah nodded, shaking her head. She couldn't even get her gestures right today. Earlier, in Coach Thomas's office, then afterward, cleaning her locker, she had been outraged, rage itching in her arms, her fingers, her hands. Her fury roiled, pounding her skull, attacking the walls of her chest. She kicked her locker, pretending she was kicking a person—Coach Thomas, her parents, her teammates— and whacked it again, harder. Gradually, her anger subsided, her fury shifting to self-pity, to indignation. Coach Thomas had no right to treat Leah this way. Who did Coach Thomas think would replace her? Surely not Cissy. Now the tears flowed in great sorrowful jags, as she thought about all the games she would miss: sectionals, regional playoffs, states, possibly nationals. For the first time in school history, Cortland was ranked. She thought about all the people she had let down: her teammates, her coach. Her parents. This news would crush her father. Leah would never play soccer in college now, not at Harvard or anywhere else. Most of all, she had disappointed herself. A part of her life was finished. *It's over*, she sobbed. *I'll never play soccer again. My. Whole. Life*, she cried, *has been soccer*.

Todd cupped her chin, kissing her forehead, the short-short hair at her crown, massaging her neck. "Don't cry, babe." With his thumb, he wiped a tear from her cheek. *It's okay.*

"What's up?" Hope asked, having emerged, half-dressed, from the kitchen.

Leah wiped her eyes with a balled up napkin. If she were not so distraught, she would laugh. Hope and Lupo stood by the coffee table, Hope's dingy flannel shirt unbuttoned to her waist, exposing a ratty pink bra, Lupo's bushy, ring-lined brows bunched in a mock-angry scowl.

"What's up?" Hope asked again. "What are you crying about?"

"Jealous." Lupo clucked his tongue, winking. "Am I right? Cause you ain't getting it on."

"Cut the shit," Todd said. "This is serious."

"Sor-ry." Hope rolled her eyes. "You gonna let us in on the big secret or what?"

"Don't you *get* it?" Todd's blue eyes flashed, electric. "She don't want to talk."

Hope licked her middle finger, and flicked it at Todd.

Leah blew her nose into the napkin. "I got kicked off the team."

"You shitting me?" Hope shrugged, stunned. "You were like the best one they had."

Were being the operative word, Leah told her. "Because of your party last weekend."

"No way, dude." Hope threw her arms in the air. "You were like the only straight one there. That's bullshit," Hope said adamantly, her cheeks and the tip of her nose turning livid.

"What a bitch," Lupo said.

"Shut up, Lupo," Hope cut in. "You don't even know her. What a *bitch*."

Yeah, well. Leah stared at the blank TV screen, down at her feet. Not much she could do.

"You used to play," Todd said, inveigling Hope into offering help. "Right? Can't you talk to her?"

Hope's gaze slid from Todd to Leah, and back to Todd. "I. I guess so," she said, probably recalling how, freshman year, before they played their first game, Coach Thomas had thrown her off the team. "Sure," she said defiantly. "I'll give that bitch a piece of my mind."

"Me, too." Lupo leapt into a boxing stance, his beefy hands curled into fists. "Let me *at* her," he said, the Cowardly Lion on steroids. "Let me *at* her."

"Thanks. You're awesome, guys," Leah said. But she had to handle this on her own.

Leah laced her fingers through Todd's. These kids in this room were her friends. She pictured her teammates, as she left Coach Thomas's office, whispering behind cupped palms, Cissy passing her, pretending she didn't exist. For the first time in her life, Leah understood what friendship was really about. Friends helped you cope; they lifted you up when you were down. True friends didn't judge you when you did something they disapproved of, didn't make you feel like a loser when you made a mistake, acting as if you had purposefully intended to hurt them.

"So, dude," Lupo said, turning to Hope. "How 'bout I open that JD I've got in the car?"

"Sounds like a plan to me." Hope glanced cautiously at Leah. "You guys?"

Leah laid her head on Todd's shoulder, grinned up at Lupo and Hope.

She had been wrong. This wasn't the end of the world. Soccer was one small part of her life. If that part was over, so be it. Why prolong the inevitable? She'd learned a valuable lesson today: She couldn't control her teammates' behavior, couldn't force Coach Thomas to trust her or believe in her again. If her teammates abandoned her, if her coach had lost faith in her, why did they matter? Why be involved with people like that? In a way, it was good this happened. At least she knew where she stood. Sometimes you need a push in order to change and adjust.

The three of them were watching intently, waiting to hear what she'd say.

Leah gestured and Todd pulled her to her feet. "I'd love some JD. Time to get this party rolling," she said, with all the hope and enthusiasm of a girl whose world had just opened up.

Eleven

Another Bad Day, II

Jerry was on his way to the forest to break up a party when the dispatcher radioed. "Juvenile. Requires medical assistance," she said. "Six Lily Farm Road. Ambulance dispatched."

It was rare for Jerry to be summoned to this side of town. Cortland was a quiet suburb of fewer than four thousand people, the sort of town where young hooligans smashed mailboxes, occasionally broke into a car, offenses that cops in bigger towns were sometimes forced to ignore. In Cortland, the police took a smashed mailbox seriously, even prosecuted sometimes. Like many old New England towns, Cortland was divided by a river. From the west, Jerry's side of town, it could take twenty minutes to reach the nearest highway. The houses in West Cortland were older and smaller than people were building today, the undeveloped land, primarily forest or scrub, isolating the neighbors, as opposed to giving them views. When people on Jerry's side of town called the police, the call often arose out of helplessness, desperation: an elderly woman hadn't answered her telephone in three days, a family member was drunk or out of control. If you were new to the area, driving west to east, and landed here, you might wonder if you'd accidentally crossed the town line. East Cortland hugged Route 2, providing easier access to Boston; here, the sub-divisions were not neighborhoods; they were "estates." Residents typically called the police to report some minor inconvenience: a lockout, a lost pet, a dead deer in the road. Not that wealth liberated people from personal problems. Rich people had their share of trouble, as Jerry could attest. Their money provided access to expensive psychologists, fancy rehabs, private clinics, places where they could address their embarrassing issues in private.

He took a shortcut over the railroad tracks, drove three-quarters of a mile, turned left, crossing over a suspension bridge, and took a right onto Old Orchard Road, a winding street flanked by stone walls. He followed Old Orchard for three miles, speeding past a fallow cornfield, the transfer station, the last working orchard in Cortland. The grade steepened. Downshifting, he stepped on the gas. In the 70's, after the state built 495, the sleepy towns that looped around the highway were sucked up by industry, and Cortland had changed. Developers bought the farmland, the orchards, erected neighborhoods of monstrous homes (mausoleums, the townies had called them) to house the influx of high-tech executives who needed places to live. As the town developed, the price of real estate shot through the roof. Few of Jerry's high school classmates could afford houses in town; most of them settled farther west or north, in cheaper, less accessible areas. Jerry was lucky. With two paychecks, he and Maura qualified for a mortgage. The house was small, but it was theirs, and it was in town. Within a few years, the town had rebuilt the post office, and the rundown package store Jerry had haunted in high school was razed. The new liquor store sold fancy French wine he could never afford. At The Natural Grocer, a hundred bucks bought two tiny sacks of food. Jerry loved Cortland. But he would be hard-pressed to say whether these changes had transformed the town for the better or worse.

He entered the Lily Farm Development through the mouth of a pompous stone wall, took his first left, and proceeded up a mildly-graded hill, past several huge contemporary colonials, with multi-gabled roofs and chimneys that housed multiple flue pipes, the houses set on level two-acre lots, with sweeping front lawns. At the end of the cul-de-sac, he slowed the cruiser, switched off the siren to avoid causing a disturbance, and eased down the driveway marked "Six." The house was enormous, especially compared to the fifties-style ranch where Jerry and his family lived. He used to wonder who lived in these houses, how they afforded places like this. Stockbrokers, a lot of them. Doctors. Lawyers. Entrepreneurs. He'd been envious of these guys, with their fine breeding and private school pedigree. Next to them, he felt like a loser. Ten years on the force had taught him never to judge from the outside. He would be impressed by the size of a house, its custom design and manicured lawn; inside, he would discover that the place was a cavernous shell. In a few of the homes he'd be in, there wasn't even a couch, or, worse, no food in the house.

Some of these people lived closer to the edge than his family had, when he was a kid. They were not one iota happier than he was. However it might appear on the outside.

He parked by the post lantern nearest the garage. The weather was changing, the nights colder, his breath visible when he exhaled. A brick walkway, illuminated by discretely placed landscaping lights, led to the front entry. He hurried up the front steps, hoping he wasn't too late.

Fluted pilasters supported the house's barrel-vaulted entry. A big man, close to six-three, Jerry was dwarfed by the entrance. A brass lion head knocker hung on the soaring mahogany door, below three stalks of Indian corn. He knocked, waited a few seconds, and rang the bell.

The room to the left of the front door was dark; ditto the room on the right. You'd think, having called for help, somebody would be watching for him, waiting. Hyperventilation, the dispatcher had said. Maybe the child had suffered an asthma attack. If they were running the shower in one of the bathrooms, to generate steam, they might not hear him down here. These emergencies made Jerry feel helpless. The Cortland police were not equipped with defibrillators, his only recourse to keep the victim calm until the EMT team arrived. He rang the bell again, waited a few more seconds, scooted down the steps, and around the garage, to the deck at the rear of the house. He took the steps two at a time, tapping the kitchen window as he passed, rapped on the slider, waited, and turned the handle. Locked. A light burned in a room off the kitchen. Someone had to be home. He heard voices inside, and knocked again.

A dark-haired woman in faded jeans and an Irish-knit sweater finally opened the door.

"Hello," he said, surprised to see Zoe Tyler. "I'm responding to a call."

Zoe smiled, her eyes tired. "Officer Johnson." She inched the glass door closed, its frame dividing her slender body in two. "We're fine. I'm sorry to have bothered you. I overreacted."

A dog poked its massive head out the door, growling. Jerry stepped back. He'd been attacked once, by a Doberman Pinscher owned by an elderly woman. A neighbor called the station, said they hadn't seen her in a few days, asked them to check on her. When she opened the door, the mutt charged. He'd needed twenty-five stitches to close the wound on his calf.

"Don't mind her." Zoe grabbed the dog's collar. "She's just a big old wimp."

Jerry noticed the Lab's weathered face and relaxed, ruffled her ears. "Nice dog. Labs make great pets. Mind if I come in for a minute, check things out? Won't take long."

"Of course. Sorry." She opened the door, stepping aside. "That's a good girl," she said, pushing the dog out of the way. The Lab lumbered to the rear of the breakfast area, settled on the floor, under a window. "This is silly. If my husband were here, this wouldn't have happened."

Embarrassed for her, Jerry averted his eyes. The place reminded him of the designer houses in the *Better Homes and Gardens* magazines Maura stored in the wicker basket in their bathroom. High ceilings, cherry cabinets, a mile of granite, a wine cooler the size of his fridge. All this, he thought, it was still not enough to keep the guy home. Go figure.

"It's easier when there are two of you. That's all I meant. I panicked."

Not a problem, Jerry assured her. "That's what we're here for."

He followed her through the eating area, into the kitchen. He caught a whiff of garlic, a subtle hint of sage. He wondered what Zoe had been cooking. Last Thursday night, a friend of his cousin, the sous-chef at a tony restaurant in Cambridge, taught Jerry and his cousin how to make sausage. The kitchen in his cousin's condo had smelled almost like this.

"She's in here," Zoe said, and pushed the sleeves of her sweater to her elbows.

An arched doorway with rounded columns led to a sunken great room, furnished with two oversized chairs, upholstered in red and gold plaid, a coordinating pillow-back sofa flanked by a pair of antique end tables with turned legs. A family portrait hung above the stone fireplace. An open laptop and several magazines sat on a glass coffee table in front of the sofa. He took in the room, his eyes skimming Zoe's bare feet, her nails painted a startling pink.

A girl approximately eleven or twelve years old, pretty, if a bit pudgy, dressed in overalls and a short-sleeved T-shirt, sat cross-legged on the floor at the foot of the sofa. The little girl fixed him in her gaze. This didn't add up. The child looked fine. Everything appeared to be in order. Husband was away. Maybe Zoe had called the station, intending to thank him for the warning, discovered he was on duty, concocted the story so she could thank him in person. Zoe moved toward the child, sidestepping the coffee table, and set a hand on the little one's shoulder.

In Leah's Wake

Jerry smelled the alcohol before he saw the older girl, curled on the sofa, a bed pillow supporting her head. Because of the angle of the sofa, she'd been out of his line of vision before. She'd probably been at the forest. He pictured her with a group of kids her age, sitting around a bonfire, passing a bottle of rum. Damn shame. Living in a place like this. Zoe Tyler for a mother.

Zoe crossed an arm over her waist, the opposite hand at the base of her throat. "She was a disaster before. Hyperventilating. I couldn't calm her down. I was afraid she'd stop breathing."

He rubbed his hands together, warming his skin, checked the girl's pulse. Sixty. Good. He laid a hand on her forehead—no fever—pulled the blanket over her shoulders. "Seems fine. Color's good. Pulse normal. Ambulance'll be here any minute. We'll have her checked out."

She flashed a weak smile. "That won't be necessary."

"It's no trouble. They're already on their way."

"No, really. But thank you."

He unclipped his radio. "Let me call in. Let them know we're set. If you don't mind, I need to take some information." His back ached. He shifted his weight.

Zoe touched his arm. "Please. Have a seat." She showed him to one of the overstuffed chairs, and lowered herself on to the seat opposite his, crossing her legs.

The younger girl, watching him warily, parked herself on the floor by her sister.

Zoe leaned toward him, uncrossed her legs, and crossed the other way, her toes pointed.

Forcing himself to look away from Zoe's feet, he radioed the dispatcher, gave her a brief rundown. "All set," he said, opening his notepad. "Would you like to tell me what happened?"

Zoe and the younger girl exchanged a troubled look. "She had a big game today." Zoe shook her head, as if she were silently scolding herself. "By the time I got there, it was over."

Jerry nodded, encouraging her to continue.

"I figured she'd gone home with Cissy. Hanson. Her best friend—her former best friend, I should say." Zoe paused, grimacing. "I don't think she ever went to the game. Leah, I mean. I don't know why her coach didn't call. Or maybe she did. The battery died in my cell, and I haven't checked my messages yet. Oh God. I'm babbling. I can't think straight. I'm sorry."

Cissy Hanson. He scribbled the name on his pad. "The girls, were they together?"

109

"I don't think so. No, definitely not." She leaned forward, her left hand massaging the opposite shoulder. "Anyway, around seven thirty the doorbell rang. I didn't hear it. I was on the phone, trying to figure out where she was. By the time I got there, they were pulling out of the drive." She gestured toward her younger daughter. "Justine recognized the car."

"It's this kid's," the little girl said. She took hold of her sister's limp hand. "Lupo."

Lupo? Jerry wrestled the emotion out of his voice. "You're sure?" The Lupo kid was trouble. Jerry tried not to judge kids. He'd been a punk, too, when he was that age. The summer before senior year, a neighbor caught him stealing his chainsaw, called the cops, and Jerry found himself facing robbery charges. In exchange for a clean record, the judge, a wise older man, had sentenced him to a "summer work-study program." That summer, while his buddies were out raising hell, Jerry worked. He mowed the judge's lawn, weeded his gardens, cleaned his attic and basement, whitewashed the picket fence in front of the judge's rambling Dutch Colonial house. Jerry hated every minute, and he despised the judge and his wife for treating him like a slave. As he got older, it occurred to him that the judge had probably paid his regular crew extra that summer, to clean up Jerry's mess. He'd spent his entire working life trying to repay that debt.

Antonio Lupo made Jerry look like an angel. Assault and battery, drunk and disorderly, three DUIs. Last March, he held up a Mobil station in Ayer—with a water pistol, it turned out— every last charge dropped or dismissed. The kid's father, a labor attorney, was constantly pulling strings to get his kid out of trouble. Jerry would hate to see Zoe's daughter tangled up with Lupo.

The little girl nodded. "He's got this Marilyn Manson sticker on the back of his car."

"They just left her," Zoe said. "In a heap, on the stoop. She couldn't even stand up."

He recorded Zoe's remarks, underscoring the words *couldn't stand up*, and closed his notepad. He wanted to say they would arrest the punks; that's what he'd want to hear, if he were the parent. Unfortunately, dumping a drunk girl on her doorstep, however thoughtless and cruel, was not a crime. Underage drinking, yes, if, *big* if, the girl agreed to testify against her friends in court (which few kids would do) or he caught the Lupo kid either drunk or with alcohol on him.

Jerry stood. "I'd be happy to take her to the hospital myself. Have them check her out."

Zoe stood, too. "No, really. I shouldn't have called. I should have known better. My mother drank." She cut herself off with a dismissive wave, as if to rid the air of an embarrassing, accidental admission. "I work with kids. I don't know. With your own, it's different, I guess."

"Teenagers are tough," Jerry said. Zoe's moxie impressed him. He couldn't imagine his wife with teens. The slightest snag paralyzed Maura. "I'm glad mine are babies," he said.

"You have children?"

Twins, he said proudly. Three month-old boys.

"How sweet." She offered a genuine smile this time. "Can I get you anything, by the way? Sorry. I should've asked before. Would you like a drink before you go, Officer Johnson?"

"Jerry."

"Jerry? Tea? Coffee?"

Coffee. With Zoe Tyler. His imagination ran wild. He pictured himself selecting a bottle of wine from the cooler, heard the clink of the glasses. "Thanks," he said, caught in a prison of competing desires—fulfillment, decency, relief. She'd had a harrowing night. He would be taking advantage, he thought. "Another time. Got to go, write up a report."

"Thank you." She touched his forearm again, her fingers charged. "You really are kind."

Or stupid, Jerry thought, and followed her to the door.

Twelve

Chase The Blues Away

Kyra set the sandwich Will had ordered—roast chicken with onion and lettuce, on a baguette—on the bar, along with a bottle of Evian and a glass. "The water's on the house," she whispered. "Don't tell my boss." She winked, and untied her apron. "I've got a short break. OK if I sit with you for a few minutes? There's a table over there." She pointed to an empty table a few feet to the right of the band. "I hate sitting at the bar. I feel like I ought to be working."

Will had polished off his fifth martini. He'd been at the bar for five hours, the time inching toward seven. Considering how little he had eaten all day, he felt surprisingly sober.

Ten minutes after Will and Kyra seated themselves, the band took a break. The musicians impressed him, their music a far cry from the watered-down bossa-pop the record companies put out. The classical guitarist, a virtuoso by any objective standard, was accompanied by a flashy, supremely accomplished American kid on drums, and a sexy Latina vocalist in a red sequined gown with a plunging neckline, whose throaty confidence reminded him of Linda Ronstadt in her early days. In the complexity of their rhythms, he heard the distinctive echo of Charlie Byrd.

Will was introduced to Bossa Nova at a beach party, in 1981, shortly after he arrived on the West Coast. A tape of the original Charlie Byrd-Stan Getz *Jazz-Samba* LP was playing on somebody's boom box. The raw sensuality and inherent optimism of the music enthralled him. He managed to finagle a copy of the tape, and listened to it constantly for six months—mostly at night, when he lay in bed, mooning over the sexy cheerleader he had left behind at Penn State.

112

"I was into Beach Boys, for pretty much the same reason. Isn't that dumb? They're not even sexy. I was all about Brian Wilson." She dunked a steak-cut fry in the ramekin she'd filled with ketchup. "Did I mention, I've got tickets to the A's?"

"The A's. You a Beane fan?"

"Big time," she said. She was a numbers girl. Before she got pregnant with Rachel, she'd earned her certificate in accounting at San Mateo Community. After the baby, it was easier to bartend—better hours. But she hadn't given up. She helped all her friends file their taxes. "Billy Beane's definitely smart. In my book, the real hero's Bill James. You guys use him now, right?"

"He's a senior advisor. The Sox brass have bought in to that sabermetrics business."

"You don't agree with them, I take it. Too cut-and-dry?" Kyra laughed, shaking her head. "From a business perspective, it makes sense to analyze stats. I mean, how do you size up a hitter without considering his walk to strike ratio? Kevin Youkilis is a great example—he had the highest on-base percentage in the league this year. I love that guy. He's got great plate discipline. All that other stuff—gut instinct, intuition—it's, what do they call it? Magical thinking."

Will agreed, to a point. Old baseball guys like Grady Little did overemphasize instinct. "Too much voodoo," he said, curling his fingers. "But, come on. Instinct gives the game heart."

Kyra raised a palm, feigning defeat. With the band on break, drinking had picked up, the queues two and three deep in front of the bar. "Better get back. The inmates are getting restless."

He followed her to the bar, stood in a corner, near the TV, waiting for an empty seat.

When the crowd fizzled, Kyra asked how he thought the Sox would do next year. They had some decent minor league prospects. Did he think they'd bring them up to the majors or try to deal them for proven players? Didn't know, he told her, and he didn't much care. "To be honest with you, I'm more of a fair weather fan, these days." When he was a kid, he'd lived and died by the Phillies. In the old days, loyalty was important. It was a badge of honor for a player to spend his entire career with one team. Players today were mercenaries, for sale to the highest bidder. One year, you're rooting for Pedro, the next he's gone. He missed the old days, Will said.

She opened the tap, poured a beer, froth dribbling onto the bar. "Funny." A hand reached from behind Will, exchanged a five-dollar bill for the beer. "You didn't strike me as a romantic."

A romantic? Interesting take.

They talked for a few more minutes. She showed him a picture of her five-year-old, Rachel. "Quite a kid," he said, and she was, a tiny spitfire blond, with her mother's curly hair and deep-set eyes. He slid school photographs of the girls across the bar. While Kyra studied the pictures, he rooted through his wallet, found his American Express, and laid the card down.

She returned the photos. "Time to go, already?"

Ten o'clock flight, he told her. "Don't want to miss it."

She returned his Amex card, wrapped in a napkin. "I wrote down my number," she said. "Call me next time you're in town. I'll take you around, show you where the locals hang out."

When he left the bar, he returned to the hotel for his carry-on tote, and headed to the airport. Everywhere, people were out, restaurants bustling, doors closing and opening, the emerging couples holding hands, laughing. He couldn't get Kyra out of his head. He kept hearing her voice, picturing her slender body, the sexy bounce in her step. He'd almost forgotten what it was like to feel at ease with a woman, to be able to talk without editing his words, without worrying that she would read into something he'd said, misinterpret his tone or be offended by a look he was not even conscious of making. With Kyra, there were no unspoken resentments, no hurt feelings, no misunderstandings bubbling under the surface. An argument about baseball was simply that: an argument about baseball. The light turned red. The limousine in front of his rental car turned into the Mark. The bellhop opened the door and an elegant middle-aged couple appeared, he in a tuxedo, she in a strapless black gown, her silver hair piled on top of her head.

The older couple made him sad. Zoe, he'd always believed, was the love of his life. When he pictured the future, she was always beside him. He couldn't imagine a future without her. The way they fought lately, it was hard to say for sure if they would be together next year.

They met in Berkeley, in the spring of '84. His first two years in California, he'd bounced from bar to bar, playing a night here, two or three there. Six months before they met, he'd finally landed a long-term gig, at one of the few bars in the Bay Area that still featured folk singers. The crowd was older than normal that night. His connection with his audience was intense, their energy feeding him. For the first time since leaving the football field, he felt invincible.

In Leah's Wake

Midway through his first set, four coeds strolled in, took a table at the back of the bar, immediately started jabbering. Now and then, one would glance at him, make a face, whisper into another girl's ear; they'd quiet down; in no time, they would be talking again. Irritated, he finished the set, nodded, acknowledging the applause, headed to the kitchen for something to eat.

When the lights went down twenty minutes later, the girls were still chattering. He took his time tuning his guitar. The folks in the tables closest to the stage began turning their heads. At last, the girls took the hint and shut up. Will introduced a song called "Chase the Blues Away," an obscure, hauntingly romantic piece by Tim Buckley. It was his first time performing the song for an audience. He had trouble with the opening verse, his voice a thick, self-conscious slur. Gradually, he came into his own. By the third verse, the girls were jabbering again.

When the song ended, he did something he had never once considered doing before: he put down his guitar. "Thanks," he said, standing. He unhooked his mike, knowing full well that he would never play in that bar again. "You've been great."

In the alley, leaning against the bar's blemished stucco wall, smoking a cigarette, he watched the crowd file out. It was raining earlier, when he rode his 1978 Honda CX down the five-mile dirt path, from his place to the bar, his guitar strapped to the luggage rack behind his seat. Now the moon was bloated, the sky a star-stippled ebony dome.

The more brazen of the audience members saw him and sneered. *Wanna be*, somebody shouted. *Ain't no Dylan*, said someone else. To the first few, he smiled and waved, his weak attempt at irony trumped by the bird. After that, he ignored them.

Three years, down the tubes. Maybe this was for the best. He'd go home, find a real job. He had no right to complain. He'd known, sitting in the office of the academic dean, the day he quit school, listening to a lecture he didn't want to hear, that he was choosing a difficult road. He dragged on his cigarette, contemplating his options, wondering what would come next.

"Excuse me?"

A small, dark-haired girl stood beside him. He hadn't heard her approach. She looked prettier than she had inside, sitting apart from her friends, her face partially hidden in shadow.

115

"Listen. Will. That's your name, right? Will?" She touched his arm. "Sorry about tonight. They were incredibly rude. I tried to get them to shut up."

He bent his right knee, pressing his foot against the wall. "They always like that?"

"Not really. Do you mind?"

He handed her the cigarette. She took a drag, handed it back. "Actually, they are."

They both laughed.

She was a senior at Berkeley. She'd enjoyed his music, especially that last song.

Within three months of losing his job, Zoe had graduated college, and they were living together, in a cheap apartment on the water. Zoe encouraged him to stick with his music. For a few months, whenever he heard about an audition he went, but his desire was gone. He still played for Zoe, but he'd lost his drive to perform. It wasn't the girls. People often dissed him when he played an unfamiliar tune. He had been kidding himself, pretending to be a musician. He was an adequate cover artist, a decent stand-in for the popular musicians the audience really wanted to hear. It was time to find honest work. He'd begun to think vaguely about marriage, not immediately, but in the future, when he found a job that paid well enough to support a family.

It was tougher than he had imagined to adjust to life outside of music. On occasion, he would try his hand at writing a song, recording the lyrics in a spiral-bound notebook he stashed in his underwear drawer. After he and Zoe married, he'd played for his family, their daughters, once they were old enough, dancing around the living room, singing along. If they forgot the lyrics, they improvised, substituting their own lyrics for the words they couldn't remember. Over the years, their lives had grown fuller, with work, family plans, activities for the kids. One day, he realized he hadn't played his guitar in over a year, and his notebook was gone.

Will made it to the airport in just under forty-five minutes. The place was dead. In no time, he was in and out of Hertz, the rental car returned and checked in, and aboard the shuttle heading to the United Terminal. He set his tote on the luggage rack, and took a seat by the central door, closing his eyes. Traveling on business to the West Coast, he was too busy to notice the three hour time change; once he stopped moving, it hit him, his joints and muscles tight, his back aching. On the ride, he drifted in and out of a fitful sleep.

He felt a hand on his shoulder, reached for it, yawning, thinking it belonged to his wife.

"Sir," the driver said, nudging Will's shoulder. "This is your stop."

Grasping the handrail, Will groggily departed the bus, the fluorescent lights momentarily blinding him as he stepped into the terminal. Partway down the ramp to Gate 2, he spotted a vending machine, rooted in his pocket, digging for loose change to buy a candy bar and a Coke. Along with a handful of coins, he pulled out the napkin Kyra had given him, scanned the area, looking for a trash receptacle, stuffed the napkin in his pocket, planning to dump it at the gate.

Before meeting Zoe, Will had never honestly believed he would marry. He'd dated dozens of women, hadn't believed he would find anyone he could live with for the rest of his life. Zoe was different from the other women he'd dated. Maybe because she was curious, constantly questioning, pushing to do more, to grow. Maybe because she pushed him. She didn't bore him and never had. A disconnect had prompted his one, as he thought of it now, inconsequential affair. Even now, thirteen years later, thinking about his infidelity produced a sharp pang of guilt.

He and Zoe were going through a rough period. On the advice of her obstetrician, she'd undergone an abortion. Afterward, she'd curled into herself, gained fifteen or twenty pounds, stopped showering, washing her hair. Her depression confused him. She seemed to be blaming herself, punishing her body, as if it had failed her somehow, punishing him. He spoke with her physician. Rationally, he understood his wife's grief. On a gut level, it made no sense. If she'd allowed it to go full-term, the pregnancy could have killed her, leaving two young kids without a mother, him without his wife. He tried to reach her, to console her, but she pushed him away.

He'd been casual friends with the woman in high school. They met again, by chance, at Logan airport. He was on his way to Boulder, on business; an ad-exec, she was on her way home from a meeting in Boston. The plane was empty. When the final person had boarded and settled, Will moved to the seat beside hers. Before the plane touched down at Denver International, they had exchanged numbers. Because they both held jobs that required traveling, it was easy to meet.

Over the next two months, they slept together a half-dozen times, in hotels all over the country. He was never in love. When it was over, he confessed the affair to his wife.

"I had a feeling," Zoe replied, her eyes betraying the strange impassiveness of her tone. While he was away, the hamster he'd bought for their daughters had died. She'd interpreted the hamster's death as a sign. She had forgiven him unconditionally, a munificence he knew he did not deserve. The anguish in her face had torn him apart.

He checked to be sure his plane wasn't boarding, and, stretching his legs, dialed the number for home. "Were you sleeping?" His wife sounded groggy.

"Wide awake. You didn't get my messages? I've been calling."

He'd turned the phone off, hadn't checked his messages yet. "What's wrong?"

Leah. She'd been trying to reach him all night.

His blood pressure skyrocketed. He'd kill the bastard who'd dumped his kid on the stoop.

"We've got to get her into counseling. Honestly, Will, I think we should all go."

He rubbed his eyelids with his index finger and thumb. He and Zoe had seen a marriage counselor for a few months, after his affair. Counseling had helped to the extent that it got them talking again. The underlying problems—his restlessness, her difficulty with trust— they had worked out on their own. Why would it be any different with Leah? "All right. Let's do it. Zoe?" He could tell, from the sound of her voice that she was fighting back tears. "You OK?"

I'm fine," she said, her voice steady again. "I'll make an appointment."

"It's late. Try to get some sleep." He would be home first thing in the morning. They would work this out, he promised. "Trust me," he said, with all the conviction he was able to muster. They would get through this together. He planned to do whatever it took.

PART TWO

THE RUNAWAY LIFE

Thirteen

Meeting Coach Thomas

In their session with the family counselor, which Zoe had scheduled for noon, Leah admitted to quitting the soccer team. Quitting at
this point in the season, after all the work she'd put in, made no sense
to Will. Where was Hillary in all this? Why the hell would the coach
allow her best player to quit? Leah was a kid. If she was having
problems, it was up to the coach to get her back on track. If Leah
performed well in the playoffs, scoring two or three points a game, as
she had earlier in the season, the *Globe* All-Scholastic award was a
lock. That she was tired, that her feet hurt, that she didn't enjoy the
game anymore—all that Will understood. For the past four months,
his daughter had devoted several hours a day, every day, to soccer. If
not on the field, playing or practicing, she was in the gym, doing
stretching and strengthening exercises. Any player who dedicated that
much to her game tired eventually. Fatigue was normal, even for pros.

They were on the way home from the counselor's office. Leah
was sitting beside Justine, in the backseat of his BMW, with her eyes
closed, her head leaning against the door. Admittedly, his timing was
less than ideal, Leah visibly hung-over. Impatient, he charged on.
"Think about the Sox. By September, most guys look like they've lost
a step since April or May."

Zoe touched his arm, asked him to hold off until they were less
keyed-up, anxious. "Please." The session with Molly had gone well.
"Let's try to maintain the momentum."

"Forget it," he whispered back. He'd already agreed to turn the
drinking and boyfriend issues over to Molly. Soccer was his
department. He refused to sit back, watching the career they'd spent

years building go down the toilet. "She's too young to make a decision like this."

"Will?" His wife's hand fell to her lap. "I really think we should wait."

They'd done too much waiting already. If they would confront situations head-on, as they arose, instead of procrastinating all the time, they wouldn't always be facing a crisis.

Zoe sighed, and turned to the window.

"You've got two weeks," he said to Leah. "Three at the most." Adrenaline would propel her through the post-season. After the playoffs, she would have plenty of time to rest and recoup.

When he finished his pep talk, he asked Leah if she understood, meaning did she agree?

She grunted.

He considered asking her to repeat the key points, to see if she'd been paying attention, and changed his mind: too antagonizing. Instead, he caught her eye in the rearview, told her he'd talk to her coach. "I'll tell her you made a mistake. I'm sure you don't feel like practicing today. I wouldn't, in your shoes. But you've got to. You've got to prove you're dedicated to the team."

"Whatever." Leah crooked her elbow, using her arm as a pillow. "She won't listen."

The door to Coach Thomas's office was closed. Through the plate-glass window, he saw her, bent over her desk, working on what appeared to be a game plan. She made a notation in pencil, erased it. A plaque designating her 2004 Coach-of-the-Year for the Hillside League hung on the wall behind her desk. He gave her credit: she had overcome a rough start to her tenure in Cortland. For four years running, the team had losing seasons. The year before the AD brought Hillary in, Cortland had gone two and eleven. When Hillary took over the program, Leah's freshman year, she'd assessed the talent, decided to rebuild. The parents of the older girls were enraged. It was unfair for freshmen to get more playing time than experienced upperclass-men, they griped, accusing her of favoritism. They wanted their kids on the field, where the college coaches would see them. From the sidelines, Will watched the battle unfold. Hillary had made some unpopular calls; he agreed. In her defense, there was not a talented athlete on the team, other than Leah. His daughter had a monster of a season, particularly for a freshman. She won Cortland High MVP, was named to the league All Star team. As long as the coach did well by his daughter, he was disinclined to make waves. When the season ended, the disgruntled parents brought their complaints to the athletic director, demanding he fire her. When the AD, who had known Hillary since she was in high school, refused to kowtow, they requested a hearing with the school committee. Hillary had surprised a lot of people, Will included, by hanging tough, refusing to be run out of town. He admired her gumption. Every year, her team had improved.

She looked up when he knocked. Gesturing, she invited him in. Hillary was built like Leah, tall and well-toned. She wore blue sweatpants, a short-sleeved T-shirt that showed off her toned arms, her dirty blond hair tied in a ponytail like a kid's. When Will met her, five years earlier, at a coach's meeting, when they were both coaching Cortland's fourteen-and-under town teams, he had been surprised by her youth. He'd guessed her to be in her late twenties. In fact, she was thirty-five, just a few years younger than he was. She still looked young for her age, her complexion dewy and clear, but her eyes and mouth showed the strain of the past several years.

"Hillary." He proffered a hand. "Do you have a minute?"

"Have a seat." Hillary showed him to the chair by her desk. "What can I do for you?"

On the drive over, he'd rehearsed this moment. With any conflict, it was best to be direct, get right to the point. He planned to ask Hillary outright why she'd allowed Leah to quit, and what it would take to get Leah back on the team. But he'd neglected to take into account Hillary's disarming persona. If he attacked too aggressively, he would look like a jerk, no better than the parents who'd complained about her two years before.

"How are you?" he asked. They hadn't seen one another in a couple of weeks.

"Fine." Her right eye blinked, a nervous tic. "You were away, Leah said. Trips good?"

"All right." He pointed at the plaque on her wall. "Took them long enough."

She turned, acknowledging the plaque. "They spelled my name wrong the first time."

"Hillary?"

"Thomas."

"Ridiculous. Why didn't they ask, if they weren't sure?"

"Good question." She pushed away from her desk. "Water?" From the cooler in the back right corner of her office, she filled two Dixie Cups with water, and set one in front of Will.

"Big game Tuesday," he said. If he wanted to be a dink, he'd make a snide remark about her team's having lost their final game of the season. But the objective was to get Leah back on the field. Alienating her coach was hardly the way to do that. "Be tough," he added. "Games get serious at this level." As a courtesy, because he was the father of her best player, also because he used to coach, Hillary often showed him her game plan. Be interesting to see what she planned.

She rotated the sheet, and pushed it toward him. "We're playing Avon."

"I heard." He leaned forward, pulling the paper closer, and scrutinized the diagrams she'd drawn. "Heavy on D. Good. They've got that stud, Silva; otherwise, their offense is weak. Good plan, Hill." Smart. He'd underestimated her ability to make such a facile adjustment. Still, he thought, in order to win big games, they had to score.

"Thanks. Listen, Will, I hate to rush." She glanced at the stopwatch she wore on her wrist. "I'm expecting the girls shortly. How's Leah? I assume that's why you're here."

He finished his water, and sat back, crossing his legs. "She's all right."

"I'm glad. We were devastated to lose her. We'll be at a serious disadvantage now."

He couldn't tell if she was making a point, letting him know his daughter had let the team down, or feeling him out, trying to gauge his intentions. A Cross pen, a gift from the team, stood in a silver holder at the edge of her desk. He pulled the pen out, read the engraving—*Coach Thomas, 2004*, and put it back. "If you feel that way, have her play," he said, calling her bluff.

She lobbed her empty cup into the metal trashcan by the cooler. "If I could, I would."

"If you could? Why can't you?"

"I think you know why," she said, a trace of annoyance in her voice. The raised pink rash that often plagued her in games spread from her chest to her neck. "She broke an MIAA rule."

"You've got to be kidding. Leah's off the team because of a *rule?*"

Someone knocked, interrupting them, and Amy Randall, one of the sophomores, poked her head in the office. Earlier this season, Amy's game had been unimpressive. She was slow, overweight, relatively uncoordinated. She'd turned into the ace on the JV team. Hillary stood as she entered the room, told the girl she would be finished shortly, asked Amy to tell the others to start the conditioning exercises. "Have Cissy do fire drills first." The girl groaned, pleading for mercy. "Go on, Amy. Five minutes." The door clicked shut. Hillary watched the window until the girl disappeared. "Leah signed a pact. She knew the consequences of violating it."

"That's bullshit, Hillary. And you know it." He gnawed the inside of his cheek. He couldn't sit anymore. He had to move, get his blood flowing.

He strode to the window, stared out at the rows of lockers, the benches littered with paraphernalia: gym bags, towels, cleats. Plastic water bottles lined the bench nearest the door. He heard commotion from the dressing room, the players changing into workout clothes. Frustrated, he turned back to the coach. "She's the best player in the state. Why the hell would you do this?"

"Why would *I* do this? I don't know what she told you. Your daughter quit the team."

"After you sat her. It was their last game. She's a competitor. What did you expect?"

"I don't know, Will. Common courtesy, maybe? Leadership?"

For Christ's sake. His daughter devoted two years of her life to that talent-starved team. Without her, Cortland High would be in the cellar. Instead, they owned a winning record. And Hillary was the frontrunner once again for Coach of the Year. She owed Leah something for that.

"Do you have any idea what this will do to her? It'll blow her chances for a scholarship."

"Look, I don't want to argue." She brushed a scrap of paper off her desk. "This wasn't my decision. Every athlete at that party was benched. If I didn't sit her, I'd have lost my job."

Finally, the puzzle was coming together. "So this is about your job."

"No, this is not about my job. If you want to know the truth, your daughter's been a problem all year."

Will felt as if he'd been dope-slapped. Leah had been bellyaching all season. He'd attributed the constant grumbling to frustrated jock talk. When he was her age, he'd moaned about football. Every time he reached the boiling point, he would threaten to quit. He never followed through. He lumbered back to his chair. "All year? What do you mean by 'all year'?"

"I mean, she's been a problem all year." It was Hillary's turn to get up. Scowling, she went to the window, looked out, shaking her head, opened the door, ordered the girls to get a move on. "Let's go, ladies, *now*," she barked, and tramped back to her desk. The flush spread from her neck to her checks, her neck and face tensing. "If you think I like this, you're wrong."

"I think I'm missing something. What exactly has she done?"

"Why don't we start with the fact that she missed practice last week." A mop-headed girl opened the door, attempted to ask a question, her voice squeaking. Hillary dismissed her, and turned back to Will. "And she's constantly challenging me. Doesn't ever want to do drills. And running is a joke. I ask her to take the girls out for three miles, they're back in ten minutes. What kind of message do you think that sends? Anyone else would've been gone long ago."

Will didn't want to believe her, but his gut said he was hearing the truth. He should have known what she was doing from the steady decline in her performances. "Listen, I'll talk to her."

"Wait." The coach held up both index fingers. "We're not done. Her slacking sets a lousy example. And it's disrespectful. If I didn't bench her, I'd have had a mutiny on my hands."

Will winced, his brain fried. "How about this?" He promised to talk with Leah, see where she stood. She was burned out. And she was involved with a class-A loser, which didn't help.

"Todd Corbett."

"The kid's an asshole."

"I know him." He'd been in her AP geometry class, her first year in Cortland. "Bright kid. I was disappointed when he quit school. A decent wide receiver, too. You knew that, right?"

Will remembered reading about him. According to the *Gazette*, the kid had good hands. Good for a second-rate high school team, Will thought. Kid never would have made it in college.

"I've got connections at UNH," the coach went on, referring to her alma mater. His grades were middling, but the UNH coach liked him, and he'd scored over twelve hundred on his SATs. "If he'd stuck around for another few months, I could have gotten him in."

"The kid's a screw-up. He'd have made you look bad."

"I don't know." She made a face he couldn't decipher. "I agree, he's not good for Leah."

He rubbed his knuckles. "Leah's seeing somebody. A therapist my wife knows."

"Good," the coach said. "That's a start."

"She's a good kid. Let her prove she deserves to be on the team. That's all I'm asking."

Hillary deliberated for a long, difficult moment. "If she's serious, if she really wants to come back, agrees to follow the rules, we'll talk. No promises. Leah's got to want this, not you."

Will nodded, relieved. As soon as he got home, he would sit down with Leah, convince her to finish the season. Once the season ended, he'd have a year to work with her, help her get her head screwed back on straight. This time next year, she'd be applying to Harvard. "Thanks, Hill. I owe you."

She brushed his gratitude off. "One more thing," she said, as he was leaving.

He turned to face her.

"I've given her captainship to Cissy."

Will bit into his cheek. Leah would have a fit when he told her. "And next year?"

"If the girls vote for her again, sure. She can have it back next year."

"Fair enough. Thanks, Hill. I owe you. I'll have her stop by tomorrow."

"I'll be here," Coach Thomas replied. "Tell her Coach Thomas is waiting."

Fourteen

Sisters Redux

Coach Thomas could keep waiting. She could wait forever, for all Leah cared.

Leah lay in bed, doodling on the wall, a swish, swish, swipe of black magic marker across the pale violet paint. She couldn't believe her parents had grounded her again. She was supposed to be going to the Ani DiFranco concert tonight. The other day, Todd had surprised her with tickets. Furious, she drew stick figures of her mother and father, and crossed them out.

For a day or two after the meeting with her coach, her father pretended he didn't care that she'd quit soccer. He suggested they discuss alternative plans, in case she decided not to go to college. On Sunday, when she informed him and her mother that she would not be keeping her second appointment with that dorky shrink, her father tweaked out. What was *wrong* with her? Nothing, she spat. "You ought to be glad I'm not as bad as other kids." *I don't care about other kids,* he shouted. *I care about you. You'll keep that appointment. Is that clear?* Uh, no.

Leah got up, plugged an Oasis CD into the player.

Leah drew a tiny star, other stars circling around it. Up close, you saw each tiny rotating prick of black, an intricate web spiraling outward. From a distance, you saw an explosion.

She set the marker on her nightstand. With a pen, she drew a three-dimensional square, a theater peopled with stick figures, the kids she couldn't stand anymore (Cissy Hanson, the girls on the soccer team) on one side, her new friends, Hope and Lupo, on the

128

other. At center stage, she drew Todd, his arms outstretched like a messiah.

"Champagne Supernova came on, Leah's favorite song on the CD. She bobbed her head to the music. Noel Gallagher was a genius: people really did change—people like Cissy. Coach Thomas. Leah's parents. Her mom always used to pester Leah to share her problems, to "verbalize" her feelings. Yet, when Leah approached her to talk, her mother couldn't be bothered. Just the other day, Leah knocked on her parents' bedroom door. She'd been upset about Cissy being captain. (She didn't admit that to her father, of course.) She wanted advice, wanted her mom to tell her how to handle the situation, wanted to know what she should do. But her mother was on her computer, working on a website she planned to launch to market her seminars. "Can I talk to you for a minute?" Leah had asked, the request purposely vague, so she could gauge her mother's response, determine whether she actually wanted to help. "Can't you do whatever it is yourself, Leah?" her mother replied. "I'm busy right now." *No.* If she could do it herself, she wouldn't have asked. "Sure," Leah had said. "Thanks anyway."

What did her parents think they would accomplish, stranding her in her room, cutting her off from the world, unplugging her landline, taking her cell phone, removing her computer? Did they really think isolating her would change her behavior? Convince her to go crawling back to Coach Thomas? Force her to dump Todd? Her soccer days were behind her. Period. And she had no intention of dumping Todd. She was a different person than she used to be, stronger, more independent. She refused to follow orders. Her parents might as well get used to it.

The telephone rang. On instinct, she scrambled to answer. Then she remembered: Her father had taken the phone out of her room. "Damn him," she cursed. "I *hate* that man."

"Jus?" Leah tapped the wall between their bedrooms. "Who's on the phone?"

"Nobody."

"You sure?"

Of course, she was sure. Why would she lie?

Justine snapped her science book shut and patted her mattress, signaling for Dog to jump up. "Here, girl," she said, taking hold of her dog's paws. With Justine's help, the old yellow Lab hauled her hindquarters onto the bed, and, wheezing, snuggled next to Justine.

Justine felt bad for her sister. Their parents were overreacting, grounding her, forcing her to see a shrink, treating her like a loser. Sure, her behavior had changed. Leah was sneaky and secretive now, and she liked different things. In the past, except for Cissy, a few other friends, soccer was all Leah cared or even thought about, really. Now she claimed to hate soccer, wanted nothing to do with her old friends. Justine understood their parents' concern—she didn't want to see Leah hurt, either—but the changes were not all bad, as their parents believed. Certain aspects of her sister's personality had improved. Leah was starting to tell her things now, for example. Not big things, not yet; she refused to say what she and Todd did on their dates. But she told Justine she'd played hooky a few times, admitted to stealing a toe ring last time she went to the mall. Leah was testing her, trying to see if she was a snitch. Justine had not breathed a word.

Justine dialed the phone. A grownup, Hope's mother most likely, answered again, and Justine hung up. Hope Lansdown was bad news. She was the real reason Leah was always in trouble. Even the kids in the junior high knew about Hope, the wild parties at her house, her weird, disgusting mother. (If the rumors were true, Hope's mother encouraged the boys to get high, and took them into her bedroom.) Though Justine would never say this to Leah, her sister's friendship with Hope embarrassed her. The kids at school were starting to whisper. She couldn't be sure they'd been discussing her sister. (Who would admit such a thing?) But they shut up whenever Justine moved into their circle, which was a pretty good sign. Lately, Justine had been taking the tack St. Peter had taken, in the Gospels. When the kids at school asked if her sister was friends with Hope, Justine always denied it.

Hope made Justine so . . . so . . . so *mad.*

Justine punched Star 67, so her number wouldn't show up on caller ID, and dialed again.

Justine enjoyed pranking people. Normally, she and Holly worked as a team. They would dial a random number. When the person answered, they would ask a question such as, "Do you have Prince Albert in a can?" Questions that had been around for decades, the same questions their parents had probably used. Sometimes, when the girls were in the mood to be mean, they pretended they were calling from the IRS. "We're calling about your recent tax statement," they would say. Or "we're calling to schedule an audit." But only when they reached an adult. Kids couldn't care less about taxes. Most of Leah's friends didn't even bother to file.

The phone rang . . . five, six, seven.

Finally, someone picked up.

"Speak," said a cranky voice on the other end of the line.

"Is this Hope?"

"Who wants to know?"

"Good. Here's a hope, Hope. Hope you go to hell," Justine said, and clicked off. "Yes," Justine squealed, high-fiving herself and then Dog. "How's that, girl? I *got* her."

"Leah." Justine tapped the wall between her room and her sister's. "Guess what."

"Go away," Leah said. "I'm tired."

Her sister was lying. Justine could hear the stereo blasting out of the tiny Bose speakers on top of Leah's bureau.

Leah *was* tired. Tired of her life. Tired of living in this crappy house, in this crappy neighborhood, with crappy parents who didn't appreciate her, who did nothing but pick, pick, pick at her every second of her life. Plus, her sister was a pain. Why couldn't Justine be a normal eighth grader, instead of this precocious kid everybody thought was a genius? Why couldn't she leave Leah alone? Leah heard a banging noise and rolled her eyes. Justine was whacking that ridiculous punching bag, probably pretending she was Buffy the Vampire Slayer.

"Cut it out," Leah said, banging the wall. "You're giving me a headache."

Leah rolled onto her back. Nearly all the phosphorescent stars she'd tacked to her ceiling had fallen off. She had about a half of a constellation left. The Big Dipper was gone. She'd have to buy a new pack of stars, next time she went to the mall. She got up, popped the Oasis CD out of the player, plugged in a Rage Against the Machine disc she'd borrowed from Todd.

Leah heard a weird scratching noise, and turned down the music.

It was only Justine, rapping again at the wall. "I want to tell you something."

"Go away, I told you."

Didn't the little geek have homework to do? Work on her science project? That project was getting way out of hand. Justine was constantly conjuring new ideas, more complicated schemata. Originally, she'd talked about constructing a papier-mâché model of the Milky Way galaxy. As far as Leah could tell, the project incorporated the whole universe now. Pictures of celestial phenomena—planets, nebula, star clusters, red giants—photographed from every conceivable direction, cluttered her sister's desk, littered the floors. Amazingly, Dog hadn't destroyed anything yet. You'd think the dog would have a heyday in there when Justine was at school. Somehow, Dog had an instinct for protecting anything that belonged to Justine.

Dog barked. Leah pounded the wall, a hint for Justine to quiet her up.

Must be hell being Leah's sister, always holed up in her bedroom, doing schoolwork, working on her project or playing on the computer, her only two friends their dog and the girl down the street. Holly wasn't a bad kid. She just wasn't cool, wasn't anyone Leah would want for a friend. Didn't her sister get bored? Being grounded bored Leah silly. The minute she came home from school, she marched up to her room, where she remained until bedtime. A few times, her mother had tried to force her to join the family for dinner. Have to eat something, she said. It's not healthy being up there all day. But Leah stood her ground. Her parents could punish her. They could take away everything she owned. But they could not force her to eat with them. At night, after the others had fallen asleep, Leah snuck downstairs, helped herself to the leftovers.

To occupy herself, Leah listened to music and doodled on her walls. Above her desk, she'd scrawled original aphorisms. *F—the world. Drugs rule. Party or die.* Next to her bed, she'd drawn hundreds of hearts, in different colors, with fancy arrows piercing their centers.

Leah lit a stick of sandalwood incense, tapped a cigarette out of the packet that lay on her nightstand, and went to her window. If she reached outside, she could touch the branches of the oak tree that rose up next to the house. The tree was practically bare, a few stray leaves clinging to the branches. Leah missed the robin that used to live in the boughs of the tree. Once, the robin landed on Leah's windowsill. She'd wanted to capture the bird, touch her feathers, had wanted to bring her inside. She wouldn't cage it, the way people caged parakeets or canaries. She would fashion a nest from a shoebox. Feed her lettuce and worms. She would keep her bedroom door closed, so she couldn't escape, so she wouldn't get lost in the house. In the end, though she was tempted to trap the bird, she didn't have the heart. Leah had known that the robin would die.

Leah dragged her futon to the window and knelt on the cushion, elbows resting on the sill. An icy breeze blew in the window. Soon winter would be here. Todd had promised to teach her to snowboard this year. His stepmother owned a cabin somewhere in Maine—near Bangor, she thought. They planned to drive up one weekend in

January, when the cottage was empty. Leah couldn't wait to go. Every Christmas, she asked her parents for skis. Every year, they denied her request. Instead, her parents showered her with expensive gifts she didn't need, luxuries she didn't want: a new stereo, a high-speed computer, a CD player, designer clothes that her mother didn't normally buy. Her parents refused to give Leah skis. A broken leg would end her precious soccer career. *Ha.* The last laugh was on them. Soccer was over.

She lit the cigarette, brought the butt to her lips, inhaled deeply. Forming an "O" with her lips, she blew rings at the screen. Her parents would kill her if they caught her smoking. Which was also a joke. They had already grounded her. What else could they do? Lock her in her room and throw out the key? Send her to boot camp? She hoped they did. Any place would be better than here. Anyway, she wasn't worried. Her parents rarely stepped inside her room anymore. Her mother had stopped making her bed. Leah dumped her dirty clothes in the laundry chute in the bathroom; a day or two later, her mother left a pile of folded clothes on the floor, outside her door. Her parents had no more desire to venture into her room than Leah had to invite them.

A knock at the door caught her by surprise. "Wait a sec," she said, fumbling with the screen. Come *on.* She jiggled the frame. It was stuck. Jiggled harder. *Open.*

Finally, the screen popped. She snubbed her butt on the shingles, flicked it away, and tugged on the screen, pulling it too far inside the frame. She righted the screen as best she could, and yanked down the sash, grabbed the perfume mister from her bureau, and sprayed puffs of perfume by the window and around her bed.

"Oh," she said, breathing hard as she opened her door. "It's only you."

Justine's heart sank. Only her? Maybe coming over here wasn't such a hot idea after all. "You didn't have to get rid of the cigarette, you know. I wouldn't have told."

"Yeah," Leah said irritably. "I know."

With the heel of her bare foot, Justine pushed the door closed and hopped onto Leah's bed. Over the past couple of months Leah's room had undergone a dramatic change, the Nike poster at the foot of her bed the only memento left from before. Leah's old soccer schedules, which she used to tape to her walls, were gone. In their place, she'd plastered the walls with posters of arrogant hip-hop artists and moody rock stars. There was a glossy picture of Sugarloaf,

133

skiers gliding down the lush, sun-dappled mountain, a smaller poster of a fat lady sitting, knees apart, on the toilet, reading the paper. On the wall by Leah's bed, her sister must have drawn a hundred hearts, pierced by colorful arrows, with her and Todd's names scrawled in the centers.

Justine crossed her legs, Indian-style. A package of Marlboro cigarettes lay on the nightstand. Justine wondered what her sister would do if she filched one. Unlike her sister, Justine had not changed at all over the years. She still had the same boring personality, still wore the same nondescript clothes. Justine was the "good one" in the family, the obedient one, the one who rarely did anything wrong. She did all her chores, often without being asked, went to school on time, finished her homework before it was due. She'd never sassed a grownup (except for her parents, of course), had never been on a date with a boy. She'd never smoked a cigarette, had never taken even a puff. Justine was tired of being Queen Dork. She didn't want to be a goody two-shoes anymore. She wanted to be like her sister. Fun and exciting and brave. Leah didn't feel obliged to follow rules. She smoked in the girls' room at school, and she drank and smoked marijuana, and she had a cool boyfriend, one their parents didn't approve of. Leah was her own person. She wasn't afraid to stick up for herself, give adults a piece of her mind. No one pushed Leah around. Justine was sweating profusely, her shirt glued to her back. It was time to make a stand, time to grow up. Time to earn some self-respect. Today, she told herself. Today is the day.

Justine rose, went to the window. "Is it OK if I open it?"

Leah shrugged. "Whatever."

"Leah?" Justine said, faltering. Why was she so nervous? So what if she wanted to smoke? Leah smoked. What could her sister possibly say? "Can I ask you something?"

Leah shrugged again.

No. That's what Leah could say.

"What, Jus? You want me to call that kid you like? What was his name?"

Justine stood alone at the window, shaking her head, her back to her sister.

Her little sister tried Leah's patience. Leah couldn't stand when people beat around the bush. Why not just ask for what you wanted? Be direct? Justine was a baby. That was the problem. Leah cleared her throat, a hint for Justine to hurry up. "Well?"

Justine turned from the window, fanning herself. "Are you hot?"

"No. I'm not hot. Look, Justine." Leah put her hands on her hips. "If you want me to do something, ask. OK?" She wasn't an ogre. She'd probably say yes. Unless her sister wanted help with her homework. "You're doing geometry, right? I can help with that. Science, forget it. I mean, I would, but I'm lousy at science." Leah picked a satin camisole off the floor, held it in front of her. Violet used to be her favorite color. She would never wear purple now. Too girly. "Want to borrow something? Is that it? A shirt? You can, but my clothes are probably too big."

Justine hedged. "Could I—"

"What? Spit it out already."

"—try one of your cigarettes?"

Cigarettes? No way her sister had asked for a cigarette. Justine was a geek. Even Todd had noticed. What, he would ask, is the little geek up to these days? Or, how's the little geek doing today? Leah had misheard her sister's request. Justine would never smoke. She was always nagging Leah to quit. She was scared of cancer. And heart disease. And all the other ways smoking supposedly damaged your health. If Justine were anyone else, Leah would think this was a trap. Justine was too honest. Leah doubted the girl could tell a lie to save her own life.

Can I *throw out* your cigarette, she had probably said.

"Can I have a cigarette?" Justine asked again, with more confidence this time.

Leah swiped the pack of Marlboros from the nightstand, tucked it in her pocket. This was absurd. Leah's sister was sweet and naïve, if a little pathetic. Leah could never allow her to smoke. Sure, she'd offered a couple of times, but that was only to tease. She never would have asked if she'd thought Justine would say yes. Their father was wrong: Leah would never corrupt her sister. Leah had taken a path that was different from the road her parents had chosen. She was glad she'd gone her own way, didn't mind that she was always in trouble. She was proud of her choices. Proud of herself for being an independent thinker. Those same decisions would spell disaster for most kids, particularly an innocent girl like Justine. So what if Justine was a geek? Geekdom was good for her sister. In certain arenas, the geeks had the advantage.

"Please?" Justine pleaded.

Leah couldn't believe this. Justine? Wanting to smoke? Yet the poor kid was so earnest. Maybe Leah should play along, let Justine see for herself why she shouldn't start smoking.

"All right," Leah said, finally. She reached into her pocket, retrieved the package of cigarettes, and tapped one into her outstretched palm. "Go for it, if you want."

Justine was a dope. No, worse that a dope. For the past thirty minutes, she'd been obsessed with the idea of smoking. Wanted to prove to her sister, prove to herself, that she was mature, that she wasn't a baby. Naturally, the second Leah agreed to let her smoke, the urge vanished. Justine could name a hundred reasons why smoking was a lousy idea. One, cancer. Two, their mother would be home any minute. Three, smoking was dumb. But she'd made such a production, practically begging. If she chickened out now, Leah would think she was a ninny. And Justine wouldn't blame her a bit. She couldn't believe she'd gotten herself into this mess.

Leah was still offering the cigarette. It was hard to tell if she was amused or annoyed.

"Maybe this isn't such a good idea after all," Leah said, closing her fist around the butt. "Let's skip it, OK? Pretend you never asked."

No, Justine insisted. This was her chance; she had to try. "Will you light it for me?"

Leah did not feel at all comfortable with this idea. Lighting a cigarette for her sister. Letting a twelve-year-old smoke. Maybe their father was right. Maybe she *was* evil. (He hadn't said those exact words, but that's what he meant.) Maybe she'd been born that way, evil to the core, evil blood coursing through her veins. Yet even evil people had limits. She could not be responsible for leading her sister astray.

Justine was staring up at her.

If the little geek wanted to smoke, Leah should probably let her. Who was she to judge? She could advise Justine not to smoke; ultimately the choice belonged to Justine. Her sister had a right to decide for herself. Besides, Leah had already said yes. Only cowards went back on their word. She opened the window, to draw the smoke out of the room, and went back to the bed, sat beside her sister, their thighs touching. "Watch," Leah said, placing the cigarette between her lips. She lit the end, took a long drag, and turned the filtered end to Justine.

Justine took a tiny puff, immediately blew out the smoke.

Oh God. She's an even bigger geek than I thought. Leah couldn't help laughing.

136

"What?" Her sister looked wounded. "Did I do something wrong?"

"You're supposed to inhale," Leah said, forcing a straight face. "Like this." Leah took a long drag, her eyes squeezed, lips pulling at the ends, and handed the cigarette back to her sister.

Justine brought the butt to her mouth, pursing her lips, mimicking Leah. Eyes closed. Sucking hard. Suddenly, she was—

Doubled over, coughing, the lighted butt dangling from her loosely closed fingers.

Leah swooped down, rescuing the cigarette before it fell and burned a hole in her rug. "Take it easy," she said, patting Justine's back. "You all right, Jus? That's it for today."

Justine wanted to die. Here she was, trying to prove she was grown up, that she deserved her sister's affection, her sister's respect, and what did she do? She made an idiot of herself. Throwing a coughing fit. Practically starting a fire in Leah's bedroom. *Think you're SO cool*, she scolded herself. *Look at you. You big stupid nerd.* She stared at her stubby feet, hanging over the edge of the bed. She was afraid to meet her sister's eyes. She knew exactly what Leah was thinking. *Baby, baby, baby.* No wonder Leah didn't like her. Justine didn't like herself, either.

Finally, she gathered the courage to look up.

"Don't feel bad." Leah took hold of Justine's hand. "Same thing happened my first time."

"Really?"

"Really. You should've seen me and Cissy, coughing. I almost barfed." Leah opened her arms, drew her sister into a bear hug. "Sure you're OK?" Leah asked, when they both let go.

Sure, Justine replied. She sort of liked smoking.

Leah ruffled Justine's hair. "Liar."

Justine giggled and Leah got up, slipped a disc by an artist called 50 Cent into her CD player. "The song's called 'Candy Shop.' Cool, huh? What do you think?"

Justine detested rap, with its repulsive chauvinistic lyrics. She hated the way the violent downbeat made her feel small. But if Leah thought rap was good, there had to be *something* good about it, she thought. The truth be told, she missed Leah's old music taste. Until a few months ago, they'd listened to the country station together. Justine loved country music, the simple songs about family, the complications of love. Justine understood the sensibilities of the singers. Now Leah listened to creepy rock bands like Pink Floyd,

137

their weird sounds emanating from an eerie background, or Ani DiFranco, her angry voice croaking, "I'm not a pretty girl." Or rap.

"It's good," Justine lied. "I like it, I think."

Leah slid her hands through her hair, her whole body pulsing with the syncopated beat.

Leah had the talent to dance professionally. Music flowed through her body like waves of electric or water or heat; she had "a feel for rhythm," as their dad used to say. Justine had no musical sense whatsoever, no timing, no rhythm, no feel. Whenever she ventured on to the dance floor, at the Halloween Ball at the middle school, for example, she was all arms and feet, the butt of everyone's joke. Justine stood in the center of the room, her sister dancing circles around her.

Leah stopped dancing. "Move your shoulder, Jus." Justine's shoulder twitched. "Good. Now your hand," she said, demonstrating a swimming motion with her hand, her fingers splayed.

Justine imitated the move, her hand limp, her arm wavering like a fish.

Leah laughed. "Good. That's the idea. Now let's see if you can time it to the music." She stopped the CD between verses and started the song over again. "Listen. Hear the beat? It goes BOOM, boom, boom— That first big boom starts the phrase. Listen again. Hear it?" She snapped her fingers. "One, two, three, four," she said, tapping her foot in time with the beat. "One, two, three, four," she said, snapping her fingers, her body pulsing again, her arms and shoulders and hips moving as one. She took Justine by the hands, and twirled her around and around. "One two three four," Leah sang. "One two three four."

When the song ended, Leah turned off the music, and, holding Justine's hand again, pulled her close. "Think you could do me a favor?"

"Sure," Justine said. *Anything.*

Leah looked Justine in the eye. "You have to swear to God you won't tell."

Justine drew an X over her heart. "I never tell."

"I know you don't, Jus. I'm sorry."

Ani DiFranco concert tonight, she whispered. Would Justine cover for her, if she went?

Was that it? Was that all Leah wanted?

Leah nodded. "I'd owe you, big time." Ani was Leah's favorite singer, ever. "I'm dying to see her." Todd had gone to so much trouble. He'd be heartbroken if she blew off the concert.

"I have an idea," Justine said, cupping her hands, and whispered in Leah's ear.

Great idea, Leah said, laughing. I can't believe I didn't think of that one myself.

Fifteen

Not a Little Girl

After dinner, Justine clattered back up the stairs. When Leah opened her door, her sister handed her a DVD of *The Princess Bride*, snagged from the video library in the family room.

"You still like this one, don't you?" Justine asked.

Definitely, Leah said, and turned the movie over to read the credits. She loved this movie. The princess reminded Leah of herself, with her fair skin and pale blond hair. Also—she hadn't shared this with anyone yet—Leah had been dreaming, lately, of becoming a bride. She glanced at Justine, lying on the bed, tiny feet crossed at the ankles, waiting for the movie to start. The wedding would be smaller than it might have been, if Leah were older. Justine would be her maid of honor, of course. Leah had two female cousins, about her age, on their father's side, but they lived in Pennsylvania. She didn't know the girls well enough to invite them to be in her wedding. For attendants, that left only Hope. And Todd was an only child. He would ask Lupo, and possibly Jamie, if Jamie hadn't fired him yet. She didn't know of anyone else.

"Justine?" She was about to ask her sister what color brides-maids dresses she should choose—blue would look great on Justine, a flattering design, nothing revealing; sexy dresses looked silly on twelve year-old girls—and changed her mind. Todd might want to elope.

Her TV sat on a small wooden table at the foot of her bed. She plugged the movie into the DVD drive, and hit *Play*, pulled her spare pillow from the shelf in her closet, and climbed onto the bed, next to her sister, rolled the feather pillow and tucked it under her head.

Her room was warm and inviting, her bed comfy. A patchwork quilt lay at the foot of her bed. She unfolded the quilt, covered herself and her sister. It might be nice to stay home, watch the rest of the movie with Justine. Her sister was giggling, getting a charge out of the movie, her face alight. Her sister's enthusiasm was contagious. She'd missed out on a lot, Leah thought, by dissing Justine. Staying home would keep them both out of trouble. Only, Leah couldn't stay home. Todd would never forgive her if she backed out now. Also, she wanted to see the concert.

Between them, Todd and Justine had ironed out the arrangements. Todd planned to wait for Leah at the end of their street, ready to fly when Leah showed up. She checked the alarm clock on her nightstand: five past seven. The concert started at eight. In ten minutes, Todd would be turning onto their street. If all went according to plan, they would be settled in their seats before the end of the opening act.

Leah hauled herself up. "Time to get going," she whispered. She snatched her Cortland team sweatshirt from the laundry pile on the floor, pulled it over her head.

Justine rolled on her side, pushing her bangs out of her face. "Are you excited?"

Leah, nodding, brought her index finger to her lips. "Wicked," she mouthed. She hiked up her sweatshirt, tightened her belt, smoothed the sweatshirt over her jeans, and laced her Doc Martin boots. Bending, she kissed her sister's forehead. "Wish me luck."

"Want some help? With the window?"

Leah shook her head. "I'm OK. I'm a little nervous about climbing back in."

"When I go down to say goodnight, I'll unlock the back door."

Leah squeezed her sister's hand. "Cool, Jus. Thanks."

Leah had no trouble climbing out the window, into the tree. Belly to the sill, she slithered under the sash and, catching hold of a hefty branch, hoisted herself out. The smell of the wood burning in their fireplace reminded her of their family camping trips, when she was younger.

Cautiously, she stood, gripping the branch above her, her feet turned outward for balance, and made her way to the trunk of the tree. So far, so good. She steadied herself, squatting. Her mistake was looking down. The drop was a good twenty feet. She thought she might vomit. Her room beckoned, the interior awash in soft yellow light. Justine lay in bed, laughing. If Leah closed her eyes, and stretched herself out on the branch, she could easily crawl back

141

inside. She would tell Todd her parents caught her sneaking out, and guarded her for the rest of the night.

Only she couldn't do that to Todd. He was probably at the bottom of the street right now, tapping impatiently on the steering wheel, waiting for her to arrive.

Do it, Leah told herself. Don't be a baby. *Just do it.*

Holding a thick branch, she dropped her right leg, foot feeling for the next lower branch.

The branch. Her foot sliced the air. *Where was the branch?*

Finally, she hit something solid. She dropped her left foot, slowly lowered her body.

At last, she reached the split in the trunk, just above the bole. She set her foot in the "y" and leaned back, breathing hard. Perched here, on a low branch, she was only five or six feet above ground, the family room window spitting distance away. Her mother was curled on a chair by the fireplace, reading. Her father lay on the sofa, watching TV. A commercial came on; her father, rising, peered at the window. *Damn.* She pushed herself backward, pressing her spine to the trunk. He moved toward the window. *Damn. Damn. Damn.* She sucked in a lungful of air, praying that her parents didn't see her.

Her mother said something. Her father, in his stocking feet, strolled toward the kitchen.

She let out a breath. *If you're up there, God, thank you.* Holding the branch directly above her, she scanned the yard for roots, searching for a safe place to land.

One, she counted, closing her eyes. *Two.* On three, she let go, gritting her teeth, and leapt.

From the foot of the tree, she monitored the movement inside the house, waiting for the right moment to split. Her father strolled back to the family room, a glass of white wine in one hand, a beer in the other. He bent, setting the glass on the coffee table, his back to the window.

Run for it. Now.

Leah sprung like a sprinter leaving the block, and dashed across the lawn, her head down, arms pumping, toward the woods bordering their property.

Once she was safely under cover, she stopped to catch her breath.

Leah walked toward the end of the street, hugging the curb, staying out of the light cast by the streetlamps. Midway down the block, she spotted Todd's Jeep, jogged the rest of the way.

In Leah's Wake

The door swung open. "You made it," he said, and leaned over the seat to kiss her.

Jerry was on duty tonight. He'd agreed to cover for Larry Hollingshead, who'd come down with the flu. He backed the Explorer into the vacant lot at the intersection of Blanchard and Old Orchard Road. Lately, Jerry often found himself parking here, in the spot where he'd been parked the afternoon Zoe Tyler's Volvo whizzed by. Coming here, Jerry told himself, had nothing to do with Zoe Tyler. Old Orchard was a treacherous road, flanked by towering oak and maple trees. The area was sparsely populated, the traffic light; people drove as if they were on a freeway, gathering speed as they sailed downhill. The oak tree at the foot of the hill marked the site of a horrific crash that happened several years earlier: four teenage boys racing downhill in a souped up T-bird, the driver losing control halfway down the hill. Three boys died on impact. By the time Jerry arrived, the T-Bird had caught fire. A fourth boy was trapped in the backseat, crying, pounding on the window. Two men were struggling to open the jammed door. Jerry, shouting, gesturing, ordered them back. He was ten feet from the T-bird when it exploded. For months, he had nightmares. He'd wake, drenched in sweat, cursing himself for having let the boy die. The friends of the dead boys nailed a cross, festooned with carnations, to the base of the tree, a shrine whose implications were lost, he felt, on the kids who'd left it. For a month or two, the kids took greater care on the roads; soon, they were speeding again. At this time of year, the road covered with leaves, the asphalt slick, speeding was deadly. *That* was why he was here.

Yet, even as he sat here, convinced that parking in this particular spot had nothing to do with Zoe Tyler, he saw her. When he least expected it, her face materialized—her translucent green eyes, her golden skin, that bewildering smile—and his imagination tormented him with images of the two of them, in New Hampshire, Vermont, engaged in some strenuous physical enterprise: hiking or riding a bike or climbing a mountain. In his fantasies, he watched her from behind, Zoe in shorts and a tank top, her hamstrings straining against the exertion, her shoulders glistening, her wavy dark hair pulled in a ponytail, exposing the graceful curve of her neck.

Jerry blinked the image away. From his station, he watched the cars coming and going. To bide time, he ran the tags on the vehicles that drove by. Already, after two weeks, he recognized most of the drivers. A white Jetta rounded the corner, sputtered up the hill. Maggie Whitefield, nineteen years-old, cautious kid, judging from the

143

way she handled her car; lived on Cortland Street, an offshoot of Winding Brook Lane. Black Honda Civic: Wayne Wilson, head of janitorial services for the high school. Dodge Caravan, pale blue: Rhoda McCabe, retired, self-appointed Cortland historian. A purple Taurus blew by. Jerry switched on his siren and lights.

Leah snapped her fingers, bobbing her head.

Ani, they shouted, a whorl of hands and hips and feet. *Ani.* The audience impatient. Opening act come and gone, a reggae recording pounding out of the speakers . . . *Ani* . . . *Ani.*

Leah's shoulders pulsed, her body rocking to the rumbling noise.

Ani . . . suddenly, the canned music died and the arena went dark. . . Matches flickered.

Leah reached for the stage, the tips of her fingers barely visible.

A roadie adjusted a speaker. And Todd handed Leah the twinkling joint.

The stage lights exploded, washing the stage in a radiant rainbow of color.

From out of the wings, she appeared . . . *there she is.* . . a tiny girl, in tan chinos and a plaid flannel shirt, dwarfed by a giant guitar.

An eerie quiet descended.

Ani stared into the audience, at the sea of faces willing her on . . . flicked a hand.

Ani, someone shouted. *Ani,* the crowd joined in. *Ani, Ani.*

She tipped her head, gazing up at the lights.

The elf-girl threw her head forward and back, and plunged into her song, the energy real and sizzling and raw.

Pausing, mid-song, she ripped off the flannel shirt, stripping to a snug black camisole, her shoulders sinewy, lithe. .. tuned her guitar. Now, she was playing again, her presence expanding. Music flowed from the core of her body, filling the stage, the arena . . . now Leah was on her feet, a raindrop in this raging river of music. . . She took the joint, sucked hard, handed it back. . .

. . . up, up, up the notes rose. . .

Todd propped his feet on the back of the empty seat in front of him. Leah grabbed hold of his hand. "Can you feel it?" she asked. "Can you feel it?"

He rolled another joint, and another. . . pulled her to him. . . the notes full and strong, reaching, reaching. . . into depths of her body. . . his tongue in her ear. . . hand on her thighs. And now she was up there, too, on the stage. She climbed onto her chair, pulled him up with her . . . her body swaying, in the swirl of sound and color and light. . .

"Oh my God," Leah said. "She was *amazing*."

Todd, holding her hand, pulled her across the lot behind the arena, where he'd parked the Jeep. The temperature had dropped, the sharp wind chafing her face. Normally, she would be freezing. She'd forgotten her jacket. Her sweatshirt, the top to her soccer warm-ups, provided little protection against the elements. Tonight, she was not the slightest bit cold.

As they left the arena, he asked if she'd enjoyed the concert. She'd responded with a terse nod, loathe to let go of the music whirling inside her head. Now, she was ready to talk.

"Oh my God, Ani was great. Wasn't she, like, incredible on guitar?"

Todd smiled, a noncommittal response.

The Jeep loomed in front of them. Todd rooted through his pocket, hunting for the keys.

She wished she'd taken him up on his offer to buy her a CD. In the concourse, they'd stopped at a table displaying all of Ani's recordings, her latest as well as the older records, all of which Ani had produced herself, under her Righteous Babe label. Leah was dying to hear the recorded version of the songs Ani had played. Also, it would have been nice to add one of the older discs to her collection. But she'd felt uncomfortable accepting a CD. Todd had spent so much money on the tickets already.

The lot was a nasty tangle, vehicles battling one another to get to the exits. Todd swore under his breath, and plugged some random jazz CD Leah had never heard before into the deck.

As they inched toward the exit, an awesome idea popped into her head. She and Todd could form a band together, a boyfriend and girlfriend team, or a husband and wife like White Stripes or Fleetwood Mac. Or maybe she'd go solo like Ani, and hire Todd to manage her act. According to the bio on her website, Ani left home when she was Leah's age, moved to New York, lived with friends. If Ani could be this huge success after all she'd been through, there was no reason in the world why Leah couldn't be a star, too. She strummed her air guitar. She would give anything to play as well as Ani DiFranco. She wondered how long it would take to learn.

"Todd?" Could he teach her to play? "You know. Guitar?"

"Sure. You can use my old guitar, if you want."

145

She pictured herself on stage, performing before a packed house, for her adoring fans. "Think I could ever be as good as her?"

"Who?" he asked, perplexed.

"Ani. If you taught me, I mean."

Todd's eyebrows curled in dissent. "Don't get me wrong. She's got great energy and all. But you've got to admit, her guitar playing's kind of simplistic."

Ani DiFranco—simplistic? Leah shifted sideways, away from her boyfriend, as if she didn't want to catch cooties. He probably thought that noise he was listening to was good. *Vital Transformation*, he said it was called, the recording by some weird seventies band she'd never heard of. Honestly, who named a song "Vital Transformation"? And Mahavishnu Orchestra? Please. What was *that* all about? Her boyfriend seriously irritated her, at times. He fancied himself this big music expert, just because his father had worked for Rounder Records for a few years. The kid didn't even *know* his father. Leah wagged her foot. Obviously, Todd wasn't all that smart if he didn't appreciate the brilliance of a talented musician like Ani. *She*, on the other hand, knew good music when she heard it.

"I think she was wasted," Leah said, once her anger had abated, and she was feeling somewhat amorous toward him again. "She seem it to you?"

Todd hit his blinker, signaling left.

"Did you see how wired she was? She used to do acid, you know."

"Actually, babe, I was paying more attention to you."

Leaning over the stick shift, Leah pecked her boyfriend on the cheek. "I loved the concert," she said. "That was so cool, you got the tickets."

Todd grinned. "Look at this traffic." It would be late, by the time they got home.

Route 2 was a long, dark stretch of road. The road of tears, her mother called it. The Jeep's headlights caught the heads and arms of the makeshift crosses lining the grass alongside the shoulder. Leah wondered aloud who they belonged to and Todd told her a story about a friend of a friend, drag racing on Route 2. "It's up here," Todd said, pointing to a small wooden cross, nailed to the stump of a tree. "You can't really see it that good."

When they reached 495, Leah's boyfriend picked up the pace.

Sixteen

The Arrest

Jerry was sitting in the lot, with his window rolled down, listening to the wind sweep through the trees, enjoying the crisp night air on his face, when Corbett's truck careened around the bend. The Jeep was traveling erratically, one minute skidding along the shoulder, the next nosing too far center. Corbett had to be drunk or on drugs. The police had their hands full, trying to contain the recent flow of heroin and cocaine pouring into the area. In the last six months, two high school kids, sixteen and eighteen, had overdosed at parties in Ayer. Thankfully, neither had died. The Cortland kids were using, too. Be naïve to think otherwise. The last thing the Cortland PD needed was some punk townie, on probation for dealing, back on the scene.

A head bobbled on the passenger side. So Corbett wasn't alone. Antonio Lupo, no doubt, Corbett's sidekick. Lupo scared the hell out of Jerry. The Corbett kid had a conscience, at least. When the El Paso cops arrested him, Corbett had balled, or so the story went. Corbett had certainly cooperated or the judge would not have let him off on probation. The Lupo kid, on the other hand, was like a coyote. Over the last ten years, the land development had driven the coyotes out of their native habitats. At first, they'd lurked at the edge of the woods. Now they slunk through neighborhoods in broad daylight, brazen and fearless. Unless they were rabid, there wasn't much you could do, except chase them away. Like Lupo, they were protected.

Jerry switched on the strobes, the light bouncing off the rear of the truck.

Finally, Corbett pulled over. Jerry eased onto the shoulder, behind him.

The wind cut across the cruiser as he pushed the door open. His sciatica was bothering him again. Pain shot through his leg. When the wind died down, he stepped tentatively out of the truck, and onto the road. He shook his right leg, wincing, and turned on the flashlight.

The passenger turned his face to the window as Jerry approached. Too small for Lupo.

While he was waiting for Corbett to produce his license and registration, Jerry shined the flashlight around the inside of the truck, checking for contraband. The Jeep was a pigsty, littered with paper, candy wrappers, cigarette packs. Probably find wads of chewing gum tacked to the underside of the seats, if he looked. He worked his way across the rear bench, and into the front.

The passenger shrank away, shielding his eyes. *Her* eyes. Jesus. A girl. She wore a blue sweatshirt; she had a blanket spread over her legs. What was wrong with parents today? Jerry would cuff his daughter to her bed before he would let her out with a hoodlum like Corbett.

The glove compartment hung open. "What's in there?" Jerry aimed the light at the door.

"Nothin'," Corbett grumbled.

"I'll bet there's nothing in there."

"Is there a problem, Officer? If not, we'd like to get going."

That voice. He recognized the voice. *The Tyler girl. Shit.* Her sister said that she'd been hanging out with Lupo. He'd seen the Tyler girl only the one time, when she was passed out, and doubted he would recognize her again. But there was no mistaking that voice. She sounded just like her mother. Zoe would be mortified if he arrested her daughter. Maybe he should spare Zoe the embarrassment, let the kids off with a warning, tell them he'd be watching their every move. In the long run, he wouldn't be doing Zoe any favor, though, would he? Somebody needed to pull this girl back, before she hurt herself. If he put a good scare into her, maybe she would wise up. As a bonus, he could put Corbett away. Get that troublemaker out of the picture, too.

"Can't detain us without reason," the girl said, and theatrically clapped the door shut.

Unfortunately, the little smart-ass was right: couldn't hold them without justifiable cause. For Zoe's sake, Jerry ignored her. "Out of the car," he said to Corbett. There was weed in that glove compartment. He smelled it. A few twigs would be enough to haul these two to the station.

"Let's go." Jerry reached for the handle on the driver's side door. "Today."

"Coming," Corbett growled. "Gimme a minute."

Jerry's back ached. He should have told Hollingshead to find somebody else to cover for him tonight, begged off, claimed he had to take care of the kids. A coyote howled, its desolate cry coming from somewhere off in the distance. He scanned the field, shrouded in darkness, peered at the bleak, empty sky. On nights like tonight, Jerry hated being a cop.

Wind lashed the Jeep, vibrating the cab. Jerry peered inside, to see what was taking so long. Corbett lifted his ass, zippered his jeans. *Christ.* No wonder the Tyler girl had a blanket spread over her legs. As Corbett opened the door, he caught her kicking a can under the seat.

Leah sat beside Todd, in the backseat of the cruiser, arms indignantly crossed. This cop was ridiculous. Officer Johnson—she remembered him now. He'd given the safety presentations at her school, when she was a kid. One stupid joint and he found it. It wasn't even in the glove compartment, where he'd obviously thought it would be. He'd seen her accidentally kick the Coke can under the seat, claimed that gave him "reason" to search. Fine. The laugh was on him.

He found nothing in the Jeep. There was nothing to find. Leah could tell he felt bad for harassing them. She was all ready to accept his apology, when he decided to pat them down. Todd was clean. They'd smoked everything they had, except for one teensy joint he'd given her, to smoke before bed. She'd forgotten about it. She would've swallowed it, had she remembered.

The cop didn't force her to spread her legs or anything, but he made her empty her pockets. He wouldn't have found the joint at all, if he hadn't insisted she turn her pockets inside out. She tried to divert his attention, hoping to buy time to dump it. The cop was a bloodhound.

He radioed the station, told the dispatcher to expect them shortly and revved the engine.

This cop would not get away with this. He couldn't search them without a warrant. What he did was illegal. It was like entrapment or something. She couldn't wait to tell her father he'd tricked them. Her father would hire a good lawyer, and get *Officer Johnson* kicked off the force.

This whole experience was surreal. She'd had an awesome night. She'd seen Ani DiFranco! Now this? She wondered if her parents realized she'd snuck out of the house. She hadn't seen her parents since breakfast. If they'd gone into her room to check on her, to kiss her goodnight, they would have noticed her empty bed. In which case they knew.

Relax. They wouldn't have bothered.

Her parents were going to kill her. Worse, her name would be in the police log, and the entire town would know she was arrested. Sweet. One more thing for people to gossip about.

There had to be a way out of this mess. She surveyed the cruiser, searching for a way to open a conversation. The monitor on his laptop blinked. Once, when she and Hope visited Todd at the store, she'd seen a patrol car parked in the lot, the cop playing video games on his laptop. She wondered if that were standard procedure.

She spotted a photo taped to the dashboard. "Are those your kids?" she asked sweetly.

"Yep."

Great. One word response. "They're adorable. How old are they?"

"Three months."

Don't give up, she told herself. He'll come around.

"Boys or girls?"

"Boys," he answered, and raised the volume on his CB.

Murder One. She could see the headlines already. Irate father hacks rebellious teenager to death. Fine, her parents might not kill her. But they would ground her for life, a fate worse than death, as far as she was concerned. This was all Todd's fault. How could he do this to her? If he hadn't brought the weed, they wouldn't have smoked, she would not have been giving him head, and he would not have been driving like an idiot. And the stupid cop would not have pulled them over. Swear to God, if she managed to get out of this, Todd was history. She planned to break this relationship off. *Please God*, she prayed. *I'll be good. So good, you won't even recognize me.* She would dump Todd. She'd play soccer again. It was too late for this year, but she'd talk to Coach Thomas anyway. She'd respect her parents. She'd help at home, earn better grades in school. And. And. Please, God? *I'll start going to church.* Every week. Whether she felt like it or not. She folded her hands in her lap and sat back, closing her eyes, waiting for God to perform one of His miracles. Fifteen seconds passed. Twenty. Twenty-five. Her stomach was on fire. She'd probably developed an ulcer already. If she cried, maybe the cop would take pity on her. Release her, right here. She'd walk home, if necessary. Tears burned hot and raw in her throat.

Grow up. She toyed with her button bracelet. *Don't be a baby,* she told herself.

Face it: this wasn't Todd's fault. She was the one who had begged for the weed. (What fun was a concert if nobody was wasted?) She'd also insisted on smoking. Seriously, why was she worried? She was totally overreacting. So the cop found a joint. What could he do? Send her to jail? For possession of a joint? She'd never so much as looked cross-eyed at a cop, let alone broken the law. The cop would be the laughing stock of the world if he put a promising high school student, *the best soccer player in the state*, in prison for possession of one joint. If she didn't live in such a backward state, she wouldn't even be in this predicament. In California, marijuana was legal. For medicinal reasons, but still. They were bound to legalize it for general use soon. Another reason to move to the West Coast: California had sensible laws.

As they approached the rotary at the town common, the cop slowed. Dry leaves swirled across the great lawn. The whole town appeared to be sleeping, the lights out in the post office, the Corner Grocer, the video store, the only light cast by the dim streetlamps. A ten-speed bike, chained to a banister, stood on the battered porch of an ancient Victorian, a rooming house now.

The cruiser rounded the rotary and turned onto East Main, heading for the station.

A light was on in Cooper's Funeral Parlor, immediately outside the center. The undertakers were probably preparing a body. Leah wondered who'd died. Somebody's grandparent, maybe. When she died, Leah wanted a bash. She intended to leave a note with detailed funeral instructions, along with a guest list. She wanted every person she knew in attendance: relatives, friends, even the people she no longer trusted or liked. Coach Thomas, Cissy Hanson, the girls from her soccer team. In the eighth grade, when Katie Roman died of leukemia, Mrs. Lubbock, the music teacher at the high school, sang at the funeral. In her death note, Leah would tell her parents to hire Mrs. L, instruct her to sing sad, sentimental songs like, "I Have Always Loved You" and "Wind Beneath My Wings," songs guaranteed to reduce the audience to tears. She imagined hordes of devastated mourners at her graveside, tossing pale pink roses onto her casket, holding hands, leaning on one another for support. *Dear, dear Leah,* they would say, their voices breaking, *even in death, she had a generous spirit.* Oh, they would be sorry for having treated her badly. It would be a blast looking down on it all.

Leah placed her hand on Todd's thigh. Thinking about death freaked her out. She needed some contact with the physical world, to touch somebody *real.* She wanted to be sure she was still alive, that she hadn't died and just wasn't aware of it yet. Her heart slammed into her throat. She was alive, all right. In the backseat of a cruiser. About to be booked on drug charges.

God, let her be dreaming.

You'd think her boyfriend would hold her hand, try to help her, provide a teeny-weeny bit of solace. But no, the big oaf just sits there, comatose, barely breathing. She poked his thigh.

Now that she thought about it, he hadn't said a word since the cop discovered their weed. She couldn't imagine why Todd would be worried. It wasn't as if he were in trouble. His mother couldn't care less what he did. He could rob a bank and shoot all the tellers; if he said he was innocent, his mother would believe him. She'd buy any lie, as long as it was somewhat plausible.

Oh, no. Oh my God. She wrapped both hands around his forearm. *His probation.*

Todd leaned toward her. "Don't worry," he whispered, "everything's cool."

The cop eased the cruiser into an empty spot close to the station's entrance. The low-slung structure, constructed of concrete blocks, reminded her of the orphanage in *Jane Eyre.* Although the outward appearance was different, the building was every bit as depressing. It was easy to imagine cruel prison guards depriving their inmates of decent clothing and food.

Officer Johnson guided Leah and Todd toward the entrance, his hands on their shoulders.

Leah hugged her chest. She hadn't realized how bitter this night was. Or how dark.

When they reached the double-glass door, the cop cut in front of them, the wind swelling his leather jacket, and held the door. Leah stepped inside, squinting against the harsh prison light.

Leah wondered how long it would be until her parents arrived. Knowing her father, he would let her stay here and rot. Todd spent the night in jail, after his arrest. In the morning, his mom flew down and posted his bail. Wasn't so bad, he'd told Leah. The cops were OK, once he answered their questions. The cot was lumpy, and he'd had trouble falling asleep. And the prison food sucked. Otherwise, he had no major complaints. He'd slept in worse places, he told her.

The cop led them to the reception area, said he'd be right back, and disappeared.

Leah stood beside Todd, before a wide, bulletproof window. A computer sat on the desk behind the window, its display blinking. She could hear muffled voices. Odd, no one was back there. Flyers for a benefit basketball game—Police Shooters Fight the Cortland High Cougars— lay in a bin on the metal shelf in front of the glass. Another bin contained applications for firearm and motorbike permits. Leah shivered. *If only they were here for a permit.*

She folded her hands, lacing her fingers to keep from shaking. In a back room, people were still talking, probably deciding which charges to press. She ached to hold her boyfriend's hand, feel the comforting weight of his arm on her shoulders. Only she was too scared to move.

"Don't worry," Todd whispered again. "It'll be OK. I promise."

Leah stared at her Doc Martins, shifting from foot to foot.

When she looked up, a towering black woman was peering down at her, glowering. According to an article in the *Globe*, the prison matrons in Boston searched the body cavities of girls the cops arrested. Leah had never heard of any strip searches in Cortland. But that was hardly something the cops would advertise. A wave of nausea swept over her. They had arrested her for possession. What if they thought she was hiding other drugs? If they decided to hunt for them inside her butt? She crossed her feet, squeezing her buttocks together. Or, *no*, in her *vagina*? She eyed the matron. No way was that horrible woman strip-searching her.

Thick glasses magnified a pair of fearsome brown eyes. "Name," the woman demanded.

"Leah," Leah stammered.

"Full name please."

"Tyler."

"Could you speak up?" The matron stopped typing. "Can't hear you, honey."

"Tyler," Leah repeated. "Leah Tyler."

The matron punched Leah's name into her computer. "L-E-A-H?"

While they waited to be printed and booked, the matron record-ed their information.

A few minutes later, Officer Johnson reappeared, accompanied by an older guy, a former athlete, Leah thought, with a bulbous nose, beetle black eyes. The Chief of Police. She recognized him from photos in the *Cortland Gazette*. Officer Johnson opened the glass door leading to the inner office, and spoke to the matron. The chief, wheezing, cupped Todd's elbow. "Let's go," he said, and escorted Leah's boyfriend away.

"Wait," Leah cried, as Todd disappeared around the corner. Where were they going?

They had questions for Todd, the matron told her. "They're sending you home, honey."

Leah burrowed into the sleeves of her sweatshirt. "What are they going to do to him?"

The matron opened her door, and stepped down into the reception area. "Come on, honey. Officer Johnson called your folks. We've got a room in back. You can wait there."

"Will they keep him?" Leah pressed. For violating his probation, she wanted to say. But she kept her mouth shut. For all she knew, the Cortland police were in the dark regarding his last arrest. "Ma'am?"

"Can't tell you that, honey." She was only the dispatcher. It wasn't her place to say.

Leah followed the older woman down a long corridor, their footsteps echoing through the cavernous hall, to a dank room no bigger than Leah's bedroom, lit by a rectangular fluorescent light. A round table sat in the center of the room, surrounded by six rigid plastic chairs. A filing cabinet, pushed against the left wall, was stacked with newspapers. On a metal desk at the back of the room, a computer idled, its low buzzing hum like the drill of a woodpecker.

"Here you go." The matron pulled a chair away from the table. "Shouldn't be too long."

Leah slumped into the chair. "What's gonna happen to me?"

The matron lowered herself onto a seat, covering Leah's hands with two large hands the color of roasted chestnuts. The matron clasped Leah's hands. She smelled of honey and almonds, her scent warm, reassuring. "Officer Johnson? Trust me. He's a good guy."

Leah's heart beat in her throat. "My parents are going to kill me."

"I'd be steamed too, if I was your mamma. But they'll get over it. They're your folks, right? They love you. I got kids myself, honey. Believe me, I know." The matron squeezed Leah's shoulder. "I'm Millie," she said. "Need anything, you come get me. You hear?"

Seventeen

All a Big Lie

The telephone jerked Zoe out of a deep alpha sleep. She had trouble placing the caller.

"Oh, God," she said, stunned. "What happened? Is she all right?"

Arrested? Impossible. Her daughter was home, Zoe argued, knowing, even as the words spewed from her mouth, that she was deluding herself. "She's in bed."

She listened for a few minutes more, collecting then sorting the details, and hung up the phone. Will was already up, sitting with his back to her, at the foot of their bed. He pulled on a pair of jeans and a Grateful Dead T-shirt, Jerry Garcia's mug screened in color over the chest.

"That shirt, Will. *Please.* They'll think we're white trash."

"What the hell do you want me to wear?" He yanked the shirt over his head. "A tux?"

Slacks and a sweater, she snapped, would be fine.

He flung the T-shirt on the bed, and stomped to their closet.

Something clunked. Seconds later, it sounded as if his entire shoe collection crashed to the floor. She flinched, ignoring her husband's antics, and smoothed her nylons over her hips. Best to stay calm, she told herself, until they'd heard the whole story. Leah could be an innocent bystander. The police had decided to release her for a reason. She zippered her skirt, stepped into a pair of high-heeled pumps, went to the bathroom to brush her teeth and put on some makeup.

155

She managed to enjoy a few minutes of peace before Will was ranting again. "I see that Corbett—" He stood in the bathroom doorway, waving his socks. "—I'll kill the son-on-a-bitch."

She swished her mouthwash, spat in the sink. "You ready? We have to get out of here."

"He'll wish he never met this family, by the time I'm through with him."

"Will, stop. You'll wake Justine." She fished a roll of antacids out of the vanity drawer, peeled the foil, and handed the roll to her husband. "I told you, they're not pressing charges."

"I've had it with her shit. We're going to do something about it this time."

"Damn it, Will." She slammed the drawer shut. "Think I like this any better than you?"

He stomped to the tub, sat on the rim, pulled on his socks. "We'll have to hire a lawyer, I guess. I can imagine what that'll set us back. I'll call Mike Delaney. At least he won't screw us."

"That's not necessary. Officer Johnson said—"

"Johnson?" Wasn't he the one who'd responded to her 9-1-1 call?

She nodded. Her husband was trying her patience.

And the warning? Him, too?

"Yes," she said, smiling indulgently.

"What the hell is it with him? What's the guy doing, following us or something?"

"Oh, for Pete's sake. Don't be absurd."

Zoe inched Justine's door open, and crept into the room. Justine had forgotten to draw her shades. She lay across the bed, her little girl body bathed in moonlight, one arm draped over the dog, the sheets and blankets bunched at the foot of her bed. Dog opened her rheumy eyes, peered up at Zoe. Zoe set her hand on Justine's forehead. Her daughter's hair was damp. "Be back shortly, sweetie," she whispered. "We won't be long. You take care of her, Dog."

Dog nuzzled Justine's chest, and Justine groaned and rolled onto her belly.

On her way out the door, Zoe set the burglar alarm.

In the garage, she nearly tripped over the box of clothes designated for Goodwill. Two weeks ago, she'd asked Leah if she would like to add anything, was still waiting for Leah's contribution. She didn't understand how the situation with her daughter had come to this. How had they raised such an irresponsible kid? Leah rarely followed through on anything. She'd quit playing soccer, right when her team needed her the most. Skipped school. Managed, God knew how, to get herself arrested tonight. Nothing worked with Leah. Reasoning was useless. Zoe could beg, scream, threaten, cajole. Her pleas fell on deaf ears. Or worse, Leah would agree—*sure, Mom, you're right, I know*—and do exactly the opposite of whatever she'd pledged.

A year ago, if someone had predicted that she and Will would be driving to the police station tonight, their daughter arrested for possession of drugs, Zoe would have laughed. *Never. You're out of your mind*, she would have said. Now here they were. There had to be a way to reach Leah, to pull her back, to help her see what she was doing to herself. Leah had been lucky this time. This police were not filing charges. Colleges looked poorly on applicants with a criminal record. If this behavior continued, Leah would destroy her future. Zoe and Will had to make their daughter understand the importance of this, make her stop screwing up. Only how?

Will pressed the button on his visor and stepped on the accelerator, ducking instinctively as he backed out of the garage. A garage door had hit him once, at their old place in Hudson. The door nicked his shoulder, knocking him off balance. He'd fallen backward, his head missing the steal beam by an inch. If not for a tricycle breaking his fall, he would have been dead. The door snapped shut. He adjusted the mirrors, backed into the turnaround, and headed up the drive.

"Warm enough?" He spiked the temperature, raising it to seventy-five.

Fine, his wife replied, "thanks," and flipped up the vents, redirecting the hot air.

This situation with Leah was driving him out of his mind. That one of his children might be arrested had never crossed Will's mind. Towns like Cortland were supposed to be islands of safety. He'd spent an extra fifty grand to buy a house here so he could avoid this kind of crap.

Traveling across town to the police station, he tried to regain control of his emotions. It was embarrassing enough that his daughter had been arrested. No need to make a fool of himself, too. But he was not having much success. His daughter was a good kid, until she hooked up with that shit-bum, Corbett. Sure, she'd disappointed them on occasion. When Leah was a toddler, his mother, one of the most levelheaded people on the planet, told him that child-rearing was a

157

bittersweet enterprise. Your children will bring you the greatest joy in your life, she'd said. They will also break your heart. "You've got to take the good with the bad." It was insightful advice. Will tried to the best of his ability to live by it. When Leah was in eighth grade, Judy Hanson caught the girls sneaking cigarettes behind the bushes in her yard. He and Zoe had sat Leah down, explained the dangers of smoking, exacted a firm promise from her to quit. In October, when she refused to study for the SAT test, he allowed her to put the test off until spring. Even her quitting soccer Will managed to rationalize. But an outsider screwing with his daughter's mind, messing her up? Not on his shift. Leah made mistakes, of course, but she'd never been in any real trouble until Corbett entered the picture.

"What's your take?" he asked, as they pulled into the station. "How do we handle this?"

"I don't know," his wife said quietly. "I think we need to hear her out."

"Figures." He withdrew the key from the ignition. "Should've known you'd say that."

Leah couldn't stop thinking about Todd. She had a sick feeling the police had discovered his criminal record on the computer. If so, they were probably in the process of transporting him to the maximum security prison, at MCI Concord. She didn't know what she would do if that were the case. She could never live with herself if Todd wound up in jail because of her.

A door opened and closed, and she heard her parents talking to the dispatcher. The jig was up. Leah was dead. Maybe she ought to confess. Tell the truth, about everything this time. Skipping school. About Hope's. That she'd tried Ecstasy once. That, on occasion, the others did crystal meth. If her parents forgave her, she would do everything in her power to live up to their expectations. She would take up where she left off last week, only this time she would do better. Work harder in school, help more at home. Study, *honestly* study, for the SATs, take every single practice test in the program. She couldn't live this way anymore. She didn't want her parents to hate her. If they'd give her a chance, one more chance, she would prove she could be trusted.

They were in the hall now, headed this way, the volume of their conversation increasing. She recognized the measured click of her mother's heels, the impatient squeal of her father's leather-soled loafers. The third set of footsteps were Officer Johnson's. Any second, they would be here. Leah felt naked, totally exposed. If only she had somewhere to hide. When she and her sister were little and their parents fought, they would huddle under a table or hide in a closet, until the house was quiet. She covered her face, pressing her knees together, hugging her chest.

Leah felt a pat on her head, and caught a whiff of her mother's perfume. She looked up, partially uncovering her eyes. Their gaze met briefly. Her mother, looking away, took the seat next to Leah. Officer Johnson nodded, acknowledging Leah's presence, slid onto the seat beside her mother. Her father remained standing, his arms crossed, refusing to meet Leah's gaze.

Her mom's eyes traveled past Leah, to a DARE poster taped to the wall over the filing cabinet. Leah had graduated from DARE; she'd been awarded a lousy bumper sticker for the effort. "Proud parent of a DARE graduate," the sticker had read, the award not even for her.

Officer Johnson cleared his throat. "Leah?" Three sets of eyes converged on her. "Want to tell your parents what happened?"

Tell them? "Don't they know?" she stammered.

Her mom coughed, covering her mouth. "We'd like to hear it in your own words, Leah."

"You can start with why you snuck out," her father interjected. "That goddamn kid—"

Her mother shot her father an exasperated look. The cop cleared his throat again. Leah wondered if he was coming down with the flu, if she should warn her mother to sit farther away.

Her mother set a hand on Leah's thigh. "Tell us what happened tonight, honey."

Leah pulled the sleeves of her sweatshirt over her hands. She wanted to answer, to tell her mother the truth. But she didn't know where to begin. The words were lodged in her throat.

Leah stared at the table, counting the scratches in its surface, chewing her lower lip.

In her peripheral vision, she saw her father cast a withering eye at the door. For one irrational instant, she thought he might leave, then she realized he was gathering momentum.

"She's sixteen years old, for God's sake. I want that asshole in jail."

Jail? Leah tugged her mom's arm, expecting an ally against such outrage. "Hear him?"

"Behind bars," her father crowed. "For as long as possible. Don't care if he rots—"

159

Rots? Leah burst out of her seat. Her father was nuts. She wasn't listening to him.

Her mother snagged Leah's wrist, as she attempted to flee, forcing her to stay put. She swiveled to face Officer Johnson. "My husband and I are exhausted. We never expected this," her mother said, and shifted her attention to Leah. "The truth, were you smoking marijuana?"

"For Christ's sake, Zoe. Of course she was." Her father's blistering eyes lit on her.

Leah cowered.

"Mr. Tyler," Officer Johnson said, "if you don't mind my saying—"

Leah thought her father might attack the cop. But Officer Johnson cut him off, diffusing the situation. "We're all set," he said, standing, his face flushed. "Why don't you go on home."

Leah's mother pressed her hands to the table like an old woman, and pushed herself out of her chair. "Thank you," she said, extending her hand to Officer Johnson. "We appreciate this."

Her father glared at the wall.

Officer Johnson paid no attention to Leah's father. "Your daughter's got herself tangled up with the wrong people, that's all." He glanced at Leah, as if to say, *you know who I'm talking about.* Lupo, she figured he meant. He ushered them out of the interview room, Officer Johnson and her mom walking ahead, her father following at a clipped pace, Leah lagging behind.

"By the way," the cop said, as they were leaving. "Your boyfriend told us the truth."

"Told you." Her father slammed his car door. "That kid's bad news."

"That's totally unfair," Leah complained. The weed belonged to them both.

Her mother stretched her arm across the back of her seat. "If you don't mind. You had your chance to talk. Now your father and I have a few things we'd like to say."

She bet they did. Slouching, Leah stared at the window, a black hole opening into a vast, empty darkness, fidgeted with the buttons on her door. Blah, blah, weed, her father was saying. Blah, blah, disappointing. Blah, blah, Todd. Was her father a retard? Covering for her was like the coolest thing, *ever.* The poor kid could end up in *jail* because of her. She imagined herself, the loyal girlfriend, trekking to the prison to visit her boyfriend, carrying a wicker basket filled with his favorite foods: whoopee pie, oatmeal cookies, devil's food cake. If they imprisoned him for too long, she'd bake a razor or a grapefruit spoon or some other sharp tool into his cake.

Her father was still harping on Todd when they pulled into the drive.

He slammed the steering wheel. "I cannot believe you managed to get yourself arrested."

I can't believe this. Cannot believe that. How many times did he plan to repeat himself? Every shred of remorse Leah felt earlier had vanished. Her parents were disappointed. Big deal. She was disappointed, too. In them. How they treated her. How they shat all over her boyfriend. She was sick of hearing how she'd hurt them, what a crappy daughter she was. She had more important things on her mind than her parents, such as determining what had happened to Todd.

"We'll look for another therapist," her mother suggested. "Someone you like."

Leah rolled her eyes. Forget it. No more shrinks. She didn't care who the idiot was.

Her father hit the button on his visor, ducking as the garage door rumbled up. Ordinarily, he pulled in and out of the garage three or four times, aligning the car perfectly, parking far enough from the wall so that you could open the doors without scratching the paint. Tonight he shot inside, the tires screeching, skidded to a stop, and cut the engine.

Leah kneed her door, opening it carefully to avoid hitting the wall.

"Hold it right there," her father growled. "It's about time you apologized."

Apologize? Was her father out of his mind? For the last fifteen minutes, he had been attacking her. Talking all kinds of shit about her boyfriend. She would never apologize now.

"Your father's right," her mother agreed. "You owe us an apology."

"And by the way," her father snapped. "It's over."

Over? Leah must have missed a link. "What's over?"

"Damn it. Have you paid any attention to what I've been saying? Tell her, Zoe."

Her mother twisted to face the back seat, her face drained. "He's not good for you, Leah. This isn't a healthy relationship. You have to break it off."

Break it off?

Her father's eyes flashed in the rearview mirror. "I see that kid. I swear to God, I'll—"

Kill him? Not if he kills you first.

"Leah?" her mother interrupted. "You're not saying anything."

"What's *wrong* with you two? Are you, like, idiots or something? The 'kid' stuck up for me. He could end up in jail because of this. You *owe* him. You ought to be kissing his ass."

Her father sniggered. "We owe him, all right. That kid's a piece of shit."

"Shut *up*," Leah cried.

"Stop," her mother pleaded. "Both of you."

"Wasn't for that asshole, none of this bullshit would've happened."

I'm out of here, Leah thought. She didn't have to take this. Her parents made her sick. She wanted nothing to do with them anymore. She rammed her door into the concrete wall.

"Goddamn it, Leah. What the hell—"

"What? I hurt your poor little door? Leah shoved her head and shoulders into the space between the seats. "Come on," she taunted, jabbing her check. "Hit me. I know you want to."

Her father swung toward her, grabbing her shoulders, her mother pulling his arms, begging him to calm down. Sweeping sideways, he lifted Leah, and threw her into the back seat.

"Apologize," her father bellowed. "*Now.*"

"Fuck you." Leah booted the back of his seat. "You pathetic *fuck*," she shrieked, and slammed the car door and bolted into the house, leaving her parents gaping at her in shock.

Eighteen

The Blame Game

At dawn, when Justine opened her eyes, she heard her sister moving around. Curious, she padded, barefoot, into Leah's room to see what was up.

Their father's nylon duffel bag lay on Leah's bed. Leah was dressed in her nightclothes, a silky blue tank top and faded Teddy Bear bottoms. She tossed a T-shirt and pair of jeans on her bed. She looked exhausted, purple moons under her sunken eyes, her skin sallow.

"What's up?" Justine asked, trying not to sound worried. "You have fun at the concert?"

Leah stuffed the T-shirt and jeans in her bag. The concert was awesome, she replied, without looking up. She trudged to her bureau, rooted through the top drawer, dug out a pair of lacy black thongs and a matching bra. "I'm out of here," she said. She stuffed the panties and bra in the bag. "I don't know where I'm going yet. I don't even care. As long as it's not here."

Justine's heart sank. She didn't think she'd messed up. After Leah left, she tiptoed to her own room, surfed the Internet until the movie ended. (She found a great astronomy site, packed with information she could use for her project.) At nine thirty, she'd gone downstairs to kiss her parents goodnight, exactly as they had planned. Their parents seemed fine, a little distracted maybe, not at all suspicious. "I didn't say anything to Mom and Dad. Honest."

Leah pulled a white T-shirt from the laundry pile on her floor, examined the armpits, sniffed, and tossed it back on the pile. "It's not your fault, Jus."

163

Justine twiddled the hem of her pink baby-doll pajamas. "Don't go, Lee."

Leah stopped packing. "I'm sorry, Jus," she said, and squeezed Justine's hand.

"Please don't go. Don't leave me here by myself."

"You won't be by yourself." Leah eyed Dog, lying on the floor by Justine's feet.

Justine ruffled Dog's ears. Dog climbed on the bed, wheezing, and nuzzled Justine's leg.

Justine loved Dog. At times, she almost believed Dog was a person, but her dog could never take the place of her sister. When they were little, she and Leah had been best friends. They'd played together constantly—school, doctor, store—Justine always in the subordinate role: student, patient, the obtuse customer who requested merchandise Leah's store didn't stock. When Leah started middle school, their relationship changed. Leah wanted nothing to do with Justine. Justine was a pest. *Go away,* Leah would say, whenever she'd invited a friend to the house, and caught Justine loitering by her door. *Find friends of your own.* Leah couldn't leave now, just as they'd finally grown closer again. Didn't Leah say, just yesterday, Justine was cool? A good kid? She could be trusted? Hadn't their parents taught them that they could always rely on their family? That love conquers all? When you love someone, their mom always said, you *find* a way to work through your problems. "I'll help," Justine said. "I'll do whatever you want."

Leah yanked a padded bra and two more pairs of panties from her top drawer. With her elbow, she pushed the drawer shut. "It's them, Jus. I can't be here anymore. I hate them."

"What happened, Lee? Tell me?"

Leah's cell phone rang. (Last night, Justine had stolen the phone from her mother's secretary, and left it on Leah's nightstand.) Leah answered on the first ring. "OK. I'll be there."

From the tenderness in her sister's voice, Justine gathered that she was talking to Todd. She wondered how long until he arrived, how much time she had to talk her sister out of leaving. Possibly, he was already waiting, his Jeep parked at the bottom of the street or in the circle. *Please, don't let him be here.* Give her ten minutes. Ten measly minutes was all she needed.

Once she'd hung up the phone, Leah dressed quickly, in low-slung stonewashed jeans, a ribbed tank top, her baby blue sweatshirt. She combed her short blonde hair, parting it unevenly, pulled the bangs to one side, secured them with a yellow plastic barrette, and swiped the mascara wand over her lashes. Her cheeks were flushed, her lips a pale buttery pink. Her sister was the prettiest girl Justine had ever seen. The thought of her leaving tore a hole in Justine's heart. The house would feel deserted without her. It was all Justine could do to fight back the tears.

"I'll miss you, Teenie." With her thumb, Leah wiped a tear from the corner of Justine's eye and gave her a hug. "I have to do this. Try to understand, OK?"

"But—"

Leah closed the duffel bag and set it on the floor by the foot of her bed. "Hey," she said, taking hold of Justine's hand, pulling her up. "Why don't you come? We can leave together?"

Justine tried to mirror Leah's smile. Oh, she wanted to go with her sister, badly. But run away? Her parents would hate her. They would treat her like an outcast, as they did Leah. She would get behind on her science project. She'd miss school. She wouldn't be here to feed Dog (and she was the only one in the house who regularly remembered). But if she went, she thought, brightening, she would be with her sister. She and Leah could do things together. Watch movies. Hang out. If Leah needed her for anything, to do her a favor, to talk, Justine would be there. Living away from home might be good for her. After all, she had to strike out on her own, achieve independence at some point. "Sure," Justine said. Give her five minutes to pack?

"Awesome." Leah went to the window, lifted the honeycomb shade. *Hurry.* She would call Todd, she said, to let him know they'd be a few minutes longer than she had expected.

Justine emerged from her room, five minutes later, dragging her bulging tweed suitcase behind her. (Thankfully, her suitcase had wheels. Since she wasn't sure where they were going, had no idea what she would need, she'd packed practically every item of clothing she owned.).

Her sister was waiting on the landing, the duffel bag slung over her shoulder.

"I'm all ready," Justine said. "We can go now. He's waiting, right? We better hurry up."

Leah took in Justine's suitcase, and looked away, shaking her head miserably. "I can't get you involved, Teenie. I'll be back. Sister's promise. Soon as I teach them a lesson," Leah said, and threw her arms around Justine, hugging her little sister as if she would never, ever let go.

165

Leah had taught her parents a lesson, all right. Here she was, lying alone, on this smelly hide-a-bed in Hope's living room, the springs poking into her back, wishing, more than anything else in the world, that she was home, in her own room, in her own comfortable bed. She missed her dorky little sister. She had no one to talk to, no one she could rely on. She was all alone here. Hope's response to her arrival this morning was lukewarm. "I *guess* you can stay," Hope had said. "I'll tell my mom it's just for tonight, so she doesn't think you're moving in or anything. But you've got to sleep on the couch." As if Leah planned to confiscate her room. Strange as it seemed, she also missed her parents. Hope's mom was cool, but she wasn't Leah's mother.

Leah could never go back to her parents' house. After her behavior in the car, she could never face her parents, could never look them in the eye. What was wrong with her? Why couldn't she keep her stupid trap shut? Her parents hadn't disowned her exactly, but she had seen their disgust. She'd read the revulsion on their faces. They were probably glad she was gone. And she didn't blame them. She had disappointed them, again. She'd disappointed everybody. Her mother, her father. Coach Thomas. The girls on her soccer team. The high school dean, who "for the life of him" could not understand why a bright girl like Leah would skip classes or let her grades slide. She'd alienated her teachers. Withdrawn from her old friends. When kids saw her approach, they turned their heads or walked away. Worst of all, she'd disappointed Justine.

Leah's eyes welled, thinking of her sister on the landing, Justine begging her not to go. When Leah asked her sister to run away with her, though her sister was obviously scared, Justine had been willing to join her. Leah pictured her sister in her denim overalls, all phony smile and fake animation, towing an enormous tweed suitcase stuffed with all of her earthly belongings.

Her parents were right. She was a loser. A worthless, no-good loser. A disappointment, the very word a knife to her heart. If only she could disappear. Fall asleep and never wake up.

Leah's duffel bag lay on the floor, by the sofa, Hope's cat curled inside. The cat arched its back, rubbing its sour odor into her jeans. Leah tried shooing her away, but the cat was too stubborn to leave. Leah suppressed an urge to throw the dumb cat at the wall. But the cat was just an animal. This wasn't her fault. Holding the cat by her belly, Leah picked her up, let the cat flop on her chest, and stroked her back. The cat lay still for a minute, mewling, and scampered away. Leah stretched her legs, pressing through the soles of her feet, and stared at the ceiling.

Outside, a car skidded around the corner, its brakes squealing, its headlights shining in Leah's eyes. Leah swallowed the bile rising in her throat, and rolled onto her side. In the next room, Hope's mother had tuned in to a sitcom. Leah felt the vibration from the laugh track. She wondered how her sister was holding up. Leah pictured her, curled at the foot of her bed, hugging Dog. How would Justine manage without her? Leah wanted to call, to talk to Justine, to hear her sister's voice. But it was eleven o'clock. Justine would be asleep. If her parents answered, and realized Leah was on the line, they'd probably hang up. The people on TV were laughing again, a low rumbling yowl that shook Hope's sad little house. Leah dug her toes into the space between the cushion and arm of the sofa, and covered her ears.

They'd had a harrowing night, last night. This morning, both Zoe and Will had overslept. When Leah didn't come downstairs for breakfast, Zoe figured she was up to her usual baloney. Any other day, Zoe would have engaged, called to Leah from the foot of the stairs. If Leah didn't show her face in a few minutes, Zoe would have marched to her room, and stood over her bed, pestering until Leah opened her eyes. This morning, Zoe had been far too angry to fight. She felt betrayed, less by Leah's arrest than by her daughter's insolence, her lack of respect. Her daughter had showed not one iota of remorse. Instead of an apology, which Zoe and Will had every right to expect, she'd raised a fit, taunting, kicking Will's seat, calling her father terrible names.

Zoe was glad Leah hadn't joined them for breakfast. She didn't care to look at her daughter this morning. She and Will were by no means perfect. God knew, they'd made their share of mistakes. But their intentions, however misguided at times, had always been good. She and Will worked hard to provide a decent home for the girls, ensure that their children received a good education. At night, she set her alarm to go off forty-five minutes earlier than necessary, so she would have time to make a healthy breakfast in the morning. She prepared elaborate dinners to celebrate birthdays and special occasions. Since the girls were in pre-school, she and Will had opened their home to their daughters' friends. Some mornings, she would wake up and find four, five, even six extra girls in the house. She and Will had encouraged Leah in her pursuits, tried to support her decisions. Will devoted countless hours to Leah's athletic career.

167

And she treated them like this? Leah could sleep the day away, if that's what she wanted. And deal with the fallout herself. Time Leah assumed responsibility, accepted the consequences of her behavior.

At breakfast, Justine was oddly morose. Zoe should have realized something was up. While Justine dressed for school, Zoe set out a bowl of Raspberry Crunch cereal and a slice of wheat-berry toast. Leah, depending upon her mood, could be impossible to feed. The year she turned three, she'd subsisted on a diet of deli hot dogs and Kraft macaroni and cheese. Zoe tried every trick she could think of to convince Leah to eat a wider, more nourishing variety of foods. She tried the airplane trick—*zoom, zoooom,* the food in Leah's mouth before she had a chance to ask what it was—tried baiting—*Mmm, yum, Mmm, Leah, good*—bribery—*if you eat this one teensy piece of chicken, Mama will make you a yummy hot dog.* She'd even tried the old bait and switch trick, sneaking shredded ham into her daughter's macaroni and cheese. Leah ate the macaroni and picked out the ham. With the exception of goat cheese or lamb, which Zoe rarely served, her younger daughter was happy with anything you set in front of her. Justine never complained. Unless she was sick or had overeaten the previous night, she ate a healthy breakfast of cereal and toast; if she'd eaten a light dinner the night before, she would often take seconds. This morning, she picked at her food. Zoe, hating to see her go to school hungry, offered to make something different, oatmeal or French toast or fried eggs, but Justine just opened a book. She's out of sorts, Zoe had rationalized. And who could blame her? With all this upheaval, she was entitled to a bad day now and again. Besides, Justine was about to hit puberty, and mood swings were normal. After breakfast, Zoe did a perfunctory sweep through the kitchen, ran upstairs, pressed her ear to Leah's door, to see if Leah was stirring yet, and readied herself for work.

Under the circumstances, her day at the office had gone reasonably well, maybe because she was still furious about last night or maybe she's simply evaded the problem, too frightened to allow herself to consider the possibilities, to contemplate what the future might hold. At any rate, she kept busy, put the arrest out of her mind. At eleven, her two o'clock patient called to cancel. Rather than taking advantage of the extra hour to catch up on paperwork, she called her patients, shifted her schedule forward an hour. She decided to go home early, planned to spend time with Justine. Before Zoe started working fulltime, she and Justine were always together. Afternoons, while Leah was at practice, she and Justine busied themselves in the kitchen. Zoe would start a quick, easy dinner, meatloaf or beef stew or chili, and she and Justine would bake a dessert, banana bread, angel cake, lemon cream pie, Zoe reading the recipes, measuring out the ingredients, Justine mixing the batter, preparing the pans. When Justine was older, they began testing recipes Zoe found in *Good Housekeeping* or *Bon Appetit*. American chop suey, gourmet chicken potpie. One day, feeling adventurous, they'd prepared a sophisticated dish of veal cutlets with shallots and mushrooms, simmered in a savory, sage-infused cream. The finished dish looked less appetizing than it looked in the picture, but it tasted delicious. It had been ages since she and Justine tackled a project together. Tonight, she'd thought, they'd make dinner together.

Anticipation, the feeling of moving forward, having something positive to think about, energized her, and the day passed quickly. Between appointments, she searched for recipes on the Web. By two o'clock, she'd designed the perfect menu: warm butternut soup, followed by garlic-roasted chicken, sweet potatoes and haricot verts, chocolate lava cakes for dessert. While she waited for her final patient, she compiled a grocery list, and tucked the list in her handbag.

Why, she wondered, hadn't she thought of this sooner? For the past two months, she had been preoccupied with Leah, almost obsessed. Every day had brought a new problem, it seemed. First Todd, then soccer, now *this*. Because Justine had always been the stable one, her problems trivial compared to Leah's, less urgent, Zoe had pushed her younger daughter aside. She'd been lucky, so far. Justine hadn't rebelled. If Zoe continued to ignore her, she would lose Justine, too.

At four fifteen, Zoe packed three new files into her briefcase, thinking, if she had the time, she would look them over tonight, before bed, and gathered her handbag and coat. Halfway home, she'd remembered that she'd forgotten to lock up. Over the past several weeks, they'd had a rash of robberies in the building. At the tenants' urging, the property manager had installed surveillance cameras. Somehow, the thief managed to evade them. An inside job, the property manager opined. Eager to get to the grocery store, Zoe considered leaving the door unlocked. What was the worst that could happen? Her patient information, the only thing in her office she could not afford to lose, was safe, her electronic files backed up and locked in the safe. But the thought of someone violating her space, fingering her photos, her books, touching her personal belongings, unnerved her enough to warrant the time it would take to go back.

Her phone was ringing when she opened the anteroom door. "Yes," she said, breathless from the short sprint to her office. "Hello."

Mindy Lansdown? Zoe struggled to place the name.

"Hope's mother?" the caller prompted. "A friend of your daughter's?"

"Your house?" Zoe flinched, repelled by the caller's coarse voice. Ran *away*?

In the family counseling session, Leah had admitted to being at a friend's house the night she'd gotten so drunk. She'd been tight-lipped regarding the name. This Hope person must have been the friend in question. Why would the Lansdown woman allow Leah to stay at their house? Any decent person would send a runaway home. During their brief conversation, to keep from lashing out, Zoe forced a tight smile. As soon as the woman paused for a breath, Zoe cut her off. She thanked her profusely for giving Leah a safe place to stay, hung up, and dialed the police.

According to Jerry Johnson, the Lansdown house was a drug den, a hangout for every petty criminal in the area. For a month, the narcotics unit of the Ayer PD had been trailing a coke ring. Last week, they'd observed one of their prime suspects, an acquaintance of the Lupo boy, leaving the Lansdown house. They did not have sufficient evidence for an arrest, but they were "closing in." Leah was a minor. They could press charges against Mrs. Lansdown, for aiding and abetting a runaway. "It would give the drug investigation a boost," Jerry added. They'd have reason to search the house. Jerry meant well. But Zoe would never allow her daughter to be a pawn in a drug bust. Never mind, sending the police to fetch Leah would only exacerbate an already bad situation. Zoe had counseled dozens of runaway kids. She knew that the choice to return home had to come from inside; otherwise, running away would always be an option. If they forced her to come home now, the first time Leah felt threatened again, she would take off.

After talking with Jerry, Zoe was determined to see the Lansdown place for herself. Visualizing the house might give her some insight, help her understand what had driven her daughter to run there. Zoe resisted an urge to call her husband. Will would insist on confronting the woman. If Jerry was right about the drugs, the Lansdown woman might have a gun in the house. If she and Will showed up on the doorstep, Will issuing threats, something ugly might happen. Zoe booted her computer, looked up the address, printed directions from *Map Quest*.

In the car, Zoe checked and rechecked her directions. She was unfamiliar with this part of town. North Cortland was a wasteland, a solid four miles from the center, on the side opposite from the schools and the highway. There were no shops, no restaurants, no gym, no ballet or jazz or tap-dancing studios. Unless you lived here or your child took riding lessons, or you lodged a horse in one of the stables, you would have absolutely no reason to be here.

As she approached the Lansdown's street, Zoe considered turning around. Maybe this wasn't such a great idea, after all. What if Leah happened to be looking out the window when she drove by? If Leah saw the car, she would assume, correctly, that her mother was spying on her. Maybe it would be better to come back with Will. Bringing Leah home, against her will if need be, might actually be for the best. At least Leah would know her parents loved her. Maybe, on Leah's part, this was a plea for reassurance; maybe Leah wanted proof that, despite her behavior, her parents still cared. A confrontation need not be violent. They could negotiate.

The house, a squalid ranch with a sagging roof and chipped cobalt blue paint, looked every inch the drug den Jerry described. A tangle of rhododendron skirted the house, partially concealing a grimy picture window. A child, trick-or-treating or selling Girl Scout cookies, would be petrified to stop here, Zoe thought, never mind knock on the door, afraid some lunatic was lurking inside. A rusted chain, tied to the trunk of a maple tree, lay in a coil in the front yard, a miserable square of pine needles and dirt. If the Lansdowns owned a dog, it was nowhere in sight. A dented black Cadillac, an ancient boat of a car (Zoe was surprised it didn't have fins), sat in the drive. "Jesus is my Savior," its bumper sticker read.

Save *her*, Zoe prayed. *Save my daughter.*

Two a.m. Zoe lay awake, staring at the ceiling.

"Will," she whispered. They had to go to the Lansdown's house. Immediately. Since this afternoon, she had been telling herself it was best to give Leah the time and space to work through this herself, to allow their daughter to return home of her own accord. She realized now that they might not have time to wait. A drug bust would most likely happen at night. If Leah was present when the police stormed the house, she would be drawn inadvertently into the whole sordid mess. She might even be arrested herself.

"Will?" Zoe switched on the reading lamp. "Wake up."

Her husband turned groggily onto his side, reaching for her, and squeezed her thigh.

"For God's sake, Will." She brushed his hand off her leg. "We need to talk."

"Morning," he grumbled, and rolled away from her again.

"No, Will." She rattled his arm. "Now."

"All right." He yawned. "Give me a minute." He patted the nightstand, reaching for his watch. "Jesus, Zoe." He brought the watch closer to his face. "It's two a.m."

Zoe got up, huffed to her bureau, fished out a pair of underpants. "We need to go there."

"Huh? Where?"

"The Lansdown's. Where do you *think*?"

Her husband yawned again. Reaching backward, he switched off the light.

Zoe stomped to the bed and switched it back on. "She's liable to get arrested."

"Tomorrow."

"So you don't care if you're daughter's involved in a major drug bust? Is that it?"

Her husband turned onto his stomach, pulling a pillow over his head. "Tomorrow."

Was he dense? Did he not see the trouble Leah was in? "Tomorrow could be too late."

Will exhaled loudly and propped himself on his elbow. "How about I give you a backrub? In the morning, if you still think we should go over, we'll talk."

"Damn it, Will. It's our fault she's there. And we have to *do* something about it."

"*Our* fault?" he repeated, as if he deserved the Father of the Year award, maybe.

"Right," Zoe snapped, outraged by her husband's inability to see this situation for what it was, his refusal to accept any blame. "You had to keep pushing. Admit it, Will, you fucked up."

"*I* fucked up?"

And round and round they went.

Justine's parents were at it again. Their bedroom sat at the end of a long hall, on the opposite side of the house. Even with the doors to both bedrooms shut, she heard them. The digital clock on her bedside table said two a.m. She'd been trying for hours to fall asleep. She'd counted sheep, tried thinking positive thoughts. Her roiling stomach kept her awake. If she was not out of bed by six thirty, she would miss the bus. She didn't see how she would ever wake up in time. Maybe her mother would allow her to take the day off. She would say the Zantac their family practitioner had prescribed for her reflux had stopped working; her stomach ached. Her stomach did ache. It ached for her sister. Justine snuggled with Dog, her legs curled around Dog's rump, her arm wrapped around her dog's waist, Dog breathing in time with Justine.

Justine lay in bed for a few more minutes, slogged to the bathroom, peed, drank two glasses of tap water, and climbed back in bed. She wanted desperately to talk to her sister. Be sure she was all right. She'd tried calling earlier. Stupidly, she used the phone in the kitchen, instead of calling from her room, where she could have talked to her sister in private. Her mother noticed her dialing, and took the receiver. "We have to give your sister some space, honey," she said. "She needs time to sort this out." In her head, Justine knew she shouldn't call her sister tonight, maybe not even tomorrow, knew that, in some weird way, calling was an invasion of Leah's privacy. Only her heart didn't always hear what her head was trying to tell her. Take right now, for example. Her head said *wait*, yet her heart ached to hear her sister's voice. "Why can't I call?" she had asked. "Because," her mother answered, the vague response infuriating Justine. Exasperated by Justine's prodding, her mother finally said, "If your sister wanted to talk to us, she would call." *That's not true*, Justine cried. *I'm not the one she wants to avoid. It's you and Dad and your stupid rules, giving her shit all the time.* Her mother raised her eyebrows when Justine said "shit," but said not a word. *You make her feel like a loser. And you never let her out. And. And. And.* There was more. A lot more. If only Justine could think. "Calm down, honey." Her mother lifted the phone out of Justine's limp, sweaty palms, and set it on the counter. "No," Justine shouted. "I won't calm down. This is your fault. Yours and Dad's. I hate you both."

Maybe her mother was right. Maybe her parents were not the only people Leah was avoiding. Maybe her sister was avoiding her, too. Maybe Leah thought it was her fault their parents were so angry. Maybe she thought Justine ratted her out, even though Justine assured her sister that she'd kept their secret. Last night, after her parents went to bed, she snuck downstairs, as she and Leah planned, and unlocked the mudroom door. At breakfast, when her father asked if she had any idea who'd unlatched the back door, she'd crossed her fingers behind her back and said, "no." Earlier, when Leah left to meet Todd, instead of racing after her, as she longed to do, instead of waking their parents and telling them Leah was gone, Justine curled up at the back of her closet with Dog, and pulled the door closed, so their parents would not hear her crying.

Justine slipped off her bed. Dog followed, easing herself to the floor. Justine had trouble recalling the last time she'd knelt to say prayers. Leah never prayed, as far as Justine knew. Her sister had stopped believing in God. God was a crutch for weak, dependent people, Leah said. "You're a scientist, Jus. Scientists believe in logic and reason." Justine listened politely, and kept right on praying. Occasionally, Justine prayed and nothing developed. In those low moments, she had to admit, she wondered if her prayers had reached God's ears, and it occurred to her that maybe Leah was right. Maybe there was no God. Or maybe, if He existed, God was not the loving father she imagined. Maybe He was inaccessible. Maybe He never paid attention at all. But, always, the instant she opened her heart and started talking to Him, her doubts disappeared.

"Oh my God," Justine prayed, "I am heartily sorry (she believed in asking God's forgiveness, before deluging Him with requests) . . . for lying, being a jerk to my mom. . ."

Please, God, take care of my sister. Bring her home safe.

Nineteen

Woodstock Momma

In the morning, Leah felt better. She'd been overtired; that was the problem. After the fight with her parents, the night before last, she'd had trouble falling asleep. She'd dozed for two or three hours, woke before dawn. A good night's sleep had cured her anxiety. Her lower back was bruised from the sofa springs jabbing into her spine; otherwise, she felt better than she'd felt in a long time, her body refreshed, her head clear.

When she was playing soccer, it was an effort to get out of bed in the morning, her legs and feet protesting in pain as she took her first excruciating steps. Now, she swung her feet off the sofa, and strolled to the window. She was proud of herself. She'd survived an entire day and night without calling her parents, without caving in. Yesterday, she wouldn't have believed she could do it; now she had.

Hope's mother, an early riser, was clattering around the kitchen, the tang of strongly brewed coffee filling the tiny house with anticipation and hope. Leah's stomach grumbled. She hadn't eaten a bite since eating the dinner Justine had brought to her room, the night before last. She wondered what Mindy was preparing for breakfast—pancakes, she hoped, or Belgian waffles. Leah's mom made the best Belgian waffles in the world, thick yet light, heaped with berries and cream. Leah winced. *Waffles are way too fattening for breakfast.* Oatmeal and wheat toast would do. Leah shooed the cat out of her suitcase, flipped through the meager pile of clothes, chose a black T-shirt and faded gray sweats, and carried her clean clothes to the bathroom at the end of the hall.

175

The door was locked. Inside, Hope was singing a top forty song Leah couldn't quite place, her sonorous alto missing the high notes. When the shower went off, Leah knocked.

"Just a sec," Hope warbled. Evidently, she was in a better mood today, too.

Steam swirled out of the bathroom when Hope opened the door. She'd wrapped herself in a threadbare terry-cloth towel, her chubby fingers pinching the edges together. Water dripped from her sopping hair into her face. She had a thick neck, wide, rounded shoulders. "Hey," she said. "How's it going?" A small butterfly tattoo decorated her right deltoid. Hope was hardly the most modest person around. She often traipsed around the house with her shirt unbuttoned, exposing her bra. Nevertheless, it was jolting to see her practically naked. "Sleep good?"

"Yeah," Leah said, averting her eyes.

"Great," Hope replied, "my mom's got breakfast," and toddled down the hall to her room.

Leah laid her T-shirt and panties on the toilet, undressed, and climbed into the shower stall, cringing as she stepped under the icy water. A thick layer of grit coated the floor. With the ball of her foot, she wiped a section big enough to stand on, adjusted the shower head, turning the spigot as far it would go, raising the temperature of the water by about five degrees, picked a sliver of soap from the floor, washed quickly, rinsed and hopped out, her body covered in goose flesh. Leah wasn't used to cold showers. When her parents built the house in Cortland, her father paid the contractor extra to install two heaters; they never ran out of hot water. Well, those were the breaks. If she wanted to live on her own, she had to put up with certain inconveniences. With a thin hand towel she found on a hook on the back of the door, she blotted herself dry.

"You look good," Hope said. "I like your shirt."

Leah stood in the doorway of the kitchen. She'd found the plain black T-shirt with fake pearls on the collar on the markdown rack at the Gap. She ran a hand over her head, her hair stiff from the cheap aerosol spray she'd used to hold it in place. "Liar," she countered. "I look gross."

Hope's mother tapped the ashes from her cigarette into a Dixie Cup. Scary how much Hope resembled her mother. Mindy was several inches taller than her daughter, and her face was wider, but their features—deep-set eyes, pug nose, rosebud lips—could have been cloned. They even carried themselves alike: shoulders erect, flat butts tucked, their bellies slightly distended, like out-of-shape dancers. "Pretty as a picture." Mindy winked. "Even in sweats."

"Really?" Leah's mother would have given her crap. *You're not leaving this house dressed like that,* she would have said. *You look like a beatnik.* "I don't look like a beatnik?"

"A beatnik?" Mindy laughed, her deep horse-like laughter rising from her belly, it seemed. "Ain't heard that word since the Village."

"Greenwich," Hope said, rolling her eyes.

"You lived in Greenwich Village?" Maybe Mrs. Lansdown could give Leah some pointers, tell her where to find an apartment, suggest places to look for a job. "What was it like?"

"Oh, you know. I'm a country girl myself. Never did take to the city." Mindy dragged thoughtfully on her cigarette. "I was at Woodstock, you know."

Hope made a snapping motion with her fingers and thumb.

"Woodstock?" Leah said, ignoring Hope's gesture. When she was a kid, her father used to play an album recorded at Woodstock, Leah entertaining him by dancing around the room, pretending she was on MTV. In those days, she cared only about pleasing her father. As she grew older, she came to appreciate the gathering itself, the atmosphere—*open, alive*—the communal spirit, the peace and acceptance and love the audience shared. Today, if three hundred thousand kids gathered anywhere, a massive fight would break out. Leah often felt out of place in her world, as if she'd been born twenty years too late, into the wrong generation. She'd never met anyone who'd been to Woodstock. Her parents were too young. "Really?" she asked. "You were at Woodstock?"

"Sure. Hope never told you?"

Leah shook her head. "What was it like?"

"A ball." Mindy fetched a bag of Wise potato chips from a bread drawer under the counter, filled two plastic sandwich bags, zipped them shut, took another drag from her cigarette, deep crow's feet puckering the skin at the corners of her eyes. "Ever seen them pictures in *Life?*"

"Mom," Hope said, drawing the *o*. "She doesn't want to hear about that."

Thankfully, Mindy ignored her (otherwise, Leah would have spoken up). "Me and Hope's dad's in one of them. We're the little people way in back."

"They're butt naked," Hope interjected. "It's gross."

"I wrote a letter, you know, asking them to send me one. When Leo left, he swiped the original. So all I got now's this faded copy we made. It's on my bureau, if you want to go see it."

"That stinks," Leah said. "Sorry about your husband."

"That's okay. Me and Hope, we're better off without him. Right, sweets?" Hope looked at Leah and shrugged. "Oh come on, you." Mindy waved her daughter's grimace away. "You know it's true. Hope was our love baby. I was thirty-eight when I had her. After she was born, her daddy pressured me to get married. Said he wanted to 'do the right thing.' Big mistake. Right, baby? Listen, sweetie," she said to Leah, "you got to eat something today, keep your energy up." She pointed at the snack-sized cereal boxes lining the counter. "Go ahead. Pour yourself some cereal."

Leah selected a package of Fruit Loops and opened the box. (Hope was using hers as a bowl.) Leah's mom would never buy Fruit Loops. She fed them weird organic cereals from the Natural Grocer, or homemade granolas with names like Rainforest Crunch or Boysenberry Nut.

While the girls ate, Mrs. Lansdown stuffed brown paper bags with boxes of Hi-C, packets of peanut butter and cheese crackers, bags of chips, all the while humming the melody to an old song, called "Strawberry Fields," that Leah's father played for her on his guitar, a long, long time ago.

When Justine went down to the kitchen for breakfast, she found her father in the nook, sulking, the *Globe*, open to the sports page, spread in front of him on the table. Her mother, feigning indifference, was scooting around the kitchen, scrubbing the counters, watering the potted ivy on the windowsill, the hem of her old purple robe fluttering around her bare feet.

"Look at this." Her father swatted the newspaper, as if the paper had done him some grave injustice. "They're talking about trading Arroyo again."

"Arroyo?" Justine repeated, as though she were outraged. It was pathetic attempt at commiserating, she knew, considering she had no clue what the implications of such a trade might be. She knew Arroyo pitched for the Red Sox. She also knew he was young—in his late-twenties, she thought. She knew he wore his hair in cornrows, even though he was white, and he played the guitar. Leah and their father were like DJs on a sports radio team. If Leah were here, they'd be trading stats, opining about the team's chances for making the playoffs without Arroyo on the mound, batting around the names of players the Sox ought to look for in a trade. "Toast?" Justine asked, lacking anything better to say.

"No, thanks," her father replied. He blew air through his teeth. "They've got their heads up their asses. It's not Epstein. That Lucchino's the problem."

"I thought you hated baseball," said Justine's mother, not quite taunting, but close.

Justine cringed. Was she the only one who realized that fighting was a waste of time? That nothing positive ever came from fighting? Couldn't her parents at least pretend to get along? Just this once? What did her mother hope to gain by goading Justine's father?

Justine toasted a slice of wheat-berry bread, set her plate on the island counter, and poured a glass of orange juice. The sour smell of the butter made her want to retch.

Dog lay on the floor by her feet. Justine tore the corner off her toast, fed it to Dog. The TV was on in the family room, the AM sportscaster also discussing Bronson Arroyo.

"Kid won fourteen games last year," Justine's father said, repeating the sportscaster.

Her mother made a devious face. "Tell me, when's the last time you watched a game?"

"For Christ sake, Zoe." He folded the paper in thirds. "Get off my case."

"I'm just saying. If you don't like baseball, why make such a big deal?"

"Mom." Justine contorted her features. "I don't feel well today. I'm gonna stay home."

Her mother, sighing, laid a hand on Justine's forehead. "You feel fine to me."

"My stomach hurts," Justine pressed. "I won't be able to concentrate."

"You're going to school, Justine. I'm sorry. We need to stick to our routine." In other words, forget Leah's not here. As if Justine could *ever* do that. "She'll be home soon, honey." With her fingers, her mother brushed the hair out of Justine's eyes. "I have a good feeling."

"Woo-hoo," said Justine's father, curling his fingers. "Your mother has a feeling." He tramped to the pantry, shaking his head in disgust, and threw the newspaper in the recycling bin. "Stick to our routine," he said, under his breath. "What's the hell's that supposed to mean?"

179

"Don't pay attention to him." Her mother slammed the dish-washer door, startling the poor dog. "Your father's a jerk."

Justine stroked Dog's ears. She couldn't decide which parent was less mature. "It's OK, baby," she whispered. "Don't be scared." She forced another spoonful of cereal (so she wouldn't pass out before lunch), and fed Dog the rest, Dog's warm, scratchy tongue licking her hand.

Justine cleared her dishes, loaded them into the dishwasher, and gathered her jacket and books. "Got to go, Puppy." She planted a kiss on Dog's nose. "You take care of yourself, baby."

"See you, guys," she called on her way out the door. *Try not to kill each other today.*

Leah's mood deteriorated steadily over the course of the day. She kept feeling as though she'd lost something, a pencil, a book. She would race back to her locker to retrieve it, only to discover the missing item among the things she was already toting. Between classes, she floated mindlessly through the halls, her eyes trained straight ahead. In class, she hunkered low in her seat, avoiding the questioning eyes of her teachers. When Mr. Mulvany called on her, in social studies class, Leah asked to be excused, and slipped into the girls' room, where she stayed, hidden in one of the stalls, until the bell rang. She had home ec the following period. She could not face Mrs. Berman today. (Bad enough the class was making frog pillows!) Mrs. Berman had a nose for trouble. She would stand over your shoulder, pretending to watch you sew. Catching you unawares, she would pepper you with embarrassing personal questions. Normally, ditching classes was easy: Leah would go to the nurse, pretend she was sick. If she did that today, the nurse would call her mother. As a last resort, she went to the front office, to visit her dean. When she arrived at the office, Dean Leahy's door was shut. His secretary said Leah was welcome to wait; the dean, however, was busy with another student and might be awhile. Leah slumped into the metal folding chair outside Dean Leahy's office, where she sat, her mind wandering, waiting for some vaguely imagined change to take place, something that would make her life different, and better. When the bell rang, she told the secretary she had to go and headed to the cafeteria.

The food line snaked into the hall. Today's main selection was pizza, the only edible food they served in this dump, the spicy odor of tomato sauce fusing with the curdled tang of the cheese. The usual hysterics, the kids shouting, laughing, horsing around, overwhelmed her. She stood outside the entrance, repelled by the swarm of gyrating bodies, searching for a place where she could be alone. At last, she spotted a table that was all but empty, its three dorky occupants seated at the far end, nearest the wall, books open before them on the table, probably discussing their calculus homework. Leah took the aisle seat and set her bag on the chair beside hers. Her head spun. She nibbled a chip to settle her stomach, staring straight ahead, ignoring the kids passing by, carrying trays loaded with pizza, plates of salad or fries, cartons of milk.

She couldn't stop thinking about her parents. What had happened to them? When she was a child, theirs had been a close, loving family. A memory of the Stoneham Zoo popped into her brain, Leah balanced on her father's shoulders, peering down into the polar bear cave. "How comes that one's so lazy?" Leah pointed to a fat white bear, sunning itself in the corner. "That's the Mama bear," her father replied. The Mama bear, her mother explained, was expecting a baby. "They'll be a family soon. Just like us." Leah pictured her sister standing in the doorway with her suitcase, ready to follow Leah blindly, wherever she went. Leah had never felt so lonely, so displaced, in her life. She forced herself to picture the ride home from the police station the other night, the rage in her father's eyes, her mother refusing to take Leah's side, the disgust on their faces when she climbed out of the car. *You have to do this*, she told herself. She had to be strong.

A tray crashed, the glasses and plates shattering. At the front of the cafeteria, two boys scuffled, fists flying. One of them fell and the other leaped on top of him. A crowd quickly gathered around them, the onlookers clapping, cheering them on. Scanning the faces, Leah spotted Cicely Hanson, who, at that moment, caught sight of her. Leah lowered her eyes. She'd heard through the grapevine that Cissy's mother had forbidden Cissy from hanging out with Leah, which galled her, frankly. She couldn't care less what Cissy thought of her. She had no use for unsupportive, judgmental friends. She had better friends now, people who cared about her. That Cissy's mother deemed her daughter too good for Leah pissed Leah off. True, the girl didn't smoke weed. She never touched drugs, in fact. Didn't drink. She'd quit smoking after she and Leah were caught. But she lied. And poked fun at other kids. And cheated on every test she took. Cissy was also a thief. Look at her, in a pink Juicy Couture shirt and Humanity jeans. That outfit had to cost three hundred dollars. How did Cissy's mother think her daughter paid for those clothes? She and the step-dad gave Cissy twenty-five dollars a week, barely enough money for gas. She had no a job. She'd stolen her outfit from the Jeans Company, a boutique in Groton. She and three of her soccer toadies sashayed in, wearing baggy sweat suits. They layered the stolen outfits under their clothes. Cissy bragged about it for weeks. Evidently, Mrs. Hanson had no problem with her precious daughter being a thief. As long as her little darling never got caught.

Cissy strolled down Leah's aisle, surrounded by a posse of fawning JV players. Leah stared at her hands, pretending to eat. She did not have the energy to engage in a battle today.

The clique crept closer, their eyes darting from one another to Leah. Leah gathered her bag, swept her crumbs off the table. If she left now, she might have a chance to escape.

"Hey," Cissy called, when they were about ten feet away. "Look who it is." As they closed in, Cissy wagged a spirited hand. The girl to Cissy's right covered her mouth.

Leah glared at them both. *Let it go*, Leah told herself. *Ignore them.*

"Did you hear?" Cissy's groupies giggled. "We won the division."

Leah's heart thumped in her ears. "Nice jeans, Cissy. Where did you get those?"

Cissy's face flushed. "So I guess you heard, we're going to states."

That girl had no idea how close Leah was to punching her.

Cissy pretended to pout. "Too bad you won't be with us."

Leah was about to invite Cissy outside when Hope, her fists clenched, materialized. "Hey friend," she said to Leah, her eyes challenging Cissy. "These jerks here giving you trouble?"

Cissy dropped her gaze, and the girls passed without saying a word.

Hope's narrow gaze followed Cissy to a table at the opposite side of the cafeteria. "What was that all about?" she asked, when Cissy's gang finally stopped gossiping, started eating lunch.

"Nothing."

"Lying sack of shit." She punched Leah's arm. "Could you spare a few chips?"

Leah handed over the bag. "What are you doing here?"

"Came to check on my bud." Hope nudged Leah's shoulder.

"You didn't cut Trig again, did you?"

"Yup," Hope said. "Just for you."

Hope gobbled the last few chips, crushed the empty bag. "OK? You look kind of putrid."

In Leah's Wake

"Sure," Leah lied. *No,* she wanted to say. *I'm not OK at all.*
"See that kid?" Hope pointed to a puckish, orange-haired boy in
the lunch line, a tray balanced on his hip. "In grade school, they used
to smoosh our tables together. You were here, right?" In Cortland, she
meant. "Anyways, my hair was *way* long." With her finger, Hope
sliced the base of Leah's spine. "I never got it cut, till I was like ten."
Leah found it hard to picture Hope as a child. In her mind, Hope
had always been exactly as she was now: tall and plump, and, well, a
bit rough around the edges. Leah had never seen a baby picture of
Hope. Except for the copy of the Woodstock photo, Leah had never
seen any pictures at the Lansdown's house. And here Leah had
believed all mothers were hopeless sentimentalists like hers, with
stacks of photo albums lining their bookcases, their attics crammed
with cardboard boxes filled with useless mementos: old baby clothes,
costumes from dance recitals the girls participated in when they were
three, pictures she and Justine had drawn when they were in grade
school. Hope's mom didn't give a hoot about pictures or photos or
school papers, evidently. Really, though, what did it matter? Mindy
thought Leah looked great, even in sweats. Plus, she was cool. She'd
been to the concert at Woodstock!
Hope helped herself to the rest of Leah's crackers. Leah tucked
the empty plastic bag into the larger paper bag and rolled the bag in a
ball. "So anyway," Hope continued. "That kid, right? Sam Ridley? He
was always pulling my pigtails. And the whole class used to say shit.
Like me and him were gonna get married." Hope made a face,
indicating the idiocy of a union between her and Sam Ridley. Or
maybe it was the institution of marriage Hope considered insane; with
Hope, it was hard to say. "And he stunk. Like poop. I swear to God,
the kid rolled in dog turds."
Rolled in dog turds? Hope would lie about anything, for a laugh.
Still, Leah cracked up.
"There," Hope said. "Gotcha. What's the matter? You feeling
OK? The truth, babes. I'm your friend, remember? I mean, we're
living together now. That makes us practically sisters."
Sisters? Leah took in Hope's overalls, the faded denim stretched
taut over her friend's massive thighs. Hope thought the overalls
flattered her figure; in fact, she looked like a cow. If Leah were a
half-decent friend, never mind a sister, she would tell her, the way she
had always told Cissy if an outfit made her look fat. If Leah couldn't
tell Hope her clothes looked bad, which, as a friend, was almost her
duty, how could she possibly say she longed to go home?
"Hey?" Hope jogged Leah's arm. "Friend? Got to jet."

183

"Sorry," Leah said. "I'm a little tired today."

"That's okay. Mr. O's still pissed at me, from last time I cut. If I tell him I got woman troubles, maybe he'll cut me some slack." She winked. "By the way," she said, as she was turning away. "Meet me after the bell. By the gym? Hubby's picking us up," Hope said, tittering.

"You talked to Todd?" Leah asked, too excited to bother playing Hope's silly game. She hadn't heard from her boyfriend since he dropped her at Hope's house, yesterday morning. "What did he say? Did he ask about me?"

"Sure, babes. He said, 'tell her I'm horny,'" Hope said, and snagged the last of Leah's crackers and cheese.

Twenty

The Runaway Life

Zoe's first patient of the day, a six-year-old, one-child wrecking crew, dumped sand by the fistful out of the box. With the crayon he begged to draw a picture of his best friend, he scribbled on the wall. After their session, while Zoe spoke to his mother, a middle-aged woman in a cashmere sweater set and pleated wool slacks, the child raced around the room, plucking books from Zoe's shelves, throwing them on the floor. "Such a creative little thing," the mother said, with a passion bordering on lust. "So curious. Always touching things, taking them apart. Ah, well"—feigned embarrassment—"That's the cross I have to bear. Trey, he's just so *smart.*"

If her seminars would turn a profit, Zoe would quit this job, or at least cut back on her hours. Running seminars was far less stressful than seeing patients day after day. She loved the kids. The parents wore her down, the mothers needy, obsessed with their children's success. Five years ago, the parents treated her with respect, listened to what she had to say. Today, parents had no interest in Zoe's diagnosis. The mothers arrived for their initial visit armed with folders stuffed with useless information they'd gathered from the Internet, seeking professional proof that the teachers were wrong in their negative assessments, written confirmation of their child's superior intellect. *Of course Janie talks in class, the poor child is bored,* they wanted Zoe to write. Today, it wasn't good enough to be smart. Every child had to be Einstein. The mothers expected Zoe to gush over their children, to minimize the underlying problems causing their kids to act out. They wanted to hear how special—no, how *brilliant*—their progeny were. *ADD?* She was supposed to say.

185

How wonderful! You've a budding Michelangelo here. The truth is, some kids with ADD are creative and smart; others are not. Parents didn't want to hear that. They had no interest in anything that might taint the inflated opinion they held of their child. They wanted a miracle, a magic pill that would zap away their child's behavioral problems, the compulsions, the difficulties in school, the ADD, the OCD, the Tourette's. A pill. *If only life were so easy.*

Zoe handed the mother a referral for a local psycho-pharmacologist who'd gladly prescribe the Ritalin she wanted, and ushered them out, closing the door, and collapsed onto her sofa, her head in her hands. Zoe saw the next three children on her list, asked the secretary to cancel her appointments for the rest of the day, packed her belongings, and headed for home.

Once she was in the car, on the road, her mind shifted to autopilot. She wove through neighborhoods she hadn't visited since they first moved to Cortland. Will traveled constantly in those days. In his absence, she and the girls had done lots of exploring, the motion of the car settling for the girls, especially Leah. They'd drive for hours some days, the kids taking turns choosing directions. "Left," Leah would say. "Wight," Justine would chirp. Despite the physical work of caring for two small children, life was relatively easy, the girls strapped in their car seats, the three of them playing silly games like "Name the Tree" or "Find the Funniest House."

Zoe passed a Victorian on Winding Brook Lane. She and Will had driven by this house every Sunday afternoon, on their fantasy house-hunting trips. "There—" She would point to the stunning moss green Victorian, with the scalloped shingles and sweeping front porch, the fairytale turret. "That's where I'd like to live." Someday, Will always said, when they could afford it. Now, all the promise of that house was lost, the siding chipped, the porch sagging, the lovely English garden gone to seed.

At the end of the street, she made a U-turn, and headed back toward the center. She'd been on the road for nearly two hours. A convoy of busses turned into the high school lot. Leah stopped taking the bus—the banana, she called it—when she was a freshman. Too much to carry, what with her backpack, her gym bag, her protein snack, a quart-sized bottle of Gatorade, her shin pads and cleats. Will chauffeured her to school in the morning on his way to the office, and Zoe drove her home after practice. By the end of her freshman year, Leah was hitching rides home with her teammates or friends. This year, Todd often picked her up after practice, a fact she attempted to hide from Zoe and Will by having him drop her off at the end of their street.

Up ahead, Zoe spotted Sullivan Farms, the ice cream shop her friend Bobby Sullivan owned. Her stomach rumbled. At breakfast, she'd forced two spoonfuls of granola with soymilk; she'd eaten nothing since. A tuna salad sandwich sat, in an insulated bag, on the passenger seat. She should really eat that. Sugar would only increase her anxiety. On the other hand, a sugar kick might do some good, help her out of this funk. At the last possible second, Zoe hit the brakes, scooted into the empty lot—in a half hour, with the kids on their way to and from their afternoon sports, the shop would be mobbed—and eased the Volvo into a space in front of the windows.

Todd was late—big surprise.

Hope and Leah waited by the gym door until two thirty. Bored, standing around, doing nothing, they begged a ride to the front of the school from the student trainer, who was tooling around the grounds in a golf cart. Hope skipped to the top of the drive. She looked silly, a fuzzy bear of a girl, in a faux fur jacket, hanging onto the post of the sign that read, "Cortland High School. Home of the Cortland High Cougars," waving like a two-year-old at passing vehicles.

It was a dreary afternoon, drizzly and raw. Over her T-shirt and sweats, Leah wore a black button-down sweater she'd borrowed from Hope. She tossed her backpack on the ground, sat on the damp lawn, stretching her legs, and chewed on a blade of grass. Soon, the grass would be dead, like everything else in this dump. Too bad fairy godmothers were a myth. And genies. If she found a magic lamp, she'd use only one wish (a totally unselfish gesture, she thought). She'd ask the genie to transport her to Florida or California, someplace sunny and warm, where she didn't have to live under a microscope, people judging her every minute of her life.

At three, Todd finally showed up. He stopped, waited for Hope to hoist herself into the truck, and turned into the drive. Leah brushed herself off, heaved her pack onto one shoulder.

"Hey, babe." Todd pulled the Jeep alongside her, and opened his window. "Coming?"

Fuming, Leah circled around the truck, dumped her pack on the floor, and climbed into the passenger seat. "What took you so long?" She thumped the dashboard. She'd bitten her nails to the quick. Pain shot through the tips of her fingers. "Where *were* you?"

"Yeah," Hope echoed, from the back seat. "Where the hell were you?"

"Hey. Whoa. Gimme a break. Me and Jamie were talking."

"About what?" Hope slapped his shoulder. "Come on, dude. Let's have it."

Todd extracted a cigarette from the pack inside the cup-holder on the console, lit it, inhaling languorously, as if he had not a care in the world, not a single thing better to do.

"What, you're not talking now?" Leah swatted his arm, too. "You get fired? Is that it?"

"Quit it." He jerked away. "I didn't get fired. Told you, me and Jamie were talking."

"About what?" Hope pressed. "Planning to tell us? Or keep us in suspense?"

"Oh, forget it," Leah said, too exhausted to wage another battle. Better late than never. At least her boyfriend still had a job. "You're here. That's all that matters, I guess."

"You tell him, girl." Hope gave Leah a derisive thumb up. "Don't hold nothing back."

Leah snorted, and Todd, thumbing the backseat, ordered their friend to sit back and relax.

"You suck," Hope said, glaring at Todd, then at Leah. "The both of you."

At the first red light they came to, Todd drew Leah into his arms. "I missed you, honey." He stroked her cheek. "They treating you all right?" he asked, eyeing the backseat.

"I missed you, too." Leah gave her boyfriend a deep, penetrating kiss on the lips.

"You guys are disgusting," Hope piped up. "Can't you save that shit for later?"

"Screw you," Leah said. "Like you got room to talk."

When the light changed, Todd stepped on the gas. "We're gonna let you off, dude," he said to Hope. "Me and my girl, we could use a little privacy. If you get my drift."

Jerry slid the tray of cubed pork out of the freezer, poking the meat with his finger to be sure it was partially frozen, so the fat wouldn't melt in the grinder and clog its blades. Locating a clean spot on the counter, he set the tray down, and shook kosher salt liberally over the pork. With his clean hand, he swept the dirty utensils into the sink. His wife would flip if she saw the disaster he'd made of her kitchen, the countertop littered with cooking equipment—a bowl, a cutting board, several knives of various sizes and shapes. When she cooked, his wife cleaned as she went along, washing, drying, and reusing everything, even the spoons.

He measured a tablespoon of dried sage and a teaspoon of red pepper flakes, mixed the seasonings in a glass measuring cup, and crushed two cloves of garlic. The pungent odor of garlic reminded him of long-ago Sunday afternoons at his parents' house. When he was a kid, his mother worked fulltime as the principle's secretary, in the office of Cortland's only grammar school, Frost Elementary. Every Sunday, she would cook a large dinner, often tripling the recipe, thus providing leftovers for the rest of the week, the spicy aroma of a hearty soup or a chicken casserole or a savory beef stew filling the house. Humming, he added four ounces of maple syrup to his measuring cup, and stirred, periodically licking his spoon, tasting to be sure he'd gotten the ratios right. Satisfied, the seasonings evenly dispersed, he tossed his spoon aside, lugged Maura's industrial-sized mixer out of the cabinet, screwed on the grinding attachment.

The babies were sound asleep in their room, the nursery door slightly ajar. This way, he would hear the boys if they woke from their nap. Maura had an appointment, this afternoon, with her gynecologist. Routine, his wife had assured him. Nothing to worry about. As if Jerry might have thought otherwise. It had been months since he and Maura were intimate. Late in her pregnancy, she'd taken to sleeping in the living room. She slept better on the sofa, the down cushions more comfortable than their ten year-old mattress, she claimed. (When he suggested they purchase a new mattress, she said they couldn't afford it.) After the babies were born, he'd assumed that his wife would return to their bed. Eventually, they would go back to making love two or three times a week, as they had in all the previous years of their married life. But it was starting to look as if he had lost his partner permanently to the sofa. His wife had a million excuses for sleeping alone: her back ached; the babies were sick; she felt a cold coming on. From an article in *Parenting,* which he'd read in the bathroom, he'd learned that a woman's sexual desire often waned after giving birth, particularly after a multiple birth. He tried to be patient. It was not as if he expected sex every night, or even every week, for that matter. But it would be nice to be able to touch his wife without her flinching. If she would sleep in their bed.

He fed the pork cubes into the grinder, its motor churning, his right hand pushing the semi-frozen cubes into the hopper, his left hand guiding the strings of ground meat into a metal bowl. Grinding the meat took less than ten minutes, stuffing the casings, because he had not yet bought the proper attachment and had to do it by hand, the time-consuming part of the job. He stirred the maple syrup concoction into the pork and put the bowl in the fridge, unscrewed the hopper and pulled it apart, tossed the blades in the sink, and began loading the dishwasher.

Loading the dishes into the washer, he heard a low whimper. He dried his hands on a paper towel, and went to check on the babies. Maura had installed blackout shades in the windows (*she* needed blinders to sleep). Several seconds passed before he could see anything clearly, then the silly lamb border came into focus. The white changing table, heaped with clean laundry. The cedar hope chest he had given his wife when before they were engaged doubled now as a dresser. The twins slept, head-to-head, in the crib, tiny legs tucked under their bellies, their backs rising and falling in sync. Jerry tiptoed into the room. He stood over the crib for a few minutes, inhaling the soft sweet scent of his babies, watching his little boys sleep. Joey, the younger by a minute, yawned, his face scrunched like a pug's. Jerry kissed his fingertips, planted the kiss on Joey's forehead, kissed his fingers again, touched Mattie's forehead this time, then he gave each boy a second kiss, in reverse order, gathered the laundry, and tiptoed out of the room.

He brought the laundry into the living room, laid it on the sofa, and turned on the TV. When he first saw the baby clothes, at Maura's shower, he had been almost as frightened of the doll-sized outfits as he was, a month later, by the babies themselves. In time, he'd learned to fold the miniature nighties, the tiny jogging outfits, the overalls barely the length of his outstretched hand. Now he made perfect creases, his folded piles almost as neat as Maura's. It was the same with the babies, when they were newborns. He volunteered to pitch in, but they'd cried when he tried to bathe them, and the smell of their shitty diapers made Jerry gag. He'd never imagined there would be so much to *learn*. You had to heat the formula to a certain temperature or the babies refused to eat, had to fasten their diapers properly or the contents would squirt out; you had to hold the babies over your lap, not over your shoulder, as his mother had done with his sister, when you burped them. And with twins, you had double-duty, twenty-four hours a day. Double the feeding, double the diapers, double the crying. Now, after only three months, he was nearly as adept as Maura. When his wife was out, he fed the babies, changed their diapers, gave them baths. He enjoyed taking care of the boys. He would help more, if Maura would let him.

Yawning, he set the pile of folded clothes on the floor, and stretched out on the sofa, his head resting on the arm, a pillow wedged under his neck. In no time, he was asleep.

Twenty-One

Wait For Me

Every year, for the past four years, Sullivan Farms had been named the best ice cream stand in the region by *Boston Magazine*. Most days, from early March, when Bob opened for the season, through mid-autumn, when the weather turned cold, all eight windows would be open, the lines snaking into the parking lot. While parents recited the long list of ice cream flavors to their little ones, the older kids would race to and from the windows, reporting on progress, the teenaged workers behind the screens moving at a feverish pace to keep up with the orders.

Today, Bob was alone. Zoe saw him behind the screens, filling the tubs of ice cream.

Zoe had met Bob ten years earlier, on the starting line of a road race, on the Fourth of July. In high school, she'd been a cross-country runner. After high school, she'd quit running—in college, she had better things to do with her time—and didn't run for years. That March, she started running again, begrudgingly at first, for the exercise, to lose the weight she'd gained when she was pregnant with Justine, to get back in shape. Within six months, her belly had flattened and her thighs had grown taut, but it was the sense of freedom she felt on the road, her heart racing, her mind clear, that hooked her. She'd started by running a mile, three times around the block, and even that was a struggle. Her strength and endurance quickly improved. Soon, she was running two miles, and gradually three. By late spring she ran five miles a day, thought it might be fun to enter a road race. The Fourth of July race, a flat two-mile course, would be perfect. Will and the girls promised to cheer her on at the finish. After the race, they'd watch the parade.

The race director called the runners to the start. Zoe squatted to tighten her laces. When she stood, slightly dizzy from the dip in blood pressure, Bob was standing beside her. She'd pegged him instantly as a seasoned runner, figured he would be among the top three finishers, if he didn't win the race outright. They introduced themselves, chatted for a minute or two, small talk. *So many runners, what a hot day for a race.* She was still talking when the gun went off.

On pure adrenaline, Zoe took off with the rabbits, ignoring every racing strategy her high school coaches had taught her. By the time she reached the quarter-mile mark, she was sucking wind, her legs wobbly, her lungs about to collapse. She would have dropped out if not for Bob, slowing his pace, urging her on. He felt her behind him, he'd told her later, knew she was dragging, couldn't let her quit. "Don't give up," he'd prodded. "Come on. I'll pace you."

"Hey, Zoe," he said brightly. "What's happening? Haven't seen you in ages."

Bob had a long, thin face, lively brown eyes she had instinctively trusted. He was several inches shorter than Will, with a distance runner's strong legs and lean torso. Though he had to be well over thirty, he could easily pass for a college kid in his twenties. He wore jeans and a Kelly green Sullivan Farms T-shirt, the number thirty-three stitched on his sleeves.

An autographed poster of Larry Bird hung on the wall behind the soft-serve machine.

"Still a Bird fan, I see."

"Even if he did sell us out," he said, joking. "I know, I know. Diehard. What can I say?"

"How's business?" In the three years since Bob opened the stand, he'd developed a loyal following, his warm, easy-going personality nearly as big a draw as the homemade ice cream.

"Not bad. Not bad."

"Run any races lately?"

A half-marathon last month. The Apple-Fest, in Hudson. "I've been trying to talk Mary Ann into running Boston next year." Unfortunately, his wife wasn't biting. He shrugged. One of these days, he would convince her. "What about you? Still out there, I hope."

"Not anymore." She felt a surprising stab of regret. She hadn't thought about running in ages. But she was glad to hear that he hadn't quit. "Hudson? That's great, Bob. How'd you do?"

"All right," he said, assuming a runner's pose. "Sixty-nine, seventeen."

Wow. Sixty-nine, seventeen? She was impressed.

Him, too. He grinned. Shifting to a serious tone, he said, "So, what can I get you?"

Small coconut almond chip, in a cup. "With extra jimmies," she added sheepishly.

A news clipping of last year's Fourth of July race hung on the outside wall, to the right of the screened windows. Bob organized the road races now, having turned them into an annual charity event. In the clipping, the frontrunner was breaking through the ribbon, fists raised in a victory V. A year ago, in their final game against Westford, in the last second of playtime, Leah had scored the winning goal, a rousing come-from-behind win. Zoe's daughter had jogged twice around the perimeter of the soccer field, the crowds cheering wildly, Leah's hands raised like the runner's, in her own victory V. Her teammates had carried her off the field.

"You okay?"

She felt a cool hand on her wrist. Startled, Zoe recoiled. "Sorry," she said, jerking back to the present. "We're fine, thanks."

Bob looked at her quizzically.

"Oh, God. Listen to me. How's Mary Ann? I didn't even ask."

"She's good. You sure you're OK? You look a little pale."

"Really, I'm fine. Maybe I'll go for a run when I get home. You've got me inspired."

Smiling uncertainly, Bob handed her a plastic spoon. From the window, he watched her walk to her car. "Take care." He waved goodbye, waiting for her to leave, before turning away.

When she left Sullivan Farms, Zoe drove straight to the Lansdown's place. She couldn't go on playing this silly game, waiting for Leah to make the first move. Her daughter wasn't safe in that drug den. Zoe had an obligation to at least talk to her daughter, do whatever she could to convince her to come home. If she went about it the right way, didn't push, she might succeed.

Zoe turned into the driveway, steering around a pothole in the asphalt, pulled her wagon behind the Cadillac. As she cut the engine, she realized that it was rude of her to block the drive, and shifted into reverse, backed out of the driveway, and parked her wagon on the street. She smoothed her hair, took several deep breaths to calm herself, and opened her door.

She looked at the foreboding gray sky, and buttoned her trench coat.

In Leah's Wake

A black and white tabby sat on the front stoop. As Zoe approached the concrete stairs, the cat hissed and scooted down the steps, its thick tail whipping Zoe's shin, and darted behind the house. Zoe brushed herself off, straightened her skirt. *Keep your cool,* she told herself. *No matter what happens, even if she cries or screams or tells you to get lost, you need to stay in control.* When she saw Leah, she would tell her daughter she missed her. She wouldn't press for any outward sign of affection, wouldn't push her daughter to say or do anything until she was ready.

If her daughter cried and leaped into her arms, well, she would act accordingly, of course.

Zoe knocked, waited a few seconds, and knocked again. In her mind, she was already pulling her daughter into her arms. This was a wake-up call. In the grand scheme of things, nothing truly terrible had happened. She and Will still had time to adjust; they could still shepherd their daughter safely through adolescence, into a caring, responsible adulthood. Zoe and Will had been reluctant to give Leah rope, worried that she would hang herself with it. But wasn't that what growing up was about? How does a child learn and grow, *except* by making mistakes? If leniency would keep Leah home, where she was safe, Zoe was prepared to grant it. Once she talked to Will, and explained her reasoning, she was sure that he would agree.

Somebody was home. She heard the drone of the TV. She'd swear she heard shuffling, people moving around. She put her ear to the grimy fiberglass door, listening for Leah's voice.

She balled her fist, about to knock a third time, when she felt a pop, the door giving way.

The door swung open, and a wave of smoke billowed out of the house. Zoe stepped back, clutching her purse as if fending off an assault.

On the opposite side of the threshold, a tall, heavy-set girl stood, with her hands on her hips, peering curiously down at Zoe. The girl looked vaguely familiar. This had to be Hope, the girl's slatternly appearance and wary demeanor the embodiment of her mother's gritty voice.

Inside, the TV was tuned to an afternoon soap, the voices fraught with drama.

"Hello," Zoe said, forcing herself not to cringe. "I'm—"

"Ms. T." The girl studied Zoe's face. "Whoa. You and her look like *twins*."

Zoe managed a "thanks" that she hoped sounded believable. It pained her to think this hard-boiled girl knew Leah well enough to

195

make a familial connection. She considered pointing out that most people thought Leah resembled her father, thought better of it, and held back.

The mother's coarse voice, calling from inside, asked who was at their door.

The girl spun toward the voice. "Leah's mom," Hope yelled, over her shoulder.

"Be there in a jiff," the woman called back.

"It's all right, Ma. I got it."

What on earth possessed Leah to run to this house? Why would she spend a minute in this God-awful place? With these *people*? "Is Leah here, by any chance?"

Hope shook her head, her long, thin face drawn into an empathetic pout. The girl would probably be attractive, if she dressed a little better. Combed her hair. If she were not so fat.

On TV, a hysterical woman accused someone of cheating her. Or cheating *on* her, maybe.

"Do you know where she is, honey?" Zoe asked, with exaggerated politeness.

"Sorry." Hope tucked a string of blond hair behind her ears. "Want me to tell her to give you a ring? If I see her, I mean."

"I know she's been staying here." Zoe peered around the girl, scanning the dingy living room, hoping she might spot her daughter inside. "Your mom called. I just want to talk to her."

"Sorry, Ms. T." Hope stared at her feet. "Wish I could help."

Or *would* help. "Honey, listen." She set a hand on Hope's forearm. "I know you're just trying to protect her." A look of uncertainty flashed in the girl's eyes, as if she wanted to do the right thing, but she wasn't sure what it was. "You're a good friend. But it would be better for her if you'd tell me where she is. She belongs at home, with her family. Don't you think?"

"I'm not lying, Ms. T. I don't know where she is." Hope stepped backward, opening a narrow space in the doorway. "If you want to wait, you can. Could be a while, though."

"Thanks," Zoe said. It made no sense to wait. It could be hours before Leah returned. "If you see her, tell her I was here. OK? I'd like to talk to her. Would you tell her that? Please?"

After Todd dropped Hope at her house, he and Leah headed for Anderson Farm, an abandoned orchard on the south side of town. He turned onto a gravel road that wound through the orchard. Two years ago, the orchard's owner had died. Since his death, the property, willed to his heirs, had been untended. No one, Todd said, would bother them here.

"Great," Leah said. "Perfect."

She opened Todd's glove compartment, pulled out the plastic bag, rolled a joint, took a long hit, and held it for Todd, the liberating smell of weed electrifying the air inside the truck.

The Jeep bumped along a dirt path strewn with decaying fruit, past a dilapidated mill where, when the orchard was operational, the farm workers had pressed cider. At the end of the path, Todd turned left, cutting across the rows of squat apple trees, and headed up a short hill toward an open field fringed by ragweed, the tall purple flowers swaying in the light wind.

"That spot looks good." Leah pointed to a clearing between two Macintosh trees, at the outer edge of the orchard. "What about there?"

Todd, following her directions, parked the truck, and they both hopped out.

A mist hung in the air, the sky darkening, rain clouds scudding in from the west. She buttoned Hope's thick black sweater, leaving the top button undone.

"Look at that." Leah pointed to a tractor parked in the adjacent field, by a decaying shed.

In sixth grade, her class studied organic farming. Enthralled by the notion of living in a sprawling farmhouse, with pigs and cows and sheep as her pets, she'd decided to be a farmer. She pictured herself riding around the fields like the old farmer in town, operating the farming machinery. (She'd changed her mind when she learned that farmers worked sixteen hours a day.) She skipped past the Jeep, leaving Todd to spread their blanket, raced over the path to the field.

She set one foot on the tractor's runner and, grasping the edge of the seat, hauled herself up. "Hey, dude," she shouted, waving to her boyfriend, who was spreading their blanket, a nasty scowl on his face. She leaned forward, both hands gripping the wheel. "I'm coming to get you."

"Come back here," Todd griped. "Help me with this."

Stretching her right leg, she tapped the pedal, trilling her tongue, making an engine noise.

"Hey," she called again, "look at me."

Holding the wheel to steady herself, Leah lifted one foot to the seat, found her balance, and lifted the other. Crouching, she extended her arms. Slowly, she straightened her legs.

Standing on the seat of the tractor, she could see for miles and miles. All the way out to the street. To her house, maybe. To Boston, if she'd known which way to look.

She flapped her wings. "One, two, three…I'm an eagle," she cried, and leaped into the air like a bird, flapping harder, harder, willing her body to remain adrift.

Leah crashed to the ground, landing on the pointed edge of a rock, twisting her ankle.

"Ahhh," she squealed. "It *hurts*. Todd. Help me. Hurry. I broke my leg."

She removed her shoe and, sitting on the cool damp earth, massaged her ankle and foot.

Todd jogged toward her, an undershirt in one hand, a penknife in the other. "Let's see," he said, squatting. He lifted her foot, set it on his knee. He turned her foot left and right, ran his fingers over the ankle. "It don't look broken," he said, after a few minutes. "Can you move it?"

"Yes," she said, irritated by his casual tone. Her boyfriend didn't care if she was dying, evidently. She examined her ankle for signs of bruising. Wiggled her toes. "I guess I can."

"Let's go back. Come on." Todd pulled her arm over his shoulder. "I'll help you."

She leaned into him, transferring her weight to her good foot, limped back to the truck.

Todd had spread their blanket under the biggest of the Macintosh trees. He lowered Leah to the blanket, propping her against the trunk of the tree, shrugged out of his jacket, and draped it over her shoulders. The sharp, bittersweet smell of decaying apples, the musky odor of the damp earth, made her feel bold and adventurous, like a mountain girl at the turn of the century. She pictured herself and Todd living in a lean-to, battling the elements, the two of them against nature. He'd shoot bear for hide, to keep them warm in the winter. But what would they eat? Wild buffalo, maybe. Or deer.

Her stomach groaned, from thinking about food. "I'm starving," she said. A weather-beaten picker lay on the ground, near the path. She motioned at the picker. "Pick me an apple?"

Too late in the season, he said. The apples were rotten. "I got some gum, if you want it."

She unwrapped a stick of peppermint gum, folded it in half, stuffed it in her mouth. "I love picking apples," she said. Her mom used to take her and Justine to the orchard every fall. Their mom would buy two large bags, and the girls would skip up and down the dirt paths, their mom carrying the bags, Leah hunting for the reddest, most perfect apples on the trees, her sister plucking any old apple in reach, no matter how misshapen or wormy or green. "That orchard near our house. It's a development now. Why would anybody sell an orchard to a developer?"

"For the money?" Todd suggested.

Leah stretched out on the blanket, laying her head in her boyfriend's lap, and looked up, through the bare branches of the Macintosh tree, at the sky. The thick flannel blanket was as soft as a broken-in sweatshirt. Todd slid his hand under her head, rubbed the nape of her neck.

She gazed up at her boyfriend. "This one Halloween, we went to the orchard, right? They had all these pumpkins with candles inside. Thousands of Jack-O-Lanterns, all lit up." She closed her eyes, thinking back. "It's weird, remembering all this. I hardly remember being a kid."

Todd lit a pipe. Leah sat, and he passed it to her.

When the pipe was empty, he laid her on the blanket, and, straddling her legs, lowered himself onto her. His eyes were clear and bright, a passage leading directly into his soul.

Todd slid his hand under her shirt. Leah groaned, shifting her torso slightly, helping him find his way under her bra. He kissed her gently. And kissed her again, his hands traveling to the small of her back. Her belly tightened. She opened her legs, felt the seam of his jeans pushing against her groin. He was breathing heavily, his smoky breath on her face, her flesh tingling.

Her entire life had been building to this moment. When she was younger, lying in bed, she imagined making love with a man. She touched herself, pretending she was being touched by a boy. On occasion, she'd allowed a boy to touch her breasts. Only with Todd had Leah gone farther. For a lot of girls in her school, sex was no big deal, just another experience, like drinking beer or smoking weed. Leah couldn't relate. To give so much of herself, Leah had to be ready. The timing had to be right, the boy special, someone she honestly loved.

Lately, each time she and Todd were together, they had come a little closer. Last week, as a precaution, she asked Hope to drive her to the family planning clinic, for birth control pills.

Todd fingered her belly ring, his hands sliding under her shirt, over her ribs. "Beautiful," he whispered, and in that moment she *was* beautiful, to him, to herself, to the world.

Relax, she told herself. *Let yourself go.*

199

Terri Giuliano Long

He fumbled with her bra. Leah dropped her sweater, and sat, pulled her T-shirt over her head, the air cool on her shoulders, her chest, her arms. Reaching backward, she unhooked her bra. She closed her eyes, her breath quickening. And he pushed the straps over her shoulders.

She felt the pads of his fingers beneath the swell of her breasts, arched her back, felt the release as he pulled the cottony fabric away. She shivered, her nipples hardening in the crisp autumn air. Gently, he pressed her to the blanket, and pushed against her, kissing her neck, her shoulders, her clavicle bones. He kissed her belly. . . unzipped her jeans.

She lifted her pelvis, felt her panties sliding over her hips.

Twenty-Two

Where Are You? Where Am I?

Dusk had settled by the time Zoe pulled into the garage. As she opened the mudroom door, she felt an echo from inside the empty house. She hated this time of day—the witching hour, she'd called it, when the girls were babies—darkness settling, both girls irritable and hungry. She flipped on the lights, the house eerily silent. Justine was nowhere in sight. Probably at Holly's. Lately, Justine had been spending every spare minute at her friend's house, working on her science project, she claimed. Last night, after dinner, Justine retreated to her room and closed her door, leaving Zoe feeling as if she were losing both of her daughters.

Zoe tossed her keys on the counter. The TV was off, the family room dark. She wandered through the dining room, into the foyer, called upstairs, not really expecting an answer. She waited a few seconds, and ambled into the living room. An old photo of the girls sat on the end table. In the picture, the girls were clowning in a wading pool in the backyard of their Cape in Hudson, Justine in her one-piece orange suit with blue stars, Leah in her ruffled pink bikini. Zoe picked up the photo, drew a box around her daughters, leaving a trail on the dusty glass.

Closing her eyes, she summoned a picture of her daughter. Leah's face appeared, and her body gradually materialized. *Be safe*, Zoe whispered, and enclosed her daughter in a protective circle of light. *That's all I ask.* Dejected, she headed back to the foyer. "Justine," she called again, from the bottom of the staircase. "You up there, honey?"

201

She called one last time, and trekked upstairs, thinking maybe Justine had fallen asleep.

Dog lay at the foot of Justine's bed. She woofed when Zoe entered the room, slid off the bed, followed Zoe to the closet. Her head nudged Zoe's legs, and they both peered inside.

"Looks like nobody's home," Zoe said to the dog, as she closed the closet door.

A bag of bone-shaped treats sat on the edge of Justine's desk. Zoe fed Dog a treat, the dog licking her hand as she took it. For a while, Zoe sat on Justine's bed, admiring the sponge-painted walls. She and Justine had painted the walls two years earlier. For amateurs, their job had turned out surprisingly well, swirls of fluffy cumulus clouds floating across the powder-blue paint. She'd been hesitant to paint clouds on the walls, sure that Justine would quickly grow out of the look and want something different, more sophisticated, more suitable for a teen. But Zoe was wrong. Two months ago, at Justine's request, she'd ordered a matching bedspread and curtains, the fabric a soft blue like the walls, spangled with bright yellow stars.

Dog had dozed off. Zoe scratched the dog's neck, and dragged herself up.

Before she headed downstairs, Zoe stuck her head in Leah's room.

The room looked exactly as Leah had left it, her top drawer open, her bed unmade. Zoe stood in the doorway, feeling strangely out of place, as if her daughter's room were somehow off-limits to her. *Decorum be damned*, she thought, and ventured inside, Dog at her heels.

The room was full of Leah's smell. Zoe ran a hand over her daughter's dusty oak bureau, feeling the gnarled grain, pushed the top drawer closed. Leah's CD case lay on the nightstand. Flipping through, she was shocked by how few titles she recognized. She studied the doodles on the walls, her daughter's childlike scroll, remembering the hearts, pierced by arrows, exactly like these, that had adorned the brown paper-bag covers of Leah's elementary school books. Zoe stripped the bed, changed the sheets, folded Leah's comforter, laid it neatly at the foot of the bed.

Zoe had given zero thought to fixing dinner. The fridge was empty. Milk, eggs, a hunk of moldy cheddar cheese, Dijon mustard. Seven bottles of salad dressing, all different, all open. She found a red onion and a bag of carrots in the vegetable drawer, a package of ground sirloin in the freezer. Chili, simple and easy. She checked the cabinets to be sure she had beans, took two cans of tomatoes from the Lazy Susan, pulled a Dutch oven from the drawer under the stove.

She crushed and sautéed two garlic cloves, diced the onion and carrots. While the onions were browning, she tried Will's cell phone, hoping for some indication of when he would be home, whether he planned to eat dinner with them, if he'd like them to wait. He had a meeting in Woburn this afternoon. When she asked him with whom, he'd evaded her question. She had a hunch he'd called a headhunter. Last week, Micronics had opted out of their contract, claiming that NAC had failed to perform. Micronics still owed NAC several million dollars for work Will's crew had completed; the client refused to pay. Supposedly, the construction delays, which no one had benefited from, had cost them a fortune. According to their project manager, "a royal asshole," in Will's words, the money Micronics had withheld barely recovered their costs.

"You do realize," Will said to her last Sunday night, "we've already been paid?" Will's boss was holding Will personally responsible for collecting the balance of the money. NAC had paid his commission in good faith. Will poured two glasses of Merlot, handed one to her. If he couldn't convince his client to pony up, Jackman expected him to return the twenty-five grand.

Twenty-five thousand dollars. Zoe set her glass on the counter. When she deposited the check, she'd placed five thousand dollars in the savings account to hold them until his next commission check; with the rest, she'd paid overdue bills. They had no way to repay the money. Refinancing was not an option: they were carrying two mortgages already. With their debt load, no reputable bank would give them a personal loan. Maybe they could take cash advances against their credit cards— *Good Lord.* "Jackman's upset. He won't go through with it, Will."

Will downed his wine in a single swallow, and poured another glass. He was too damn old to be humping contracting jobs. This wasn't like the old days, when people were good for their word. You couldn't trust anybody, today. The entire industry was corrupt. "They're vultures, Zo." He didn't want to deal with this goddamn crap anymore. "I talked to a guy today, about finishing that space over the garage. I'm thinking about starting a rep business." A company in Michigan manufactured moldings for the high-end housing market. They were looking for an East Coast rep. He'd called yesterday, was waiting to hear back from their VP.

"Housing market?" she said, reeling. He'd be calling on *Home Depot*, for God's sake. Who did he know at Home Depot? Did he really want to start over, build a new client base from scratch? "You can't just quit." They'd go broke. "At least get something solid lined up first."

"You're right," he'd replied. "Maybe I'll do the rep thing part-time, till I'm up to speed."

Good grief. Please, she thought now, don't do anything drastic. This was not a good time.

When the vegetables were soft, she browned the beef, poured a can of organic tomatoes into the pot, a large can of kidney beans, a sprig of parsley, a bottle of medium-hot salsa, added three heaping teaspoons of chili powder, a sprinkling of cumin. While she waited for the chili to boil, she washed the counter, folded a load of laundry. Maybe she should go for a jog, try to clear her mind. She hadn't run in so long. She didn't know if she had the energy. *Go*, she told herself. Running would do her good. She turned the chili to simmer, covered the pot, wrote a short note, in case she was gone when Justine returned home, and changed into her running clothes.

Zoe had trouble catching her breath. Her muscles tight, she stopped at the end of the street, to stretch. Holding onto the post of the street sign, for balance, she stretched her Achilles, folded her left leg, stretching her quads. Leaning forward, reaching for her toes, she stretched her hamstrings and glutes. When she finished, she shook out her legs, and turned left, onto Old Orchard Road. She loved running in this weather, the air damp and cool. It felt good to be out, breathing hard, her feet pounding the pavement, her nylon jacket flapping behind her.

In the dark, the surface of the road seemed to bank and shift. She considered returning home for a flashlight, a reflective vest, and thought better of it. Once she was in the house, she'd find a reason to stay. The road sloped downhill. She hugged the shoulder, taking the hill slowly, finding her stride. Finishing that first race on the Fourth of July had given her a shot of badly needed confidence. For a few years, she'd run a race nearly every weekend. At the end of a tough five-miler, she imagined herself finishing a marathon, chasing Joan Benoit to the finish.

Zoe breathed deeply, pumping her arms, her legs in a rhythm. She lifted her face. *Let go.* Breathed through her nose, exhaled through her mouth. The image of Joanie morphed into a vision of Leah, racing up the soccer field, her ponytail bobbing. *Wait,* Zoe called. *Wait for me.*

A van careened toward her, the driver honking his horn. Startled, she blinked into the headlights, and sprung back, onto the shoulder, her sneaker hitting a mound of wet leaves.

Watch it, asshole, the driver bellowed, poking a finger through the open window, as the van swerved around her.

Zoe must have passed out for an instant. When she opened her eyes, she was lying, face down, in the road. She took a breath, pulling herself together. Stupid, running after dark without a reflective vest. Rolling sideways, she pushed herself to a sitting position, brushed away the damp pine needles clinging to her jacket, and, gritting her teeth, tried to lift herself onto her hands and knees. Pain shot through her leg. And she passed out again.

Todd and Leah sat on the ground, wrapped in the blanket, while Todd refilled the pipe. Leah felt stupid, sitting here naked, but she was too flustered to suggest getting dressed. She'd never made love before. Maybe being naked together afterward was part of the deal.

Leah was disappointed in herself. She'd expected to feel different after losing her virginity. She was bleeding a little. She was a tiny bit sore. That was it. She'd gleaned no secret carnal knowledge. Shared in no deep, cosmic revelation. She'd crossed no hidden boundary, felt no sudden immersion into womanhood.

Oh, no. What if she'd done something wrong? Todd was *far* more experienced than she. On the road, traveling with the rock band, he had been surrounded by groupies. They were skanky, he told her. He'd hooked up with only a few of them, he claimed, but she didn't believe him. She'd asked him, one time, for a count. She wasn't interested in hearing specific descriptions or names. She wanted a number. "Fifteen?" Leah pushed. "Twenty? Twenty-five?" she asked timidly, hoping he would counter with a far smaller figure. Todd only smirked.

"Was I OK?" She winced, hugging the blanket. *Please don't say NO.*

"Yeah, babe." He handed her the pipe. "You were great."

"Thanks." She bit down on the pipe, inhaling deeply, filling her lungs with smoke, held her breath until she couldn't hold it another second, coughed up a cloud of smoke. "This tastes funny. What is it?"

"Weed." He brought the pipe to his lips.

"It tastes like plastic."

He raised his eyebrows, handed the pipe back. "It's only weed."

"How come it's this color?" She tipped the bowl to show him.

"*What* color?"

"Red." She took another long hit.

He'd laced it with opium, he finally admitted.

"Opium?" Todd knew very well that opium scared her.

"Chill out, babe. Opium's cool." He dragged on the pipe. When he tried to hand it back, she pushed it away. "Hey, you trust me?" he growled, his words ringed in smoke. "Or not?"

"Guess so." Of course she trusted him. He would never let anything bad happen to her.

"So chill out already."

When they'd finished the first bowl, they lit another. After the second bowl, Todd set the pipe on the ground, scooped her up, and, kneeling astride her, lowered her onto the blanket.

She giggled, scrunching her shoulders. "Stop." His tongue tickled her ear. "Cut it out." Her voice had a hollow ring, as if she were talking into a microphone that wasn't turned up.

He loomed over her, his piercing blue eyes boring into her brain.

Terrified, she pushed him off, and wriggled out from under him, tugging at the blanket, pulling it over her face. "He's watching," she whimpered. *If he found them, he'd kill them.*

"Who?" He yanked at the blanket. "Nobody's here."

"The farmer's." She gripped the edge of the blanket, hiding her eyes. "Looking for us."

"*What* farmer?" He ripped the blanket away from her. "Nobody's here."

"He's watching." Leah curled into a ball, crossing her ankles.

Todd stood with one hand on the tree trunk, his blistering blue eyes tearing into her skull. Leah's head spun, the earth slanting under her. All at once, his penis started to shrivel.

Leah tried to keep a straight face. But she couldn't help herself. His penis was a shriveling snake, the snake shrinking into a teensy, weensy, baby blue *prune.*

"I don't friggin believe this." Todd snapped the wheel, veering onto the dirt road, heading out of the orchard. He plugged a Nirvana CD into the player, an angry, frenetic rush of sound, increased the volume, turning the music up, up, up. She could barely hear herself think.

She covered her ears, trying to ignore the tin soldiers mauling the inside of her brain.

In her hurry, she'd pulled her T-shirt on backward. She pulled her arms out of the sleeves, spun the shirt around, put Hope's sweater back on. The music raged, a strident march into oblivion. "Turn it down. Todd? Please?" She squeezed her throbbing temples. "I'm sorry." For laughing at him, she meant. "I didn't mean it. I'm sorry. Todd, listen to me. Please?"

Rain pounded the windshield. A dense fog had rendered the headlights useless.

Todd pumped the accelerator, the truck crashing over the ruts.

"Todd," she pleaded, straining to be heard over the din. "Slow down."

He popped the CD, plugged in a rap recording. *Don't fuck with me bitch*, the MC railed.

"Do we have to listen to this misog, misog. I hate this music."

"Fuck it." He pounded the steering wheel, his keys jangling. "What the hell did I *do*?"

"Nothing," Leah lied. "You didn't do anything."

He lit a cigarette, sucked hard, and handed it to her. She pulled the scalding smoke into her lungs, held it as long as she could, and gave it back. He ground the butt, lit another, his hands shaking.

They were headed toward Main Street, the road a winding asphalt blur. *Trees, field.*

He swiveled to face her. She flinched, and he overcorrected, swerving into the oncoming lane. He wrestled the Jeep back to its lane, the abrupt shifts in direction flinging her around the cab like a rag doll.

She gripped the dash. "Slow down. Please?"

"Can't pull this shit," he snapped, spewing spit. "It ain't right."

Her heart beat in her throat. "Todd, please?" *He was going to kill them.*

"You don't want to do it again, tell me. No, you fucking laugh at me."

Rain hammered the windshield, the wipers sluicing, back and forth, back and forth, her brain drowning in a watery fog. Couldn't take this anymore. She had to get out. Get away. Be alone. Think things through. Seizing the door handle, she swung her legs sideways.

"You *nuts*?" Todd lunged right, pinning her in place. A pickup skidded around them.

"Let me go," she whimpered. Just let her out.

He switched on the defroster, the whirring fan drilling into her skull.

"Taking you to Hope's." He drove, leaning sideward, his arm strapping her in place.

"Not crazy," she cried, gulping back tears. With her fist, she pummeled her thigh.

"Stop," he croaked. "I never said you're crazy." He loosened his grip, and Leah grabbed for the door. The Jeep nosed into the gutter again. "Don't do this," he begged. He rotated the wheel, his free hand clinching her legs. "I won't let you do this."

Let me out of here," she cried. She was drowning, a whirlpool sucking her into its depths. "Let *go*." She punched at his arm. "Not going anywhere with you." Pitching left, she took a swing at his face, kicking the dash. "Let me *out*," she wailed, and wrenched herself free.

"Go." He jammed the brakes, the Jeep fishtailing. "Get out. I don't need this shit."

Leah eased herself out of the truck, the door squealing. Limped onto the street. She heard Todd call. "Wait. Leah? Come back." Heard him hop out of the truck. "Leah, Wait." She set one foot in front of the other, her eyes focused ahead, refusing to listen, to look. Heard her name again. *Leah*, his voice breaking. He called her one last time, swore, and slammed his door shut.

The Jeep's engine roared, and the truck skidded around her. She watched the taillights, shrinking to pinpricks. A sharp wind cut past her, the frigid gust slapping her cheeks. Her head hurt, her ankle, her feet. Move, she told herself, one step at a time, one foot in front of the other. She stretched her arms, her hands strangely ghoulish in the dim light cast by the streetlamp. Leah barely recognized her own hands. She wasn't herself anymore. And she didn't know this crazy, lost girl she had become.

PART THREE

IN LEAH'S WAKE

Twenty-Three

Wake-Up Call

In Jerry's dream, he and Zoe Tyler are at a campground. She's swimming in a body of water, a lake, an ocean, sometimes a pond. He hears a cry, sees her floundering, dives in to save her. He carries her, cradled in his arms like a princess, out of the water, lays her warm body on the dewy grass. Her eyes are closed, long lashes brushing her cheekbones. He kneels beside her, plants a deep kiss on her lips. That was as far as he'd ever progressed. Just as the dream heated up, someone or something always managed to wake him. He slung his arm over his face, and tightened his eyelids, willing himself back into the dream.

"*Jerry.*" He felt his wife shaking his shoulder. "*Jerry*, wake up."

"Huh? What?" he said, blinking against the artificial light. He'd fallen asleep around four. Now the house was lit like a circus, and the curtains were drawn. "What time is it?"

"Six. You got a call." She pushed the receiver into his out-stretched hand.

Jerry pressed the phone to his chest. "Who is it?" he mouthed.

"Station," she snapped, and stormed into the kitchen.

Jerry listened carefully as Millie explained the situation. *Urgent*, she said. *Tyler girl.* Could he come? In his mind, before he'd even clicked off, Jerry was on his way to the station.

His wife was hovering over him again. "You're supposed to be off," she complained. She'd put the boys down for the night. She and Jerry were supposed to have dinner together.

Maura stalked him to the bathroom, stood outside the bathroom door, whining, as he checked himself in the mirror. He ran his fingers

211

under the faucet, tamped the stubborn hairs at his crown, brushed his teeth, and took a leak, in case he didn't have a chance to go for a while.

His wife's behavior was utterly absurd. She'd married a cop. She knew exactly what his job entailed. If he received an emergency call, he had to respond. He opened the bathroom door, squeezed by her, excusing himself, advanced to the coat closet by the house's formal entrance, in the living room, his wife looming over his shoulder. He was dressed in worn jeans, a blue flannel shirt. Casual clothes would have to do. He had no time to hunt for a clean uniform. He reached for his leather bomber, the wire hangers jangling as he pulled. Flinching, he steadied the hangars.

"You're not leaving," his wife cried. "You can't do this to me." In the kitchen, her arms spread, blocking the back door, she said, "Look at this pigsty you made. Who's going to clean up, Jerry, huh? *Wait.* Aren't you going to change?'

"I'll stuff the sausages later," he said, as if his wife cared, and asked her nicely to move.

Lousy night, raw, typical of late November. It was raining earlier. Now the world had gone stagnant. He gazed up at the heavens, searching for some sign of life—the moon, a few stars. Nothing but clouds. A gust of wind tore the last of the sodden leaves from the sugar maple in the side yard, sent them swirling into the driveway. He'd parked on the street, leaving space in the drive for Maura to pull her minivan up to the door. He felt a pinch in his sciatica as his foot hit the asphalt driveway, stepped carefully around Maura's van, avoiding the wet leaves.

They lived in the sticks, on the western border of town, neighbored by trees. This far out, they couldn't even get cable. Given a choice, he would live in a development closer to town, a neighborhood of young mothers with kids, an area less isolating for Maura. Choosing to stay in Cortland, opting to buy rather than rent, had left them no option; this was all they could afford.

According to the dispatcher, O'Leary had seen the Tyler girl wandering along the shoulder of Main Street, pulled over to give her a ride. O'Leary didn't recognize Leah. She was out sick the night Jerry brought Corbett and the Tyler girl in. When she asked Leah for a name and address, Leah refused to answer. Leah's attitude toward O'Leary surprised him. O'Leary was good with kids. She was young, closer to their age. The kids sensed her genuine concern, and they knew she cared. The girls in particular responded to that.

If O'Leary had failed, Jerry doubted he could get through to the girl, but he would certainly try. Leah had left the Lansdown place. That was a start. Except in serious cases of abuse or neglect, kids, *even older kids,* he said, talking to himself, *kids Leah's age,* fared best at home, with their parents. Jerry had run away when he was a kid, so he knew. After his arrest, his parents, or his mother, actually (his father the more lenient of the two), banned his friends from their house. Incensed, Jerry tossed three changes of clothes into a pack, rolled his sleeping bag, grabbed his portable tape deck, and hopped in his Mustang, heading west. He'd always liked horses, figured he'd find a job on a dude ranch. In Wyoming, he slept outside under the stars. He'd never imagined the world to be so big—or so lonely. He lasted all of two weeks. He would do his best to convince Leah to go home, try to work things out with her family.

Millie was bent over the front desk, writing. When she saw him, she held up a finger.

"Thought you ought to know," Millie whispered, "her momma's had an accident."

Zoe? Jerry's mind reeled. *What kind of accident?* "When? How? What happened?"

"Whoa. Slow down, honey. Don't want you having a heart attack here." Millie glanced in the direction of the holding tank, and lowered her voice another notch. "She fell. That's all I know. Hollingshead's with her. Chief will fill you in. We were hoping you'd tell her little girl."

"Punk dumped her out of the car," the chief groused. "Up on Main."

Jerry swung toward the chief's gravely voice. The chief stopped a few feet from Jerry, coughed, covering his mouth with a fist. "Pardon." He crossed a hefty arm over his chest. A hulk, Martin Healy was a former nose tackle at Rutgers. Would've played pro, had he not blown out his knee. He'd never lost the weight he'd gained playing ball, and the extra bulk put pressure on his airways; he was constantly wheezing. "Believe that?" He coughed again. "Bastard dumped her," he said, and wiped his watery eyes. "Lucky some idiot didn't run her over."

Who the hell would dump Zoe Tyler anywhere? "We get a name?" Jerry asked.

"Corbett," Healy wheezed. "Get with the program. Been spending too much time with them kids of yours. Noggin's turning to oatmeal, big guy." He hacked again. "Should've locked that punk up last week, when we had the chance."

"I heard that," Millie said, from across the room. Unlike Jerry and his coworkers, who shared a more pragmatic opinion of the men they detained (it was mostly men), Millie believed *all* suspects, however unlikely, regardless of the evidence stacked against them, were innocent until proven guilty. Though experience had taught Jerry differently, he respected her views. But Millie's "liberal bullshit" rankled the chief. *She* didn't have to deal with the fallout, Healy said.

"Kid's got herself a load of trouble with that piece of shit," the chief said.

"Excuse me," said Jerry, who had more important things on his mind. "Is she all right?"

"Fine." The chief wagged a finger at Millie, still razzing. "Shook up. Otherwise, fine."

Jerry relaxed—until the chief lobbed another cheap shot at Corbett. "The mother," Jerry said, injecting a sense of purpose into his voice. "Mrs. Tyler. Is *she* all right?"

"Whoa." Healy knuckled Jerry's chest. "Almost sounds like you're doing the broad."

Jerry let the chief's crass remark pass. Defending himself would only implicate him.

Something was wrong here. Less than a week ago, Corbett had risked his neck for the Tyler girl. They could have sent the kid away for violating his probation, if they'd been so disposed. Tonight he dumps her out of the truck? Didn't add up. "We get any details?"

"O'Leary's on the computer. Talk to her."

Coughing, Healy cut across the reception area, opened the glass door to Millie's station, sauntered to Millie's desk, logged onto her computer, and said something Jerry didn't catch.

Millie removed a manila folder from the top drawer of the filing cabinet and gave it to Healy. Jerry attempted to catch her eye. He wanted to hear her take. He trusted her instincts. She had an uncanny ability to cut to the heart of a matter, and she often saw things the rest of them missed. A call came in, a 9-1-1. Rather than wasting time waiting, he left to pay O'Leary a visit.

O'Leary sat at the desk in the interrogation room where they'd brought Leah, a few days earlier, to wait for her parents, her back to the door. O'Leary was young and bright, two years out of college. Like him, she studied criminal justice at Northeastern. With her ambition and talent, he didn't figure her for long on the street. In a few years, she'd wind up in law school.

He tapped the door, to let her know he was there. "Meg?"

O'Leary stopped typing, swiveled to face him. "Jerry. Hey. Glad you're here."

Normally, he'd ask how she was doing, crack a joke about her boyfriend, a rookie ADA, assigned to the courthouse in Lowell. Tonight, he cut to the chase. "Tyler girl? What happened?"

O'Leary looked puzzled. "We were hoping you'd figure it out." Basically, she said, she'd noticed Leah limping down Main, offered to drive her home. The girl refused to give her name or tell Meg where she lived. O'Leary had brought her here, for her own protection. She'd given Leah a blanket, a cup of hot chocolate. "I tried talking. I couldn't get through to her."

"She doesn't know about her mother yet, right?"

"Not yet. I put her in the tank, Jer. I hated to do it. But the poor kid was in such a state."

"I'll see what I can do. She trusts me. Or I think she does, anyway."

Healy, motioning for Jerry to hold on, spat in a tissue. "Hollingshead radioed. Looks like the Tyler broad got nicked by a truck. Bet it's that bastard from East Main." Last week's hit and run, Healy meant.

"Witnesses?"

"No, unfortunately." Healy was hacking again.

Jerry rubbed his neck. "How bad?"

"Fracture." Gesturing, Healy excused himself and waddled to the cooler.

Fracture. Thank God. Jerry didn't know what he would do if Zoe had died.

Healy returned, carrying a paper cup filled with water. "Like I said, we'll know more once Hollingshead gets a statement."

"She say anything else? Mention a make? A color?"

Nada.

"So what the hell was Hollingshead doing out there? Did he get anything useful?"

Healy grimaced. "Sure you're not doing her, Johnson?" Before Jerry had a chance to respond, Healy clapped him on the back, laughing. "It's a joke, big guy. Relax. I told you, we'll know more once we get a statement."

Leah was sitting on the floor, by the toilet, hugging her knees, hands cradling the cup of hot chocolate, the smelly blanket the female cop had given her over her shoulders.

She knew the instant Officer Johnson poked his head in the room that something was up.

Accident, she heard the cop say. The Jeep's fishtailing lights flashed before her eyes. "No." Leah covered her ears. She didn't want to hear about an accident. Todd had been driving erratically. He must have hit the stone wall. She pictured him, ejected on impact, rocketing through the windshield, blood splattering over the glass. This was her fault. They'd been fighting. She'd upset him. She covered her face. Tell her this wasn't true. Please?

Officer Johnson stood a few feet away, staring down at her with those pitiful eyes.

He probably wanted her to go to the morgue, identify the body. Leah didn't have the strength to look at Todd's dead, lifeless body. She'd be sick. She would pass out. This wasn't fair. How could this happen? She loved Todd. He was only twenty years-old. Too young to die. Leah felt like a widow. She would never stop grieving. Ever. Even if she lived to be a hundred.

The cop set a hand on her shoulder, his features blurred by her tears.

She watched his mouth working, the words oddly detached. Everything around her had stopped. She was still breathing, but whatever part of her lived inside—her soul, Leah, *herself*—had gone flat. The room twisted, the floor heaving. She couldn't get her bearings. Her ears rang. A strange sound—a school bell, a fire alarm—went off in her head, drowning everything else.

He crouched beside her.

If only this day would end and she could start over. Take today back. Everything would be different. Todd would still be alive. She clutched her stomach. She was going to vomit.

"Let's go," the cop said, taking her by the hand, helping her up.

"Where?" Leah squeaked. "Where are you taking me?"

The cop gave her a soulful look.

"Where?" she asked again. She couldn't go to the morgue.

"Gum?" Jerry offered Leah a stick of spearmint gum from a pack he found in his jacket.

The Tyler girl was sitting beside him, in the passenger seat of the cruiser, her head leaning against the window. She had not uttered a word since they left the station. He was taking her to the hospital, to visit her mother. For her own protection, given her irrational state of mind, he probably should have put her in flexible handcuffs, only he didn't have the heart. Poor kid took the news hard. He didn't blame her. He'd have had the same reaction if Zoe were his mom.

Leah had misunderstood him, at first, thought he'd said her mother was dead. He felt like a clod, scaring her. Most of the time, he was good with people, but he was a disaster when it came to bearing bad news. He never knew how to broach the subject, what he should say. He always felt as though he'd stuck his foot in his mouth, even when logic told him he hadn't.

She shivered, poor kid. He shouldered out of his jacket, laid it awkwardly over her legs, and turned up the heat, adjusting the vents, directing the airflow her way.

"I have a niece your age," he said, digging for something to say.

She pushed his jacket off her legs, onto the console between them.

At first, he'd worried that she might be in shock. What he'd mistaken for shock, he realized now, was guilt. He felt for her. She'd upset her mother, running away. Emotionally, it was easy to link one event to the next. But the accident had nothing to do with her. Her mother had been jogging, the accident a crime, if it turned out to be a hit and run. Not Leah's fault. "My wife, I mean. It's her niece. She has a nephew, too. I have a sister. She doesn't have any kids." *I have a sister, she doesn't have any kids.* This would not be as easy as he'd hoped.

Leah tugged at a silver hoop in her ear. A trail of silver earrings ran, from the base of her lobe, halfway up the helix. "That's a lot of earrings, there. Did it hurt?"

"Not really," she said, her voice barely audible.

He understood how she felt, Jerry told her. "I'd be out of my mind, if she was my mom."

A call came in, over the CB. Millie spoke in code, avoiding names. While he talked with Millie, Leah fiddled with the automatic button on her window, up and down, up and down.

The window business annoyed him. He chose to overlook it. He glanced over at her, pleased to relay positive news. "Mom's doing good. Looks like she broke a bone in her shin."

"Is that bad?"

Doesn't sound too bad, he told her. "She'll probably be on crutches for awhile. Getting around might be a pain in the neck."

The heat had fogged the windshield. Jerry switched on the defroster, activated the wipers. At the intersection, he slowed, noticed her peering at him. "Don't worry," Jerry said again. Had she ever broken a bone? She shook her head no. Wasn't too bad. Painful at first. Inconvenient.

She listened politely, asked him quietly if her mom had seen the guy who had hit her.

If he told the truth—he doubted that Zoe could ID the guy— Leah would be devastated. If he lied, well, he would be lying. "Maybe," he said, opting for the middle ground.

Her chin puckered. She picked at her nails. To reassure her, he decided to embellish a bit. "I think we've got enough to go on. We'll find him."

Leah turned to the window again. Poor kid. Broke his heart to see her so worried. Jerry pumped the brakes, mentally abusing himself for being so tongue-tied, wishing he could do something to make her feel better. The rain had ended, but the temperature was dropping, the visibility steadily decreasing. "You all right?" Any moron could see she wasn't. "Not too cold?"

She answered with a barely perceptible shake of her head.

The cold made Jerry think about Maura, who was always cold. From there, his thoughts turned to the boys, which in turn brought Zoe to mind. He pictured the two of them raising his children together, envisioned them in the park, playing catch with the kids. Zoe's girls could baby-sit, on occasion; that way, he and Zoe wouldn't be stuck in the house all the time like Maura and him. Divorcing Maura could pose a slight problem. "Over my dead body," she'd told him one day, out of the blue, when she was seven months pregnant and picking a fight, the one and only time in their married life that the subject had ever arisen. On the other hand, she might be glad to be rid of him. She was hardly amorous toward him these days. Getting custody of the boys would be tough. Maybe he could pay his wife off, give her alimony in exchange for the kids. She complained constantly about the twins, how their demands drained her, how tired she was. Having to take care of the boys only on weekends might be a relief.

He flicked his blinkers on. As he was turning into the entrance to St. Michael's Hospital, Leah broke the silence. Was he sure her mom was OK? It was the third time she'd asked. Really sure? Positive? Yes, he promised. He hadn't seen the medical report, so didn't know the full extent of her injuries, but he had no reason to believe otherwise.

"What's gonna happen? You know, to the guy who hit her?"

In Leah's Wake

Nothing, Jerry thought. The bastard would probably get off scot-free. A fine for driving to endanger, if they located the son-of-a-bitch. Even if they caught the guy, it would be hard to get a conviction. According to Hollingshead, Zoe claimed she'd fallen, and she was sticking to her story. Poor kid had been through enough for one night. He wasn't about to tell her the truth. *We'll nail him*, Jerry started to say, and caught sight of Tyler's BMW, parked in the visitor's lot.

Today was the worst day in Leah's entire life. She felt disloyal, assuming that Todd hit her mother. But it all made terrible sense: Todd had dropped her off less than a mile from where her mother was hit. He'd been driving like a maniac. According to the police, she'd been hit by a truck. If Todd was involved, their relationship was obviously over. She could never forgive him. But it would break her heart. She loved him. Seeing her boyfriend in jail would destroy her.

This morning, despite the lumpy sofa she had slept on, she'd woke feeling alive and refreshed, proud of her gumption, pleased with herself for proving she could get by on her own, that she didn't need her parent's support. She'd eaten a decadent, unhealthy breakfast of Fruit Loops, listened eagerly to Mrs. Lansdown's wild stories of Woodstock. Years seemed to have elapsed since this morning. She felt like an old lady, climbing out of the cruiser a challenge.

The parking lot was frenetic tonight. Accidents, Leah surmised, because of the rain.

An ambulance screamed by, the siren wailing. At the emergency entrance, its doors snapped open and an attendant hopped out. He and another paramedic lowered the gurney to the ground, a medical team rushing outside to meet them, the team all barking their orders at once.

The temperature must have dropped twenty degrees since this afternoon. Leah was freezing, the brittle air cutting right through her. This time, when the cop asked offered his jacket, she accepted.

When he was her age, Officer Johnson was saying, he'd run away, too. She knew that he was trying to establish a bond, but his story depressed her. Leaving the security of her parents' home had been the only interesting aspect of running away. Plenty of kids her age ran away, of course, but they usually hailed from marginal families, families any intelligent person would leave. Among kids like herself, from solid middle-class families, she was a leader, she'd felt. Except for Todd, possibly Lupo, Leah did not know a single person brave enough to strike out alone. Listening to Officer Johnson, one of the most average people she had ever met, talk about running

219

away, forced her to face the awful truth: She was totally ordinary. Nothing special at all.

"You're limping." Officer Johnson pointed to her foot. "What happened?"

Leah shrugged. The accident was dumb, not worth talking about. He'd broken his foot once, he told her. "Jumping off a roof."

"Off a roof," she repeated.

Now that she knew her mom was okay, she was tempted to press the cop for details, see if she could figure out what else they knew about the hit-and-run. Only she wasn't sure how to go about it. If she asked too many questions, she'd raise his suspicion. Pointing the investigation in Todd's direction was the last thing she wanted to do. If Todd was at fault and they caught him, she would have to live with the outcome. But she was not about to rat the kid out. She dug into the sleeves of the jacket, burying her hands in the folds. She would have to play the cop, let him think she wanted to see the guy caught. "Officer," she said sweetly, and lost her nerve.

When they reached the revolving door at the ER, Officer Johnson set a hand on her shoulder, gestured for her to go in ahead, his prompt stopping her in her tracks. Go inside? Alone? Until this instant, she hadn't considered what would happen when she entered the hospital. She had been focused entirely on the future, worrying about her mom, thinking about Todd, wondering what the outcome of all this would be. She'd skipped right over the present.

Jerry placed a hand on Leah's shoulder. "Go ahead. They'll be glad to see you."

She looked up at him, her face the face of a frightened child. He thought she might run.

He put his arm around her, to calm her, to keep her from running away. Family can be tough, he told her. People are familiar, it's easy to take advantage. You don't meant to, but it happens. Hurtful words, misunderstandings, you let them slide, take on a life of their own. "Pretty soon, you feel like you're on opposite sides of a valley. It's like there's a mountain between you." He pictured his wife at the living room window as he climbed in the cruiser, the curtains parted, Maura watching him leave. "There's too much distance, you tell yourself—"

"To run," Leah said softly.

"Try to patch things up," Jerry said. "Might not seem worth it, but it will be in the end. Family, believe me, they're the ones who'll be there for you—no matter what." Leah offered a weak smile. "Your folks are crazy about you," he said, and pulled her into a fatherly hug.

"Thank you," she said, when they released. She withdrew her arms from his jacket.

He took the bomber, shook it out, draped it over her shoulders. Hang on to it, he told her. He'd swing by in few days, to check in on them, to see how they were. She could return it then.

"Here," he said. "Before we go in." He handed her his card, with the phone number and e-mail address where he could be reached. "Call me. Day or night. Even if you just want to talk."

He escorted Leah through the revolving door. He was proud of her, a young woman, suddenly poised, striding purposefully through the waiting area, past the sick people hunkered in their metal chairs, some napping, others listlessly watching TV. At the intake desk, he spoke with a wary administrator. Took him three tries, the words arranged in three different ways, to convince her that Leah was neither a convict nor a danger, Jerry's intent simply to reunite the child with her mother.

Within minutes, a triage nurse emerged from her glass-enclosed office to greet them.

Jerry followed Leah and the nurse through double doors, to the central desk in the ER.

Nurses and doctors, dressed in scrubs, were congregated around the desk, discussing cases. Others sat inside the U-shaped station, in front of buzzing computers, entering test data, recording patient information. The triage nurse spoke briefly with one of the doctors on call, then she led Leah to Room 6, the cubicle where, behind a green curtain, Zoe lay, awaiting her care.

His back to the desk, elbows resting on the counter, he watched Leah weave through the bustling staff, dodging the rolling gurneys. The triage nurse pushed aside the curtain shielding Zoe's cubicle. Leah stopped. He saw the staccato tic of her thin shoulders as she pulled off his jacket. From where she stood, though she would have heard voices, she could see nothing.

Tyler sat on a rotating stool, feet apart, his hands between his knees, staring at the heart monitor beside his wife's bed. He nodded when he saw his daughter, rose, touched her shoulder. Leah tiptoed to her mother's bedside, pecked her mother timidly on the cheek, as if she were afraid of hurting her, afraid of getting too close. Zoe squeezed her daughter's hand. Now she and Leah were crying. Tyler drew Leah into a hug, as Jerry had done, just a few minutes ago. In an hour or two, once Zoe had been treated and bandaged, they would ride home together, a family again. A wave of depression swept over him. Then, strangely, Jerry felt better.

Though it may not seem so at the moment, Leah's troubles were minor, a pit stop on the bumpy road to adulthood. She was a good kid. Good head on her shoulders. Decent family. So much love, such positive energy on her side. One day soon, they would discover that she had grown up, and all this would be over, these hard times fading to a distant memory, a story to be pulled out when the family gathered at holiday time, Leah's teenage rebellion good for a laugh.

Twenty-Four

In Leah's Wake

According to the emergency room doctor, Justine's mother's injuries were relatively mild. Their mother, Leah told Justine the following morning, had joked about how dumb she had been, jogging in the dark. Her leg hurt, she'd said, but it wasn't too bad. In a few days, everyone agreed, she would be up and around. By that afternoon, when Justine arrived home from school, her mom's knee had swollen to the size of a small beach ball and she could hardly talk, her face sallow, pinched. Justine burst into tears. When she was ten, Justine had fallen off the jungle gym at her school, spraining her ankle, and she remembered clearly how much pain she had been in.

Her mom was in worse shape, it turned out, than the ER doctors suspected. The orthopedist Justine's father consulted the day after the accident ordered an MRI. The test confirmed the original diagnosis, a hairline fracture of the tibia bone, a minor problem, requiring a cast for four weeks. She had also strained the anterior cruciate ligament in her knee. Freak accident, the orthopedist said. She'd fallen just the right way. Unfortunately, there was no quick fix. For now, he preferred to watch it. That night, surfing the Net, researching ligament injuries, Justine learned that, if her mother lost the stability in her knee, she might need surgery. Until her next visit with the orthopedist, her mother was to stay off her feet and elevate the leg. Her doctor prescribed OxyContin to help her manage the pain, told Justine's father to order a wheelchair.

Three days after the accident, at six in the morning, her dad's boss sent him an e-mail message, informing him of a company-wide management meeting Mr. Jackman had called to address the

223

Micronics issue. Her father, of course, had no choice except to attend. The visiting nurse he'd hired to care for Justine's mom during the day was unable to start until the following week. If they had notified her father a day in advance of the meeting, he would have arranged for a neighbor to stay at the house. Reluctantly, at Justine's insistence, he allowed her to stay home with her mom. Justine rarely missed school. With five honors classes, she could not afford to fall behind in her work. But she never could have concentrated on her studies today, knowing that her mom was home alone, barely able to move, and Leah was isolating herself in her room.

Justine was sitting, with Dog, on the family room floor, by the sofa where her mother was dozing, half of her watching *Fire Starter* on cable, the other half daydreaming. She'd made the first major decision of her life, today: she decided, when she was older, to be a physician. Since the accident, Justine had been spending all her spare time on the Internet, surfing medical websites. Her initial research on ACL injuries had led her to a site hosted by the Yale Medical School's anatomy department, where she learned that the quadriceps and hamstring muscles stabilize the knee. The site provided detailed pictures of the human body and its systems. Hoping to contribute in some way to her mother's recovery, Justine undertook a study of the body's muscular structure. The human body, she'd discovered, has six hundred skeletal muscles. Muscles work in pairs (one contracting while the opposing muscle relaxes), and are attached directly or indirectly to bones. So far, Justine had learned the names and functions of fifty of the body's six hundred skeletal muscles, but *that*, she bragged to her dog, just as the doorbell rang, was only the beginning.

She was vaguely surprised to see Officer Johnson on the stoop, though she wasn't really sure why. He was the officer in charge of investigating her mother's accident, after all.

"Hello, Justine," Officer Johnson said. "How are all you Tylers today?"

"We're fine," said Justine uncertainly. "What can I do for you, Officer?"

"If she's around, I'd like to talk to your sister. I came to see how she's doing."

"I'll get her," Justine replied, not at all sure Leah would agree to come down. Her sister had not left her room since their parents returned from the orthopedist's office, two days earlier.

Justine found her sister curled in the corner of her bed, wearing nothing but black silk panties, washed to translucence, and a rumpled blue T-shirt, her button bracelet encircling her wrist like a flexible handcuff. The policeman's leather jacket covered Leah's lower legs, the grimy soles of her feet poking out from under the waistband.

"Lee?" Justine nudged Leah's shoulder. "That policeman's here. He wants to see you."

Leah's foot moved slightly, under the jacket.

"The policeman's here, Lee. What do you want me to tell him?"

Nothing.

"Lee," Justine said again, shaking her sister's foot. "What do you want me to say?"

In one violent motion, Leah scooped up the jacket and hurled it at Justine, the bomber slapping Justine in the chest. "Take it," she cried. "And tell that fucking cop to get lost."

The incident with the cop left Justine off balance. To clear her head, she took Dog outside to do her business. For ten minutes, Justine watched Dog race around the yard, darting in and out of the woods. Justine hated to call the dog she was having such fun, so she snuck inside alone.

Justine's mother lay on the sofa, her head and feet propped on goose-down bed pillows, a third, smaller pillow rolled under her knees. She blinked up at Justine, motioning for the bottle of pills on the coffee table. Justine fed her mother a pill, and brought a glass of water to her mouth, encouraging her mother to drink. Her mother took one short swallow, and closed her eyes. Justine covered her mom with the mohair blanket, and switched off the TV. When she was sure that her mom was asleep, she went to the kitchen, to fix a turkey sandwich for her sister.

"Leah?" She knocked, waited briefly for a response, and opened the door. "Hungry?"

"Go away," Leah croaked, burying her face in a pillow.

Justine set the plate on her sister's nightstand and padded to the window, lifted Leah's shades, letting some daylight into the room. "Oh, my God. Look at *Dog*," she said, amused. "You've got to see this, Lee." Dog raced across the backyard, chasing a squirrel. "She's going nuts out there." It was good to see Dog running around. All the poor thing seemed to do lately was sleep. "Wake up, Lee. Come on. You've got to eat something."

Justine stole a potato chip from her sister's plate, and popped it in her mouth. "At least drink the Pepsi," she said, and lowered herself to the floor, by Leah's bed. She crossed her legs, Indian-style, took a handful of chips, and started talking—about nothing, really. The weather: Cold again. Her geometry teacher: Kind of a dope. *Silas Marner*, the book she was supposed to be reading for English. "It's so *bor*ing, Lee. I hate it. Why can't they assign fun books? Like *Harry Potter*. Or *Lord of the Rings*? I'm not finishing it," she announced.

Leah rolled over, a palm shielding her eyes from the light. "Why are you *do*ing this?"

"What?"

"Bitching. You're like a reading machine."

Justine shrugged. "I want to pick my own books." She hated being told what to read.

Snorting, Leah pushed herself up, her T-shirt crawling up with her, exposing a path of downy blond hair that began at her belly ring and snaked under the waistband of her panties. "Get used to it," she said. "They never let you pick your own books. Hey, can I have that Pepsi?"

Justine unscrewed the cap. "Mom seems a little better," she said, hoping she might finally be able to draw Leah out. "She watched TV for a while today."

Leah took a sip of the Pepsi, set the bottle on her nightstand, and picked at her nails. "I can't do this, Jus."

"What do you mean?" Justine asked, alarmed.

"I shouldn't have come back here."

"Because of Dad?" Their father had been cool toward Leah since the morning after the accident. He hadn't said anything directly, his not addressing the problem indicating his anger.

"Not just him, Jus." Yes, Leah hated fighting with their parents, walking on eggshells, always worried that she'd say or do something to set them off. "Mom's accident. It's my fault."

Justine climbed onto the bed, next to her sister. "It was an accident, Lee. Nobody's *fault*."

"You know as well as I do, she was out there, running, because of me."

"That doesn't make it your fault."

"I broke up with him," she mumbled, her words directed at her feet. "I couldn't sleep."

"Oh, Lee." Justine wanted to hug her sister, to let her know she wasn't alone, but she could see that a hug was not what Leah needed right now. She needed a sympathetic ear.

It was the right thing to do, Leah told her. It was time for her to pull herself together, get her life on track. As long as she was with Todd, nothing would change. She'd called him this morning, before he left for work. They'd talked for over an hour. "He kept repeating himself. Saying he loves me." He tried to convince her to change her mind. "He cried, Jus. Like a little kid. It was so *hard*." She took hold of Justine's hand. "But I've got to make this right. I can't have you guys hating me, Jus. I just want things to be the way they used to be."

Justine's eyes welled. She would be lying if she didn't admit that she was angry with Leah, for running away, for abandoning her, for all the trouble she'd caused. But Justine was proud of her sister, too. She heard the catch in Leah's voice. She saw the pain in her sister's eyes when she talked about Todd. "I could never hate you," Justine said, her own voice breaking.

Together, they decided Leah would talk to their parents tonight. She would apologize, tell them she'd broken up with Todd. She would let them know she regretted all the mistakes she had made. She would promise to be good from now on. She would ask if they could all start over.

Leah twiddled her belly ring. "The truth, Jus. You really think this'll work?"

After dinner, Justine scooted back upstairs, to her sister's room. Leah had changed into a pair of Levi jeans and a clean white T-shirt, the words, "Sexy Babe," scripted in blue sparkles across her chest. She was sitting on the edge of her bed, staring blankly at her feet or possibly at a speck of dirt on the floor. Justine's heart sank. She was afraid her sister had lost her nerve, that she'd decided not to apologize. Apologies were risky business. Adults could never be satisfied with a simple apology. To grownups, an apology was like a victory, a chance to pile on.

Leah giggled when she caught sight of Justine's face, and tussled Justine's hair. "Don't be so paranoid. I was just thinking." She'd been rehearsing what she wanted to say, psyching herself up. She never heard Justine enter. "Ick." She wrinkled her nose. "The house reeks from that codfish Dad made. Glad I'm not hungry tonight. So what do you think, Jus? How are they?"

"Good," Justine replied. "Mom ate a cup of soup. They're watching TV."

With her baby finger, Leah hooked Justine's pinky. "Wish me luck."

Justine followed Leah to the landing, and lowered herself onto the top step. "Oh my God," she prayed, squeezing her eyes shut, her hands folded nervously in her lap. *Let this work.*

227

Her sister approached their parents respectfully. Leah asked if she could please talk to them for a minute. Their mother invited her into the family room, and their father turned off the TV. Justine breathed a sigh of relief. Thank goodness. They were off to a positive start.

"Contract?" Justine heard Leah say, a minute later. "I told you we broke up. Isn't that good enough?"

"A guarantee," their father roared. "In writing."

Their mother, through her stupor, objected. This was a family meeting, not some war tribunal. Supposed to trust one another, she said, her words slurred. Without trust, what good was a piece of paper?

"For Christ's sake. Zoe," her father shouted, his voice cutting right through Justine. "Didn't you hear me on the phone? I'm not putting up with this shit anymore. You tell that kid," he said, redirecting the onslaught at Leah, "he calls again, I'll put his scrawny ass in a sling."

"Todd called?" Her sister, Justine could tell, was shocked. "When? What for?"

"Jesus, Zoe? You hear that? Talk about trust. She probably put him up to it."

"No," Leah protested. "Honest. I had no idea he called."

"Piece of shit," their father said, talking over Leah. "Kid calls here, acting like he gives a damn how your mother's doing. Tell her I asked for her," their father said, mimicking Todd, his voice high like a girl's. "Next thing I know, he's badgering me, telling me he loves my daughter. He's changed. He's nothing like he used to be. What's the asshole think? I'm a moron?"

Justine covered her ears. Still, she heard the voices churning, her family tearing one another apart.

"Out of here," Leah stammered, her voice choked with tears. "Can't take this anymore."

Will, stop," her mother pleaded, her thin voice careening out of control. "Leah, too."

"For God's sake, Zoe," their father kept saying. "They planned this. Can't you see that? I'm telling you, this kid can't be trusted. Wants to live under this roof, she'll sign the contract."

"Not signing—"

"Freaking kid calls, trying to round up sympathy. And she pretends they broke up."

"I did break up with him. Why won't you listen to me? We didn't plan anything."

"And we're supposed to let the two of them carry on like nothing happened," their father shouted. "Listen up, sister. You can tell that Corbett your little plan backfired."

"I hate you," Leah screamed, kicking something—a table, a chair, maybe the wall. "I hate you. I hate you both." Something thudded to the floor. "I wish you were *dead.*"

Silence descended over the house. Then Leah was hurtling out of the room.

Every year, from the time Justine was a toddler until she was eight, her family rented a summerhouse on Squam Lake. Justine and Leah spent the weekdays with their mom, in New Hampshire, while their dad, in Massachusetts, was working. The owners of the cottage moored an outboard motorboat by their dock. Their mother never unlatched the boat. She was not a strong enough swimmer, she said. In case of an accident, how would she save two little girls?

Weekends, their father would unmoor the motorboat, take the family for long, fast rides on the lake, the boat crashing over the waves, the water splashing like rain. Leah, in the bow with their parents, would hang on the back of their chairs, begging to steer, her bright blue life vest slipping over one shoulder, her bikini bottoms riding over her butt cheeks. Justine never cared to drive. She would spread her towel over the deck in the stern, lie on her belly, sunning her back, watching the motor cut through the water, the waves churning behind them. Justine felt sorry, back then, for the fish, their habitat all agitated, roiling. Now, here they were, in Leah's wake, living just the same way. She had no idea how to save her family. What they would do. How they would survive.

Twenty-Five

Sisters III

With their mother laid up, Justine went into overdrive, trying to help. She did her own chores as well as her sister's, kept her mom as comfortable as possible, took care of the house. After school, when the bus dropped her off, instead of stopping at Holly's house, hanging out until dinner, she went directly home, started supper, washed and folded the laundry, cleaned the kitchen and bathrooms, damp-mopped the floors. She didn't mind that no one noticed. Helping her mom, covering for Leah helped maintain some semblance of peace in the house, and peace was worth double the effort, she felt. Don't get her wrong: It would be nice if someone said thank you, on occasion. If her mother tried to wean herself off the pills. If her father came home from work on time, for a change, so they could eat dinner together. Instead, she put his food in the microwave. In the morning, she would find his dish in the sink, and he would be gone.

A week after the accident, Justine's father hired a carpenter to build an office over their garage. He called a plumber to install a bathroom, ordered a cot. Justine had seen him browsing the Internet, looking at shelving, paint colors, hardware. Evidently, he planned to live there.

Leah's birthday, on the twenty-first of November, came and went with little ado. Their father gave her four CDs (which Leah immediately exchanged) and an iPod with headphones that she wore morning and night. No one bothered with cake. Technically, Leah was living at home, but she was rarely around. Her sister, Justine suspected, was spending her time at Hope's, though Justine had no way of knowing for sure; nobody asked. On the rare occasions when

Leah *was* home, she moped around the house, acting all angry and hurt, refusing to talk. Plainly, she didn't want to be here. Justine often heard Leah, alone in her room, crying. She wanted desperately to console her, to let her sister know someone cared. When Justine knocked on Leah's door, her sister shooed her away.

Two days before Thanksgiving, Nana and Poppa Tyler called, and offered to drive up from Philly to spend the holiday with them. They would arrive on Tuesday afternoon, they said, and stay through the following week, if that would help. Nana would cook dinner. Poppa, who'd taken up baking after he retired, would bake the holiday pies. After her father hung up the phone, he and Justine had gone shopping, to purchase the supplies on her grandparents' list. They drove to the Stop & Shop in Ayer, picked up dry goods and cranberry sauce. At the Natural Grocer, they bought a twenty-five-pound free-range turkey, an assortment of vegetables and fruit. While her father organized the pantry, Justine washed the linens, and made the bed in the guest room.

The night before her grandparents were due to arrive, Justine heard her parents fighting. Her father, in fit of frustrated anger, threatened divorce. The next morning, he called his parents, asked if they would mind postponing their trip until after the first of the year. "My wife isn't up for company right now," Justine heard him say. But what about us? she thought. *What about me?*

Thanksgiving dinner was a total disaster. The dinner she and father made was disgusting: dried-out turkey ("big freaking waste," her father muttered, scrubbing the pan, *four bucks a pound*), a boring mushroom and artichoke stuffing in a casserole dish, limp gray string beans, and lumpy mashed potatoes, the garlic overpowering the potato. They forgot the cranberry sauce. At her father's insistence, they ate together, at the dining room table, her mom nodding off every few minutes, Leah pushing the vegetables around her plate, barely eating, no one saying a word.

Justine's mother continued to rely on the OxyContin her orthopedist had prescribed. According to his nurse (Justine heard her dad telling her grandmother on the phone), her mom shouldn't need drugs anymore. After her father clicked off, her parents had their worst argument yet, her mother, through a jag of tears, demanding to know why he'd spread those dreadful lies about her to his mother, Justine's father insisting it was out of concern. Exasperated, he pounded the counter. "Time to snap out of it, Zoe." There was no getting through to her, though.

Justine soon grew tired of taking care of the whole house by herself. No one noticed all she had done; now, no one noticed all she left undone. After school, she dragged herself to her room, where she spent her afternoons and most of her nights at her desk, with Dog at her feet, surfing the Web, researching facts for her Milky Way project. She'd given up on being a doctor.

On Thanksgiving day, Justine's friend's stepfather had wound lights around the columns on their front porch, and Holly's mom had put electric candles in all their windows. A huge pine wreath, adorned with a red satin bow, hung over the Begley's garage. And a glittering electric menorah decorated the Lieberman's front yard. The Sunday after Thanksgiving, the Girl Scouts strung lights on the giant spruce tree on the common. Gradually, twinkling holiday lights had gone up all over town.

In the past, in the weeks leading to Christmas, the entire Tyler family had pitched in with the holiday preparations. Justine and Leah helped their mother shop and bake cookies and address the holiday cards. Their father, in charge of the tree, trekked from nursery to nursery, traveling as far as New Hampshire some years, in search of the biggest, fullest tree he could find. Her father would haul the tree home, tied with a bungee cord to the roof of her mother's car, drag it up the back steps, across the deck, and into the family room, where he would eyeball the space, making weird faces until he'd found the best spot to erect it. Every year, the spot he chose was exactly the same as the spot he'd chosen the previous year: three feet to the left of the fireplace, so you would see the tree as soon as you entered the kitchen, no matter how you approached.

Now, the white lights her father always strung through the bushes in the front yard were packed away in a box. The banisters, normally festooned with holly, were bare. They'd gotten no tree. Justine's father kept promising to buy one, but whenever she asked, he said he'd forgot.

On Saturday morning, Justine took it upon herself to decorate. She carried the Nativity set, stored in a cardboard box filled with packaging peanuts, down from the attic. She unpacked the rustic wooden stable, set it on the family room mantle, sliding it left and right, until it was centered. She cut a brown paper bag into thin strips, making straw to line the stable's cracked wooden floor, and unpacked the people. Over the years, the shepherds and Wise Men had vanished, leaving only a miniscule Jesus, a cherubic infant lying in a manger the size of Justine's thumb, a seven-inch ceramic Mary, in a lustrous sky blue robe, her blue veil trimmed in white, and a featureless Joseph, carved from wood, several inches shorter than his dazzling wife.

Justine unraveled the artificial holly, wove the silk strands through the banisters in the hallway leading upstairs. Last year's ribbons hadn't fared all that well. She tugged the flat, wire-reinforced loops into reasonably good shape, attached them to the newel posts with garbage bag ties. When she'd finished decorating the landing, she went to her bedroom to check on the dog.

Dog lay at the foot of the bed, nuzzled on Justine's bathrobe.

"Hey, baby." She waved a rawhide treat in front of Dog's nose. "Hungry, my sweet?"

Dog lifted her head groggily, licked the rawhide, and settled down on the bed.

As usual, her father had left for work early. Her mom and Leah were still in bed. Justine enjoyed the quiet, her mind wandering freely, thinking of nothing, really. In the kitchen, she prepared apples for crisp. When she finished peeling the apples, she sliced them into a bowl, added cinnamon and sugar, scooped the fruit into a buttered Pyrex dish. The apples looked skimpy. She peeled and cut two more. In a clean bowl, she measured the flour and oatmeal, added a stick of butter, pinching the butter into the flour until she had crumbs, sprinkled the crumbs over the apples, and brought the Pyrex dish to the oven, and slid it inside.

Maybe she and Leah could go to the nursery together, when Leah woke up. Leah didn't have her license yet. If they paid for the gas, maybe Hope could borrow her mother's car, give them a ride. They would select the fullest, prettiest tree on the lot, a tree so magnificently tall, it would stretch, like the tree in the *Nutcracker*, to the family room ceiling. Justine had saved her birthday money and most of her allowance; she had three hundred dollars stashed in her bureau. Plenty of money, she thought. If she had money left over, she would buy a wreath for the door.

"Morning, sweetheart. Looks gorgeous around here."

Justine spun around, startled by her mother's voice. It was barely eight thirty. For as long as Justine could remember, her mother had been an early riser. Justine, an early bird herself, would wake at dawn, find her mother in the living room, reading a book or staring into space, daydreaming. These days, her mom slept late, especially on weekends. Justine hadn't expected to see her for another hour.

"Thanks, Momma," she replied. "I made apple crisp. Are you hungry?"

Her mother propped her crutches against the center island, and lowered herself onto a barstool. "Not yet," she said. "It smells awfully good."

Justine's mom set her elbows on the counter. She was dressed in the threadbare terrycloth robe she'd been wearing for years, a washed-out violet color, cinched at the waist. Despite the robe, she looked different this morning, though Justine could not quite put her finger on how. She'd combed her hair. Maybe that was what it was. "How about some coffee?" Justine asked.

"Sure, honey. That would be great."

At half-past eleven, Leah clopped down the stairs. She'd borrowed Justine's baby doll pajamas. Her sister looked silly, Justine thought. The bright pink pajamas clashed with her hair. Two days ago, just as it finally started looking decent again, Leah dyed her hair a hideous rust-orange red.

"Aren't you cold?" Justine was wearing a thermal T-shirt and a long-sleeved cotton turtleneck under her angora sweater, with fleece-lined jeans. Even in layers, she was freezing.

Leah finger-combed her stubbly orange hair. "Never, little sister. I don't get cold. So what's up with Dog? How come she's not down here?"

Justine frowned. She didn't know, really. Dog was lazy today. "Maybe she's tired. Do you think it's normal for her to sleep so much?"

"How should I know? She *is* pretty old."

Dog wasn't old. She was only thirteen, a few months older than Justine. That was not *old*.

Leah pranced across the kitchen, flung open the pantry doors, plucked a box of cream of wheat cereal from the shelf, and turned the box on its side, inspecting the ingredient list. "Did you know cream of wheat's got thiamin mononitrate in it?"

Justine had no clue what thiamin mono—whatever Leah had said—even was.

Some additive shit. "I thought this crap was supposed to be good for you."

"Maybe that thiamono-nono stuff is a vitamin."

"Maybe," Leah said doubtfully. "But I'm not eating this crap. I don't believe in eating anything that isn't one hundred percent natural. It's against my religion."

"Since when?" Leah always begged their mom to buy Cocoa Puffs or Fruit Loops or Trix.

Leah put her hands on her hips, the cereal box angled away from her body. "Since now. I'm gonna eat really healthy, from now on." She lowered her voice. "I quit smoking, you know."

"Seriously? That's awesome, Leah." Justine was thrilled.

"Thanks," Leah replied, with a self-satisfied nod. "Starting today. Actually, I've been thinking about joining a commune. I found this really cool community on the Internet. Anybody can join. They're like totally open-minded. It's up in Vermont. You can come, too, if you want."

Justine hedged. She loved her sister. The house felt empty when Leah wasn't around. But a commune? Communes were filthy, with all those people living under one roof. Besides, Justine was only twelve. She was supposed to live at home. "I don't know. Maybe when I'm older."

"Come on, Jus. You don't want to croak, eating all this rotten stuff, do you? Want to know what I think? Why they put all this crap in our food?" Leah sent the cereal box sailing across the counter; it landed with a soft thud on the floor. "The rich dudes, right? Like in the Senate and shit, the ones that run the big corporations? They're trying to get rid of the rest us. So they can rule the world. Think about it. They radiate the food they ship out here from California, right? Like veggies and fruit. They're preserving your food with the same shit they use to make atom bombs. Don't believe me, if you don't want to. I'm telling you, they're trying to kill us."

Leah returned to the pantry, reappeared a minute later, waving a box of Mallow Treats cereal. "Look at this. I bet Mom doesn't know he buys this crap. Wait a minute. *You* didn't tell him to get it?" she asked, in a tone Justine found insulting. "You don't *eat* this stuff? Do you?"

Justine cringed, afraid of what her sister would come up with next.

Leah tugged Justine's arm. "Look." She pointed to the ingredient list. "Marshmallow, sugar, gelatin, artificial flavoring, color added." Emphasis on the word "color." "Malodextrin. That's another kind of sugar, in case you were wondering. I don't know why they can't just say it outright, so you know what you're eating. Look, sugar again. That'd be the real sugar. Partially hydrogenated soybean oil, salt, natural and artificial flavoring. What exactly is natural flavoring? Isn't that like an oxymoron or something?" Leah clucked her tongue. "High fructose corn syrup, malt flavoring. This shit's bad, Jus. I don't know which is worse, the artificial shit or all that sugar.

Your stomach's probably poisoned. Imagine what your intestines must look like?"

"I never thought about it," Justine replied, nervously considering the state of her innards.

"I'm telling you, dude. I wouldn't trust anything that came out of a box."

"Want me to make you some eggs? Eggs are good, aren't they?"

"Cholesterol? I don't think so." Justine could see her sister's brain working. She hoped Leah didn't ask for some weird ingredient they didn't have, like tofu, for instance. "Oh, why not," Leah said, finally. "Bacon, too. As long as it's not that turkey crap Mom used to buy."

When Leah finished eating, she put her plate in the dishwasher, and helped Justine clean the kitchen. While Leah washed the pans, Justine scrubbed the stainless steel stovetop.

Leah flung the dishrag on the counter, and shook out her hands. "Who's *she* talking to?" She cocked her head, tipping it toward the family room. "Can you hear?"

Justine pricked up her ears. Their mother was talking about her knee. As long as her strength returned, she said, it didn't look as though she would need surgery. Their mother lowered her voice. Justine winced. The conversation must have shifted to Leah.

"I don't believe this." Leah slapped the counter. "It's that *cop*."

"No way," Justine replied. "Why would she be talking to him?"

In fact, their mom talked to Officer Johnson every day. If Leah were around more often, she would know. At first, Justine thought it was nice, Officer Johnson's taking a personal interest in their family. Now, almost a month after the accident, she was starting to think it was weird. Justine never mentioned the calls to her sister. Leah had it in for Officer Johnson. It was almost as if she blamed him for her problems with their parents, which made no sense at all.

"Yeah, it's him. I heard her say his name. What's she talking to *him* for?"

"Maybe he wants to make sure it was really an accident. That nobody hit her."

"Didn't they determine that already?"

Justine squirmed. She wished her sister would let this go, talk about something else. "I don't think it's him, Lee. I think it's one of her friends, from work."

"Sure. So where's the D-man?" Leah bent over the counter, scrubbing aggressively. "Give me an SOS. There's something disgusting stuck on here. Dried beans or something."

Justine fished an SOS pad out of the box. "Dad's at work."

"On a Saturday? He's avoiding us, Jus. The way they've been going at it, lately, it won't surprise me if they got a divorce. I've heard them both threaten. More than one time."

A sharp pain shot through Justine's belly and under her rib cage. She doubled over, clutching her stomach. "He's working," she said, once the pain faded. "He had to return calls."

"Since when does he call people on Saturday? You're so *gullible*, Justine. If he had to make calls, he could do it from here. He's got that stupid office over the garage now." Leah rubbed the counter with the steel wool pad, set the steel wool aside and worked at the spot with her thumbnail. "Not that I blame him for wanting to get away. She's like addicted to those stupid pills. I bet she called that cop," Leah spat. "The phone never rang. What a jerk."

Please, Justine thought. *Stop.* "The phone did ring. I heard it," she lied.

Leah gave her a dubious look. Well, anyway, she countered, that wasn't the point. "By the way, what's wrong with your stomach? You're not on that Zantac again, are you? Oh my god, *I* know." Leah shook Justine's arm. "You're getting your period," she said, dancing in a circle around Justine. "Aren't you? You *are*. My baby sister's finally getting her period."

If only she was. Justine was practically the only girl in the entire eighth grade who didn't have her period. Leah wouldn't let up. To change the subject, Justine said, "We should get a tree today. Don't you think? If we wait for Dad, it'll be New Year's."

That got Leah off on a whole other tangent, giving Justine a few minutes of peace.

"So," Leah said. She was perched on a barstool at the island, laboring over a crossword puzzle, picking at the bowl of apple crisp, while Justine finished the rest of her homework for math. Their mother had fallen asleep on the family room sofa. Leah had called Hope, fifteen minutes ago, to see if she'd drive them to a nursery to pick out a tree, but Hope, it emerged, was out for the day. "Jus?" Leah scribbled an answer to one of the questions, crossed it out, and wrote another answer above it. "Why do you think they hate him so much?" She meant Todd.

Leah knew very well why their parents hated her ex-boyfriend. First, he'd encouraged Leah to run away. Second, since they began dating, Leah was constantly in trouble. Third, the kid was defiant. He stopped by the house one day, after the accident, when Leah wasn't around, supposedly to visit their mother. He'd given their mom a bouquet of fresh flowers, asked a lot of questions about her injuries, how she was feeling. The second she dropped her guard, the wheedling started. He said the same things he'd said to their father, when he called that day. He tried to talk her into allowing Leah to see him, told her how sorry he was, said he'd never meant to hurt Leah. He pointed out all the ways he had changed. Her father happened to come home while Todd was still at the house. Todd refused to look at him, a tactic even Justine found offensive. It was hardly the way to win their father's approval. All the same, their parents went overboard, blaming him for any little thing Leah did wrong. Her sister was seventeen, too old for her parents to be blaming other people for her behavior. Leah was responsible for herself. It dawned on Justine, suddenly: Todd and her sister had never stopped dating. He hadn't called the house in awhile, and Justine had assumed that they'd stayed broken up. He must have been calling Leah's cell phone. "You're not back together? How could you, Lee? After what he did to you?" The day they broke up, Leah had told Justine what had transpired that night at the orchard.

Leah sniggered. "We broke up, for like two *days*. It was stupid. I mean it was mostly my fault. I'm the one who made him pull over. Besides, he said he was sorry." With her fingers, she picked a gooey apple out of the bowl. "They're crazy if they think they can keep me away from him. I'm stuck here right now. I don't feel like going back to Hope's and I don't have anywhere else to go. Believe me, the second I turn eighteen, I'm out of here."

"You'd do that again? You'd leave me alone?"

"Alone?" their mother echoed. She stood awkwardly on her crutches, her shoulder leaning against one of the columns in the archway between the family room and the kitchen. "Did I hear somebody say something about leaving?"

"Hi, Mom," Justine said.

"So what's going on?"

Leah sniggered.

"Justine?"

"Nothing," Justine answered. "Feel better? Want us to take you for a walk?"

Her mother massaged her neck. "I have a headache. I do feel a little better, though."

"You guys aren't seriously going outside, are you?" Leah pointed at the window over the sink. "Look out there. We're supposed to get like six inches of snow."

Justine glanced obediently at the window. Wind shook the tiny dogwood tree their father had planted in the backyard the year before last, bending its trunk nearly in two.

"I wouldn't go out there. You might get caught in a snowstorm."

"It's not supposed to snow till tonight," Justine said. "Why don't you come with us, Lee? You could push the wheelchair."

"That's a great idea," their mother said. "We hardly see you lately."

"I don't know." Leah poked the cabinet with the nubs of her toes. "Maybe. I guess so."

"Honey," her mother said, once Leah was gone. "Could you get my sweats? They should be in the laundry room. On top of the dryer." When Justine returned with her mom's sweatpants, her mother said, "Your father isn't avoiding us, honey. He's busy with work. That's all it is."

Justine glanced nervously at the hallway. "I know."

"By the way, sweetie. Where's Dog? I haven't seen her all day."

"Up in my room."

Justine's mother untied her robe, and Justine helped her into her sweatpants.

"I tried to get her to come down," Justine said. "She didn't want to budge."

"Has she gone out today?"

For about two seconds, Justine reported. Dog scooted to the trees at the back of the yard, ran right back, and sat on the steps, crying, until Justine let her in. She'd peed. Justine didn't think she'd had time to do number two. "I don't know what's wrong with her, Mom. All she wants to do lately is sleep. She won't even fetch when I toss her the ball."

"She's thirteen, honey. She's getting old."

Justine lifted her eyes, fighting back tears. "Why does everybody keep saying she's old?

"Why don't we take her with us," her mother suggested. "The walk will do her good."

Dog lay at the foot of Justine's bed. She hadn't budged since Justine checked on her, hours ago. Justine ruffled her ears, joggling her bright red collar. Dog lifted her head, yawning.

"Go for a walk, Puppy?" Justine cooed, and patted the bed. "Come on, girl."

Dog hobbled off the bed. Justine stroked Dog's head, and, taking hold of her collar, pulled her gently toward the steps. It wasn't fair that animals had such a short lifespan. Parakeets lived for only five or six years, goldfish for just a few months. Even horses had a shorter lifespan than people. When they were little, Justine and Leah had hamsters. Their parents bought the hamsters all sorts of paraphernalia: mirrors and tunnels and exercise balls. They even bought a rubber mouse, so the hamsters would think they had friends. That made no difference, however. The dinky gray ones had been particularly prone to disaster. The hamsters kept dying and Justine's father kept buying new ones. One day, their mother insisted he stop. "This is too hard on Justine," her mom said, "she gets too attached." To be honest, Justine wasn't all that fond of the hamsters. She'd cried because crying, she thought, was expected. Dog was different. Justine scratched the old Lab's ear and Dog bounded down the stairs after her. Dog was her friend.

Justine's mom was resting on a barstool when Justine led Dog into the kitchen. Her mother did reasonably well with the crutches. She could do almost everything now, except activities that required her to stand for a long period of time or that needed two hands. She also needed help navigating stairs. Justine put her arms around her mom, and lifted her to her feet.

Leah was waiting for them in the back hall, snapping her fingers, reciting the words to a rap tune. Justine did a double take. Her sister had changed into a pair of flannel pajamas, an ugly red and green plaid, that Justine would swear belonged to Todd.

"Pajamas, Leah?" their mother said. "Can't you dress like a normal person for once?"

Leah extended her leg, gathering a wad of fabric. "What's wrong with them?" she asked, as if she honestly did not understand. "They're no worse than those clown pants you have on."

Their mother let out a sigh and shook her head.

In the garage, Justine lowered her mom to the top step of the utility stairs, pressed the button, raising the garage door, and, rounding her mother's car, went to the back of the garage, where the wheelchair was stored. She unfolded the chair, pushed it to the stairs, and helped her mother into the chair.

The wind had died down, the air brittle. Her mom drew a black, knitted cap out of the pocket of her down vest, pulled it over her head. She looked like a dork in the cap, which she'd managed to pull over her eyebrows. Justine tugged the cap, combed her mom's brows into place.

It had snowed twice this week, a dusting both times. Although the driveway was not particularly steep, it was slippery and long.

Justine should have worn her snow boots. Grasping the handles behind her mom's shoulders, she pushed the chair up their hilly drive, leaning forward, into the grade. She was out of breath by the time they reached the cul-de-sac.

The Ridley girls across the way shot across their front yard. The girls reminded her of herself and Leah when they were younger, always playing together. Justine waved and headed down the street, Leah zigzagging down the road, dragging Dog with her. Leah dropped the leash and swung her arms, side-to-side, fists slicing the air like a speed walker, carrying weights.

"What's she doing?" their mom asked.

Who knew? "Hey," Justine called. Leah had gained ten yards on them. "Wait up."

Leah spun around, arms frozen in mid-air. She looked comical, really, in her goofy clothes, doing silly things to draw attention to herself.

Dog stood at the end of the Begley's driveway, sniffing the snow. An engine rumbled, and Mr. Begley backed his Jaguar out of the drive.

A schnauzer dashed out of the Begley's garage, chasing the car. Dog trailed after her.

"Leah," Justine hollered. "Get Dog. Her leash. She's gonna get hit."

Leah crouched, coughing. "Here, Dog," she called. "Let's go, Pups."

Dog skidded to a stop, planting her paws.

"Come on, Dog." Leah extracted a piece of cheese from the pocket of her pajamas. "Come to Lee-Lee." Dog scooted across the street. As she closed in on the cheese, Leah jacked up her hand. Dog jumped, not quite high enough to reach the cheese, and flopped back down.

"Cut it out, Leah," Justine said, and brought the chair to a halt. "You'll tire her out."

"What are you talking about?" Leah dangled the cheese. "Dogs are supposed to jump. It's like their job. Come on, Dog," she said, again. "Jump."

Dog wheezed.

"Stop that," their mother scolded. "You're right, honey. This is too much for Dog."

Leah broke the cheese into two pieces, hid her hands behind her back. Dog nudged Leah's leg. Leah bolted, Dog at her heels, wheeled around, and skated back toward the wheelchair. A yard or two from the wheelchair, Leah hit a patch of ice and pitched forward, slamming into Justine.

"Oh no," Justine cried, grasping futilely at the air. Her feet slipped out from under her, and she lurched forward, arms flailing, and landed on Dog, who let out a wounded yelp.

"You OK?" Leah grabbed Justine's hand, pulling her up. "Didn't mean to run into you."

Justine gasped for breath. Falling knocked the wind out of her. She brushed herself off.

"Sure you're all right, honey?" her mother asked, twisting in her chair until she was facing Justine. She offered her hand, though Justine didn't need it. "You took a pretty good fall."

"I'm sorry," Leah said again, her eyes filling. "I didn't mean it. Honest. I'm sorry."

"You shouldn't tease like that," their mother scolded. "Somebody could have been hurt."

"Sorry," Leah mumbled, her entire face downcast. "That was dumb."

Justine wasn't hurt, really. Her knee stung a little, from hitting the ground. Their mom was making too big a fuss. Justine felt bad for Leah. Her sister looked as if she were about to cry. "I'm fine," Justine told her. "It was an accident." She stretched, arching backward, turning left, and right. "Hey," she said, suddenly realizing that her puppy was missing. "Where's Dog?"

"Don't know," Leah said. "Did you see her, Ma?"

Their mother shook her head.

Justine scanned the neighboring yards. No sign of Dog. "Leah," Justine said. "Could you take Mom home? I'm gonna go look for her."

"Sure," Leah said, exchanging an indecipherable look with their mother. "No prob."

Justine cupped her hands over her mouth. "Dog," she called. "Dog?"

Justine headed down the street first. She stopped in front of each house, calling Dog's name. Maybe Dog had gone home, she thought, switching direction. The Ridley girls were still playing. They hadn't seen her, they said. Justine had fallen hard on poor Dog. She hoped she hadn't hurt her. The whole thing happened so fast. She'd lost her balance. She hadn't realized she was falling until it was too late. She couldn't do anything about it. Dog was in the way.

A half hour later, disheartened, Justine gave up, and headed for home.

She was standing by the window in the dinette, her mind wandering, when she spotted the old Lab, lying under the oak tree beneath Leah's window. Dog must have fled through the neighbors' yard, then cut through the thicket near the top of their drive.

Dog was shivering when Justine reached her. Justine shot into the house, snagged a blanket from the sofa, and raced back outside, draped the blanket over her trembling dog.

She placed her hand on Dog's chest. Dog's heart was racing.

Dog laid her head on Justine's lap, whimpering. Justine stroked her neck and Dog looked up at her, her red-rimmed eyes closing and opening again.

"It's okay, Puppy," Justine crooned, running her hand over and over Dog's head.

Dog licked Justine's hand. Justine picked a thorn out of the fur under her neck. "I'm gonna take you inside," she said, helping Dog to her feet. She tried to lift Dog, intending to carry her, but the dog was too heavy for Justine. "It's OK, my puppy," she said quietly. "Justine will take care of you." Taking hold of her collar, Justine led her dog into the house.

Leah and their mother must have argued after the walk. When Justine came in with Dog, her sister informed her that she was leaving. She would be out for awhile, she said. Their mother, apparently realizing at the last minute what Leah was up to, called after her, demanding to know what was going on. Leah kept walking, never turning around. The front door slammed, and their mother, talking to herself, swallowed a painkiller, and settled on the sofa, a Mozart concerto for the violin playing softly in the background. Ten minutes later, Justine heard Todd's truck in the circle. After Leah left, Justine brought Dog upstairs, to her room, and helped her onto the bed.

Justine sat by the living room window, alone, in the dark, waiting for her father to arrive. At seven, her father's car pulled into the circle. She watched the BMW roll down the hill, its headlights arcing over the lawn as it rounded the bend in their drive.

The garage door snapped up. Justine shuffled to the mudroom.

"Found a *great* one this year," her father announced, as the door swung open. The buttons of his sports jacket were undone, his tie loose. His hair was damp, his face flushed from the cold. "Best ever, Jus," he said. "It was worth the wait, baby doll. Blue spruce. This big." He stretched, reaching for the ceiling. "It's in the garage."

"I was waiting for you." She struggled to get the words out, her voice barely a whisper.

"Mom asked me to stop for a tree." He patted her head. "You all right, sweetheart?"

Justine's lips quivered.

"What happened?"

She shook her head, her throat aching.

"Wait till you see our tree." He headed toward the garage. "That'll make you feel better."

"Dad?"

Her father turned toward her. "Yes?"

"I need you to bury my dog."

Through everything that had happened with her family this fall, through all their trials and travails, her mother's retreat into the fuzzy world of her pain pills, her family's dizzying fights, even while Leah was away, though she'd missed her sister terribly, Justine had stayed strong. Now, the tears fell, releasing all that pent-up emotion. And there was no holding back.

Twenty-Six

Lonely Days Are Here Again

Zoe's younger daughter was not the same since Dog died. Justine moped around the house or sat in her bedroom, in front of her computer screen, oblivious of her surroundings. After the accident, Justine had taken over for Zoe, cooking, cleaning, doing laundry. Justine was the one person Zoe could count on to keep her company, to cheer her up when she was down. It was not fair of Zoe to depend on Justine as she had. She wished she could find a way to reach her daughter, to set things right. But the weight she'd placed on Justine's shoulders seemed to have caused some deep, irreparable damage. When Zoe spoke, Justine listened politely, and accepted Zoe's apologies, her words accompanied by a disconsolate half-smile that broke Zoe's heart.

It was time for Zoe to go back to work. She could bear the pain in her leg now, was able to get around, more or less, on her own. And the family needed the money. Since the Micronics fiasco, Will's sales had dwindled; his last commission check had barely covered their mortgage. Their savings would take them through January, if they were careful; after that, she didn't know what they would do. Either reason should have been enough to motivate her to call Jean, the secretary for the practice, ask her to start booking appointments again. The truth was, the very idea of returning to work overwhelmed her. It wasn't the workload. In her absence, a colleague had taken on Zoe's caseload, eliminating the backlog of appointments that, otherwise, would have been hanging over her head. What Zoe dreaded was the routine. She couldn't imagine spending eight or ten hours a day in an office, doing work she no longer enjoyed. It was hard to imagine how

245

she'd managed to do it for so many years. On vacation, she'd always fantasized about quitting her job, buying a Bed and Breakfast in Vermont, opening an organic restaurant, where she grew her own food. Fantasizing, for that one week, imagining herself in a new role, was the true purpose of taking a vacation, she'd felt, sort of an adult version of Disney World or Fantasy Land. Within a day or two of returning to clinic, she would be back in the swing of things, those silly notions of starting a new life set aside for another year. Now, having been away from work for over a month, she saw that these fantasies about quitting her job were not fantastic at all, but rooted in concrete desire. Funny, how different things looked from a distance.

If she had little enthusiasm for returning to her job at the clinic, she had even less for tackling the workshops. In the months before the accident, her numbers had dropped. She'd considered the falloff to be a normal, if at times disquieting, part of the business: She'd made few changes in her presentation of late, was essentially rehashing old material. Fluctuations in attendance were to be expected. Besides, she'd rationalized, the local market was not big enough to support the program long-term. If she wanted to grow, she had to start traveling. A few days before the accident, at the clinic, of all places, on her way to the restroom, she overheard Molly talking up the workshops to one of her patients. "Isn't she that soccer player's mother?" Zoe heard the woman ask. "From what I hear, she needs to get her *own* life in order."

Instinct told Zoe to confront the woman, demand to know where she'd heard such drivel, and she'd spun on her heels, about to stalk off in the direction of the voices. Fortunately, she'd taken hold of her senses, sparing herself the further humiliation of mounting too strong an objection, thus personally confirming the worst. It irked her, knowing people were judging her, boycotting her workshops because of rumors about her personal life. (Plenty of professionals, free-spending accountants, for example, offered advice they failed to follow themselves.) Part of her was tempted to restart the workshops, just to prove everyone wrong. But the thought of going through the process again, reestablishing a clientele, explaining herself, overwhelmed her.

She'd tried any number of times to discuss their work situations with Will. Her husband brushed her off. Couldn't she focus on something positive, for once? Meaning, steer clear of anything important, skate over the emotional surface. When they talked (which, lately, was rare), his end of the conversation revolved around two subjects: Sports: Would the Red Sox sign a stud in the off-season? (Too early to tell.) Would the Patriots make the Super Bowl this year? (He thought so.) And moving. He went on *ad nauseam* about moving, dropping out of the rat race, moving the kids to a healthier environment, his idea of which included only the most desolate areas of the US: Northern New Hampshire, Maine, Idaho, Montana, Wyoming. Her husband didn't want to move. He wanted to hide. She often found herself wondering if she and Will spoke the same language anymore, why they stayed married when they had so little in common.

After Will's affair, when the kids were babies, Zoe had seriously considered divorce. In the end, she'd decided to stay because saving the marriage, she'd felt, would be better for the girls. Her children needed a real father, a constant force in their lives, not a part-time dad, an interloper they would see on the weekends. To maintain her sanity, she created a calendar in her head, ticked off the days. When Justine graduated high school, she would be free. To bide time, she'd enrolled in graduate school; after grad school, she'd started her practice. With the extra money she earned, plus the additional income afforded by Will's promotions, their economic situation improved, relieving their stress, helping her to forget. Zoe was older now, stronger. This time, unless she and Will found a satisfactory way to settle their differences, Zoe would leave.

On Tuesday morning, five days before Christmas, Zoe sat, with her legs crossed, in the oversized chair by the fireplace, flipping through the stack of glossy holiday catalogs she'd been collecting, trying to motivate herself to finish the shopping. The day Dog died, Justine had set up the Nativity set, strung lights over the mantle; in the front hall, she'd threaded holly through the balustrades and banister leading upstairs. For Justine's sake, it was time for Zoe to do her share. If Leah was in a decent mood this afternoon, maybe Zoe and the girls would bake cookies. The schools, because of a teachers' workshop this afternoon, were operating on a half-day schedule today. Baking cookies would give the girls something to do. Even if they baked only a few of their favorites, sugar cookies, gingerbread, butterballs, the colorful tin cans stacked on the counter, marked "Don't touch until Christmas," would give the whole family a much needed lift.

Never the type to enjoy a day at the mall, not even with friends, Zoe dreaded buying gifts. Money was tight, but that was not the issue. She'd already justified using the credit cards this one last time. The problem was, she had no sense of what she should buy. Will was no help. He'd bought the tree and retreated. Zoe had attempted to rally the girls. She'd asked them, separately and together, what they would like for Christmas, their answers frustratingly vague.

She closed the catalogues, and opened her laptop, hoping to find inspiration online. While she was waiting for *Windows* to boot, the phone rang. Nine twenty, too early for Jerry. Jerry's daily calls were her lifeline these days. Jerry was the only person outside her immediate family who was privy to their current state of affairs. After college, her girlfriends had scattered across the country, and she'd lost contact with all but her two closest friends, their communications limited to an occasional e-mail, a birthday card, if one of them happened to remember. It took time and energy to be a good friend. With Will traveling, Zoe bore the majority of the responsibility for the house, the kids. With all that, plus her work at the counseling center, she hadn't had time, *hadn't made time*, she scolded herself, for establishing new or maintaining old friendships. Her closest friends were her colleagues at the office, and they were acquaintances, really; she would never tell them the truth about Leah. At lunch, she listened to their litany of superficial complaints. Someone's three-year-old refused to eat veggies; a third-grader was snubbed by a friend; a six-month-old had croup, and the mom hadn't slept in three weeks. *Three weeks?* Zoe thought. *Try not sleeping three months.* But it was unfair, she knew, to one-up the parents of younger children. Even if they listened sympathetically, she would hear the bitter edge in her tone and hate herself for it. Sometimes, to give something back, she joked or rolled her eyes or made pointed remarks about the difficulty of raising teens. She never let down her guard, never admitted to doubting herself or questioning her fitness as a mother. Except for Jerry, she'd never told anyone, outside her immediate family, that she was frustrated or scared.

"Hello," she said. "Hello?" *Shoot.* The line went dead, just as she answered. She checked the caller ID. Anonymous, a telemarketer probably.

She logged onto AOL, surfed a few Internet stores. Nothing jumped out at her. For no good reason, except that it was easy, she logged onto Saks, ordered an Armani jacket from the sale page for Will, a pair of overpriced Seven jeans and a cashmere sweater for Justine. In passing, Will had mentioned buying skis for Leah this year. Leah had asked for skis every year, since she was a kid. With soccer no longer an issue, they might as well buy them, Will said.

Zoe browsed the Dynastar site, visited Atomic, Rossignol, K-2. On each website, she selected a pair of parabolic skis, finished in vibrant reds and blues, colors she thought Leah would like, and copied and pasted the pictures in *Word*, to show Will, once they were talking again. On impulse, she typed the address for Tiffany's site into her browser.

Leah loved the button bracelet Zoe had bought her. She rarely took the bracelet off. Like the bracelet, a birthstone ring would be special. Zoe selected the page for rings, scanning the offerings, scrolled to the bottom of the page. In the last row, she saw the perfect ring for Leah. For kicks (the ring far too expensive to buy), she hit the link to enlarge. The dazzling Topaz, its platinum setting encrusted with diamonds, reminded Zoe of a ring a princess might wear. As she imagined the look on Leah's face on Christmas morning, when her daughter opened the velvet jeweler's box and saw her birthstone, she relived another Christmas. Leah was five. Beanie Babies were all the rage that year. On one of his trips to the West Coast, Will stopped at a mall, bought dozens of the tiny beanbag animals for the girls, lions and tigers, monkeys, dolphins, birds. He bought snakes; he bought a giraffe. Christmas Eve, after the girls had fallen asleep, she and Will constructed a ship, nearly five feet in length, from particle board. They painted the frame crimson, scripted the words "Noah's Ark," in black, across the boat's stern. They used the pole of an old fishing rod for a mast. From an old white pillowcase, they'd made the boat's sails. The project grew more involved as they went along, and took far longer than they had anticipated. By the time they fell into bed, it was nearly dawn. Zoe would never forget the look of wonder on Leah's face that Christmas morning. No amount of money could ever replace that.

She bookmarked the Tiffany's site, and logged onto her e-mail account. At the head of the list, she spotted a message from Jerry. "Hi," he wrote. "Thought I'd swing by this morning. Let me know if you'll be around. J."

She hoped nothing was wrong. During an officially scheduled visit, a week after the accident, she, Jerry, and Officer Healy, the chief of police, had gone over the accident in detail. Jerry had stopped twice, over the next few weeks, to check on things, to see how she felt, to see how Leah was faring. That was the extent of their physical contact. Although they spoke every day and corresponded regularly by e-mail, they never got together in person.

"Sure," she replied. "Everything OK? Z."

Within minutes, she had a response. "Everything's fine. An hour?"

She answered two short messages, one from a coworker, writing to say "hi," the other from one of her past workshop attendees, asking the date of Zoe's next seminar. (No date yet, but she appreciated the interest, would keep her informed.) Zoe closed her laptop, and headed upstairs for a shower. She hobbled up the stairs, frustrated with her faltering steps, her body's refusal to respond to simple demands, limped down the hall to the bedroom. She tidied the room, made the bed, threw the laundry into the wire hamper in their closet, removed her walking cast, took a long hot shower, lathering her body with lavender soap, and washed and conditioned her hair. After her shower, she smoothed almond-scented body butter over her arms and thighs.

Zoe stood in her closet, wrapped in a towel, waffling over what to wear. Black slacks? Too dressy. Chinos? Boring. Skirt? This was a friendly get-together, for God's sake. Not a *date*.

Zoe felt as giddy as a schoolgirl, her stomach in knots. *Repeat after me*, she told herself. *Jerry's your friend.* The man was married, with infant twins. Even if he were interested in her, which he was not, she found Jerry only marginally attractive. He was too, too *earnest*. His face was too wide. And he had funny-shaped ears. And burred hair. And his hands were too big. Silly, criticizing his hands. Nevertheless, clunky hands bugged her. Will had elegant hands, his wrists graceful, his fingers slim. His hands were the first thing she'd noticed that night in the bar. She'd found it arousing, watching him pluck the strings, his deliberate fingers pressing the chords.

At ten thirty sharp, Jerry rapped on the sliding glass door off the kitchen.

When she slid the door open, a rush of cold air blew through the loose weave of her scoop-neck sweater, chilling her belly and chest. She hugged herself. "Well," she said, squinting against the glittering mid-morning light. She made a show of checking her watch. "Aren't we punctual?"

"Yeah, well." He stamped the snow off his feet. "Had to drive around the block a few times." His nose and cheeks were flushed from the cold. "Didn't want to seem too eager."

She raised her eyebrows, teasing. "That right, Jerry?"

He laughed, and she stepped aside, to let him in.

He handed her a small package, wrapped in brown paper. "This is for you. It's sausage. I made it myself. I hope you like garlic and sage?"

She turned the package over. "I love garlic and sage. Thank you." She pecked his check. "I can freeze it, right?"

"Sure. It should keep fine." He scanned the kitchen. "It's nice in here. Warm." His eyes traversed the length of her body. "You look great." He cleared his throat. "Feeling good?"

She felt herself blush. "A lot better. Can I take your jacket?"

He peered over her shoulder, into the empty family room. "Thought it might be nice for you to get out, get some air."

"That's tempting," she said, stalling. It was a hassle, going out in public. She felt awkward, bothersome, people constantly forced to wait for her, groups splitting as she approached, people moving right and left, kind-hearted strangers holding doors that took her forever to reach, the holder's pleasant face invariably dropping into a poorly concealed frown. "Why don't I make some tea? Let me see what I've got." She shuffled to the pantry. She'd begun to favor her gimp leg, the cast more of a nuisance now than a help. "We have blackberry currant," she said, sticking her head out of the pantry. "Or lemon. Or plain, if you'd rather."

"It would do you good to get out. It's a beautiful day. If you don't mind the cold." A great new coffee shop opened last month, he told her, in Ayer. "The coffee's incredible."

"I don't know." She felt uncomfortable going out with Jerry. She'd prefer to stay here.

"They roast their own beans."

The coffee shop occupied the lower floor of a newly renovated two-family house, across from Ayer's town common. The shop was more sophisticated than it appeared from the outside. The dark paneled walls and honey-colored ceiling evoked the wistful feeling of a lazy weekend brunch or a Miles Davis song on a rainy spring afternoon. A fire crackled in a stone hearth on the far wall, the smell of the burning logs mingling with the heady aroma of freshly brewed coffee.

The shop was empty this morning. Behind the bar, a young woman, in her early-twenties, Zoe guessed, was scooping beans from a small paper bag into the canister of a magnificent stainless steel coffee machine. Zoe loosened her knitted scarf, tucked her gloves in the pocket of her suede jacket, rubbed her hands together. "I wish I could do this with my feet." A thin athletic sock covered her left foot, inside her walking cast. "My toes are like ice."

Jerry joked about rubbing them for her. "I'm impressed," he said, cupping her elbow as they stepped down onto the wide-planked pine floor. "You're getting along pretty good." He let go of her elbow. "Don't need much help at all."

Thanks, she told him. Though it felt too slow to her, she *had* made progress.

He led her to a wrought-iron table, pushed into a corner, away from the other tables, and pulled her chair. "If you tell me what you want, I'll order."

"That's OK. I'll go."

"Really, stay. Make yourself comfortable."

She dug in her purse. She'd brought her leather hobo bag, the inside a disorganized mess. She pushed aside a small notepad, her checkbook, her house keys, the keys to her office. She was hunting for her wallet, which she realized, *oh, God,* she'd forgotten to bring.

From one of the bag's interior pockets, she produced a crumpled five-dollar bill.

Jerry had been standing over her, waiting patiently. He set his hand over hers. "My treat," he said. "I invited you, remember?" She reluctantly put her money away. "So. What'll it be?"

Zoe studied the menu on the wall behind the counter: regular coffee, house blend, coffee of the day. They were serving Guatemalan Antigua, today. They also served decaf, espresso, cappuccino, mochaccino, latte, plain, pumpkin or vanilla. "'Mocha Marvel?' Sounds interesting. What's the 'Marvel' I wonder?"

He didn't know, he said, but he'd ask. If it sounded good, he'd order one for each of them. If she trusted his judgment, that was.

All the discomfort Zoe had felt when Jerry first arrived had disappeared. In the car, they'd talked briefly about her accident. She'd surprised herself, telling him the accident had changed her life. How melodramatic, she thought, though it had. She felt like a different person, someone she was not sure she liked. She talked about her ambivalence about returning to work. "I don't know what's got into me," she said. "I've never thought of myself as irresponsible." She wasn't irresponsible, he told her. She was honest. "Most of us live on auto-pilot. Get up, go to work. Don't think about whether we like what we're doing or not. If we're good at it, even. You're lucky, you had a chance to think." Thinking can be paralyzing, Zoe replied. It can also be freeing, he told her. It felt strange talking philosophically with Jerry, the words stilted, like a new suit or a hairdo she was trying on to see if it fit. As the conversation evolved, the words began to feel urgent and real, and she'd realized that, for the first time in a long time she was talking about feelings, thoughts, that mattered to her. Not about her family. Not about Leah. About herself.

"Mocha Marvel." Jerry set a tall paper cup in front of her, the coffee topped with whipped cream. He'd sprinkled the cream with cocoa powder. "Chocolate syrup swirled into 'vanilla-bean-*infused*-coffee.'" He put on a goofy, highfalutin accent, a Cockney version of Brahman. "It kills me when people talk like that." They laughed together, easy with one another. "Just kidding. They're good people, the owners. They're usually here. I hope you like cocoa."

With her finger, she scooped a dollop of cream. "I love cocoa."

He sat across from her, his hands on the table. His knuckles were chapped, raw, as though he'd been out for too long in the cold. "So," she said, returning to the conversation they'd begun in the car, "what made you decide to be a cop?"

He looked at her as if he were trying to figure out how to answer the question.

She was sorry she'd asked. It was a dumb question, too personal, too hard to answer without being glib. After all, why her own professional choices? An observant person might guess and Zoe might supply some half-baked, self-conscious reason. The truth was, she'd fallen into the field, drawn to psychology courses in college, sort of like following a path to see where it led, rather than making a thoughtful decision. Maybe she and Jerry were both masochists, drawn to professions that offered fewer rewards than jobs of a similar caliber, drawn to jobs that afforded little respect. These thoughts flitted through her mind, partially formulated, semi-conscious. Still, they endeared her to the large chapped hands clasped in front of her on the table.

"I was a punk," he said finally. "My parents didn't deserve the crap I put them through." In high school, he'd been brought up on robbery charges. Instead of prosecuting the case, the judge had assigned a "summer work-study program." He chuckled, describing his feeble attempts at weeding the judge's garden. "I think I pulled up more flowers than weeds." One day, the judge pulled him aside. "He said I had promise. I could make something of myself, if I chose. Or I could end up in jail. I took him up on the challenge." For the next five years, he worked full-time, as the night guard at Wang. Days, he attended school. Eventually, he'd earned his degree in criminal justice. The judge passed away last spring. "Must have been a thousand people at his funeral. The line went around the block. He touched a lot of people, that man."

Several customers had wandered into the shop while Jerry was talking. Zoe edged her chair closer, so she could speak without raising her voice. "You're a good cop, Jerry," she said.

He wiped her chin with his napkin. "Cream." He shrugged, grinning.

She let out a small, uncomfortable laugh, and backed up. "I'm such a slob. I wear whatever I'm eating."

"Seriously, thank you." He covered her hand with his own. "I love what I do."

"I wish I could say the same."

He squeezed her hand. "You'll figure it out."

Zoe rarely allowed anyone outside her immediate family to touch her. She recoiled from even her friends. Part of her protested, her legs uncomfortable, her thighs twitching. *Don't be ridiculous,* the other part said. This was the way friends interacted. She forced herself to relax. "Is it always this slow?" she asked, meaning the shop. How did they make any money?

"In the morning, the line's out the door."

She wrapped her hands around the cup. He'd put the paper cup into a sleeve.

The bells on the door jingled and a man entered, a construction worker, about her age, a good-looking guy, too scruffy for Zoe's taste, with a dark mustache and hair, dressed in a navy parka and jeans, his steel-toed boots caked with mud. At the counter, he ran a hand over his head. She watched him flirting with the barista, the young woman basking in the attention.

She sipped her coffee, wiping her mouth afterward. "How are the boys?"

"Good." She lost him for an instant. "Getting big. Last time Maura— Last time the kids were at the doctor's, they weighed eighteen pounds. That's huge for their age. When you think, they were less than two pounds each when they were born." He opened a hand. They'd fit in his palm. "Blows me away."

Kids grow fast, she agreed, especially babies.

"And Leah? How's she doing?"

Zoe tipped her free hand, *so-so,* set her cup on the table. "She's still with that kid."

"Corbett." Jerry's concern registered on his face. "Sorry to hear that."

"I've never hated a kid. But I can't help it. When I hear his name, I cringe."

"I was just like Leah," he reminded her. "Had to get it out of my system, I think. Wish I could tell you differently. Some kids just need to rebel. It's how they find their own way."

Zoe considered this for a moment. It was a good point. She had no respect for people who followed the party line, people who couldn't think for themselves. When Leah was a baby, she'd made a conscious goal to raise independent children, she told him. She'd let Leah get away with too much. "I didn't want to stifle her, you know? My father always told me to be careful what I asked for." She laughed. "It's just scary. If I had a crystal ball— Be so much easier if I could see her ten years from now, know she was all right. Know for *sure* nothing awful would happen—"

"You've taught her right from wrong. When she's ready, she'll come back."

"Thank you." Talking helped, she told him, diverting the conversation away from herself, and turned her attention to the silver roasting machine. "They roast the coffee here, you said? That machine really works?"

"Every Monday and Friday. Usually in the afternoon."

"Must smell nice."

"It does." He reached again for her hand. "On Friday, I'll pick you up. You can watch."

She slid her hand from under his, confused by the closeness she felt to this man, who wasn't her husband, ashamed of having shared such intimate details of her life. He probably thought she was leading him on. "I've got to get back. It's an early release day."

On the way to the house, they talked about the weather. The forecasters were calling for snow again. Didn't feel like snow. But look. See the clouds scudding in? Jerry pointed to the dash. The temperature had dropped to thirty degrees. The sun slid behind a cloud, diffusing the light, the sky turning gray. It was too early for snow, she complained. If it were up to her, they would live on the equator. She'd gone to college in California. She'd loved the weather out there.

"Why didn't you stay?"

"Oh, you know."

"I had a job offer in Houston, after college." He signaled the turn onto Lily Farm Road. "Maximum security prison."

"You?" She raised a brow. "A prison guard? You don't strike me as a hard ass."

"Oh yeah?" He pumped the brakes, turned into the drive. "You'd be surprised.

She poked his arm playfully, comfortable again. "Tough guy. So what happened?"

"Stayed here." He backed into the turnaround, shifted into park, letting the engine idle. "I was tempted. Thought it'd be nice to see another part of the country. Maura didn't want to go."

"That must have been tough."

"I didn't blame her. Her folks would have gone nuts. Money-wise, it would have made sense. They paid pretty good. Better than a rookie cop." He stared at the drive. "I couldn't do that to her, after she stuck with me through college. Figured I owed her that much. What about you?"

"What?"

"Any regrets?"

Zoe laid her head on the rest. "Regrets?" She toyed with her wedding ring. A doe leapt out of the woods, a yearling tagging behind her. The deer bounded across the yard and over the drive, white tails lifted, their gray coats camouflaged by the fading light. "Sure. I guess. But I'm glad I came back." She pictured gritty Fisherman's Wharf, the brick warehouses, the glittering water, Alcatraz in the distance. The harbor had changed since they left, Will had told her. They'd revitalized the Embarcadero, put in fancy restaurants, upscale shops. Though the development was surely good for the city, it was hard to imagine appreciating that sort of change. "I miss it sometimes. San Francisco, especially. But, I don't know. I never felt centered out there."

"Do you now?"

Jesus, these questions. Yes, she felt centered. No. Maybe. Why couldn't they talk about the weather again? Something simple and easy. "I don't know, Jerry. Do you?"

"Maybe." He studied her face.

Her breath quickened, warmth radiating into her chest, her belly, her legs.

Zoe pulled back. She couldn't do this. However wrong her marriage felt at the moment, however badly she might want to escape. She couldn't plunge into adultery the way she'd plunged into a career, an impulse driving her into another man's arms. It wasn't fair to any of them—Will, Jerry, especially to Jerry, or his wife, wasn't fair to their children—to enter a relationship she wasn't ready for, a relationship she wasn't even sure she wanted. "You're a good man, Jerry. A good friend," she said quietly, hoping he would understand, that she hadn't gone too far, crossed a line, that they still had room to retreat. "That means a lot to me."

He wrapped her hands in his. "Me, too."

She returned his smile. He let go of her hands, and she accepted a kiss on her cheek. And sad, flustered, angry with herself—mostly relieved—she bid him cheery, melancholic goodbye.

Twenty-Seven

You'd Better Not Cry

Leah got off the stupid Twinkie at the bottom of her street, and walked home, alone as usual, dragging her feet through the gutter, kicking dead leaves with the toe of her Doc Martin boots. She was halfway up the hill when the cruiser blew by. She didn't recognize the driver at first. Without the cop hat, he looked about twelve. She did a one-eighty, caught his face in the rearview. What was *he* doing in their neighborhood? It wouldn't surprise her if he'd stopped at the house to tell her parents some juicy new tidbit, to see if he could get her in *more* trouble. Or else he was there for her mom. Which was worse. "Screw you," she spat, and flipped him the bird. *Stay away from my house.* It felt good, flipping him off. Too bad he hadn't seen her.

The wind howled, and it started snowing again, big wet flakes that stuck to her cheek. This weather was ridiculous. Worst winter in years, the *Farmer's Almanac* had predicted. Too bad her family didn't live in Florida, someplace where you didn't get snow. She'd had enough snow for one winter already. She dropped her chin into the collar of her peacoat. Of all years, her junior year, to have to ride the dumb bus. Nobody her age took the bus. Only the nerds. Her father had driven her to school last year and the year before, years when it would have been perfectly acceptable to ride the stupid banana. Now that, if she were to retain one *shred* of pride, she needed someone to drive her, her father refused. Her parents were like that. They only wanted to do favors for you when it didn't matter. If you called them on it, they always had a gazillion lame excuses. Her school, her father claimed, was out of his way.

In Leah's Wake

She stepped over a mound of petrified dog dung, Dog's probably, hopped over the curb and onto the grass on the neighbor's lawn. Leah was sad Dog had died, though not nearly as sad as her sister. Leah was more pragmatic than Justine, more mature in her outlook. Her sister had been unreasonable, believing Dog wouldn't die. Naïve, in her little kid way, refusing to accept the inevitable. Leah had tried to tell her differently. Dog was thirteen years old, ninety-seven in dog years. She was bound to die, sooner or later. Nothing, after all, lasted forever. Not dogs, not hamsters, not people. Nothing, except maybe mistakes. Mistakes lived forever.

The Ridley girls across the street were singing again. "Oh, you'd better not cry. . ." They danced around a tree, Sarah, the younger one, hanging on her sister's belt loop. The yard in front of their house tilted toward the street. The girls spotted her, and raced down the hill, two little snow-bunnies in their matching blue snowsuits, hurtling toward her. Leah leapt out of the way.

Santa Claus is coming to town. Humbug. Christmas was supposed to be this magical time, a time of kindness and generosity and cheer. What a joke. It was all a pretense, a big competition, a show. Nobody *cared* about anyone else. The mall, the other night, was nothing but a disgusting display of consumerism, bells jangling, shoppers tearing down aisles, shoving you out of their way, zipping in and out of the stores. Real Christmas spirit. They'd bowl you over, if you didn't move out of the way. Cheesy red and green decorations had taken over the world. Everywhere you turned, you saw inflatable Santa Claus dolls and plastic reindeer, and ice cycle lights. Everywhere except *their* house, that was. All they had were those pathetic decorations Justine had put up. As far as Leah knew, her mother had not done a stitch of shopping. Leah had checked all the usual hiding places, in the attic, under her parents' bed, behind her father's workbench in the basement. Nothing. Not a solitary gift.

"Hey, Leah," Sarah called, "wanna play snow fight?"

Leah shook her head and kept walking. There was a time when she might have joined them. There was a time when Leah would have done a lot of things she wouldn't do now. She had hung out with Cicely Hanson, for instance. Leah couldn't imagine how she and Cissy had ever been friends. Other than soccer, they had nothing in common. Leah was cool. Cissy was a tool. Pathetic Leah laughed at her own stupid rhyme. It was true, though. Cissy *was* a tool. She didn't think for herself, didn't do anything she hadn't been told to do by somebody else. Not even the clothes stealing scheme was Cissy's idea (though you'd never know it, listening to her). All the girls she

259

hung out with stole their clothes. She only did it so they'd think she was cool.

Leah turned down their snow-dusted driveway, slogged past the giant rock she and Justine had played on when they were younger. Once, when she was bored, Leah had drawn stick figures with black and red magic markers (swear words written in code underneath) across the front of the rock. When her father came home, he'd given her a bucket of soapy water and a brush and made her scrub it off. He used to be anal about the property. Now he didn't bother.

Leah picked up a stone lying in her path and tossed it in the woods. Dog used to love to play catch. You'd throw a stick or a small stone, and she'd race off to retrieve it. She would find it too, always, no matter where the thing landed. Weird not to see Dog racing out of the garage, skipping up the driveway to greet her. Maybe her parents would buy them another dog, maybe for Christmas. Something big, Leah hoped, a dog that would scare people off. A rottweiler or a mean German shepherd. Or maybe a cat. Hope's alley cat, Tabby, was pregnant. The kittens were due any day. Maybe, if she asked permission, her parents would allow her to bring one of them home. *Right. Fat chance.* Her father hated cats. Too finicky. Too stuck up. You had to work too hard to earn their affection. Of course, she could always sneak one home, under her jacket. The idea of a squirmy little kitten hiding inside her jacket made Leah laugh. She pictured herself stealing past the dinette where her parents sat, drinking their coffee, a tiny fur ball curled on her belly. She could probably keep the kitten a secret forever, as long as he lived in her room.

Leah schlepped into the empty house, through the dark mudroom and into the kitchen. She shouldered out of her backpack and peacoat, and tossed her jacket in the general direction of the island counter. The jacket landed on the edge of a barstool, and slid to the floor.

Strange, a light was on in the family room.

And there was Leah's mom, on the sofa, her laptop balanced on her thighs, assorted catalogs fanned out around her. Most afternoons, when Leah came home, her mother was napping. Nice to see her awake. Maybe, Leah thought, she was finally coming around.

"Hey." Leah slouched into the arched doorway, rounding her shoulders, and stretched her lower back, sore from lugging her backpack. "What are you doing? How come you're awake?"

"Answering some e-mail," her mother replied. "What do you mean, how come I'm awake? Come in here for a minute. How was your day?"

Leah shrugged. "All right. What are those?" she asked hopefully, meaning the catalogs.

"Oh, nothing." Her mother gathered the catalogs into a pile and set them on the floor, shielding them with her feet. "Busywork. Just trying to keep myself occupied. How was school?"

"I don't know," Leah snapped. For a minute, she'd let herself believe that her mother had started the Christmas shopping, that her family might actually have a Christmas this year. "Why do you bother asking? What do you care, anyway?"

"Honestly, Leah. Can't you at least try to be civil, for once? I asked a simple question."

Leah snorted. Her feelings hurt, she launched into interrogation mode, her face pinched, accusing. "So, what was that cop doing here, anyway?"

"Why are you *doing* this?" Her mother's face curdled. "Please," she said, and held up her hands, acting all hurt and perplexed. "For once, could we please just have a polite conversation?"

"Oh, sure," Leah barked, "like it's all my fault." She snatched a bag of barbecue chips from the pantry, and stormed up to her room, ignoring her mother's pleas to wait, to come back.

Leah shut her door, turning the lock. She plucked a towel from her laundry pile, rolled the towel into a snake and stuffed it into the crack under her door, a trick she'd picked up from Hope, not that Hope had to hide anything from *her* mother. Irritated, she selected a Nirvana album, called *Nevermind*, from the list in her iPod, and plunked onto her mattress.

When the CD ended, Leah reached for the mesh purse under her bed. She'd found the bag, a taupe macramé with red and yellow flowers embroidered on the flap, in Hope's closet. Hope had seen Leah with the purse. Hope had so much new stuff that she probably didn't even realize the handbag was hers. Leah dug her pack of Marlboros out of the inside pocket, shook out a butt. A week after Officer Johnson brought Leah and Todd to the police station, the cops arrested Hope and Lupo for drinking in public. Tons of kids partied on the common. Hope and Lupo were the only ones the cops busted. Since her daughter's arrest, Hope's mom had been on a mission, bribing her with shirts, jackets, purses, trying to buy good behavior. Hope was having trouble coping, her mom held, a delayed reaction to her parents' divorce. "Which suits me fine," Hope had boasted. "She can buy me all the shit she wants." *Her* parents, Leah thought, might want to take a page out of Mindy's book. Leah's mother and father never cut her a break.

Terri Giuliano Long

Leah smoked the cigarette, pulling hard, holding the smoke inside until her lungs burned. She couldn't wait to get out of this dump. Her sister, the only person in her family who liked her, spent the majority of her time at her friend's house. Leah's parents despised her. They had always hated her, Leah saw now. A couple days after her mother's accident, she had attempted to apologize to her parents for all the trouble she'd caused, hoping to set things right, hoping they would give her a chance to start over. Her parents were in the family room watching a pay-per-view movie they'd rented on cable. She stood on the precipice between the kitchen and family room, steeling herself for the job. It had taken every ounce of courage she was able to muster to open her mouth. She was terrified that her parents would think she was lying when she told them she'd broken up with her boyfriend, afraid they would tell her they were finished with her, that she had disappointed them one too many times. "I'm sorry," Leah mumbled. She'd been shocked to learn that Todd had called their house that afternoon, hoping, he told Leah later, he'd be able to convince her parents to change their minds about him. If he could talk to her parents in person, he'd thought, they would realize he was good for Leah, he looked out for her, he would do her no wrong. At the mere mention of Todd's name, Leah's father had gone ballistic. He insisted she sign this ridiculous contract he'd written. It was insulting. She shouldn't have to sign a contract to prove that she could be trusted. She told her parents she would be good. That should have been enough. They should have believed her. They should have realized she was good for her word. If he so much as heard that kid's name, her father screamed, he would— He left the threat hanging, but it didn't take a brain surgeon to fill in the blanks. Her father would cut her off, too, in a heartbeat. After the fight with her parents, she'd called Todd, to ask why he'd called. Within a few days, they were together again. She would never leave him, now. Todd was her only true friend. She wondered if her parents realized that they had pushed her into his arms.

Leah crushed the cigarette butt in the palm of her ceramic ashtray, and lit another, took one drag, touched the smoldering tip to her thigh, and held it there, her breath quickening. Repulsed by the smell of her burning flesh, she flicked the butt into the ashtray, and picked at her bubbling skin. Leah had made mistakes—many, many mistakes. Still, she didn't deserve to be treated like a pariah. Not by her own family. Leah wasn't a loser. Not in her heart. Her parents had certain ideas about what she should do, how she should behave. They refused to accept anything less. When she was a little girl, her parents forgave her for botching things up. Once, when she was seven, she missed the bus and her father had driven her to school. Leah frequently missed the bus, sometimes twice in one week, and her father always drove. Normally, he didn't mind. That morning, he had a meeting with an important client, and couldn't be late. About a mile from the elementary school, she remembered that she'd left her spelling homework on the kitchen counter. If she forgot her homework again, her teacher had threatened to make her sit on the "naughty bench," to teach her to be more responsible. Her father had driven home to retrieve it. For the rest of the ride, he had berated her for making him late. All day long, sitting in class, she tried to think of ways to apologize. That night, at dinner, Leah presented her dad with a note. "DeEr Dad," the note read. "I diNT's mean A be late. I luv you. Hugs and kSSes from Leah Tyler." Her father, delighted with her note, pulled her into a bear hug. Sometime between then and now, her parents had stopped forgiving her. They had no interest in apologies or excuses. They failed to see how tired she was of trying so hard to be perfect. She would never be perfect.

Exhausted, Leah retrieved a joint from the small wooden jewelry box hidden in her top drawer. She changed the music in her iPod, switching from Nirvana to a Radiohead album called *OK Computer*, lit the joint and brought it to her mouth, tipping her head back, inhaling deeply, losing herself in the languorous strains of the music. She smoked until her fingertips burned, put the roach in the silver clip Todd had given her. When the roach burned out, Leah removed her headphones, dropping them on the floor, and pulled the down comforter over her head, the room silent but for the soft hum of warm air blowing through the heat vents. Her breathing slowed. Soon, she was outside, on the street, plodding through the snow, her backpack flung over her shoulder. The icy wet snow seared the pads of her bare feet, and she began to limp. Worn out, she could think of nothing but sleep. She longed to lie down in the snow, like Sleeping Beauty, and close her eyes. She walked for miles, it seemed. Suddenly, a car whizzed by, an old black Cadillac, its window open, the driver whistling, calling her name.

Todd.

The car zipped around a corner and doubled-back. He'd noticed her limping, he said, and swept her off her feet. Cradling her in his arms, he carried her to the car.

The radio was blaring. Snapping her fingers, she gave her body over to the music.

All at once, it was dark. Snow whirled in the beams of his headlights. He stepped on the gas. . . *faster, faster* . . . the car morphed into his truck, the Jeep speeding down the hill like a rollercoaster ride. Leah was awake now, alive, shouting, urging him on.

Faster, faster.

Out of nowhere, a deer. . . a jogger . . . oh my God, Leah cried . . . *her mother.*

Todd turned the wheel, twisting. The disk snapped off its column. He pumped the brake, pressing his foot all the way to the floor. His brakes were gone, the car spinning out of control.

Leah woke, sobbing, her face buried in her pillow. This was her life—careening out of control. She had made terrible, unforgivable mistakes. And she had no way to make amends. No way to apologize. No way to turn back.

Twenty-Eight

And To All A Good Night

Christmas morning, Justine woke at dawn, golden sunlight, from the skylight over her bed, streaming into her room. The second her eyes popped open, she got up, put on her slippers and robe. She couldn't wait for the others to wake up. She couldn't wait to see the look on her sister's face when Leah opened her present. Selecting gifts for her parents was easy: a Brahms CD for her mom, weightlifting gloves for her dad (she overheard him one night, talking about joining a gym). Finding a gift for Leah was tough. Last year, Justine gave her sister a Tim McGraw CD they'd heard on Country 98. Choosing a CD for her sister would be impossible now. Justine had no idea what Leah would like. Ani DiFranco? 50 Cent? Some rapper she'd never heard of? Last week, Justine and her friend Holly had wandered around the mall, poking in and out of stores, searching for the perfect gift. "A shirt?" Holly suggested, in Abercrombie and Fitch. "Sweat pants? A belt?" Nothing felt right. Finally, in Wicks and Sticks, Justine found exactly what she had been hunting for: a wax figurine of Merlin the Magician.

Justine lifted her bed-skirt, digging for the shopping bag she'd hidden under her bed. She set the gifts for her parents aside, lifted the candle out of its box. The magician was small enough to fit in her palm. He wore a pointy, star-studded hat, a flowing ebony robe. A crystal ball sat in his outstretched hand. Justine touched his eyes, sparkling sapphire glass, ran her fingers over the smooth black wax of his robe. This was the perfect gift, this magician. He would make all her sister's wishes come true. Justine laid Merlin back in his box, and folded him inside the tissue.

265

With all they'd been through this fall, Justine was afraid her parents might forgo their Christmas celebration this year. Her mother, despite her physical improvement, spent the majority of her time in the family room. Instead of watching TV or lying on the sofa listening to music, she surfed the Web or e-mailed friends at her practice. She'd stopped seeing patients, had postponed her seminars indefinitely. It was almost as if she were trying to figure out what she was supposed to do next. Justine's parents hardly ever talked. When they did converse, they argued. Her father went upstairs to his office before Justine woke in the morning, was there when she went to bed. He still worked at NAC, she believed. She had no idea why he didn't go into the office in Waltham, why he wasn't traveling anymore. Nobody said.

A couple days ago, her parents rallied. Justine overheard her mother and father talking about Christmas. One night, they'd even gone shopping together. The next morning, her father set-up the tree he'd left, nearly two weeks ago, in the garage. Even Leah was unusually perky. At their mother's insistence, Leah had gone to their family practitioner, and the doctor had put her on Zoloft. The prescription seemed to help. Maybe their lives were finally turning around.

The minutes dragged. Their parents insisted that Justine and Leah stay in their rooms, on Christmas morning, until they were called. Their parents liked to be the first downstairs, so they could see the girls' faces when they saw the tree, and their dad could videotape their reaction. Each year, while they were waiting for their parents to get up, Leah would sneak downstairs. Back in her room, she would describe for Justine what she had found. For Justine, the anticipation, imagining the brightly wrapped piles of gifts, was better than unwrapping.

She knocked on Leah's wall, hoping to wake her. But Leah wasn't budging today.

Justine curled up at the foot of her bed, covered herself with a blanket. To pass time, she told herself stories, meandering narratives that eventually put her to sleep. When she opened her eyes, she heard someone in the kitchen. She hopped off the bed, and hurried downstairs with her gifts.

"Merry Christmas, Sunshine," her father said. "Look who's up, Zo."

Justine's breath caught in her throat. She could hardly believe her eyes. *Fairies* had visited, it seemed, sprinkling their golden dust. The family room shimmered. Her father had lit a crackling fire. In the corner stood a magnificent tree, white lights twinkling, trimmed in purple and gold. The floor was a sea of exquisitely wrapped gifts, the packages silver and purple and green. Her mother had donned a new white robe, put her hair in a twist. She even wore makeup.

Justine laid her presents on the family room floor. While her father poured coffee, she raced upstairs to rouse Leah.

Justine tapped on her sister's door. "Leah?" She waited, tapped again, opened the door.

Leah's room smelled putrid, a stew of stale cigarettes and old sneakers, masked by a syrupy, floral perfume. Justine nearly tripped on a chunky black sandal at the foot of Leah's bed. She stepped around the shoe, over a pile of dirty laundry, picked a blue silk blouse off the floor.

"Wake up, sleepyhead," Justine said, shaking Leah's shoulder.

Her sister grunted and rolled onto her belly.

"It's Christmas," Justine said gaily. "Time to get up." She danced to the window, and rolled up the shades. Light poured into the room.

Leah pulled the pillow over her head. "Go away."

Justine sat on the bed next to Leah, stroked her sister's head. "Come on, Lee. We're opening presents. You're gonna love what I bought you."

"You guys open." Leah yawned, and pushed herself onto her side. "I'll be down after."

"Please?"

Leah flung her arm over her face. "I don't feel like it."

"Come on, Lee." She tugged on her sister's arm. "Please?"

"Fine," Leah grumbled, and pushed the covers aside.

Leah was naked, except for purple thong-backed bikinis. Her tiny breasts sagged. Justine sucked in a breath. She hadn't seen her sister undressed in weeks, was appalled by how scrawny Leah was. When her sister played soccer, her body was strong and athletic. Now her elbows were knobs and every bone in her body protruded, her hips, her ribs, every disk in her spine.

"You've lost so much weight." Justine felt horrid. How did she miss this? "Feel OK?"

"I'm fine." Leah stood near the window, combing her wispy burnt-orange hair. In the light, Justine saw the thin blue veins under her sister's skin. "I've been this weight for ages."

Leah lifted her bed-ruffle, sending a cloud of dust mites into the air, lowered herself to the floor, and reached under the bed, raking her fingers over the carpet. "I know they're under here," she said, stretching farther, her cheek pressed to the box spring.

She dragged a pair of black satin slacks from under the bed, brushed off the lint. "Think I can wear these?" she asked, holding the slacks by the belt loop. "They too dirty?"

"No," Justine lied. "They look fine."

Leah threaded a black patent-leather belt through her belt loops and yanked, pulling the buckle to the very last hole, the fabric bunching at her waist. "So that cop was here last week."

It took Justine a second to realize who her sister meant. "He was? When?"

"When we had that half-day." Leah raised an eyebrow. "I think she's doing him, Jus."

Justine rocked backward. How could her sister say something so outrageous? Their mother would never have an affair. "No way," Justine said, annoyed with her sister for slandering their mother. "She's not like that."

"Yeah." Leah smirked. "You're right." She pulled on the blue silk shirt Justine had laid on her bed, stuffed her shirttail under her waistband, and grabbed a handful of plastic butterfly barrettes from the yellow can on top of her bureau. With one hand, she separated her bangs into sections, securing each section with a different color barrette. From a box on her nightstand, she removed a thin silver ring shaped like a serpent, and strode to the mirror to check her reflection.

Justine had never seen the ring before. The ring was a Christmas present, she suspected, from Todd. "How was Mass last night?" she asked, hoping Leah would tell her the truth.

"It was good," Leah said, fingering the ring. "So. I pass inspection, or what?"

"Sure. You look awesome," Justine mumbled, and headed downstairs.

When she stepped into the kitchen, her father thrust the video camera in her face. Justine waved, clowning for the camera. Leah appeared, a few minutes later, and stuck out her tongue.

The girls took turns opening their gifts, shirts and sweaters and jeans for them both, computer games for Justine. In a shirt box tagged Leah, there was a promissory note for a pair of skis. "So many options," their mother said, "we thought you might like to choose for yourself."

"Thanks," Leah said, without much emotion. She had wanted skis for a long time.

"There's something else," their father said. "Right, Zoe?" He focused the video recorder on their mom, slowly turned it toward Leah, twisting a knob, recording a close-up of Leah's face.

From the pocket of her robe, their mother produced a small box, wrapped in a metallic silver paper, tied with a red satin ribbon. Smiling, she handed the gift to Leah.

Justine watched her mother, watching Leah intently.

Leah untied the ribbon, slid a finger under the tape, pulled off the wrapping. "It's pretty." She turned the box, displaying a stunning topaz ring in a diamond-encrusted platinum setting.

"Your birthstone," their mother pointed out. "Did you know, the ancient Romans associated topaz with Jupiter, the god of light?"

Leah listened until their mother finished talking, thanked their parents politely, and tucked the velvet box, with the ring still inside, into a larger box, under a pair of jeans.

Their mother glanced at the girls' father, and looked away.

Justine opened her final gift, a telescope for her room. She set the telescope on the floor, and leaped into her mother's arms, planting a kiss on her cheek, and turned to her father, gave him a hug and a kiss. "Oh my god." She pranced across the family room floor. "I love this," she sang. "I love it. I love it. I love it. Thank you *so* much," she said, settling uneasily on the floor.

Leah opened Justine's present last. She set the ribbon on the floor by her feet. Justine held her breath as her sister lifted the shiny green and gold-flecked paper away from the box. "Thanks." Leah turned the wax figurine over in her hands. "This is really thoughtful. I love it."

"Really?"

"Cross my heart. Only I feel bad. I didn't get anything for you."

Justine threw her arms around her sister. "You're here, Lee. That's the best present ever."

After breakfast, their mom carried her coffee into the family room, and Leah offered to help their father clean the kitchen. "I went to Mass last night. I'll stay with Mom," Leah said, and shooed Justine upstairs to shower, and get ready for church.

Justine and her father left late. By the time they parked, it was quarter to twelve. The church was packed, the double doors propped open, the congregation spilling onto the steps.

From the outside, St. Theresa's was an incongruous building, all angles and slopes. As she stepped inside, her heart swelled. Their church felt like a cathedral, cool and dark and smelling of incense, with vaulted ceilings, and stained glass windows, adorned with holly, depicting the lives of the saints. The wooden plaques lining the walls told their own story, of the agony of Christ. Justine and her father worked their way through the crowd, settling into a space near the vestibule door. Justine loved Christmas Mass, the majestic red and white poinsettias, the earthy smell of the pine wreaths and greens. She loved the scratchy sound of brand-new holiday outfits, the families all decked out in new clothes, the fathers in suits, the mothers in festive holiday skirts, the little girls in smocked velvet dresses, the boys in trousers and bow ties and vests. Even the most bedraggled teenagers looked presentable today.

At St. Theresa's, the children's and adults' choirs sang together on Christmas. The choir, a multitude of voices accompanied by hand bells and violins, sounded like a chorus of angels. A girl from Justine's school sang "Silent Night," her high clear voice raising goose flesh on Justine's arms. The cantor gestured, urging the congregation to join in the singing. Justine hesitated. Like her mother, she couldn't hold a tune. A scroll depicted on one of the stained-glass windows read, "Singing is praying twice." God knew, she needed the prayers. And so Justine sang along, timidly at first, and gaining confidence.

A baby cried off and on throughout the sermon. Justine had to strain to hear the priest's voice. After a while, she gave up, let her mind wander. Mostly, she thought about Leah. It was nice to have her sister around, even if she did dress and act rather strangely.

As she stood at the back of the church, reflecting, it occurred to her that Leah had probably been teasing her earlier, egging her on. Justine was a terrible sister, always judging, assuming the worst. And she wasn't much of a friend, these hasty assumptions a shortcoming of hers, probably even a sin. At communion time Justine stepped aside, let the others pass by.

When they returned home, Leah was stretched out on the sofa, watching a cartoon Christmas special. *Frosty the Snowman*, Justine saw. She'd changed into the faded pajama bottoms she wore every day, a ratty gray sweatshirt. Their mother sat on the oversized chair, fists clenched, feet propped on the ottoman. Though she was looking at the TV, she didn't appear to be watching. Her eyes were glazed, her face drawn. A *People* magazine lay on the floor next to her chair. From their pinched expressions, it was clear that a fight had occurred.

"So," Leah said, "how was it?"

Their mother perked up when she noticed Justine. "Sweetie," she said, and patted the side of her chair, an invitation for Justine to join her.

Justine looked from her mom to her sister. "Good," she said, addressing her sister. "Did I tell you, Miss Green asked me to speak at Confirmation? I was thinking about it in church."

"For *real*?" Leah gave their mother an accusatory look. "How come you didn't tell me?"

Leah folded her legs and Justine settled on the sofa, by her sister's bare feet.

Justine shrugged. "I'm not sure I want to do it. All those people. I'll feel stupid."

"Are you kidding me?" Leah folded one of the down pillows and wedged it behind her back, repositioning herself. "I remember when I made mine. I wanted so bad to be the one who gave the talk. But they didn't pick me." Leah smirked. "It's like this huge honor. You can't blow it off. I know." Leah's face lit up. "What if I help? Do you know what you want to talk about?"

Justine glanced at her mother, who shot an exasperated look at Leah.

"The entire Confirmation class wrote essays," their mother said, her words directed at Leah, her eyes on Justine. "Miss Green and Father McCarthy picked the two best essays."

"I know," Leah interrupted. "We did the same thing."

"Yes, well. Your sister did a nice job. Dad and I are proud of her."

"A nice job? You're using the speech you already wrote?"

Justine hesitated, too embarrassed to tell her sister the truth.

"Jus? Are you gonna tell me what you wrote about, at least?"

"It's about you, kind of." Justine blushed. "I said all this stuff about how our family helps me know what it's like to be part of God's family," she said, the words spilling out in a rush. She covered her face. When she wrote the essay, maybe because she'd felt the sentiment so deeply, or maybe because she'd written the essay in CCD class, where it was natural to associate feelings with God, the words seemed appropriate. Now she felt like a cheese-ball. She spread her fingers, just far enough apart to see her sister's face. "Dumb, huh?"

"No." Leah sounded genuinely pleased. "Not at all. It's sweet. Really. I'm touched," she said, and sprung out of her seat, grabbed Justine's waist, and started tickling her, Justine doubling over, laughing.

At four, they ate dinner. Their parents, working together, prepared turkey with cranberry stuffing (Nana Tyler's recipe), garlic-mashed potatoes, asparagus, a salad of field greens and olives.

While Justine and her father were at church, Leah had baked apple pie. She'd forgotten to cover the pie with foil and neglected to turn on the timer, and the crust had burned. Despite their mother's repeated pleas—*it's a waste, Leah, please*—she refused to cut it. Instead, she served the anemic lemon meringue pie their dad had bought at the supermarket, two days before.

After dinner, Justine's father called his sister, in Philly. Passing the phone, they wished her, her husband, and their six children a merry Christmas. Next, their dad called his parents.

Leah asked to talk first. She spoke with their grandmother for five minutes, and asked for their grandfather. His apple pie, she said, shooting an evil eye in their mother's direction, was "way better" than hers. Would he give her a lesson next time she saw him? She laughed at his response, said goodbye, passed the phone to Justine, excusing herself, and went to the bathroom.

Justine hopped on the counter. "When are you and Poppa coming up?" she asked, swinging her legs. "I miss you guys."

"Soon," her grandmother replied. "In a couple of weeks, maybe. Your dad asked Poppa and me to stay at the house, so he and your mom can get away for a few days."

Justine shot a heated look in her father's direction. They didn't need their grandparents to baby-sit them. She and Leah were old enough to stay home alone. Leah would be furious when she found out. "You're going away?" she asked, agitated, when her parents hung up the phone.

"Nothing's definite," her father said. "We haven't decided anything yet."

"Calm down, Justine," her mother cut in. "There's nothing to get riled about."

"What's up?" Leah asked, having emerged from the bathroom just as Justine was about to demand an explanation. Leah cut into the center of the pie, pushed the filling off the knife with her fingers. "This about the grand-rents?" Leah popped the pie in her mouth. "They coming up?"

"They were here in August," their mom said. "Don't tell me you've forgotten already?"

Leah shrugged. "Seems longer than that."

"Cut me a piece of that, would you?" Their father pulled a dessert plate from the top shelf of the cabinet, handed it to Leah, and set a second plate on the counter. "And one for mom."

Leah cut two wedge-shaped slices of pie, removing the burned sections, and pushed the plates toward their father. "Something's up," she said, holding the knife in one hand. "You guys are acting all weird. Nana and Poppa are OK? They're not sick, are they?"

Tell the truth, Justine said to their parents, with her eyes. *Tell her the truth.*

"Nothing's up, Leah," their mother snapped. "Would you change the subject, please?"

Leah glared at their mother in defiance.

This was wrong. Their parents expected the truth from Leah, from both daughters, about everything. Leah deserved no less from them. "They're going away," Justine told her sister.

"Justine," her father warned. "That's enough."

No, Justine thought. It wasn't enough. "They asked Nana and Poppa to stay with us."

"Are you serious?" Leah's eyes widened. She spun toward their father, pivoted, turning to their mother, looked back to their father. "You guys aren't *ever* gonna trust me? Are you?"

"Lower your voice, Leah." Their mother reached for Leah's arm. "Nothing's definite yet." Leah shrugged her away. "It's Christmas," their mother pleaded. "Don't ruin the day."

Leah hurled her knife. It hit the sink with an echoing clang. "Don't *you* fucking ruin it."

"Goddamn it, Leah," their father bellowed. "Watch your mouth."

"Why are you mad at *me*? She's the one you ought to be pissed at." Her face turned pink, then purple, the veins in her temples bulging. "Why don't you tell him, Mom?" Leah smirked. "When you guys were at church, I was checking my e-mail. I found love notes to that cop."

"Nice, Leah. Good. Should I tell him what *I* found, now?" From her pocket, their mother produced a blue plastic case. "You know what these are, Will?" Her mother waved the packet.

Leah pounced at their mother, pawing for the birth control pills.

Her mother snatched her hand back. "You know what this means, Will. Right?"

They were crazy, this family. Justine wanted to run. To hide. To go—anywhere. To Holly's. To the moon. Anyplace where people were normal. But her feet were plastered in place.

"Might want to talk to your daughter, Will. Unless you don't care she's having sex?"

"Why are you *do*ing this to me?" Leah slid to the floor, burying her face in her arms.

"To you?" their mother shouted. "Why am I doing this to you?"

Their father crouched in front of Leah, taking hold of her arms. "Leah, listen to me."

"Why? Does? She?" Leah asked, between sobs. "Hate me so much?" With the back of her hand, she wiped her teary eyes.

"She doesn't hate you, honey." Their father pushed a hair away from Leah's forehead.

"Jesus. Don't coddle her, Will. She knows I don't hate her."

"Damn it, Zoe," their father shouted. "Would you just shut up."

"I don't believe this," their mother hissed. "You're playing right into her hands."

Leah struggled to her feet. "Liar." Leah pushed past their father. "You don't love me. You never loved me," she cried, her face contorted, and bolted out of the room.

Justine tore out of the kitchen, after her sister. "Leah, wait."

"Lee, she didn't mean it." With her fist, Justine pounded her sister's door. She heard her sister inside her room, talking to someone, her drawers opening, slamming shut. "Lee, open the door." *Please,* Justine prayed. *Don't let her run away. Not again.* "Leah, please?"

All of a sudden, the door swung open, and Leah swept by, her nylon bag swinging.

Justine chased after her sister, taking the stairs two at a time. In the foyer, she skidded into her father, who was blocking the door. "Leah," Justine called. "Leah," she hollered. Her sister sprinted to the top of the drive, toward the Jeep idling in the circle "Leah, come back."

"Let her go," Justine's father said. Setting both hands on Justine's shoulders, he moved her gently away from the door. "She'll be back. She just needs to blow off some steam."

No, Justine thought, not this time. This time, her sister was not coming back.

Twenty-Nine

Where There's Will, There's A Way

"I'll pound the *piss* out of that kid if I see him." Will rammed his fist on the bar, a thick slab of shiny, poly-urethaned oak. His daughter was a good kid before Corbett got hold of her.

First his kid, mixed up with that lousy piece of shit, Corbett. Now his wife.

His wife wasn't mixed up with Corbett. His wife was involved, he'd learned three nights ago, with that cop. Goddamn Johnson, moving in on his wife. Kill that son of a bitch, too, if the opportunity presented itself. But Corbett was the responsible party. The punk got the ball rolling.

"You okay?" the bartender asked. "You hit that hand pretty hard."

"Yeah, yeah. I'll have another one." Nother un, it came out, meaning a Bud. He was drinking Bud now. Shows you how far down he'd dropped on the beer drinker's food chain.

The bar, a dive he'd discovered off Route 40, was called Lahey's. The bartender wasn't a Lahey. Henry was a Hooter or a Holter or a Howler. Used to be a Hell's Angel, before he moved East. Will knew because, the first time he drank here, he'd asked Henry about the mermaid tattoo on his forearm. He'd figured Henry for a weightlifter, with those thirty-inch biceps. He didn't know who the hell Lahey was. He ought to ask. Probably ought to know. "Who's Lahey?"

Behind the bar, Henry was drying a glass. "Kid sister's old man." He swirled a paper towel inside the cheap crystal bowl, wiped off the stem. "Pain in the ass. You sure you're okay?"

Just dandy, Will assured him.

Not all bars are created equal, he thought. This was an ace. Didn't smell too bad, a little funky, depending on who all was drinking here, how long since they'd bathed, what the guys did for a living. The wallpaper, an indifferent blue and green plaid, kept the hostility down. Paneling under the chair rails. No neon. No neon was good. Henry kept the lights dim, which allowed for a certain degree of anonymity, a plus in any good watering hole. A string of colored Christmas lights blinked through the bottles behind the bar, the lights twinkling in a way that struck Will as sad. Christmas had come and gone, and nothing had changed. People pinned too much hope on the holidays. Six billion bodies and counting. Couldn't all get what they'd wished for. Santa never could make it all the way around, the jolly old bastard just one more eighty-percenter.

Will drummed the bar, to catch Henry's attention. *What do you think of me, bruiser?* Will wanted to know, *had* to know, it was vitally important for him to know, if Henry respected him or not. If Henry saw him as an equal, if he looked at Will as a real man. A good bartender could tell you a lot about yourself. If Henry had divined some deep, dark secret, something Will didn't perceive in his being, he wanted to hear it. Figure out why his wife was screwing around.

The bells on the door jingled. *Jing-a-ling, jing-a-ling,* Will sang, *hear them ring, hear them ring,* his mind lighting on a cartoon image from some Christmas special the kids used to watch. *Frosty the Snowman,* he thought. *A ve-ry hap-py soul.* Stupid jingle, lodged in his head.

Pair of lowlifes in wool hunting jackets, the gray hoods of their sweatshirts pulled over their collars, stamped their feet on the mat, kicking the sludge off their boots, and swaggered to the bar, ordered Silver Bullets with a shot of JD. Henry served their drinks, and they strutted to the pool table in back, lifted a couple cues off the wall, racked up the balls, and instantly began bickering. This joint was the real deal. The balls, Will thought, because of bastards like them.

"The kid ain't worth it," Henry said. Without Will's even asking, he'd produced another Bud. "Touch that kid, your ass goes to jail. Hear me, Tyler? You ain't saying much tonight."

Will dug a twenty out of his pocket, and laid it on the bar.

"Where you off to, buddy? All this yakking, you got me on the edge of my seat."

To take a piss, Will told him.

He'd left his cell phone in the car. He stood by the pay phone, in a dark hallway that, if you trailed the overpowering odor of piss, eventually led to the men's room. Swaying, he fished through his coat pocket for the crumpled bar napkin he'd been carrying around, Kyra's number scrawled in faded blue ink. When he came home from California, he discovered the napkin in a stash of receipts he'd collected on the trip. He'd meant to throw it out; he'd accidentally put it in his armoire, instead. Two days ago, rooting through his underwear drawer, he'd found it again.

They needed a light in this corner. He could barely make out the numbers: 526-6647. He dialed, got a recorded message. A male voice. Must have been four-*nine*. Tried again. What—

—the hell did he think he was he doing? He plunked the receiver on the hook, and staggered back to the bar, said bye to Henry and left.

The lot was a sheet of black ice. The soles of his leather shoes slid all over the place.

He wandered around the lot, hunting for his car. Some asshole must have moved it on him. Took one more spin around. Hot damn, the beamer was right by the door. Crazy bastard, must've returned it when Will looked the other way.

He fumbled with the lock, loaded himself into the car, and switched on the headlights.

He drove, with no particular goal in mind, down winding, poorly lit roads. Hard to see in the dark. He leaned into the steering wheel. After awhile, he found himself on Main, heading in the general direction of home. It occurred to him, as he was driving, that it was pointless to go home without Leah. If he could find her, bring her home, everything would change. They would work on things, Zoe and him. He missed his wife. He loved her. Fuck Kyra. He wanted his wife back. Couldn't keep living this way. Had to bring Leah home. First, he had to find her.

He'd pressed a Springsteen disc into the changer. The Boss was singing a haunting tune about a freight train inside his head. *Whoa-ho.* Will rubbed his neck, the rumbling pain pressing from the back of his skull into his temples. He knew exactly what the Boss was talking about.

He bagged a left onto a residential street, an oversized horseshoe that eventually dropped him a block from where he'd started. He'd been driving for an hour, his head just about clear.

Up ahead, he spotted a cop. Sneaky bastard. Parked his cruiser at the edge of a field, behind a thicket, only its nose exposed. Will veered onto another side road, heading west.

The houses on the west end of town were pieces of crap. Run-down Capes. Ranches. Deck houses, seventies-style. He passed the

277

entrance to a lower income housing development, Spartan brick townhouses, the brick sandblasted to give the illusion of age.

He checked his gas gauge. Quarter of a tank.

A light flashed in his rearview. Corbett's Wrangler. *What the frig do you know.*

The Wrangler signaled a left-hand turn. Will swerved onto the shoulder, did a U-ie, and tailed the Wrangler into the development. Christmas night, at his wife's insistence, he'd tried to chase down the kids. But he'd dawdled too long at the door. By the time he got to the circle, the Jeep was gone. He'd parked in front of the two-family where he thought Corbett lived, sat there until midnight, eyeballing the place, waiting for nothing, it turned out. Pissed him off at himself. A father ought to have more than a general idea regarding the whereabouts of his daughter's boyfriend. Afterward, he'd looked up the address, online. Right street, wrong Corbett, evidently.

This time, he'd hit pay dirt. He pulled into an illegal spot behind the dumpster, and cut his engine.

This spot afforded him a partial view of the Wrangler, the tail end, the interior obstructed. *Let's go, Corbett*, he grumbled. *Get a move on.* What the hell was he doing? Fixing his makeup?

After five, hour-long minutes, the driver's door crawled open, and a pair of tiny orthopedic shoes swung out. Will slapped the steering wheel, and backed out of his spot.

When he left the development, he drove to the road where he'd parked Christmas night.

The street, an offshoot of the center, had been left to decay. The stately Victorians that once housed the bigwigs from the tannery had been converted to two- and three-family homes, most of them rented. The street was lined with pickups, sedans appeared ready for the junkyard.

The street was nearly pitch-dark. For a second, he wondered if a transformer had blown, knocking out the power. A third of the way up, he spotted Corbett's Jeep, parked under the lone operational streetlamp. Well, I'll be, Will thought. He'd had the right place all along.

The Corbetts had left the Victorian to rot, its front porch sagging, the balustrade warped, half the balusters missing or cracked. Since Christmas, someone had nailed a sheet of plywood over the broken window in the attic. This two-family conversion was recent. The contractor had done a lousy job. Will could see where he'd patched the shingles around the front doors.

In the front yard, an inflatable Santa Claus stood by a scruffy white pine sprigged with red and green bulbs, the same tacky lights blinking on the miserable tree inside the front window.

Lights burned on all three floors of the house—which meant they were in there.

Will drove around the block, parked near the foot the street, where he would be less conspicuous, and slid into the passenger seat. He turned off the CD, switching to "Sports Talk" on AM radio, the callers pulverizing the Celtics for losing again, and settled in for the duration.

He needed a solid plan for getting his daughter out of this place. He surveyed the area, calculating the distances from the house to the truck, and from the truck to his side of the street.

As soon the front door of the Victorian opened, he decided, he would slip out of his car. If he stayed low, behind the vehicles parked along the curb, Corbett wouldn't spot him until they were face-to-face. Unless the kid had shotgun reflexes, which Will doubted, considering the kid's profligate lifestyle, Will would be on the kid before he had time to react.

The seconds dragged.

Half an hour went by. Forty minutes. Maybe he should call the house, tease Corbett out.

Finally, the front door of the Victorian opened, and Corbett stepped out, alone.

Relief shot through him. Maybe his daughter had come to her senses, and given up on the asshole. Be something, if Leah were home.

Corbett headed down his front walk, his head bobbing, a gloved hand on his headphones.

Will slowly, quietly, opened the BMW's passenger door.

He crouched behind a Buick, directly across from the Jeep, his adrenaline shooting into high gear, his hands jittery, his breath rapid. He could almost smell Corbett's bad vibes.

Wait, he told himself. *Be patient*. Don't move until Corbett's got his hand on the door.

As Will waited, counting the seconds, the front door of the Victorian opened again, and a hulking, bald-headed kid stepped onto the porch. At one time, he could have handled these two punks together. Hadn't worked out in years. If he separated them, he thought, he might be all right. Generally, when an older guy raised his fists to a kid, it took the kid an instant to psych himself out of the parent-child role. That split-second hesitation would give Will the advantage.

Better yet, he would call the cops. Leave an anonymous message, say he'd witnessed a drug deal. The objective was to get Corbett out of the picture. What difference did it make how Will accomplished his goal? Great idea, Will thought. He felt good about this one.

He'd punched all but the final digit for the Cortland police when the door opened a third time, and Leah trotted out. *Damn.* If something seems too good to be true, it's because it's not. He should have known she was in there. He stuffed the phone back in his pocket.

Leah tucked her chin inside the collar of her peacoat, her hands pushed deep in her pockets, her breath rising like smoke. Halfway down the sidewalk, she made a face, as if she had forgotten something, turned toward the door, and spoke to someone inside.

The door swung open again. Cases of beer were stacked, four feet high, in the front entry.

From behind the stack of beer, Will's younger daughter appeared.

Will froze, the shock of seeing Justine immobilizing him.

The sidewalks were poorly shoveled. Justine slipped on the ice-crusted snow. Leah snagged her sister's arm, pulled Justine to her feet.

The burly kid, crammed in the passenger seat of the Jeep, was fiddling with the radio. Corbett stood at the curb, waiting for the girls, the driver's seat of the truck pulled forward.

Will found this scene impossible to comprehend. What was Justine doing here? What did these punks want with an innocent kid? He couldn't let his girls get away. Had to do something.

Will shot across the street, banking on the element of surprise.

Todd was holding the door for Justine, his back to Will.

"Oh my God," Leah cried. "My father. Todd, *look out.*"

Todd wheeled in Will's direction. He stared at Will, his eyes glinting.

Will stared right back. "Let's go, Corbett. Have it out. Let's see what you're made of."

The Jeep's passenger door swung open, an old Mother Love Bone song blaring from the stereo. The bald kid, twisting backward, stood half-in, half-out of the truck, a thick hand on the roof.

"Daddy." Justine skated across the sidewalk, her ponytail bobbing. "Daddy, wait."

Overalls and a sweatshirt. No jacket. *Jesus.* "Get in my car." He pointed down the street.

"Daddy. Wait. It's okay. We were—"

"Now, Justine. In my car."

"What do you want?" Leah waved her fists at Will, her features distorted by the shadows. "Justine," she shouted. "Come back here."

"Stay where you are, Justine," Will ordered. "You're going with me."

"Don't listen to him, Jus." Leah extended a hand to her sister. "You're with us."

Todd held his ground. The big kid, circling behind the truck, made his way to Corbett.

"It's OK, Lupo." Todd tipped his head at the Jeep, his eyes on Will. "It's under control."

Todd and Leah stood a few feet apart, the base corners of a triangle, Leah a foot or two closer to him than Todd. If he startled them, he could reach her before Todd had time to react.

"Leah. Watch out, behind you," he called, and lunged for his daughter.

All at once, Todd was on him. Will jerked his elbows backward, flicking him off, the kid fumbling in the snow. "We're going," Will shouted, and seized his daughter's arm.

"He's *drunk.*" Leah, struggling, dragged Will onto the lawn. "You stink. Let me go."

Todd spun toward Will again. Enraged, Will swung right, one hand grasping Leah's arm, and batted the kid off, knocking him to the ground.

Somehow, in the scuffle, he'd let go of Leah. She attempted to escape, feet slipping out from under her. Will swooped down, grabbed her arms and legs, and hoisted her over his shoulder, Leah kicking, squealing, her Doc Martin shoes pounding his thighs, fists pummeling his back.

Corbett swiped at his nose, streaking blood onto his cheek.

"Todd," Leah wailed, smashing her head into Will's neck. "Your *nose.* Call the cops."

Todd swore and charged again, the bigger kid rushing into the fray, grabbing Todd from behind, holding him off. "Let's *go,* man," the big kid yelled. "Get out of here. He's psycho."

Leah, hanging over Will's shoulder, screamed for help. It was a wonder the neighbors hadn't called the police. Or maybe they had. Will didn't know if the arrival of cops would be good or bad. Good, he thought. If they didn't haul him away, too. Distracted, he loosened his grip on Leah's legs.

Leah pulled free, her hands and feet hitting the pavement at once.

"Come on, Jus." Leah rushed to Todd's side, and reached for her sister.

Todd waved Justine into the idling truck.

"Justine," Will pleaded, a last ditch effort. "Come home with me."

Justine hesitated, not quite sure, it seemed, where she should go.

"Let's go, dudes." The big kid, Lupo, waved a cell phone. "Cops are on their way."

"Well, Dad. I guess this is it." Leah brushed herself off. "Looks like your *friends* are coming for you. Like to see you get out of this one," she spat, and pulled her sister into the Jeep.

Will stood stupidly on the sidewalk in front of the Victorian, watching the Jeep pull away. It was not the police or the aftereffects of the beer or even watching his daughters leave with Corbett and Lupo that turned his blood to ice, that kept him from moving. It was the realization that he was fighting a losing battle—no matter what he did or how hard he fought, he could not save his daughter this time— that paralyzed him.

Thirty

Snow Angels

After they left Todd's, the four of them rode around town, the window on the passenger side of the Jeep rolled down, the song "Stardog Champion" pounding out of the stereo, blasting Justine's skull. Lupo rode shotgun, his elbow crooked on the lip of the window. He lit a joint, and passed it to Todd. Justine sat in the backseat, huddled under a blanket, with her sister.

"You believe the dude fell for that shit?" Todd guffawed. "The cops? What's he, stupid?"

"Shut up," Leah griped. "It's not funny." Justine silently seconded the motion.

"What's with him, anyhow?" Lupo asked, for the third time. He turned his head, peering at them. *His* father would never do something like that. (His mother, it emerged, had died when Lupo was four.) "Because he doesn't care what you do," Leah had grumbled, the first time Lupo brought up his father. *Cause he ain't nuts, you mean*, Todd and Lupo had responded in unison.

"Pussy," Todd interjected. "You see him floundering? I could a had his ass, if I wanted."

"Dude?" Lupo punched Todd's upper arm. "That's how come you're covered in blood."

Todd blotted his nose. His cheekbone and the bridge of his nose were swelling.

Lupo sniggered. "What do you care, anyhow? The goon was wasted."

"Was not," Leah said peevishly. "My father was a little buzzed. He wasn't wasted."

283

"Fucking psycho." Todd sucked on the joint, offered it to Leah, who refused, claiming she was not in the mood, and passed it to Lupo. "Psycho," he said again. "That's all I got to say."

Justine felt like a traitor, sitting in silence, listening to the boys bashing her father. She ought to stick up for him. Only it was impossible to defend what her father had done. What did he expect to accomplish, showing up at Todd's house unannounced, smelling as if he'd taken a bath in a vat of beer? She'd brought her cell phone with her. If he wanted to convince Leah to come home, why not call? Tell her he missed her? Offer to smooth things over with their mother? Justine and her sister had talked for a good hour, this afternoon. Living in Todd's basement depressed her, Leah said. Todd and his mom tried to make her comfortable. His mom had even bought her a toothbrush. But this wasn't her home. She hated being alienated from her family. She wanted to sleep in her own bed, surrounded by things of her own. "I miss you guys, Jus. I miss my room. Stupid, I miss Paddington Bear. I can't believe I'm saying this. I even miss *Mom.*" But she couldn't go crawling home. She needed to be sure their parents wanted her back.

Todd had called earlier, to invite Justine to his house, to visit with Leah. He dialed Star 6-7, in case Justine wasn't around. If one of her parents answered, they wouldn't know it was him.

"We can pick you up, if you want," he had said. "She's scared to call you herself. Your sister thinks you hate her." They agreed to meet in forty-five minutes, at the end of her block.

Justine told her mother that Holly had invited her over. "I might be late," she had said.

Their father had no right attacking the boys. They'd done nothing wrong. They'd spent the afternoon watching *Reservoir Dogs,* one of the movies Todd's mother had bought him for Christmas, drinking Diet Coke, eating stale chips. When they'd first arrived and she'd seen Lupo on the living room floor, propped on his elbows, playing Nintendo, Justine had to admit, she was scared. On Halloween night, the only other time she had seen him, Lupo had struck her as evil. But she was wrong about Lupo. Yes, he was a little messed up (he *had* to be, to sell drugs), but he wasn't a bad kid. He was actually sweet, in a way. She hated the movie, the awful people, not a redeeming character among them. She hated the violence. Lupo noticed her eyes closed, and nudged her awake, challenged her to a game of checkers. A lot of boys would be ticked, being beaten six times by a junior-high girl. Lupo shook his head in awe, asked for her secret.

"Would you shut that window?" Leah complained. "We're freezing back here."

"Want to go to my house?" Lupo asked, out of the blue. "My old man's out of town."

Lupo lived with his father, in a converted condo, on a property that was once an estate owned by a member of the Caldwell family from Boston—banking people, Lupo informed them. The main building, nestled on a knoll at the end of a winding drive, reminded Justine of a castle, with its airy portico and stucco walls. They parked in a pebbled lot behind the building, in front of a ten-car garage. Lupo's apartment occupied the right wing of the estate. The apartment was nearly as big as the Tyler's whole house, with a soaring entry, a sweeping spiral staircase.

The kitchen was equipped with the same restaurant-style appliances the Tylers owned. "The old man—" Lupo smirked. "Fancies himself a cook." Lupo's father never cooked for them. He cooked for his girlfriends. Lupo opened a refrigerator, stocked with fifty or sixty bottles of white wine, scoured the contents, scrutinizing the labels on five or six bottles, closed it, opened the temperature-controlled closet on the other side of the room, and filched a bottle of red.

"Rothschild," Lupo announced. "He's got a case. My old man will never notice it gone."

"Careful," he said, handing out Wedgwood glasses. "Suckers cost fifty bucks a pop."

The wine was "superb," evidently. Lupo and Justine's sister babbled on and on, applying snobby words like *nose* and *tannin* and *complexity*, words she'd heard their parents toss around with their friends. Todd looked on, bemused. Justine took a sip, and set her glass on the counter.

"What's the matter?" Leah asked. "You don't like red wine?"

"No, I do. It's—" Justine sniffed, and forced another sip. "Good."

Lupo offered her a hunk of whitish-yellow cheese. The blue streaks running through the cheese reminded her of Nana Tyler's varicose veins. "Try it with this," he said. "Gorgonzola."

The cheese smelled like BO. "Thanks." Justine pushed it away. "I'm not really hungry."

When they'd emptied the bottle of wine, Lupo opened another, and led the three of them, expensive crystal glasses in hand, to a marble room behind the kitchen that housed their Jacuzzi.

Black and white photographs of Lupo and his father, shot in Jerusalem and Beirut, lined the marble-tiled wall directly across from the hot tub. After his mother died, his father had joined the army, Lupo explained. He'd worked as a lawyer for JAG. In one photo, Lupo and his dad were in Kosovo. Lupo, who appeared to be seven or eight, was perched on the seat of a tank.

"That must have been scary," Justine said, picturing Lupo and his dad dodging bullets.

The question seemed to call up some grave disappointment. "The war was over," he said.

Justine studied the photos, while the others undressed.

"I don't have a bathing suit," she said, when Lupo asked if she'd like to go in.

Leah shot her a look.

"'S OK," Todd said. He pulled his T-shirt over his head. When they first arrived, he'd washed his face and iced his nose. The swelling had gone down significantly. "Don't need one."

Justine winced. Maybe *they* didn't.

"Don't be shy," Lupo said. "It's just us."

Justine shrugged, without turning around. In the mirrored glass, she caught a glimpse of the huge white moons of Lupo's butt. "I'm looking at the pictures. They're cool."

Through the looking glass of the picture frames, Justine watched her sister unhook her bra, and slip out of her panties. Leah climbed the steps, nipples erect, and slithered into the tub.

"Don't be a ninny, Jus," Leah said. "Least put your feet in."

Lupo was sitting in a corner, his arms spread. He turned in Justine's direction, treating her to a full-on view of his hairy chest, caught her staring, and laughed. Mortified, she averted her eyes.

"Come on," Todd teased. "We don't bite, you know."

The bubbling water made a loud, gurgling noise. Reluctantly, Justine rolled up her jeans and took a seat on the edge of the hot tub. Gradually, she submerged her feet in the steaming water. Leah laid her head on the rim of the tub, her knees breaking the surface, fluttered her feet.

The boys splashed each other, soaking the marble walls.

"Yo. Dudes." Todd rose like a phantom, wet blond hair in ringlets, water dripping from the hairs on his chin. He waded through the chest-deep water, shoulders hunched, his elbows crooked. "Look," he called. *Quasimodo.*

"Weirdo," Leah shrieked, and dove, grabbing hold of his leg, dragging him under.

"Hey," Todd crowed, when he came up for air, and then Leah was under the water too.

Lupo splashed and Justine splashed back. Justine's jeans were soaked, the water-logged denim glued uncomfortably to her legs. She pulled off her jeans, stripping to her panties and T-shirt, and laid her jeans on the floor to let them dry them out.

The kids stayed in the tub for a good hour. By the time they emerged, the skin on Justine's fingers and toes had shriveled. The kids, shivering, their bodies covered in goose-pimples, pulled their clothes on quickly, and retreated to the living room, where there was a gigantic flat screen TV. The boys selected an old slasher flick from a floor-to-ceiling shelf.

The movie grossed her out. Justine watched for a few minutes, and fell asleep.

Justine felt her sister's hand on her shoulder. "Wake up, Jus. Time to get you home."

Justine yawned, blinking. "Are you coming, too?"

"I can't, Teenie. You know Dad. You're with him or against him. What if he saw me?"

"Please, Lee? Just for tonight? You can go back to Todd's tomorrow."

It took some doing, but Leah agreed, haltingly. "Just tonight. For you. But only tonight."

Todd covered the five miles from Lupo's house to the Tyler's in less than ten minutes. At the top of the circle, he lifted his foot from the pedal, and let the Jeep roll down the drive. As they rounded the bend, passing the stand of trees that obstructed the view of their house, they noticed the light from the living room lamp. The rest of the house was dark.

"Shit," Leah said. "Figures, he'd be awake."

Justine wondered what he would do. Apologize for his embarrassing behavior? Or yell because they were late? Well, she thought, with escalating dread, they would know soon enough.

Todd offered to walk them to the door. How nice, Justine thought. He wants to protect us.

Her sister flatly refused. "Just go. "He's—" She twirled a finger next to her temple. "He'll freak if he sees you."

The girls waited in the shadows until the truck disappeared, opened the garage door slowly, and crept into the house. To get to their bedrooms, they had to pass the living room, where their father was waiting. At the head of the hallway, they stopped. "I'll go first," Justine whispered. "Maybe he won't notice you." Leah squeezed her hand. Holding their breath, they tiptoed down the hall. As they approached the living room door, they heard their father quietly snoring. He had fallen asleep, they saw, in his recliner, a book lying, face-down, in his lap.

Justine shrugged. Leah made a face, her palms upturned.

That night, with her bare feet tucked between Leah's shins, Justine dreamed the most wonderful dreams. In her dreams, she and Leah were little girls. In the first dream, they were playing fetch with their dog. Dog, a puppy again, bounded after the stick, scooped it, and charged back, dropping the stick at their feet. Now they were lying in the front yard, waving their arms, making snow angels. Holding hands, they stared at the deep blue winter sky, naming the clouds. In the last, long dream before she woke, Leah was pushing her on the swings. Up, up, up, Leah sang, the swing soaring over the grass, Justine giggling, pumping her legs.

Justine hugged her pillow, holding fast to the dream.

When she opened her eyes, sunshine was pouring into the room. And her sister was gone, the drawers of her bureau flung open, her closet stripped bare. Leah's cell phone, lying on the nightstand next to a full bottle of Zoloft, the only signs that she had been home.

Thirty-One

The Waiting Game

Zoe never dreamed she could feel so distant, so alienated from one of her children. After their hideous blowout on Christmas night, Leah had run off to Todd's. Will spotted Todd's Jeep, waiting in the circle. Infuriated, Zoe persuaded her husband to follow the truck, chase the kids down in his car. She wasn't thinking straight. She couldn't stand the thought of their daughter escaping, enjoying the rest of the night, while she and Will sat at home, in a funk because of Leah, stewing. Once Will hauled their daughter home, Zoe planned to force her to retract her allegations, her silly lies about Jerry. Leah had read a few friendly e-mail messages, which, for the record, she had no business opening: she'd been snooping in Zoe's *Outlook* account. Stupidly, Zoe had never bothered to password-protect her computer. There were no *love* letters. Zoe had never in her life written a love letter.

Zoe lay in bed, half-thinking, half-dreaming about Leah, the morning noises, the hiss of the heater, the water gurgling in the pipes, burrowing into the outer reaches of her consciousness. Leah's running away was her fault. She should have left the room the minute the silly squabble about Will's parents began, behaved like an adult instead of a child. The argument was pointless: she and Will had made no definite plans for a trip. But the phone call was merely a trigger. She and Leah were already circling, waiting for a battle. A blowout was the only possible outcome.

Zoe's anger had been building all day. While Will and Justine were at church, she'd gone into the girls' bathroom to gather their towels for the laundry. A smarmy Hallmark card sat on the vanity, in

289

plain view. She'd known, without even looking inside, that the card was from Todd. Fuming, she picked it up. The card belonged to Leah. Set it down. She had no right to snoop. But Leah had left the card in plain view, where Zoe could easily find it. Maybe, for some reason, she wanted Zoe to read it.

The note he'd written inside was utter drivel. *You're the best thing that's ever happened to me, Babe. I will love you for the rest of my life. Forever yours, Todd.*

Nice. Corbett and her daughter were discussing marriage. God help her.

It took an instant for the full punch of the word to hit, another for Zoe to grasp the fact that her daughter, her beautiful, smart, talented daughter, might actually *marry* Todd Corbett.

Reeling, she'd gone on a rampage, opening cabinets, rooting through drawers, hunting, for what? Drugs? Paraphernalia? An incriminating letter? Anything she could use as evidence against her daughter's boyfriend, to prove to Leah, once and for all, that he was no good.

Instead, she'd found birth control pills. Any other time, she would have addressed the situation calmly, shared her concerns, explained the dangers of sexual involvement at too early an age. She would have told Leah she loved her, assured her that she was there for her, no matter what. In a rage, she stormed into the family room, waving the packet, demanding an explanation, by which point Leah had already dug up the so-called "love letters" on Zoe's computer.

She heard a pop, their bedroom door opening, she realized a few seconds later.

Justine hovered over their bed, screaming hysterically at Will. Something about Leah. Something about Todd. Something, something, *big jerk.* Justine was beside herself; she wasn't making much sense. Zoe rubbed her eyes. "For heaven's sake, Justine," she said. She'd woke them for this? To tell them Leah was gone? Her sister had left days ago. "Justine, honey." It's early, she planned to say. Go back to bed. Get a little more sleep. The fury in her daughter's face terrified her. "Sweetheart, what's wrong?"

"She took her stuff," Justine sobbed. "Because of *him.*"

Finally, Justine calmed down enough to tell Zoe the story. When she left the room, Will confessed to a drunken escapade at Todd's. "Idiot," Zoe screamed. How could he? They knew where Leah was. They'd agreed to give her space. Had he made it a goal to push her away? *Oh, and she was a saint? Did she think she deserved the peace prize for that outburst on Christmas?* Generally, Will was not combative. Once he started, he dug in deep, and didn't relent. She was a goddamn drug addict, he snapped, a "low blow," she cried, seeing as how, the day after Dog died, she had flushed all her pills down the toilet. Enraged, she yanked on a pair of Levis and a T-shirt, and tore out of the room. "You're an asshole to boot," she shouted, slamming the door.

In a fog, she rushed downstairs to the kitchen, began pulling bowls, spatulas, measuring spoons out of the cabinets. She broke three large eggs into a plastic mixing bowl, beat the eggs with the hand-whisk, froth rising in waves up the sides of the bowl. When the eggs thickened, she added oil and buttermilk, whisked the wet ingredients together, poured flour, sugar, baking soda into a larger bowl, dug a well in the center, stirred in the egg mixture. She defrosted a bag of blueberries in the microwave. With her teeth, she ripped the plastic bag open.

Justine was in Leah's room, listening to music, the stereo turned to full blast, the song's repetitive bass rattling the ceiling. Zoe winced. When did Justine start listening to rap?

She'd turned the stove on too soon. The griddle overheated. She dumped the first batch of pancakes, the tops raw, the undersides charred, in the garbage disposal, ladled six more onto the griddle, fried the second batch to a deep golden brown. With the edge of the spatula, she cut the smallest of the pancakes in half and stuffed it in her mouth, flipped the pancakes onto a plate, and ladled six more. She'd used all but a cup of blueberries. She couldn't refreeze them, hated to waste perfectly good berries, decided to make muffins, to freeze, for later in the week. As she slid the pan into the oven, she saw that the bananas hanging on the wooden banana tree by the sink had turned brown, and mixed batter for bread. While the banana bread was baking, she made a batch of chocolate-chip cookies. She mixed the ingredients for a pecan pie last, Leah's favorite, in case Leah had a change of heart, and decided to come home.

By late afternoon, the house looked and smelled like a bakery, the counters lined with sweets: banana bread, chocolate-chip cookies, lemon poppy seed cake, mocha fudge, pecan pie.

"Who's going to eat all that?" Will asked, as she pulled the pie out of the oven.

"*We* are." She set the pie on a hotplate, tossed her towel in the sink. "Who do you think?"

"Planning to drink that?" Will asked. The Budweiser she was twisting open, he meant.

She handed him the bottle. "I don't know why I took it." She never drank beer.

He took a long pull, and, holding the bottle by the neck, wiped his mouth. "Can we talk?"

She poured a glass of orange juice for herself, added two shots of vodka, and followed her husband into the family room. He moved the magazines fanned out over the coffee table—the December *Atlantic*, an issue of *SI* with Peyton Manning on the cover, this week's *New Yorker*—set them on the end table by the arm of the sofa, and placed a log in the fireplace, prodding it with a poker. When the fire caught, he plugged a Keith Jarrett CD into the player.

"We should take the tree down," she said. The tree looked like yesterday's news, the branches drooping, the carpet a bed of dry needles. If a spark from the fireplace ever hit the tree or landed on the needles littering the floor, the whole house would go up in flames.

"Maybe tomorrow," he said. "I hate fighting with you, Zoe. It's not right."

Zoe hated all their quarreling, too. "Thanks for driving over again"—to the Corbetts' house, she meant. He'd gone to the Corbett place, forty-five minutes ago, without telling her where he was headed or what he planned to do. He'd phoned from his car to let her know that Corbett's Jeep was parked by the curb. "I tried calling, this morning. Nobody answered."

He swallowed the last of his beer, set the bottle on a coaster. "Maybe they were out."

Maybe, she thought. Or maybe they'd recognized the number on caller ID and ignored the call. "Mind if I change this music?" The piano solo depressed her. Maybe it was the dreary weather. The sun had not been out in days. The house felt like a cave. "It's dismal."

"Sorry. I thought you'd like it. Let me find something different."

"That's all right." She motioned for him to stay seated, got up, turned on a light.

Zoe scanned the rows of CDs lining the bookcase. Will had spent the entire morning organizing his CDs. It felt odd to see the bookcase, normally a mishmash of books and discs, some standing, others lying in piles, looking so neat. He'd placed the books on the bottom shelf; on the upper shelves, he'd alphabetized his CDs, arranged by genre, each genre subdivided by artist. She selected a Jan Garbarek disc, loaded the changer, and joined Will again on the floor.

She picked a glob of batter from her arm. "I never thought I'd say this. I feel better knowing she's there." She balled the batter, flicked it away. "At least we know where she is."

"We can't keep fighting, Zo." Taking her hand, he scooped a pillow from the sofa, and pulled her with him to the floor. "We're in this together. We've got to remember that."

Zoe leaned back, against the sofa. "She doesn't really think I hate her, does she?"

"Of course not," Will replied patiently. "She's a kid. Kids exaggerate."

"I can't stop thinking about it."

"You've got to let up on yourself. This doesn't help anybody, Zo."

Zoe smiled, and promised to try. She harped on the parents she counseled for this very same thing. "Focus on your children," she told them. "Get out of yourself. Think about *them*." If she listened to her own advice, her thoughts and energy would be directed toward Leah. But that would be too logical, too rational, she thought, wouldn't it? Beating herself up was instinctive.

The toilet flushed. Ten or fifteen seconds later, the bathroom door opened, and Justine clumped to the landing, turned into her bedroom, and began walloping her punching bag, her strikes fast and hard. *Thwap. Thwap, thwap.* "Listen to her up there. She's killing that thing."

"Good for her," Will said. "She's getting the negative energy out."

The quiet music helped Zoe to relax. For the first time all day, her heart wasn't racing. She reached for her drink. "She was lying about the love letters. If you want, I can show you."

"You don't have to show me."

"Jerry's a friend. That's all, Will. Nothing more."

"I believe you."

Zoe drained her OJ and vodka, set the glass on the floor, and clasped her husband's hand. "He was here, though," she said tentatively, hoping to fully clear the air. "That part was true."

He pressed his index finger to her lips, lifted her hair, massaged her shoulders.

"Wait," she said, reaching for his hand. "I want to tell you. We went for coffee." She felt his warm hand on her neck. Her heart quickened. "Nothing happened. You need to know that."

He pushed her hair off her shoulders again. She bent her neck, accepting his kiss.

He kissed her forehead, the bridge of her nose, the tip of her chin. His hands supporting her back, he pressed her to the floor. In the scent of his hair, his neck, his ears, she smelled the man she had fallen in love with so many years ago. "What if Jus comes down?" she whispered.

"She won't."

Afterward, zipping his jeans, he said, "Should we drive by the house again?"

She twisted her hair into a bun at the nape of her neck. "What do you think?"

For a few minutes, they mulled over the possibility of driving by Corbett's again. If Leah saw them, she would think they were spying. But at least she would know her parents loved her. She would know they cared. Which was better? they wondered. Hard to say. Leah was fickle. A gesture that induced gratitude one day might enrage her the next. In the end, they agreed to wait until morning.

Justine had spent the better part of the day lying on her sister's bed, absorbing the heat of Leah's angry music. On fire, she returned to her own room, began slamming her heavy bag, the huge blue bag crashing into her wall, pitching back. *Leah.* She rammed the bag harder. *I need you.* Now, in the heavyweight ring, lights flash. *Ladies and gentlemen, to your right—Cinderella Woman.* The hot lights bear down on her, and the audience goes wild. She stripped to her panties and bra, her thighs and shoulders glistening, shuffled her feet. *Pow.* Under the chin. *KIA-HA.*

Her hair was soaked. She pushed her stringy bangs out of her eyes. Heart racing, she ripped off the gloves, whacked the bag with her bare fists, and punched until her hands felt like stumps, her knuckles turning white, and then purple, her hands ballooning.

When her hands gave out, she switched to her feet.

Justine collapsed onto her bed, exhausted. Rolling onto her side, she reached for her phone, dialed Todd's number, heard a busy signal, tossed the phone on the floor, and lugged her aching body to the TV, plugged in the DVD her father had recorded on Christmas morning.

For ten minutes, you could almost believe they were a normal, happy family, the house glittering, their mom beaming while the girls opened their gifts, their dad's teasing voice in the background. Leah stuck her tongue out at the camera, making an effort to smile, pretend she was happy. When their mom handed Leah the silver box, Justine pressed *Fast-Forward*, skipping the part where Leah unwrapped the ring, watched her sister open Merlin.

Justine was sorry she had come home last night. She should have insisted on staying with her sister. If she were not such a coward, she and Leah would be together right now, at Todd's, playing a game or watching TV. Maybe they would go to Lupo's again, swim in his Jacuzzi. She pictured the kids, splashing in the water, the water droplets like crystals in Todd's goatee. She wouldn't be a ninny, this time. This time, she would strip naked like the others.

Stretching listlessly, Justine plucked her phone off the floor, dialed Todd's number again. This time, an older woman answered, her voice gravelly, as if she'd been sleeping.

"Hello," Justine said. "Would Leah Tyler be available, please?"

"No," the woman snapped. "And please stop calling here."

Leah picked through her suitcase, flinging underwear, T-shirts, jeans into a heap on Todd's bed. It was time she unpacked. She had been living with Todd, in his basement bedroom, for two days—an arrangement Todd's mother had encouraged, once she realized that Leah would be living with them for good. To be honest, despite Mrs. Corbett's kindly efforts to make her feel at home—*la mia casa è la vostra casa*, said Todd's mother, who, as far as Leah was aware, had not a drop of Italian blood in her—Leah felt awkward, mooching off her boyfriend and his mom. Unfortunately, she had nowhere else to go. With Mrs. Lansdown still in a tizzy over Hope's arrest, staying with them, though she knew that she would be welcome, wouldn't feel right. And she could never go home. The night her father drove here, looking for her, the possibility of her ever living at home again vanished. Her father had drawn a line, forcing her to take a side, to choose between him and her boyfriend. Leah had chosen her boyfriend.

Inside the cup of a wireless bra, she found the wax figurine Justine had given her for Christmas. "Hey, dude?" she said, to Todd. "Look at this." She held up the figurine, the crystal head of her serpent ring catching the light. The serpent ring was a temporary engagement ring, Todd had told her, when he presented it to her on Christmas Eve. As soon as he could afford one, he would buy her a diamond, he'd promised. Her boyfriend couldn't seem to get it into his head that Leah didn't give a hoot about a diamond. The serpent ring suited her perfectly. She swung the magician to and fro, as if the figurine were a puppet, making him dance. "Isn't he cute?"

"Sure." Todd rolled his eyes. "Guess so."

She set the wax magician on the stereo speaker next to Todd's bed.

Todd had this incredible, top-of-the-line system, worth two thousand dollars. The stereo was a bribe. After his mother bailed him out of jail, she'd offered to buy any stereo he wanted, if he would agree to move home. She'd wasted the money, in Leah's opinion. He would have done it without a reward. It wasn't as if he'd had someplace better to go, or anyplace to go, actually.

A month after he moved in, his mother suggested that they turn the basement into an apartment, to give him more privacy. Todd had done the work himself. The hardest part, he'd told Leah, was moving the headboard and dresser from his attic bedroom, down the three flights of stairs. He painted the walls a cool midnight blue, bought a Persian rug from the Salvation Army, hung a tapestry from the ceiling. And, *voila*, he had an apartment. The apartment smelled a little funky, being in the basement and all. And the exposed pipes would look better painted. But those were minor details, considering that his mother allowed him to live here rent-free.

"Todd?" Leah waved a pair of jeans she'd received from her parents, for Christmas. She'd never heard of the brand, New Line Genes, but they looked expensive. Her mom bought them at Saks. Which was too bad: the gigantic rainbow embroidered on the right butt-cheek was heinous. She was thinking about taking them back, returning them for the cash. "What do you think?"

"Whatever." Todd tuned the stereo, pulling the bass forward, and slogged to his bureau. From a small silver can in his bottom drawer, he extracted a plastic sandwich bag.

"What's with you?" Leah hollered, over the music. "Why're you such an asshole, today?"

He shot a sour look her way, reduced the volume on the stereo a few decibels, plunked on a squat three-legged stool, balancing the mirror on one knee, and spooned powder onto the glass.

"Your parents are a pain in the ass, calling ten times a day. My mom's sick of that shit."

"They called five times," Leah said, correcting him. "In three days."

"We can't stay here forever," he said, refocusing his attention on the mirror.

"Why not?"

With his debit card, he cut the powder into lines.

"Todd?" she yelled. Why couldn't they stay here? For now, until they'd saved some cash, this was a perfect arrangement. The apartment was *free*.

Fine, she muttered, don't answer. It's a free world. Think whatever he pleased. Their butts were staying right here, until she was working and they were both making decent money.

He sniffed, lifting the mirror by its handle, and offered Leah the straw. Dilated, his wet black eyes scared her a little. "I got to get a job," he said bitterly.

"You *have* a job." Leah squinched her nose, dumping her jeans on the bed.

She knelt on the threadbare carpet, next to his stool. "Put it on your lap?" she asked, meaning the mirror. Some athlete she was. She was too big a klutz to hold both mirror and straw. Holding one nostril shut, she brought her face to the glass, pushed the end of the straw up her nose, and inhaled sharply, her septum tingling.

"Supposed to go *in* your nose, not on it." Chortling, he wiped her nose with his thumb.

"Shut up." Leah coughed, her allergies triggered by the mildew. Too jittery to stay put, she pushed herself up, pressing her hand on his knee for leverage, and strolled across the room, put the mirror back on his bureau, where it belonged. "So what's this about moving?" she asked, when she returned. Her hands had a mind of their own. Her fingers refused to stay still. She picked up the magician, put it down, twiddled her sweatpants.

"I got fired. Told you yesterday."

Fired? He'd mentioned something about him and Jamie having words. He'd never said he was fired. He must have done something major for Jamie to fire him.

Shit. Leah sank onto the bed. The serpent ring. He must have stolen the two hundred dollars. He'd told her he'd borrowed the money. Out of the register, he must have meant. She fingered the ring. "Tell him why you took it?" Her shoulder ticked. "You know he likes me."

If looks could kill, she would have been on the express train to Hell. He wanted to move to Maine, he told her. His stepmother owned that cabin, outside Camden. They could stay there.

"Camden?" She swiped her runny nose, coughing again. "I thought it was Bangor?"

Yeah, well. He hadn't been there since he was like twelve. Anyway, at Thanksgiving, when he talked to his stepmother, she'd mentioned that she and her new husband planned to spend the winter in southeast Asia. The husband was an antique dealer. They were leaving for Thailand, on a buying trip, the day after Christmas. From there, they would be traveling through Vietnam, Cambodia, Indonesia, and possibly Malaysia, depending upon the political climate. He knew where she kept the key. "Might as well use it," he said. "It's just gonna sit there, empty."

"Maine?" Leah repeated. This was a lot to take in all at once.

He needed a job, he told her again. Forget about a reference from Jamie. Be easier to find a job in Maine, where nobody knew him. Where he had a clean slate. Where he could start over.

Start over. Leah's mind reeled. In Maine. *Four hours away.*

A few minutes passed before a solid picture took shape. Camden was a resort town, on the water. If they lived in Camden, they could work in a restaurant. In the summer, she and Todd would work the dinner shift, spend their days on the beach. They would take diving lessons, as soon as they could afford it. Once they felt comfortable diving, she and Todd could trap lobsters. When she was a little girl, her family had driven up to southern Maine every September. They would spend the day at York, collecting shells on the beach. On the way home, they would stop at this funky, outdoor restaurant on the water, order lobster in the rough. For dessert, they ate Boston Cream Pie. "Maine." Leah tossed the jeans in her suitcase. "Why not?" Obviously, if they planned to get married, her boyfriend needed a job. Besides, it would be fun to start over, she thought, her mind flashing forward, the movie of their brand new life already on *play.*

Thirty-Two

The Existence Period

Zoe sat by the fireplace, staring at the palladium window, the gold undertones in her button bracelet glittering in the ray of a sunbeam shooting down from the upper panes. Will was somewhere in the house, puttering. He puttered constantly, when he was not locked away in his office, her husband as lost as she was, these days. Leah had been gone for a week, and, still, they had no idea where she was. All their efforts, every attempt they made to find her, had failed.

The day Justine woke them, crying, saying Leah had packed her things, Will had driven by the Corbett place. Will had seen the Jeep. Because they knew where Leah was, Zoe and Will tried not to worry. This was a temporary setback, they promised each other. That was all. In the week leading to Christmas, though her conduct had improved only marginally, Leah's mood had lifted. Change never occurs in linear fashion. Setbacks, they told each other, were normal. As soon as she cooled off, Leah would come home. By day two, anxiety set in. By the end of the third day, when Justine had not heard from her sister, either, Zoe and her husband were frantic.

After several tries, they reached Corbett's mother, who confirmed their worst fear: her son was gone, too. After a good deal of prodding (and a pointed threat concerning her son's probation and recent drug use), Corbett's mother provided Will with a list of people the kids might try to contact. They'd handed her list, along with a detailed list of their own, to the police.

That afternoon, they filed the missing person report, and Sergeant Healey, the Chief of Police, issued a state-wide "Be On the Lookout" bulletin, and registered Leah's name in the FBI's national database. "If an officer runs a check, anywhere in the country, he'll get a hit, saying she's a runaway," Healey informed them. The chief pledged the full cooperation of the Cortland PD. Unfortunately, resources were limited. Law enforcement agencies did not consider runaways to be critical missing person cases. Amber Alerts were used only in abduction cases. Teenage runaways were ineligible. "She's an adult," Healey said. "Running away isn't a crime."

"We'd be better off if she were kidnapped," Zoe said dismally, on the way home. From working with teens, she knew that if the police located a runaway Leah's age, unless they'd caught the child breaking a law, their only option was to contact the parents. "They can't send them home. Can't even detain them." If she and Will hoped to find Leah, they would have to mount an aggressive campaign of their own.

Together, Zoe from their home line, Will from his office extension, they called every person they could think of who might have the slightest clue about where the kids were. They called their relatives. They contacted Coach Thomas, the Hansons. Zoe called Mrs. Lansdown and spoke with the daughter, who told Zoe exactly nothing. "Sorry, Ms. T.," Hope said, "Didn't know they ran away." Will *Googled* the Lupos, bought their unlisted number from a tracking service, called and talked to the father. Yes, the elder Lupo admitted, his son knew Corbett, but Tony had nothing to do with their daughter's disappearance. If he heard anything, he would pass the information along. "The scumbag's a natural-born liar," Will told Zoe, afterward.

Immediately after their meeting with Healey, Will called a colleague, who'd put them in touch with a private investigator. Desperate, they borrowed the five thousand dollar deposit from his parents. The PI, a squirrelly looking guy named John Dunham, had done undercover work for the FBI, on the Whitey Bulger case. So far, neither Dunham nor the police had had any luck.

Some days, Zoe's anger consumed her. She wished the strength would return to her legs. If she were able to run, she would have some form of relief. This morning, shortly after Justine left for school, she'd tried punching the heavy bag. The bag barely moved when she hit it. She laughed at herself, at her weak arms, feeling utterly foolish. The few times she tried to let go of the anger, Zoe drifted into despair. She needed to be doing something productive to find Leah. By now, their daughter could be anywhere in the country—or even, God forbid, out of the country. Where do you look if you have no clues? How many times could she and Will call the same people? Zoe had filed Leah's name with every runaway hotline, left messages with halfway houses and clinics all over New England. She monitored Internet chat rooms, checked the files in all the computers they owned. She kept tabs on Leah's e-mail account. What else could they do?

She tucked her feet under her legs, resting her elbow on the arm of her chair.

The oak tree outside the palladium window had grown taller than the house. Ten years ago, the tree, in a heavy growth period, was beginning to attain its girth, the low branches ten or twelve feet in length. Leah, seven then, begged for a rope swing. A rope swing was dangerous, they'd told her, knowing that the instant Will hung it, Leah would be climbing on the rail of the deck, leaping like Tarzan into the air. One of Leah's friends had a zip line, the wire, eight or ten feet above ground, running from the corner of the family's house to the trunk of a maple tree in the backyard. The kids, sitting in a basket, rode the zip line as if it were an amusement park ride. *Please,* Leah begged. A rope swing would be *so* fun. *Mom? Way more fun than a zip line. Dad? Pretty please? With sugar on top?* Leah pleaded, cajoled, nagged. Finally, they had given in. The rope swing was a mistake. The swing was dangerous. They should have stood their ground.

The floor vibrated, the floorboards creaking. She looked up, surprised to see Will with his guitar, the leather strap slung over his shoulder. Last she'd seen the guitar, it was in the attic, lying atop a pile of junk. "You found your guitar?"

Her husband lowered himself to the floor by the fireplace, positioning the guitar's body in his lap. "I had a song in my head," he said, strumming a chord. "I wanted to play it for you."

She would love to hear a song. "Leah used to love when you played. Remember?"

"Especially this one." He strummed a chord. "Let me take you down," he sang, and Zoe joined in, her teetering voice blending with his.

He stopped singing, tightened a peg. "She was a cute kid," he said, "wasn't she? I loved how feisty she was. I always thought she'd do something great. Really great. Like run the UN. Or find a cure for cancer. All that energy, you know?" He laughed. "I still do," he said seriously.

"Me, too," she said, almost convinced. "Remember the rope swing?"

How could he forget? "Damn swing was a bear to put up."

"She was such a daredevil." Zoe gazed out at the tree, and there she was, seven-year-old Leah, flying over the yard, shrieking joyfully, one hand clinging to the rope, the other stretching to the sky. "I was sure she'd fall and break her neck. Got to the point, I couldn't watch her play."

Will laughed. "Same with that big wheel. Remember how she used to stand on the seat?"

"No wonder she's the way she is," Zoe said. Since Leah ran away, she'd spent a lot of time rethinking the past, wondering what she and Will might have done to prevent this, how they might have kept their daughter on track. A strong-willed child like Leah needs solid boundaries, she believed. She and Will were always changing their mind, giving in. In effect, they'd taught their daughter that her will was stronger than theirs. If she kept pushing, kept haunting them, Leah would eventually get her way. "This is our fault, Will. We should have stuck to our guns."

Will laid the guitar on the floor, and got up.

"Where are you going?"

"To get a drink," he said flatly.

Sure, she thought, walk away. Don't talk about Leah. Don't talk, period. Better to pretend: Their daughter hadn't run away. Will was back on track at work, selling again. Justine was fine, thank you very much. Their younger daughter wasn't depressed. *If you don't want to talk, don't.* But she did. She needed to make sense of this. And she expected common courtesy, she said to his back, scolding him from behind. He didn't have to gush over her. "Listen to me," she said, dogging him out of the room. "I'm trying to talk to you, Will."

In the archway, he hesitated, his shoulders rising and falling, in agitation maybe, or maybe that was resignation in her husband's stiff posture and labored breath. Or maybe rage.

"Damn it, Will." She poked his shoulder. "Turn around."

"Jesus Christ." He turned to her, brushing her hand away. "What do you *want* from me?"

Want? Nothing. "I just want a friend."

He threw up his hands. "I *am* your friend."

"Like hell you are."

He squeezed past her, shaking his head.

She watched him shuffle across the family room, to his book-case. Her husband looked as if he had lost the ten pounds she'd gained since her accident, his jeans sagging in the seat.

He ran an index finger across the top row of CDs. When he turned his head, she noticed his sharp cheekbones, his hollow eyes.

When had his jaw gone slack? My God, she thought, he looks old. "I'm sorry. We shouldn't have put it up. That's all. Should've been more consistent."

He plucked a CD from the shelf—blues. "You like this, right?" He loaded the CD into the tray, pushed the tray into the device, hit *Play*. "Albert King." He reached for her hand.

"Not now, Will. I'm sorry." She crossed her arms over her chest. "This sort of thing doesn't happen overnight. A child doesn't wake up a rebel one day. It happens a day at a time."

"Right. Hemingway—'gradually, then suddenly.'"

"That's all I meant."

"I knew what you meant." He took hold of her hands. "It's not that I don't want to talk to you. I don't see the point in kicking ourselves in the ass all the time. This isn't only about us, what we did or didn't do. Some of this is her personality, Zo. She's been like this since she was little." He pulled her into his arms, pressing her head to his chest. "I wish we could change things, too."

She felt a rumble under his ribcage, smelled the tang of anxiety on his breath. "She's our baby," she said softly. "I can't let her go."

He stroked her head. "Tell me what to do, Zo. Tell me. I'll do whatever you want."

"I don't know what I want." She pulled away, hugging herself. "I just want her back."

Leah's head throbbed. She remembered part of last night, the pizza shop, the shouting match on their way back to the cabin, Todd insisting they stay here until they'd sorted things out, Leah pressing to move closer to home. A bottle of eight-dollar champagne, uncorked in the secluded clearing in the woods, where they had been parking the Jeep. Bottles two and three in the cabin. Strip poker. As usual, she'd lost. She remembered pissing Todd's stepmother's bed. Todd had lifted her off the bed, her head lolling like a rag doll's. The rest of the night was a blur.

She should have kept taking her Zoloft. She'd quit because she missed the excitement, the highs and lows. The anti-depressant medication made her feel flat. Instead, she wanted to die.

Todd was already up. She heard him, climbing to the loft, the stairs squeaking.

Leah felt uncomfortable up here, in Todd's stepmother's room. The first night, she'd had trouble falling asleep. A snapshot of Todd's father and stepmother, shot before the divorce, hung on the wall directly across from the bed, their line of vision shooting like a laser beam to the mattress. When she complained, Todd lifted the photo from its hook, laid it upside-down on his stepmother's antique bureau. Don't worry about it, he'd said. He hadn't heard from his old man in years and his stepmother would want them to make themselves at home. Besides, the loft was the safest place in the cabin. From up here, they would hear an intruder before he heard them.

Leah patted the nightstand, groping for the box of Hi-C, her brain in a fog.

"Hey. You're up."

She felt the mattress slope under his weight and rolled onto her belly, arms over her head.

A cold, metal object touched her shoulder. Flinching, she turned onto her back, shielding her eyes. "Oh my God." She pushed herself to her elbows. *A gun.* "Where'd you get that?"

"Found it last night, under the mattress." He turned the gun over, and pointed to the engraving on the side of the barrel. *Colt 38*, it read. The pistol had a tall front sight blade, a polished wooden grip. He pointed out the lanyard ring, the ejection pin under the barrel. "It's a .38 Special. She's a beauty, huh?" Todd ran his hand over the pistol, caressing its shiny six-inch barrel. "Baby's a classic. Here." He pressed the wooden grip into her palm. "Feel."

"Get that thing out of here," she snapped, and pushed the gun away. Guns scared her.

He brought the pistol to eye level. Squinting, he pointed the barrel at the wall.

"What are you *do*ing?" Leah wrestled for the gun, slapping at his hand. "Don't shoot."

"Chill out." He pulled the trigger. *Click.* "See?" Fired again. *Click.* "She's empty."

"Put it back," Leah pleaded. "Guns are dangerous." She relayed a story about a widower her father knew. One night, when the old man was nearly asleep, he heard his front door open, and reached for the pistol on top of his nightstand. He aimed the gun at the door, cocking the trigger, prepared to shoot the instant the intruder set foot in his room. "He killed his own son."

Todd scoffed at the story. "Right, like I never heard that one before."

Maybe, Leah replied, but this story was true. When her story failed to persuade him, she asked how his stepmother would feel if she discovered that he'd stolen her pistol.

"Lay off the fucking guilt trip. I'm going in town, for some lunch." He stuffed the pistol in the pocket of his anorak—his Eskimo coat, Leah called it. "Need anything?"

After he left, she cocooned herself in the blankets, tucking a pillow between her knees. She should have asked Todd to buy Advil at the store. Her cramps were killing her, the shooting pain in her abdomen and lower back ten times worse than the pain from a strained muscle or a broken foot. Her period was all out of whack, lately. The birth control pills regulated her cycles, when she took them regularly. This month, she'd forgotten three times. She ought to be more careful, she thought—not that a pregnancy would be a disaster. After all, she and Todd planned to get married. Still, it would be nice to have time to themselves before they had kids.

She rolled out of bed, and, holding her stomach, felt her way to the bathroom.

The master bath was the size of her bedroom closet, at home. If the cabin belonged to her, she would enlarge the vanity, add a second sink, replace the fiberglass shower stall with a tub, rip up the puke-colored floor. The skylight Leah would keep. She rooted through the drawers of the vanity, hunting for tampons. In the cabinet below the sink, under the rusted coils of a plumbing snake, she found maxi-pads, the box wilted from the dampness. Leah hated sanitary pads, the feeling like a towel between her legs. Since she had no supplies of her own, they would have to do. She peed, taped a pad to her panties, pulled on a T-shirt and sweats, and headed downstairs.

The main floor of the cabin was a like an antique shop, with teak tables and hand-painted chests from all over the world. Todd's stepmother would die if she saw how Leah and Todd were destroying the place. They'd dripped salsa on the carpet, spilled crumbs on the wood floor. Todd had been lighting fires in the massive stone fireplace every day since they arrived. Except for a few twigs, the wood-box was empty, the hearth covered in soot. A picture window, between the living and dining areas, looked outside at the woods, the glass smeared with their prints. One of these days, when she had the energy, Leah would have to do some serious cleaning. She gathered the glasses and plates they'd left on the floor, and carried them to the kitchen.

A Princess phone with a rotary dial sat on the tiled counter, next to a red, apple-shaped clock. Leah eyed the phone, wondering what Justine was up to, thinking maybe she'd call. She vaguely recalled drunk-dialing her sister last night. When Todd left their poker game to go to the bathroom, she had snuck into the kitchen. She saw a flash of herself, dizzy from the champagne, leaning against the stove, shivering in her panties and bra, her head down, her hands cradling the handset. On the fourth ring, her mother picked up. Leah froze when she heard her mom's voice.

It was only one thirty. Justine would still be at school. If Leah called now, her mother would answer again. She emptied a box of Hi-C into a goblet, and wandered back to the loft.

This morning, Justine helped her father take down the tree. The tree had died a miserable death, the branches sagging, the skirt a bed of dry needles. Justine removed the ornaments, and her father unstrung the lights. Together, they dragged the prickly tree to the deck, leaving a trail of pine needles and dirt. While her father vacuumed the mess, Justine unwound the holly and untied the ribbons, packed it all away, and disassembled the Nativity scene. She laid the stable in a box filled with peanuts, and swaddled the figurines in tissue. She wrapped the faceless Joseph, his outsized wife, Mary, and, last of all, the poor baby Jesus, permanently trapped in his manger.

Now, she and Holly sat cross-legged on Holly's bedroom floor, putting the finishing touches on Justine's science project. Before Thanksgiving, Holly's mom had hired a decorator to renovate Holly's room. The decorator, a weird lady with fuzzy black hair, dressed in gauzy bellbottoms, and sang Beatles songs as she worked. She'd covered the walls in green paper the shade of a leprechaun's hat, the accent color in the striped curtains and matching comforter that same unfortunate green. Justine would kill her mother if she paid someone to do this to her room.

"Sprinkles?" Holly shook silver sprinkles onto her palm, testing the shaker.

"Sure," Justine said. She could use the sprinkles.

The fair was two weeks away. If she were allowed, Justine would retract her entry. The science fair was the last thing she wanted to think about. The past two weeks had been the worst in her life. She couldn't eat, couldn't sleep; she had trouble concentrating in school. Even now, Justine found it hard to believe that her sister was gone. Leah was playing a game, she told herself. As soon as she'd rounded the final stretch, as soon as she had been away long enough, time having worked its magic, dissipating her anger, she would be home. But even when she fantasized about her sister, reality nagged her. "You're a scientist, Jus," she heard Leah say. "Scientists believe in logic and reason." Maybe, she thought. But she didn't want to give up yet.

On Friday, her guidance counselor called Justine to her office, asked if there were anything she'd like to discuss. Justine shook her head, fighting back tears. "Your teachers are concerned," the counselor said. She'd received a C- on her social studies exam. "That's not like you, honey. What's going on?" Justine stared at her feet. What could she say? She didn't feel like doing the work.

The refrigerator box housing Justine's project lay on its side, in the center of the room, between Holly and her. Justine wrote her name on a crepe-paper star and taped the star above the oval-shaped opening in the box. She'd painted the box's interior in swirling blues and black to create the illusion of space, glued on thousands of sprinkles to represent stars. Using iridescent puff paint, she'd designed the various celestial phenomena: asteroids, supernova, nebula, red giants. The planets, suspended like a mobile from the ceiling, were held in place by a web of pipe cleaners and string. In her accompanying video, Justine described each planet, detailing their peculiar characteristics; she named each identifiable star and discussed their development, approximating their ages. This final version of her project was baby work compared to what she'd originally hoped to produce. She'd envisioned a complicated scientific endeavor, something all-encompassing, something grand: An analysis of the probability of life on other planets. A research project on Pluto. In an article in *Science*, she'd learned that Pluto had shifted after the Milky Way was formed, into the elliptical orbit it followed today. The finding posed fascinating possibilities about planetary movement. She'd intended to research it further, learn the specifics. But she had lost interest.

The *Brady Bunch* movie was playing on Holly's plasma TV. The empty DVD case lay on the floor by Holly's knees. Holly worshipped the Bradys. She liked to pretend she was Marcia. (In Justine's opinion, her friend bore a stronger resemblance to Cindy.) The movie was a joke. Six perfect kids in a perfect stupid family. Totally unrealistic.

"Sprinkles?" Justine repeated. "Holly?" *Duh?*

Holly brushed the silver sprinkles off her arms, casting a pitying look in Justine's direction. She leaned over the box, and handed over the sprinkles, pale yellow bangs drooping in her eyes.

"What's *that* look about?" Justine snapped, and instantly regretted her words. Holly didn't deserve to be treated badly. It wasn't her fault that Justine's family was falling apart.

"Need any more?" Holly asked, avoiding Justine's eyes. "I've got gold, if you want."

"No thanks," Justine said sweetly. "This is perfect."

"Your project is awesome," Holly squealed. "Think you'll win? I do."

Justine winced. "Maybe," she said, without the slightest conviction. Who really cared?

Zoe was lying on the family room sofa, half-awake, half-asleep, dreaming of California. Last night, Hope Lansdown had finally come clean about Leah's disappearance. Leah "might" be on the West Coast, Hope had informed Zoe. Apparently, Leah had mentioned California "a bunch of times." Leah, evidently, "digs the weather out there." Good grief, Zoe thought—*California*. How would they ever find her out there?

The phone rang, jangling her nerves. She grabbed for the cordless she'd left on the coffee table, her trembling hands missing the first time. For the past three days, they'd been receiving hang-up calls, sometimes four or five in a day. According to the police, the caller was probably someone they knew, playing a practical joke. Zoe could not imagine anyone being that cruel. If the caller would stay on the line, she intended to give the jerk a piece of her mind.

The police had advised them to record all of their incoming and outgoing calls. Zoe shoved her feet into her sheepskin slippers, and hurried to the kitchen, where she'd left the notepad, the phone bleating.

Dialing Star-57 after the caller hung up, Jerry had told her, would initiate a trace. She had attempted to trace the last three calls; each time she failed. When she called the phone company, the rep claimed the tracing device sometimes misses calls from certain cellular or rotary phones.

"He— Hell—" *Get a grip*, she told herself. "Hello?"

The mudroom door swung open, and she heard Will scurrying down the hall.

"Who is this?" she shouted, into the static-filled line. "Tell me who you are."

Her husband loomed over her shoulder. "Is it him?" he asked, breathing in her ear.

So Will was talking to her again. Last night, after the call from Hope, they'd had an ugly row. Obviously, he said, Hope had known all along where Leah was headed. "You're the child psychologist," Will spat, the inflated job title better fodder for his accusation. If Zoe had managed to pry the information out of the girl the first time around, they'd have had the PI on Leah's tail, and might have found her by now. Pry? she repeated. *Pry* it out of the girl? "For your information, my dear, therapists don't *pry*. Therapists listen. But it's all the same to you, I suppose." She smirked, shaking her head indulgently. How silly, she implied with a wave, to expect him to differentiate. "You're not familiar with listening, are you, dear? You never listen."

Static, she mouthed. She couldn't make anything out.

As she was about to click off, she heard a voice on the other end.

"Sorry," Jerry said. "New phone system. How are you?"

"All right." She slouched against the counter, her legs tired, her knee sore. Last week, the orthopedist told her it was time to start physical therapy. She'd never made the appointment. What she needed were pills to calm her nerves. Maybe she should go back to the orthopedist, tell him the pain in her knee was unbearable, ask him to refill her OxyContin prescription. Or maybe she could convince their family practitioner to hook her up with some Xanax.

Checking in, Jerry told her. "Any idea yet, who the caller might be?"

No, she replied. And the calls were driving her out of her mind.

Nothing from the detective yet, either?

Will lumbered to the fridge, took a Bud from the six-pack on the top shelf. He was wearing his Harvard soccer camp sweatshirt again, the sleeves pushed to his elbows, with ill-fitting gray chinos, scuffed loafers, no socks. He twisted the cap off the beer bottle, shoved the cap in his pocket, stood by the sink, staring out at the snow, the front end of a nor'easter.

Zoe hobbled to his side, her knee tight. "Jerry," she whispered, pulling the receiver away from her face. The stench on the mouthpiece, a mix of garlic and stale perfume, nauseated her.

"What's he want?"

She shrugged. *Nothing new.*

The wind howled, rattling the window, spraying snow crystals on the vibrating glass.

Have to be patient, Jerry was saying, as he always did when he called. Runaways are notoriously hard to find. This morning, he'd phoned a classmate of his from Northeastern. His friend was a trial attorney in L. A. "I asked him to put out some feelers. Might take a little time." They would catch a break one of these days. He hadn't given up hope, and neither should they.

What?" Will tossed the empty beer bottle in the recycling bin and opened another.

Zoe raised a finger. Shivering, she buttoned her cardigan. When she hung up, she said, "He called a friend in California. The guy's a lawyer. He promised to check their databases."

"Goddamn cop." Will snorted. "Databases, my ass."

Get off it, she growled, and limped to the refrigerator. She scrounged up a tomato, a head of iceberg lettuce, a third of a Vidalia onion, and set the vegetables on the counter. She sorted through the cheeses and deli meats, tossing several outdated packages in the sink, opened a plastic bag of pepper-roasted turkey, sniffed, and threw the turkey in, too. Rooting through the freezer, she came across the package of sausage from Jerry. She'd forgotten all about it. "Are you hungry?" she asked. "I'll make sandwiches."

"How can you be hungry? We just ate."

She consulted her watch. "An hour ago."

"I've got a mind to call Healey, let him know what his boy's been up to."

"For God's sake, Will. He's only trying to help."

Will snorted again. "Help? Bastard's trying to move in on my wife. You call that help?"

She hacked off the ends of the onion, her eyes watering. She wished she'd kept her mouth shut about having coffee with Jerry. By telling Will, she'd hoped to clear the air. Instead, it had elevated his suspicions. She wiped the tears on her sleeve. With her elbow, she flipped the lever on the faucet, held the onion under the water. "Look at me, Will. Read my lips. We're *friends*."

Will took a reproachful slug of beer. "Right. So how do you explain the sausage?"

The sausage was a sweet gesture. She refused to defend it. "Want a sandwich or not?"

Will blew out his cheeks in disgust, and huffed to the living room.

Zoe repackaged the sausage in a Zip-Lock bag, sealed the vegetables in a Tupperware container, and cleaned the counter. She and Will had too much time on their hands. They were at each other constantly. They needed to start working again. Truthfully, she was surprised NAC hadn't fired him yet. Since the Micronics fiasco last fall, he'd sold one job, worth six million dollars—twelve grand in commission to him. This morning, paying a stack of bills, she'd been shocked by how little money they had left in the savings account: three thousand dollars, enough to last maybe a month, if she juggled the charge cards. Luckily for them, just before Christmas, Micronics had paid the balance on the California project, the twenty-five thousand no longer hanging over their heads. But they still owed his parents the five thousand they'd borrowed. And God only knew how much more they would rack up in charges with the private detective. She and Will had to get their act together soon or they would be headed to bankruptcy court.

After she'd finished paying the bills, she'd climbed the stairs to Will's office, above the garage. They'd been avoiding this discussion for weeks. They could not keep putting it off.

Will's door was closed. For ten minutes, she'd stood outside his office, listening for scraps of conversation, his keyboard, the buzz of the fax, anything to prove he was in contact with the outside world. The only sound she'd heard was the click of electronic solitaire cards.

She brewed a pot of coffee, filled her mug, adding skim milk and a teaspoon of sugar, carried her mug to the living room. Will was immersed in a novel, called *Independence Day*. The guy in the novel, he told her yesterday, reminded him of himself. She had been afraid to ask how.

She cleared her throat. "We need to talk, Will."

Her husband closed the book, and set it on the windowsill.

Curiosity getting the better of her, she set her mug on the sill, and picked up his book, scanned the blurb on the jacket. *Frank Bascombe, in the aftermath of his divorce and the ruin of his career, has entered into an "Existence Period," selling real estate in Haddam, New Jersey.*

Zoe sighed, and set the book down.

"Well, Zoe? Let's have it. Something's obviously on your mind."

A gust of wind ripped a branch from a birch tree, the branch sailing across the drive.

"I'm sorry," she said. "I don't know how to put this nicely." She paused, weighing her words. "So I'm just going to come out with it, all right? You and I both need to start working."

"I don't work?" He whisked the paperback from the sill, pretended to read for a few seconds, and slapped the book down, toppling the picture of the girls in their wading pool. He righted the photo. "I don't work, she says. Don't freaking work? What's that supposed to mean?"

She rubbed the back of her neck. "Forget it, Will. I'm sorry I brought it up."

He snapped his chair upright. "I'm going up to my office. I've got paperwork. If it makes you feel better, I was on the phone all morning. I've got appointments every day next week."

"That's great." Her knee and legs ached. She reached for her mug, coagulated skim milk floating on the surface. "I'm glad to hear that, Will. I really am."

Justine lay in bed, her comforter tucked under her chin, watching the Christmas DVD.

Her parents were downstairs, bickering again. All her parents did, lately, was fight. One of these days, they would call her into the living room, ask her to sit, tell her they were getting divorced. Parents all used that tactic to spring their divorce on their kids. It was like the divorce notification MO. They probably all read the same rulebook: Sit your kids down. Say you've got something important to share. "They tell you it's not your fault," Holly told her one time, "you know it's not true." Each time one of her parents mentioned a sit-down, Justine's heart lurched.

Maybe Leah was right: maybe her mother *was* fooling around with that cop. Even so, that didn't mean they had to get divorced. Her parents could always see a marriage counselor. Holly was miserable after her parents separated, never knowing whose side she was supposed to be on, constantly shuffled between the house she'd lived in since she was a baby and her dad's tiny apartment, never really at home. As soon as the divorce was final, Holly's mother remarried and Holly had moved, with her mom and stepfather, to the house two doors down from the Tylers. Holly loved their oversized house, the expensive things her stepfather bought, but she'd give up everything, she was always telling Justine, if she could just have her dad back. Justine couldn't imagine her parents divorced, her family scattered.

With her remote, Justine turned the DVD player off, and, stretching sideways, reached for her backpack, on the floor. She emptied the contents of her binder onto her bed, and sifted through the pile of paper. Math test: B-. Science: 78. She scanned the book report she'd written last week for Honors English, on *Wuthering Heights*. She'd received an A+ on the paper, a congratulatory note, the words "excellent job," scrawled across the top in red ink. The A+ was demoralizing. This was the first time she'd ever written a report on a book she'd neglected to read. You'd think her teacher would be smart enough to realize the paper was based on a movie. It probably never occurred to her that Justine would do such a thing. The teacher saw only what she wanted to see, just like everyone else. Justine crumpled the essay, and tossed it in the trash.

Justine pretended, sometimes, that Leah was taking a semester abroad, studying in Paris or London or Florence. It was easy to picture Leah in Europe. Justine had looked up the cities on the Internet, and knew what they looked like. Other times, she imagined her on an adventure, on a sailboat, sailing around the world, on a trip to Antarctica. Always, in her fantasies, she put her sister someplace exciting. When she returned, Leah would be satisfied, and want to stay home.

Every night since Leah disappeared, Justine had lowered herself to her knees, and prayed for her sister's return. Every morning, feeling Leah's presence beside her, Justine woke smiling. Every morning, she was disappointed again. Maybe Leah was right. Maybe God was a figment of her imagination. Another of her fantasies. Maybe her faith was nothing more than a crutch.

Justine unclasped the chain that held her gold cross, put the necklace in her jewelry box, and logged onto her computer. She launched the *Word* file with the Confirmation speech she had written, and scanned the opening paragraph. *I've learned from my own family what it's like to be part of God's family.* Learned from her own family what it's like to be part of God's family? How naïve could she be? She hit *Delete*, and, typing feverishly, began a new essay, the words tumbling out, describing how miserable she felt. And how very, very alone.

Thirty-Three

Misguided Angel

Tuesday Afternoon

Zoe and Will were in the family room, sitting on the edge of the sofa, studying the map spread out on the coffee table. At noon, Chief Healy had called to say that the Corbett woman had phoned with information regarding a cabin in southern Maine, owned by Todd's stepmother. Why any parent of a missing child would retain such vital information for more than two weeks Zoe could not begin to fathom. She couldn't decide if the woman was a total psycho or just plain stupid. The Cortland PD were working in conjunction with the Maine State Police. They'd issued an All Points Bulletin. "If they're in the area," Healey had pledged, "we'll find them."

According to Corbett's mother, the stepmother's cabin was located somewhere in the vicinity of Bath. Her descriptions of the house and surrounding area were frustratingly vague. She'd never been there herself, she'd told Healey. An hour ago, they'd learned from Dunham that the stepmother was out of town, whereabouts indeterminate. The woman and her husband, both currently unemployed, lived in a high-rise in lower Manhattan. No one in the building was aware of an impending trip; no one he'd contacted knew anything regarding a home in Maine.

A check of the county's Registry of Deeds also proved fruitless. When they spoke with Healey at two-thirty, Will suggested they look for a deed in the stepmother's maiden name. Naturally, Corbett's mother had no clue what the stepmother's maiden name might have been.

Corbett's mother, it occurred to Zoe, was protecting her son; for some reason, she didn't want the kids to be found. She straightened her back, rolling her shoulders, shook out her wrists, her right arm numb from leaning on her elbow. She was being paranoid. That couldn't be true.

Will planned to leave for Maine shortly, do some digging on his own. He had no faith whatsoever in "those incompetents," as he called Dunham and the police. The investigation was progressing too slowly; Zoe agreed. In fairness, she pointed out, Dunham and the cops had been focusing their efforts on the West Coast. "It's hard to find people who don't want to be found."

"Obviously," Will said sarcastically. "Bulger's been on the loose for how many years?"

"Could we not trash Dunham?" For the first time, they had a solid lead. "This is great news, Will. *Really* great news. We're going to find her. Let's focus there. Let's not jinx it, OK?"

"Jinx," Will repeated, rolling his eyes. He circled Bath on their map. "If he can't turn up a stepmother, can't even locate the goddamn cabin she owns, what are we paying the guy for?"

"Maybe he hit a road bock," Zoe offered, to diffuse him, though, frankly, her husband did have a point. "This is a busy time of year. A lot of people take vacation now."

"I should pack," Will said. "It's late." As it was, it would be dark before he arrived.

"Maybe we should give it a day, see what develops. What if the kids are in California?"

"I'll fly to California," he said, as if the possibility of Leah's being there were absurd. In the meantime, he'd check into a motel in Bath. "Nose around. Somebody's bound to know something."

"OK. I'll go with you." It was a four-hour drive from Cortland to Bath. They could take the Volvo. She bought new tires last fall, remember? Her car handled better than his in the snow.

"There's no point in both of us making the trip."

"Are you listening, Will?" She wiped her palms on her jeans, rubbed her sore knee. She couldn't bear to stay behind, waiting for news. Leah was as much her daughter as his. "I want to be there, too. We'll find a Residence Inn. Jus can stay with Holly. She's always there, anyway. Or she can come, if she wants. We'll ask as soon as she gets home. I'll bet she wants to come."

"We can't rip her out of school every time we get a lead."

"I don't think you heard me. I said, I'm going with you."

315

Will set a hand over hers. One of them had to be home, in case Leah tried to reach them. He folded the map. "I'll keep you posted. I promise."

Reluctantly, she agreed to stay home, in case Leah called. "If you hear anything, I mean *any*thing, call immediately. I'll drive up. She'll need me, Will. I want to be there for her."

Thursday Night

"Coming or not?" Todd demanded. He was headed into town, for a bottle of Daniels.

"Go," Leah said, too tired to move. "And shut the door. It's fucking freezing in here."

Her boyfriend exhausted her. Only a few weeks ago, she had been consumed by the prospect of marrying Todd. She'd planned their entire future. She'd imagined their house: a cabin by a lake. Named their children: Brittany, Taylor, Ashley, and Gina, four beautiful little girls with her silky blond hair and Todd's piercing blue eyes. They had talked seriously about starting a band. Todd promised to teach her to play the guitar. Watching MTV, she'd picked up several cool dance moves to incorporate into their first music video. Now, there were moments when Leah thought she might hate him. The least consequential things annoyed her—his long, tapered fingers, which constantly seemed to be grasping at something, the cowlick at his crown, the space between his two front teeth. The shape of her boyfriend's *head* (too narrow, she felt).

The Jeep's engine roared, and the truck rammed into reverse and skidded out of the lot.

This room was an icebox. Leah hauled her body, a hundred ten pounds of dead weight, out of bed, and adjusted the thermostat, raising the temperature from eighty to ninety degrees.

She and Todd had been living in this dump for close to a week, a nineteen-dollar-a-night room, in a skanky motel called Northern Lights, one of those low-slung, chain-style jobs where all the rooms were connected. The sign in front of the building read, "Vacancy. Free Colored TV." Not Internet. Not cable. Free *TV*. Leah swore, she heard rats scrambling inside the walls.

The town, a former logging community located thirty miles south of the Canadian border, was a hell-hole. Except for a filthy Mobil station, a Mini-Mart that could easily double as a crack house, a boarded-up non-denominational church, and the rundown doublewides parked alongside the river, there was nothing for miles around. Just trees. Trees, trees, and more trees.

She waited a minute for the heat to kick on, turned the knobs on the convector, twisting right and left. When it failed to respond, she booted the aluminum casing, her big toe whacking the corner. "Shit," she said, hopping on one foot. *Shit, shit, shit.* Her toe was probably broken.

She swiped a Power Bar and a Coke from their stash on the desk, limped across the room to Todd's backpack. She rummaged through his pack. Sitting on the floor, she pulled on his long johns and a pair of heavy wool socks, then sat on the bed to put her sweatpants back on.

A snowplow thundered down the street, the vibration rocking the motel's flimsy walls. Leah had never seen so much snow. It had been snowing since they arrived in New Hampshire, the snow piles along the sides of the road taller than Todd. At night, the plows kept her awake.

She went to the window and watched the plow, its headlights cutting through the coal black night. They'd been forced to leave Camden last week, after Todd held up the deli on the outskirts of town. He'd been to the store four times before he conjured the idiotic notion to rob it. From a densely treed bluff above the deli, he watched the customers coming and going. He knew exactly when the old man who ran the store was alone. Every time Todd went in, the old man asked his name—as if Jed Clampet were all that hard to remember. When the old geezer failed yet again to recognize him, something, Todd told her, had snapped. "It was like opportunity knocking," he said. "The old fart pissed his drawers when he got a load of the gun."

Leah was appalled. She'd felt horrible for the poor, frightened old man. Briefly, she had considered ordering Todd to return the two hundred twenty-three dollars he'd stolen, the way her mother had forced her to return the package of cherry-flavored bubblegum she'd filched from the rack by the checkout counter at CVS, when she was five. "We're not a stealing family," Leah had informed the amused clerk behind the pharmacy counter. But returning stolen money, saying you're sorry, is different for adults than for children. The most heartfelt apology cannot release adults from responsibility for their crimes. Todd would be caught, and jailed, and what would *she* do? She had made her own bed, as Nana Tyler would put it. Now she had to lie in it.

At the first town they came to in northern New Hampshire, they'd stopped at a hardware store, and bought a hotplate, an aluminum pot, a set of plastic dishes, two ceramic coffee mugs, and a package of cheap stainless-steel utensils. Since then, she and Todd had been bouncing from one fleabag motel to the next, existing on ramen noodles and soup, eyes and ears tuned in to the news. As far as they could tell, they were in the clear. The robbery never made headlines.

Lately, she'd been having trouble remembering why she left home. At night, as she lay in bed beside Todd, her brain replayed a continuous loop of home movies: afternoons in Boston, the *Make Way for Ducklings* tour their family had taken every spring when she and Justine were small. She saw herself and Justine climbing on the bronze ducklings in the park. Saw her family riding the swan boats, Justine perched quietly on their mom's lap, taking everything in, Leah, enchanted by the sun-dappled water, leaning over the rail, her father gripping her ankles. And there she was with her father, in their front yard, playing catch. Soccer: her dad on the sidelines, calling her name. Her teammates had envied Leah, her parents among the few who had attended every game. Her parents were always there to support her, "especially your dad," her teammates always said. Leah remembered the tournaments she and her father had flown to, in Colorado, Arizona, California, her mom and Justine in the terminal at Logan Airport, waving goodbye.

Leah saw flashes of herself on her mother's lap, her mom reading stories from *Grimm's Fairytales* or Leah's *Bible For Children*. She remembered the day her hamster died. Though she was only four at the time, she had been devastated, knowing she'd killed him. They'd buried the hamster in a shoebox, in the backyard. Afterward, her mother held Leah in her arms, read her a story, sang her a song. Hammy's death was an accident, Leah's mom said. *Sweetie, it isn't your fault.* Sometime between her childhood and now, she and her family had grown apart. The few times Leah had called home, her mother's voice sounded like the voice of a stranger. Leah couldn't bring herself to speak up. Leah missed Justine most of all. She'd started at least fifteen letters to her sister, ripped them all up. She considered calling, e-mailing from a public computer. But she knew that making contact with anybody from home would be too big a risk. Besides, if she contacted her sister, Justine would ask when she would be home. And what would she say?

The plow disappeared over the hill beyond the motel. For a while, Leah stared out at the darkness. Never in a million years would she have imagined herself holed up in a place like this. She'd never dreamed that she would be engaged to an armed robber, either. There were a lot of things she had never dreamed, Leah supposed. The things she did dream about—the cabin by a lake, her pretty little girls, being a rock star—none of those fantasies would ever come true. Seventeen years old, and so much of her future was already decided. Wasn't life strange?

From the list in her iPod, Leah selected a Cowboy Junkies tune called "Misguided Angel," and put on her headphones, yanked the musty blanket over the mattress, fell on the bed. She worked her baby finger into a moth hole, spun her finger around and around. Leah's heart ached, missing her family so much. She wondered if her family missed her, too. Since she and Todd left, she'd been combing the papers. She watched the morning and evening news. In all this time, she'd read not one article about herself. She'd never heard her name. There was no missing person story. No Amber Alert. No FBI search. She wondered if her family thought about her at all. Or if, this time, she'd pushed them too far. If they had forgotten all about her. If they'd simply gone on with their lives.

Sunday

Justine had lost eight pounds since Christmas. Her child's size sixteen jeans were too big for her now: she could easily slide three fingers into the space between the waistband and her belly. This morning, she'd snagged a pair of Levis that Leah had left in her closet. The inseams were too long, but Leah's jeans fit Justine almost perfectly through the waist and the hips. She rolled the hems over her feet, exposing only her toes. Claiming her sister's jeans was not exactly stealing, Justine rationalized. It was time to face the truth: Leah was not coming home.

Her father's trip to Maine was a bust. He'd spent a night in Bath, a night in Bar Harbor. From six a.m. until midnight, he'd hunted for signs of Leah and Todd. He canvassed every store, every restaurant, every real estate office. He wandered through the streets, showing everyone he met pictures of Leah. Not one person recalled having seen the Wrangler or the kids. No one had heard of the stepmother, either. A photo would have helped: possibly they knew her by face.

On Wednesday afternoon, while her father was driving home, the private detective had called, spoken with Justine's mom. He'd located the cabin, in a wooded area outside Camden. Todd and Leah had taken off in a hurry; he'd found skid marks by the front door. Earlier in the week, the deli in Camden had been robbed. The victim, an elderly man with a faulty memory, was unable to provide a positive ID. Logic, the detective said, told him the kids were involved.

"No *way*," Justine spat, when her mother relayed the news. "She'd never rob anybody."

Once the initial shock had worn off, Justine realized that her sister and Todd probably had robbed that deli in Camden. Why else would they have left in such a big a hurry? Even so, that didn't make her sister a bad person—did it? What if Leah were hungry? If she'd robbed the deli so she could buy food? What if she or Todd were sick or hurt? In need of medical attention? Couldn't circumstances turn *anyone* into a thief? She had always believed that right and wrong were absolute. Now she wasn't so sure. The questions rolled round and round Justine's head.

Along with her sister's jeans, she'd brought Leah's ceramic ashtray into her room, and also a picture she'd found in the attic, of Leah on her Confirmation day. In the snapshot, Leah, in her white gown, a crown of daisies in her hair, is clowning, leaning toward the camera, in a classic tap dancing pose—arms spread, her left knee forward, right leg extended. She looks as if she might dance right out of the picture, Justine thought. Justine set the photograph on her desk, and pressed her hand into the palm of Leah's ceramic ashtray, her fingers curling over the edges. Hard to believe she'd made the ashtray herself. Hard to believe her hands were ever that small.

Squatting, she lifted her comforter, and slid her hand between the mattress and box spring, the mattress crushing her arm. She extracted a flattened cigarette from the pack, tapped the filtered end on her palm to reshape it. That she had conjured the nerve to buy cigarettes still shocked her. She'd heard kids at school talking about a guy, at the Citgo station down the street, who sold cigarettes to anybody, never asked for ID. During her lunch period, she trekked to the station. Until she had reached the counter and handed the attendant her money, she could not have said for sure if she would go through with it. She had thought she might chicken out.

Her room was stuffy. Justine raised her window, to let in some fresh air. At the edge of the yard, just beyond the perimeter of the woods, she spotted a fox. Dog, when she was younger, loved chasing foxes. She was a wimp with animals her own size. Whenever she saw a coyote, for instance, she cried. If they were walking, Dog would stop cold. Justine would kneel beside her, her arms wrapped protectively around her dog's neck and chest, until the coyote retreated into the forest. Anything smaller—cats, mice, foxes, squirrels—was fair game.

For the most part, Justine tried not to think about Dog. It was easier to avoid thinking about things you had no control over, no power to change. Thinking about Dog made her sad, and what good did that do? Maybe that was the reason Leah had played soccer for all those years. So she didn't have to think. With sports, you have no time to reflect. You just do.

She lit the cigarette, and took a long, languorous drag, inhaling as Leah had taught her, tapping the ashes into the open palm of the ashtray. A breeze blew across her room, a faint odor of burning logs in the air. When she had smoked the cigarette down to the filter, she crushed the butt in the palm of her ceramic hand, and spritzed the air with Leah's cloying floral perfume.

Bored, Justine turned on the Christmas DVD, for the background noise, not to watch. She couldn't bear to watch, anymore. Seeing her parents acting like normal people made her too angry. Her parents' behavior, these days, was bizarre. The day her father returned from Maine without Leah, Justine's mother finagled a prescription for Xanax. Her mother was downstairs in the family room, now, sleeping. Her father had gone "out for a drive," meaning he was headed to Todd's. Her father drove to the Corbett's house every day. He never did anything but sit in his car, watching the house. A boy in Justine's geometry class lived on Todd's street. The boy had seen her father, and told her. As far as Justine knew, neither parent was working. For the first time in her life, she worried about money. Soon, *I'll* have to resort to stealing, she thought.

She launched *AOL*, and traded instant messages with Holly for awhile. Today was Holly's day with her dad. Her father was taking Holly for lunch, then to Cambridge to visit his mother. Holly had invited her to tag along. Holly's grandmother was sweet, but she asked too many questions. Justine was in no mood to talk to or smile at or be fussed over by anyone, not even a sweet old lady with purple curls. When Holly signed off, Justine shut down her computer.

Flipping through Leah's CD case, she found the 50 Cent disc, slid it into the Discman she'd also found in the attic, and put on the headphones. Closing her eyes, she listened for the beat. BOOM, boom, boom . . . ONE two three four. "One, two," she counted aloud, starting over each time she messed up the phrasing. "One, two, three—" She listened to the entire CD, and played it again. In the second stanza of the fourth song, the lyrics drifted away from the instrumentation. *One two three four.* There it was. *One two three four.* She heard it. She finally heard it. Justine extended her arms— *one two three four,* she counted—and, rolling her shoulders into the music, danced across her room.

Tuesday, early evening

"Where is she?" Will checked his watch. "She said she'd be here by five, didn't she?"

Justine had stayed after school to set up her science project for the fair. Holly's mother had offered to drive the girls home. It was five o'clock, Will pointed out. "It's getting late."

His wife was sitting on Leah's bed, in the dark, facing the window, a photograph of the girls in her lap. She wore a gray, long-sleeved T-shirt and baggie black sweats, her hair tied in a ponytail, curls falling in her face. In the shadows in the dark room, she looked like a ghost.

Leah's room also felt ghost-like to him. Since their daughter ran away, he and Zoe had touched nothing. The Nike poster still curled off the wall. Leah's bed was unmade; her clothes and shoes littered the floor. A layer of dust had settled over the room. Even the carpet was dusty.

Through the branches of the barren trees, he saw the streetlamps in the circle wink on.

"Zoe?" She blinked when he flipped on the light. "Did Justine say anything to you?"

His wife was pissed at him—again. He'd left toothpaste in the sink. Forgotten to pick up his socks. Turned his head the wrong way. If he was quiet or reflective, Zoe wanted to talk. If he talked, she wished to be left alone. He was constantly trying to gauge her moods, afraid of setting her off. His wife was like this after the abortion. It scared him, watching it happen all over again. Last night, she overheard him on the phone, asking his mother for advice. "You told your *mother* about me?" she demanded, the instant he set the phone down. "Why would you do that to me?"

The roots of depression are complex. Still, he couldn't help feeling that this was partly his fault. He had known, when Healey told them about the cabin in Maine, that his chances of finding the kids were slim. He'd driven to Maine for Zoe's sake—for himself, too; for Leah, of course; for Justine. Mostly, he'd gone for his wife. In the first weeks after Leah's disappearance, though Zoe's mood deteriorated, she'd managed to hang on, to stay hopeful. Each setback had taken a little more out of her. By the time they received the tip-off about the house in Maine, she was, in his estimation, close to a breakdown. He should have voiced his concerns. Instead, he'd taken the cowardly route, allowing her to believe in the impossible. When he returned without Leah, she'd given up. She blocked out news from the police, the PI. Yesterday, Johnson stopped by to check on the them, and Zoe had rudely sent him away. Will had called, later, to apologize.

Will had never before felt so helpless, so out of control. He stared at his useless hands, the bulging blue veins showing signs of age. If Leah were desperate enough to participate in a robbery, she was scared. That vulnerable, frightened image of his child terrorized him. And there was not a thing he could do. Will was a fixer. That was his job. He'd let his entire family down.

Zoe ran a finger over the photo in her lap. "Think I should dust?" she asked quietly.

"If you want to, I guess."

"Remember this?" She flipped the photograph, showing him the picture of the girls in their wading pool. "I took it on her last day of first grade. She was always so happy when summer rolled around. She hated school. I never understood why. She was such a smart kid."

"She didn't want to be trapped?" Will suggested. He'd hated being tied down, too.

"She was a great student—straight A's every year. Whenever Justine's teacher hung her paper on the wall, she was ecstatic. She'd have to show me, when I went in. Leah never cared."

"Speaking of Jus," he said, "we're going to a movie. That sci-fi flick she wants to see. Why don't you come? If she gets home soon, we'll have time to stop first, for something to eat."

"Not tonight," she said, her face clouding. "She thinks I hate her. It's the last thing she said. You hate me." She wiped a tear from her cheek. "How could I let her leave, thinking that?"

"She doesn't think you hate her, Zo. Kids say things. She knows you don't hate her."

"She's my daughter. I could never hate her."

"Come with us, Zoe." He squeezed his wife's shoulder. "Be good for Justine."

She edged away. "I don't feel well tonight."

"Tell you what, we'll keep the cell phone on. We won't miss a single call. I promise."

"You can't do that. It's rude."

Will cleared his throat. "I need to talk to you, Zo."

With her index finger, she drew a circle on the glass picture frame, enclosing the girls.

"I think we should move." It probably sounded as if the idea had come out of the blue. But moving had been on his mind for months. "A change of scenery would do us all good."

She looked at him as if he were out of his mind, got up, and stomped to the window.

"Think about it, hon." The house was too big, too expensive to maintain. Their last gas bill was seven hundred bucks, and winter had barely begun. They hadn't had a cold spell yet. In April, they would be hit with a bill for eight grand in property taxes. Where would they come up with eight grand? They were leveraged to their eyeballs. If they sold the house, their financial problems would disappear—he snapped his fingers—overnight. Be a relief to unload this place, to move forward again. He joined Zoe at the window. He would go anywhere—another town, another state. Hell, another country, if it made her happy. "Anywhere, Zo. You pick the place."

"That branch. If I opened the window—" She brought her face closer to the glass. "I could touch it. No wonder she got out so easily, that night."

"We need to move forward," he charged on. This holding pattern was destroying them. He could not continue to stand by and watch his marriage slowly dissolve. Look at the up-side, he told his wife: selling the house would give them freedom, an opportunity to make changes, to consider their options. All sorts of possibilities would open up if they were not strapped for cash. They could change careers, find jobs they enjoyed. And think about the benefit to Justine. She didn't want problems with Jus, did she? "Have you seen her, lately?" She listened to Leah's music, wore Leah's clothes. Her grades had dropped. She was losing interest in school. One of these days, they would learn she was smoking. Or doing drugs. Did Zoe not see where they were headed? "We have to do something, Zo. We can't let this happen. We've got to protect her."

"I'm not moving," she said, her shoulders squared. Her hands, he noticed, were fidgeting.

"Why not?"

Her eyes flashed. "Because we're not," she hissed, and turned her back to him again.

He circled around her, wedging himself between her and the window, placed both hands on her shoulders. She owed him a reason. "One reason. That's all I'm asking. One good reason."

Zoe brushed her hair out of her face. "This is her *room*, Will. That's the reason."

"OK, good. That's good. We're making progress. Look at this—" He pointed to a creeping water stain on the ceiling, a pull in the carpet, the chicken scratch on the walls. "It's a mess. If we moved, she'd have a new room. A better room. A *much* better room. Any color she wants.

Something vibrant. We'll buy a new bedroom set, too—white. You know, that white furniture you always wanted to buy for the girls? She can even have her own bathroom. And a walk-in closet. *A walk-in closet*, Zo. Leah would go nuts over a walk-in closet. How about it?"

"I said no," she croaked. She stared at the window, her mouth set, refusing to look at him, her arms crossed stubbornly over her chest. "We're not moving," she repeated.

"What about Justine? Huh, Zo? What about Jus? You don't care about her?"

Zoe met his eyes, her lips quivering. "We can't move, Will. How would she find us?"

Thirty-Four

Home Is Where the Heart Is

Thursday

Last night, Leah dreamed about soccer. Her high school team was playing in the state tournament, held in the coliseum at Harvard. She scanned the crowded stadium, the spectators standing two and three deep along the sidelines, searched their faces, hunting for her parents. Coach Thomas had switched her position from forward to goalie. Leah crouched in front of the net, paralyzed. She'd forgotten how to play. A buzzer sounded. Within seconds, the opposing team scored. The scoring forward danced in front of the net, the crowd cheering. Leah willed her body to move, tried to force herself to block the balls flying at her. But the balls kept coming.

In no time, the score was 20-0, and both teams were taunting her. The crowd, led by the players, erupted in a chorus of boos, the mob jeering. *Get her out of there. She stinks.* From the sidelines, a spectator lobbed a rotten apple at the net. She flailed her arms, dodging the apples splattering on her shoulders, whacking her chest, the infuriated fans waving their fists. *Tyler sucks.* Bam, another apple. The reporter from the *Gazette* stepped onto the field, Nikon camera in hand, followed by a photographer from the *Globe.* The photographers aimed—

The blinding flashes woke her. Leah blinked, shielding her eyes.

Todd was dragging the heavy woven drapes across the window, the clips scraping the metal rod, harsh white light shooting into the room. "Hey, babe," he said. "Rise and shine."

The room spun. For dinner last night, they'd split a package of *Reese's Pieces* and a twelve-ounce bag of barbecue chips. They'd eaten their last real meal at breakfast, yesterday morning. After

326

dinner, they polished off a bottle of JD. Every bone and joint in her body ached.

A plow rumbled by, the racket jarring her brain. She clapped her palms to her ears. She was never drinking again. Ever. Groaning, she rolled sideways, pulling her knees to her chest.

Squinting, she saw her boyfriend at the foot of her bed, the image fuzzy. He was staring down at her, amused. He must have been up for awhile. He'd already showered and shaved. He'd even washed his hair, damp blond ringlets like a curtain above his flaming blue eyes. He pulled a sweatshirt over his head, and, grinning stupidly, gestured for her to get up. "Let's go, babe."

"What's wrong with me?" she whined. "How come you don't feel like crap?"

"Some of us can handle our liquor, dude." He tugged at her blanket. "Time to get up."

"Go away," she cried, gripping the covers, batting his hands away with her feet.

With a jerk, he stripped the covers, let them fall in a heap at Leah's feet. "Let's go, dude. It's two o'clock. My old lady's loaning us five hundred bucks. I said we'd drive down today."

She pushed her bangs out of her eyes. "We can't," she started, but the point slipped away.

"Hope's throwing a bash," he was saying. "Figured we'd stay at her place tonight. Tomorrow, we'll go to my mother's. It's getting late. We've got to get moving."

"Are you crazy?" she asked, suddenly alert. "Can't drive down there." They'd get caught.

He shrugged. "Stay here, if you want. But we need the dough, babe. I'm going down."

Alone? Was he joking? Twice, when Todd went into town for supplies, the pervert who managed this dump knocked on their door, under the guise of providing new linens, and tried to corner her. Luckily, she'd managed to convince him that Todd was on his way back. Staying here by herself overnight would be like giving that psycho an invitation to rape her. She lugged her aching body to the edge of the mattress, a wave of nausea washing over her as she sat.

With her bare foot, she knocked her Doc Martin shoe away from the bed.

She vaguely recalled having stashed something edible inside her suitcase—a *Power Bar*, something chocolate, a bag of chips—in case they ran out of food. Carefully, she lowered herself to the floor, her stomach groaning, knelt, and rooted through her clothes, squeezing each item as if she were hunting for gold. She slid her hand across the interior pocket. "We're not taking money from your mother," she said. They were not a charity case. If they planned to build a life together, they had to learn to rely on themselves. "Have some pride, for God's sake."

"Right." He sniggered. "Pride tastes pretty good, I heard. We're broke, dude, remember?"

She was set to blast him—*most people work for money; they don't call mommy*—when she saw a mouse dart across the floor. "Told you"—she scooped up her shoe—"we've got rats," she screamed, and hurled her shoe, the rodent skittering under the baseboard. Her shoe slammed the wall, and ricocheted off, the vibration knocking a watercolor of a covered bridge off its hook.

Stunned, she gaped at the shards of glass on the floor, the silhouette on the empty wall where the painting had hung, her shoe, lying on its side. "You didn't believe me," she muttered.

He picked up the painting, plucked a sliver of glass out of the frame, and hung the painting back on its hook, not quite centering it, the bridge tilting sideways. "This ain't Wonderland, babe," he said irritably. "It's time for you to grow up."

She whisked a pair of jeans from the clump of dirty clothes in her suitcase. Screw him. If anybody had to grow up, it was Todd. She flung the jeans on the floor. She had a *Power Bar* in there. She remembered saving it. Or a *Three Musketeers* bar. She pitched a pair of panties, a bra, several unmatched socks, a T-shirt she'd stolen from Todd, her clothes flying in every direction.

At the bottom of her suitcase, wedged in a corner, peaking out from under the folds of the nylon lining, she spotted the bracelet her mother had given her. *Stormy.* She slipped the blue button bracelet over her wrist. *Stormy*, she thought, her heart breaking—*wild, raging, intense.*

The Jeep, parked in the motel lot for the last two days, was frozen, the seats hard as slate.

"It's freezing in here," Leah complained, and cranked the heat.

Todd wrested the blanket from the backseat, dislodging it out from under their suitcases, and tossed it in her direction. "Found some change under the seat," he said, and lowered the heat. "We'll split a burger." He poked a cigarette in the lighter. "I'll stop in Plymouth. It's two hours."

The cigarette's stale odor turned her stomach. When he offered it, she waved it away.

The world outside the motel looked like a tundra, the icy parking lot shimmering in the glare of the radiating sun. A thick layer of snow sheeted the roofs of the trailers, the farmhouses, the barns, blanketed the fields, the shrubs; tall, snow-laden pines bowed like supplicants to the massive oak and maple and birch trees, the boughs sagging under the weight of the glittering ice.

A snowmobile ripped across the frozen river and over the bank, its skis airborne.

Leah put on her sunglasses, and rested her head against the window, the icy glass searing her cheek. She wondered what the weather was like at home. She'd stopped watching the news, quit keeping track. An image of the town center flashed through her head—the great lawn, the stone wall covered with snow. She saw people bustling in and out of the post office, the video store, everyone bundled in parkas, their cheeks flushed, the cheerful colors of their hats and mittens—red, yellow, orange, cerulean blue—so different from the dolorous olive and navy, the gunmetal gray favored by people up here. She wondered what her parents were doing. Three o'clock, Thursday—they were at work. Justine would be on the bus, doing homework or reading.

Stop. She turned her bracelet, her lips quivering. *Don't do this to yourself.*

This was insane, driving to Cortland. Even if they stayed on the back roads, as Todd had promised, someone was bound to see them, or to recognize the Jeep. Someone at Hope's party would rat them out. They'd run into someone they knew at the gas station. There was something fundamentally wrong with her boyfriend. She didn't get him, taking these risks all the time. Like robbing the deli: there had been no good reason to rob that old man. They could have driven to Canada, found jobs in Montreal or Toronto. As long as they stayed out of trouble, kept a low profile, no one would have found them. They'd have been safe. They could have lived decent, law-abiding lives, gotten married, started their family. In time, her family would have forgiven her, and they could have gone home. Instead, they were fugitives. Even running from the law wasn't dangerous enough to satisfy Todd. He had to taunt the police. Leah closed her eyes, her breath slowing to the rhythm of the jazz CD in the player. In her dreams, she ran and ran.

When she opened her eyes, Todd was pulling into Hope's driveway, snow flurries swirling in the headlights. Leah yawned, not quite awake. For an instant, in her sleepy haze, she forgot why they were there. Hope's cat was perched on the sill of the living room window, pawing the glass. The colored lights around the front door blinked on, the red, green and yellow bulbs flashing like a neon sign. An electric candle flickered in Hope's bedroom window.

Todd opened his door, admitting a rush of frigid air. "Let's go," he said. "You coming?"

Leah buttoned her peacoat, and stuffed her hands in her mittens, a button catching on the cuff. *We're here to borrow money*, she thought miserably. *From his mom.*

Todd knocked once and opened the door. "Anybody home?"

"Hey." Hope threw her arms around them, hugging and kissing them. "Missed you guys."

Lupo clapped Todd's back, and drew Leah into a bear hug, lifting her off her feet.

"So?" Hope spread her arms. "What do you think?"

Hope and Lupo had pushed the furniture against the living room walls, creating an open dance floor. Bubbles gurgled out of a machine in the center of the room, the soaring bubbles turning iridescent colors in the black light from the strobe lamp on the TV. They followed Hope into the kitchen. On the counter, she'd set out plastic mixing bowls filled with Tootsie Pops, and liter-sized bottles of soda—Coke, Diet Pepsi, Orange, Sprite. At one end of the counter, she and Lupo had set up a keg. On the other sat a cut-glass punch bowl containing a vodka and citrus drink Hope had concocted, a frozen strawberry ring floating on the frothy lime green liquid.

"What's up with you guys?" Hope asked, pulling Leah aside. "You OK?"

"Fine." Leah managed a weak smile. "Place looks great. I'm psyched about your party."

Hope ladled a vodka drink for Leah and one for herself, and set their plastic cups on the counter. From her pocket, she produced a small pink pill, with a butterfly stamped on top. She pressed the tablet into Leah's palm. "Go for it, girl. Seriously. You look like you could use it."

By eight thirty, Hope's tiny ranch was rocking. The kitchen was jammed, kids drinking, smoking weed. Three girls, waving rackets, challenged their boyfriends to a game of beer pong. Lupo's friends— a scruffy-looking blond, around Leah's age, and four older boys, in their mid-twenties, Leah judged—were sitting on the floor, backs to the cabinets, passing a crack pipe.

Leah wandered from the kitchen to the living room, where the band had rigged a stage against the far wall, the raging tempo of the electric guitars tempered by a hypnotic 4-4 backbeat. Dozens of kids, Tootsie Pops bulging inside their cheeks, were dancing, waving glow sticks.

Leah cupped her hands. "Awesome," she shouted, into Hope's ear. "Best party, ever."

The Ecstasy buzz wearing off, Leah pushed her way through the mob, into the kitchen, downed four cups of punch in quick succession. Giddy, she hunted for her boyfriend, found him in the bathroom, and pulled onto the dance floor, where they danced in slow circles, his head on her shoulder, hands on her butt, her arms locked around his neck, the bubbles floating all around them as if they were under water.

At ten, on top of the world, she swallowed a second hit of E.

Shortly after eleven, a carload of out-of-towners showed up. Hope noticed the strange car parked in front of her house, and ordered Lupo to get rid of the kids. Leah beat Lupo to the punch. "Hell-*lo*," she said, fanning herself as she opened the door. She welcomed each new guest with a hug; wobbling on her tiptoes, she kissed the boys square on the lips. *All these cute guys. Ought to have an orgy*, she thought. Or maybe she said it. Either way, it was a brilliant idea. Tapping shoulders and ribs impatiently, she dragged the coffee table toward the center of the room, its feet scraping the hardwood floor. The crowd parted, kids moving left and right.

"S'cuse me," she said, clapping to get the crowd's attention. She climbed onto the table. Someone whistled; someone else handed her a Coke. She waved the bottle. *Let's have some fun.*

A crowd gathered, the musky odor of the sweat-drenched bodies intoxicating, sexy.

I love you baby, she sang. She unbuttoned her blouse, shoulders pulsing with the music.

"Dude." Todd snagged her wrist. "What the hell are you doing?"

Leah snatched her arm back. "Love, love, love," she sang.

Todd lunged for the table. Two linebacker-sized thugs went after him. The smaller one tackled him. Together, they lifted him to his feet, twisting his arms behind his back. Out of the corner of her eye, she saw them, one on each side, shove him out the front door, her boyfriend fighting, his neck and back arched. She caught his eye, her hips gyrating, and cringed.

The band raged, the bass pounding. From the sea of faces, she located a pair of friendly eyes. Holding their gaze, she threw her head back, raking her hands through her hair, her torso moving in time with the music. *Whoa, whoa, whoa, ba-by.* Kids poured into the room, the boys crowding the stage, the girls dancing. Leah had never in her life felt so alive, so empowered. *Hap-py birth-day, Mis-ter Pres-i-dent.* She unhooked her bra, tossed it into the frenzied crowd, lifted her arms over her head. The audience cheered, waving their hands. "Go, go, go." *See? The audience loved her. She was no loser. Love, love, love.* Her fingers slithered over her belly—

The door crashed open, slamming the wall. "A gun," someone shouted. "He's got a gun!"

The music died. Leah dropped her hands, her hardening nipples mortifying her, crossed her arms over her chest, covering herself.

"Let's go," her boyfriend shouted. He cocked the pistol.

Terrified, she covered her breasts. *Todd,* she tried to say—he was out of his mind—*don't.*

He pointed the gun at the boys closest to the table. "Get away from her," he ordered. "All of you." The crowd heaved and the entire room, it seemed, pushed backward. "Leah, let's go."

"Dude," Lupo pleaded, raising both hands. "Put it down, before somebody gets hurt."

Todd shrugged Lupo off. Bending, he swept up Leah's clothes, his eyes fixed on the crowd. Waving the gun, he took hold of her arm, and backed away, dragging her out of the house.

Friday, 3 P.M.

Leah squeezed her eyes shut, willing away the previous night. This can't be happening, she thought. This is a dream. I'm remembering a movie. This isn't my life.

"About *time*," Todd said. "Thought you'd never wake up."

Leah pulled the sheet over her head. Her body ached. On the way out of the house, she'd hit her knee on the edge of the door. The knee had swelled. She had trouble bending her leg.

Todd pulled the covers off her face. "Come on. Let's get out of here."

"Don't touch me." She batted his hand away.

"Talked to Lupo, awhile ago. Everything's cool."

She closed her eyes, nauseated, opened them again, squinting. "What time is it?"

"Three. Come on. Let's go. We've got to get out of here."

"Feel like shit." Leah hugged the blanket to her chest as she sat. "I need some aspirin."

"Don't have any." He'd go to CVS, if she went, too. He was going nowhere alone.

It was a depressing afternoon, dank and raw, yesterday's snow turning to mush.

For ten minutes, from the time they climbed in the car until they reached the center, Todd tried to strike up a conversation. *What did she want from him? Fucking strip tease? What the hell did she expect? Fine. His fault—OK?* Leah stared at the window. *Stupid. Never should have gone for the gun.* "Listen to me, Leah." They had nothing to worry about. *Coke, crack. Who'd call the cops?* At last, he gave up, and they rode in insulated silence, listening to one another breathe.

He turned on the radio, flipped through the stations—his mother's cheap-ass radio, as he called it, received only AM signals. "Shit," he said, "fuck it," and turned the radio off.

The center was clogged, people honking, everyone in a rush to begin the weekend.

Leah hunkered down in her seat. He'd borrowed his mother's Taurus. No one would recognize them in this car. Still, she felt exposed. She kept waiting for someone to spot them—another driver, one of the kids milling around the common or sitting on the stone wall. Expected sirens, a chase, cruisers skidding to a stop like the movies, blocking the Taurus.

Todd pulled into the busy lot, pulled the Taurus into a space between two SUVs.

"I'm not going in," Leah announced. She looked like shit in his sweats, her hair greasy.

Todd cut the engine and, glaring at her, climbed out, slamming his door.

The CVS store occupied the space at the far end of the *L*-shaped strip, next to the Natural Grocer. Harried mothers wheeled carriages in and out of the market, their toddlers, perched in the seat of the cart, clutching bagels, packets of raisins or dried fruit, their older kids, in oversized parkas and bright rubber boots, stomping gleefully through the puddles.

To bide time while she waited for Todd to fetch her aspirin, Leah conjured phrases to match the number-letter combinations on the license plates of the other cars in the lot. A blue Escort backed into the spot in front of the truck, spewing oily fumes. 93RJMA. Ninety-three royal jackasses moving to Alaska. Ha! With her long, horse-shaped nose, the driver looked like a jackass.

Someone tapped on the window.

Leah slid lower, hiding her face inside the hood of her sweatshirt.

She heard another tap, then her name. She turned her head slightly, exposing one eye.

Cissy Hanson. Of all people to run in to today. "Hey." Leah pressed the button, lowering the window three or four inches, pulled off her hood. "What's up?"

"Hey." Cissy waved her pharmacy bag. Typical fashion plate Cissy: suede jacket, doeskin gloves a shade darker than the jacket, silk scarf, in a bold geometric design, tied loosely around her neck, the scarf striking set against her dark hair. "Where've you been hiding?"

Leah swept a hand over her head. Why had she agreed to come here? She should have skipped the aspirin, done without. Pain shot through her knee, into her thigh. Cissy had probably heard all about last night, the gun, her mortifying strip tease. The whole town probably knew. Her stomach heaved. "What are you doing here?" she asked, eyeing the glove compartment, thinking how funny it would be to wave the gun at this twit. If she said a *word* about last night—

"My mom's heart pills," Cissy purred, lifting the bag. She stole a furtive glance around the lot, and stepped closer to the window. She must have taken a bath in perfume. She reeked. "I heard you quit school," she whispered, into the open window. "It's not true," she said, "is it?"

"Who told you that?"

"I don't know." Cissy shrugged, flashing a smug grin. "I just heard."

"Don't bullshit me. You didn't just *hear*."

"Actually," she spat, in a reciprocal tone. "I did."

"Liar," Leah said, infuriated. "I want to know who said that about me. Who told you?"

"Got to fly. My mom's waiting for me." Cissy waved the bag again. "I feel bad for you, Leah," she said, as she was turning away. "The kids are right. You are pathetic."

Friday, 5 PM

Justine and her father were sitting in a booth at the Ninety-Nine restaurant, pushing food around their plates. The restaurant stank of raw beef and smelly, packed-in people. The reception area was mobbed, a bunch of nerds milling around the hostess stand, waiting to be seated, the boisterous, Friday night regulars gathered around the bar. The door swung open, admitting a rush of frigid air followed by four preppy, college-aged kids, rubbing their hands together, chattering.

Justine picked her burger from its bun, dropped the slab of partially cooked beef on her plate. She was considering becoming a vegan. A girl in her English class had switched to an all-lettuce diet, and lost twenty-five pounds. If Justine lost that much weight, she would be almost as skinny as the girls in the *Seventeen* magazines Holly collected. With her finger, she poked a hole in the burger, and filled it with ketchup.

A plate of thick, greasy onion rings sat at the center of the table. Her father speared a ring. "Think I'll ask for a doggie bag, bring some of these to school. Mom would like that, I bet."

"Sure." Justine said dully—*as if.* She twirled her mother's button bracelet.

"Hopefully, she'll get to eat them before they get cold."

Why couldn't he be honest? Justine had no illusions about tonight. Since her father's trip to Maine, the only time Justine's mother left the house was to go to the doctor, to weasel another prescription. Justine pitied her mother, sitting by the window all day, waiting for the phone to ring. Justine wanted to shake her. *You have two daughters*, she wanted to say. *What about me?*

With the back of her fork, she pushed at her fries.

"You look nice, Jus. I like that sweater."

"Thanks." Justine smirked. "It's Leah's."

Her father had gone ballistic the first time he saw the baby blue sweater on Leah. She looked—like *a slut*, Leah said. *He told me I look like a slut.* He'd ordered her to return it. After that, Leah wore the sweater only when their father was out of town. Justine fingered the plunging V-neckline. She felt sexy tonight. She'd stuffed white socks in her bra, to give herself cleavage.

Her father caught their waitress's eye, ordered a second Bud Light. "Excited?" he asked, once the waitress had turned away. "You never did show me your project."

Justine mashed the burger with her fork, working until the meat resembled a pile of barf.

"Jus?"

"Huh?" She lifted her eyes. "Yeah. Sure."

"Want to tell me about it?" Her father swished a ring through a puddle of ketchup, smearing the bloody red goop all over his plate. "Something about the Milky Way, right?"

She grabbed her purse. "Go to the bathroom," she said, gagging, and slid off the bench.

"All right," her father said, with a thin smile. "I'll be here."

In the restroom, Justine pushed her mother's bracelet over her forearm, and knelt on the cold, tiled floor, her head bowed over the bowl. She pushed her index finger deep into her throat, anticipating the release, the exhilarating emptiness she would feel in her stomach, lodged her finger deeper and deeper, until her stomach heaved. And she puked.

Friday, 7:30 PM

Todd propped himself against his headboard, stretching his legs, his right foot twitching. A Machine Head disc blared from his stereo, the driving music wracking Leah's skull. On their way home from CVS, he'd stopped for a pepperoni and mushroom pizza. They'd eaten upstairs, with his mother. She'd convinced Todd to spend the night, leave in the morning. It was safer, she'd told him, to drive in daylight.

Todd brought the JD bottle to his lips, sucking it down as if it were water.

Leah held his mirror close to her face, rotating the etched glass to the light. She patted her cheek. Her face was bloated, her skin gray. She looked like a freak, with her hollow, bloodshot eyes. She picked a zit on her chin, splattering pus on the mirror. She couldn't go on this way. If she continued to live like this, she would be dead in a couple years. Or in jail. She tightened the drawstring on Todd's pajamas. "I'm such a *loser*," she said, and flopped back on the bed.

"Fuck that bitch, Hanson. You ain't a loser." *Loother.*

Shut up, she thought. She didn't want to talk to him, right now. Didn't want to hear his voice. She missed her parents, Justine. *Your family loves you*, Officer Johnson told her, that night at the hospital. *They're the ones who will always be there for you.* A tear rolled down her cheek.

She missed the silly stuffed animals in the net over her bed. Missed the smell of their house.

"Come over here, babe." He patted the bed. "Got a surprise for you," he said, snagging her wrist. He dragged her hand over his bulging crotch. "What do you think, huh?"

"Let *go*." She ripped her hand out of his. Time to get her life together, go back to school.

"Can show it to the world." He lifted her shirt, groping her breast. "What about me?"

"Stop, all right?" She yanked her shirt down. "Just let me alone."

"Thought you loved me," he moaned. He tossed the bottle in the rubbish can by his bed. "We're a team, me and you." He pushed her to the mattress, humping her leg.

"Get off," Leah said, struggling to free herself. "You stink. I can't breathe."

"Fuck you." He rolled off, swatting the bed, his gestures sharp, and stomped to his bureau, withdrew his stash, shoved the drawer shut with his shin. "'s your problem tonight?"

Her problem? *Him. Her. Everything.* "I want— I want to go home."

8 PM

Justine and her father trundled around the noisy gymnasium, her father ogling the exhibits. At each table, he stopped to ask a question, offer a compliment. *Socially conscious, I see. How original, recycled garbage!* Her father's false enthusiasm embarrassed her. When she and Leah were little, he'd refused to attend their school functions. On the few occasions when their mother prodded him into going, he'd parked his butt in the chair closest to the rear wall, and sat there, bored, with his hands folded, looking grim. It was bizarre to see him trying so hard.

"Look at this," he said, loud enough to be heard in China. "What an impressive project."

The cloud chamber was bogus. The designer, a gangling, pock-faced dork, hung on her father's every word. "Project sucks," she said, under her breath. "Who made it for you? Daddy?"

"Got to tell you, Jus. You've got some talented kids at your school."

"Mmm," she said, trailing her father down the outermost aisle.

He said something else, his words lost in the din.

When they reached Justine's table, her father stepped back, stroking his chin, his eyes wandering. He scanned the room, his gaze lingering on the door. "Phenomenal," he proclaimed, turning his attention back to her project. He patted Justine on the head, as if she were six. She deserved better than third place, he whispered. Judges were dopes. "I'd give it second, anyway."

"Thanks." Justine rolled her eyes. "Can we go now?"

"Let's give your mom a few more minutes." He insisted on circling the room yet again, in case they had overlooked one of the projects on their first, second, or third time around.

337

By eight, everyone except for Justine and her father had begun packing. Kids toted cardboard boxes while their parents, conversing across the tables, disassembled the projects. At last, her father agreed to go. Looked to him like this shindig was about to break up. He flashed a fake grin, and snuck another peak at the door. "Sorry, hon." Her mother had probably lost track of the time. "What do you think, Jus? What should we do with this box?"

Whatever. "Throw it out."

They'd stowed their coats under the table. Crouching, she reached behind the fabric panel for her father's overcoat. Justine was zipping her parka, when she spotted her mother, by the gym door. Her mother peered around the room, grinning broadly. Under her hooded black coat, she wore navy sweatpants, an old pair of running shoes. Thankfully, she had combed her hair.

Justine waved, directing her mother to their table. Her mother, shifting to the right, said something to the person following her. Justine's heart surged. The girl's face was hidden. But she recognized the blue peacoat, her sister's distinctive, slouch-shouldered gait. *Leah had come home. For the fair.* Justine had to pinch herself, to prove this was real. *Her sister remembered.*

Her father was busy pulling her project apart.

"Be right back," Justine said, and took off.

The janitors had waxed the floor to a sheen. Her feet slipped, her cartoon legs propelling her body forward, ahead of her feet. Her mom turned to the girl again, her lips moving. Justine's heart ripped through her chest. She was dying to know what her mother said. What Leah said back. "Lee," she called, from about ten feet away. *Lee—*

"Jus?" Her mother looked at Justine quizzically, and turned to the girl behind her.

"Mom." Justine's eyes pooled. "I thought she was Leah."

8:30 PM

The Jeep plowed down Main Street. The temperature had plunged since this afternoon, the road a slick sheet of black ice. Leah leaned against the door, her heart hammering.

Before they left, when Todd was in the bathroom, Leah called home. It was only fair to give her family a warning. She reached voice service. "It's me," she said, disappointed. "Leah," she added, in case they failed to recognize her voice. She was coming home. "I miss you guys."

Todd gripped the wheel, the staccato tick of his shoulders timed to the bleating music. "We're a team, you and me. We're supposed to get married. We're starting a band."

He skidded onto Old Orchard Road, the moonlight illuminating the icy fields.

The truck skated around a corner, and shot over the crest of the hill.

Leah grabbed the dash, bracing herself. "Slow down," she begged. "You're scaring me."

"What about our band? What about us?"

They'd have their band, she promised. After high school. "Don't do this, Todd." *Please.*

A cruiser nosed out of a clearing, at the foot of the hill. "Look—" She tugged his arm. *A cop.* They had coke in the glove compartment. A gun. "We'll go to jail."

He didn't give a shit about a jail. "We had plans," he bellowed. "We're a team."

A deer leapt over the stone wall, and stopped dead, caught in the headlights.

He didn't give a shit about anything—except *her.*

"A deer," Leah screamed. "Stop."

His eyes widened, and he slammed on the brakes, sending the truck into a spin.

A blue light pulsed, the cruiser's siren screaming.

Oh my God. Her hands flew to her face. *The wall.*

The impact rang in her ears, the gruesome sound of metal—grinding her ribs.

A light flashed. She pulled for a breath. Justine floated above her, her sister's eyes twinkling like stars. Now they were running, she and Justine, chasing each other. Into the sun.

Todd howled, his voice braying.

Leah gasped, struggling for air. She was cold, cold. Spittle dribbled out of her mouth.

Her door squeaked open. "Leah?" She reached for the policeman, her arms heavy. He brushed her forehead, lifted her gently out of her seat. "I've got you, baby. Help is on the way."

"Mommy?" she gurgled, the words ringing in her ears. "Want my mommy."

"She's on the way, baby." He laid her on the cold pavement, the deep dark sky overhead.

Starry, starry night.

Am I gonna die?

Shuffling, a struggle. "Got him," she heard a cop say. *Gun. Coke. Back up on the way.*

Officer Johnson covered her with a blanket, his face hovering over hers.

Am I dying?

That's it, Jus. Listen. One two three four. Let the music lead you. She held Justine's hand, and she and her sister danced around her room. *BOOM, boom, boom. One two three four.* They were lying in the yard now, making snow angels, the brilliant blue sky overhead, their mother calling from the front door, offering hot chocolate. With her foot, her mom pushes a shovel into the dirt in their backyard. She's digging a grave for Hammy. "Not your fault, baby," she says. "All creatures die. That's part of God's plan."

She felt policeman's lips. Tasted his hot breath in her mouth. "That's it, Leah. Hang on."

A door slammed shut. In the distance, a siren rang, its scream drawing closer.

She moaned, pain shooting through her hips. Her toes were numb.

Officer Johnson straddled her. "Come on, baby." Pushed on her chest. "Stay with me."

Leah danced into the sun, the warm light on her face, her flowered skirt swishing around her thighs, a halo of daisies in her flowing blond hair. *Ring around the Rosie.* She's holding hands with Justine. Her dad, her mom. In a circle, twirling. *Pocket full of posies,* her mother sings, her voice pure and sweet as a hand bell. *One. Two. Three.* They bend their knees, all four of them together, and leap, holding onto one another, laughing. *We all. Fall—*

"Breathe. Stay with us, baby. Breathe."

She felt a warm hand on her forehead. Leah—her father's voice. Her head floated. *Hi,* she said. *Hi.* Her sister was crying. *Jus— it's OK. I'm right here.* The weight again on her chest.

"Come on, baby." *Breathe.*

My God, her face. Her mother squeezed Leah's hand. "Leah, sweetie. I'm here."

Mommy. A board slid under Leah's back. *I love you,* she whispered, and felt body, on the stretcher, being carried away. *Mommy, I love you.*

Epilogue

Confirmation

March

It's snowing, unseasonable weather for late-March, a swirl of spiraling crystals. The weather steadily worsens as Justine stands, to the left of the doors, in the vestibule at the back of the church, waiting for the Confirmation Mass to begin. A door opens, an icy wind rushing in. A family enters the church, huddled together to shield themselves from the eddying wind, the father stamping his feet. Through the open door, Justine watches the whirling snow, blanketing the sidewalks, the trees, covering the sign on the lawn in front of the church. All around her, her classmates whisper behind cupped palms about the parties, the fancy receptions their parents are hosting after the Mass. Justine's parents and grandparents are seated in the pew directly behind the pews reserved for the Confirmation candidates. Yesterday, her grandparents flew up from Philadelphia, checked into a nearby hotel. Her parents invited them to dinner after the Mass, at an Italian restaurant in Westford, for "an intimate celebration," her mother had called it.

Leah is supposed to be here today. Since her accident, Leah refuses to leave the house. She spends all her time in her room, reading or listening to music—soulful, introspective songs by the Cowboy Junkies or Lucinda Williams or Sarah McLachlan or Emmylou Harris. Once a week, she takes a taxi to the home of the tutor the town of Cortland provides. Leah is lucky to be alive. The pelvic fracture, her doctors said, could have killed her. When the air bag deployed, she'd also broken her nose. After the reconstructive surgery, scheduled for early next week, she will look normal again.

Now, Leah says, she looks like a monster, her nose buckled, the bridge flat.

The Cardinal wears a white chasuble trimmed in gold; a precious Mitre sits on his head. In his right hand, he carries a staff. He assumes his place at the head of the line. The pastor slides into line behind the Cardinal. The lector lines up behind the pastor, and behind the lector, Justine.

Justine adjusts the wreath of baby's breath in her hair. Her white Confirmation robe falls to mid-calf. Under the robe, she wears Leah's plaid skirt, her sister's blue silk blouse.

The organist strikes the first note, and a hush falls over the church.

The congregation stands as the Cardinal steps into the nave. The church is packed. Parents at the centers of the pews crane their necks, for a better look at their children. A camera clicks and a lone soprano leads the choir in song. The cantor raises her hands and the congregation joins in. Justine enters the church proper. To her left, someone snaps a picture. She stares straight ahead. Sprays of white lilies in gilded vases line the steps leading to the sacristy. On the altar, white lilies decorate the marble candle-bench below the crucifix. Near the podium burns a thick white candle etched in gold—a symbol of life, a symbol of light. At the foot of the altar, Justine bows her head, takes a sharp left. The candidates behind Justine process in pairs to the end of the aisle, and the lines split, one turning left, the other right. The candidates file past the pews, proceed to their designated rows.

When the song ends and the candidates are settled in place, the Cardinal spreads his arms majestically, and recites the opening prayer. "The Lord be with you."

"And also with you," the congregation responds.

Justine is scheduled to speak immediately after the Gospel. She takes her cues from the cantor, standing and kneeling when she does. Justine's mind wanders, her fingers numb.

She stares at the pale purple paint on her nails, pushes her cuticles, picks at a hangnail on the side of her pinky. Justine feels like a hypocrite. Someone else should be giving this speech, someone whose family is normal, whose family hasn't fallen apart. Someone who isn't a mess.

She tried to beg out. This morning, when she went downstairs, her mom was in the kitchen, setting the table, the griddle warming, a bowl of batter for blueberry pancakes on the counter. Her father was upstairs in his office, checking his telephone and e-mail messages.

A month ago, her father found a new job. He makes less money, but he enjoys the work, he told her. He likes the people he works with. Best of all, he said happily, "no more traveling." From now on, he would be working out of his office at home. Her mother has returned to work, too. They've put their house on the market. All these changes, Justine thinks, and for what?

"Morning, sweetie," her mom said. "Today's your big day. I made pancakes for you."

Blueberry—Leah's favorite. "I don't feel good," Justine said. "I can't do that talk today."

"You don't have a choice, Justine. You made a commitment."

"I think I have a fever."

Her mother placed her hand on Justine's forehead. "You do feel a little warm."

Justine perked up.

"But you don't have a fever."

I should have put a hot cloth on my forehead, she thinks. *Should have barfed on the floor.*

When her father returned to the kitchen, Justine aired the same complaints.

"Sorry, sweetie." Her father exchanged a look with her mom. "But we have a surprise."

As a Confirmation gift, her parents had bought her a puppy. Justine forced a tight smile.

She feels a tap on her shoulder, blinks, not quite sure where she is. When she looks up, she sees Miss Green smiling down at her. "Luck," whispers Miss Green. "You'll be terrific."

Holding on to the rail in front of her pew, Justine drags herself up. Her body tingles, her knees weak. She thinks she might faint. She steadies herself, glides across the front of the pew, to the sacristy, up the two steps. On the altar, she bows her head, bending a knee.

She crosses herself, takes a ceremonious left, and approaches the lectern.

There must be a thousand people in the audience. Justine scans the crowd, picks out the faces she recognizes. She smiles when she sees Holly, with her mother, in a pew near the back. Officer Johnson, his wife, each of them holding a baby. Hope. Hope's mother, Mindy. Bobby Sullivan, his wife, Mary Ann. Coach Thomas. The principal of Justine's school. The principal of the high school. Leah's old dean. Cissy Hanson is here. The girls from the soccer team. All of these people have come here for someone, a sister, a cousin, a niece or nephew. A neighbor.

She lays her folded sheet of paper on the slanted desk of the lectern.

Her classmates fidget in their seats. Justine's grandmother is beaming. Her mother adjusts her wide-brimmed hat, her hair neatly swept back, stray curls framing her tired face.

Her father sends Justine a silent message. What's going on? Why hasn't she started?

Justine swallows, blessing herself. "My dear friends," she begins. "The Holy Spirit—" She planned to say "in receiving." *In receiving the Holy Spirit.* Her father nods, encouraging her to continue. Two thousand eyes are focused on her. She breathes deeply, looks out again at the audience, down at her paper, her cheat sheet. She'd intended to recite the speech by heart. But the words have slipped away. She flattens the paper, the crackling amplified by the microphone.

"My dear," she stammers. She can't do this without Leah. Justine wrote this speech for her sister. What will happen if she simply steps down? Says thank you, and returns to her pew?

Incense drifts across the sacristy, the smell pungent, sweet.

The director winks. "Doing fine," she mouths.

Am not, Justine wants to say. *I'm not fine at all.*

Her mother's eyes are partially closed, her lips moving. Her mother is praying. She's saying a prayer. Justine's throat catches. She swallows again.

"Dear Friends, in receiving the Holy Sp—"

The wind howls, rattling the stained glass windows depicting the agony of Christ, and the church falls silent. Beyond the stained glass windows, the snow roils, whipping in circles.

Somebody coughs.

The audience waits patiently.

Justine's eyes sting. She stares until the words on her paper dissolve. All her life, Justine believed God would take care of her. If she prayed, long enough, hard enough, if she believed, truly believed in Him, God would answer her prayers—a child's misguided beliefs, she sees now. She prayed fervently. She had faith. Yet, in her time of greatest need, God abandoned her.

A baby cries. His mother lays him over her shoulder.

Justine takes in the altar, hard and sturdy and real, constructed of wood, material—like her—born of this earth. She takes in the white eyelet cover, the golden chalice she once believed, literally believed, held the blood of our Lord. Whose blood is it, she wonders, inside that cup? Leah's? Her own? The blood of the parishioners?

The blood of them all.

In the balcony, the lone violinist, in front of the choir, tucks her instrument under her arm. The choir shuffles. Startled, the violinist turns toward the wing. Smiling, she nods, and steps aside. Justine's breath catches as Leah takes the violinist's place at the rail. Leah raises a palm, her face lit by a radiant smile. Justine raises her hand. Her sister, Justine thinks, is the most beautiful person she has ever laid eyes on. *And she's come here for me.*

The congregation follows Justine's gaze to the balcony. The Cardinal smiles beatifically.

"In receiving the Holy Spirit," Justine says, her voice wavering, "we become full-fledged members of God's family."

A young man, not more than twenty years old, in the row behind Justine's parents, nods in agreement. Justine's mother reaches for her father's hand, their faces finally at peace.

"We're a family," Justine continues, "children. Brothers and sisters."

A family. All of us. The beautiful and the ugly. The perfect, the broken.

Her pulse echoes inside her temples, blood pulsing through her neck, her shoulders, the tips of her fingers. At home, Justine's brand new puppy, a golden retriever, waits in her crate. I'll call her Daisy, Justine thinks, for the crown of flowers Leah wore the day she was confirmed.

This is who we are. "Family. For God. For one another. . ."

As she speaks, her voice grows stronger, the words flowing into the microphone, and out through the speakers. Justine imagines a sound, from somewhere deep inside, a sound rich and full, a nameless sound, ethereal, free of words, drifting in waves, rolling outward, touching her parents, her grandparents, her friends, the people here, in this church, rippling farther, beyond the church, through the trees and the swirling snow, through the center, across town, to all people and all places under the sun, reaching past pain and affliction, beyond the confines of this crazy, wonderful, battered old world, the sound, like the beat of her heart, circling back. *Touching her sister.* For the moment, Justine is perfectly calm. *Brothers and Sisters.* Justine places her hand over her heart. *Sisters,* she thinks. And rising to the balls of her feet, she goes on.

Author's Notes

Real People, Real Places, Real Things

I am grateful to Bob Sullivan, owner-operator of Sullivan Farms Ice Cream in Tyngsboro, MA, and Dorothy Klein, owner and designer of Ruby Slippers Designs, in Newton, MA, for allowing me to include them in this book.

Bob Sullivan

I met Bob Sullivan in 1990, when our eldest daughter, Jen, began working at an ice cream shop owned by his older brother. A kind, generous, good-natured manager, Bob inspires the devotion of his employees, many of whom work for him through college and even into their late twenties.

For more than 10 years, Bob has sponsored, organized and directed the annual John Carson Fourth of July 2 Mile Road Race. This memorial event for John Carson, a talented Chelmsford High distance runner hit by a train during a practice run, began as a fun race for local runners. Today, this highly competitive event draws 2000 athletes from across the US and 60,000 spectators.

Bob and his wife, Mary Ann, opened Sullivan Farms Homemade Ice Cream, on the bank of the Merrimack River, in 1997. Customers immediately flocked to the store. With thirty employees and eight serving windows, Sullivan Farms makes and serves over 100 flavors of ice cream— my favorite, Almond Joy—as well as sherbet, Italian ice and many varieties of yogurt. For info about the John Carson 2 Mile Road Race or directions to Sullivan Farms Homemade Ice Cream, please visit their website: www.sullivanfarmsicecream.com.

Interview with Terri Giuliano Long

Q: How did you come up with the idea for "In Leah's Wake?" What was it that stuck with you so much that you just had to grow this idea into a novel?

A: Years ago, I wrote a series of feature articles about families with drug and alcohol-addicted teens. Their heartbreaking stories stayed with me. When I began In Leah's Wake, our daughters were teenagers. I knew, as a parent, the feeling of being frightened, concerned for your children's future, I observed the kids around us, and I remembered the families I'd met years before. While Leah goes to an extreme that, thank goodness, we never experienced, all of this played on my conscious and subconscious mind, so her rebellion was easy to imagine.

Q: How have your own experiences as a mother of four factored into the plotting and characterization of the novel?

A: Our daughters grew up in the same family, yet at times their perspectives are wildly divergent. Naturally, being older, my husband and I see and experience situations differently from any of our children. I tried to show this with the Tyler family by switching point of view, at times retelling and overlapping their stories.

Q: Is there any of you in "Leah's Wake?" Which character did you identify with or admire the most?

A: Tough question! I love all the characters. And there is a part of me in all of them. It was Justine, though, who kept the book alive in my mind. I worked on this novel for years; whenever I'd think about letting go, moving on to something else, I'd see her image or hear her voice in my head, and feel compelled to keep going.

347

Q: **The Tylers are a well-to-do and relatively happy family; their environment does not seem like a hotbed for teenage rebellion. Why did you choose this family as the setting for your story?**

A: I don't see socioeconomics as a determining factor. Poor kids are more likely than the wealthy to be victimized by drug- or alcohol-related violence, so we hear their stories more often. That doesn't mean kids in well-to-do towns don't rebel. Kids drink, often in secret, and the current trend is to abuse prescription drugs.

It's terrifying, I know, to watch kids get off track. Frankly, though, the young are supposed to rebel. The notion that kids ought to be perfect, clones—or worse—best friends of their parents is crippling to them. If kids are to become creative, independent adults, they have to set their own agenda, think for themselves, which often means breaking away from parental rules. I thought, and still think, zero tolerance polices are ridiculous. It's wrong to ostracize kids who rebel, and cowardly to shame them. Instead, communities should pull together, support and encourage all kids—that's one of the social issues I tried to address in my novel.

Q: **What is the take-away message of "In Leah's Wake?" How would you like the reader to feel upon exiting the world of the Tylers?**

A: The epitaph, from The Grand Inquisitor, says it best: "everyone is really responsible to all men for all men and for everything." The Tyler family is far from perfect, but they love one another. Our flaws make us human and that humanity connects us. I hope readers feel that sense of connection—and hope.

Q: Looking at the bigger picture, what do you hope to bring to the literary world? How will your work have an impact?

A: While my stories differ—I'm currently working on a psychological thriller with a historical twist—they always tie back to the family, the ways we love, yet too often hurt one another, the grief, sorrow, revelation, the joy. I hope to entertain readers, while sharing a sense of lasting hope and deep emotional connection.

Q: What's next for Terri Giuliano Long? Do you have any other novels in the works? When will they be ready for the readers' enjoyment?

A: My new novel, Nowhere to Run, takes place in the White Mountains, in northern New Hampshire. A year after the brutal, unsolved murder of her six-year-old daughter, Abby Minot, once an award-winning writer, now on hiatus, accepts her first assignment—a profile of the philanthropic Chase family, kin of the popular New Hampshire senator and presidential hopeful, Matthias Chase.

In her initial research, Abby glimpses darkness under the shiny veneer. Digging deeper, she uncovers a shocking web of lies and betrayal, dating back to the nineteenth century. Abby finds herself trapped—between an editor obsessed with uncovering the truth and the town and family who will stop at nothing to ensure it stays hidden.

I hope to complete the novel this fall.

Discussion Topics
In Leah's Wake

1. "In Leah's Wake" is told from the perspective of five characters—Zoe, Will, Leah, Justine, and Jerry. With whom did you identify the most? Which character did you have the most difficulty understanding? How do the multiple viewpoints weave together to form a cohesive story?

2. Leah often changes her mind. One moment she misses her family, the next she hates them. She alternately wants to marry Todd and to break up with him. Why is Leah so fickle? Is this common of teenagers, or something unique to (or excessive in) Leah? Did you ever find yourself wanting to yell at her through the pages—to warn her that she was making the wrong decision?

3. If Leah had remained on the soccer team could the events of the story been prevented? What about if she had remained friends with Cissy? Are there any other what-ifs that stand out to you?

4. How does Leah's cutting her hair serve as a turning-point for her character? Which other changes to Leah's appearance, thought process, and behavior redirect the story?

5. The first time Leah runs away Zoe insists upon giving her space. Was this the right decision? Would you have reacted the same way had it been your child?

6. In the end, Justine presents some worrying behavior. What causes her to unravel? Is it her desire for Leah to think she is cool? The impact of her sister's abandonment? Having to act as the caregiver while both of her parents struggled with their own issues? Will Justine revert back to her old self, or is she destined to follow in Leah's Wake?

7. Zoe and Will have very different ideas of what it means to be a good parent. Zoe wants to keep the peace, she wants to be liked. Will desires to keep his children safe, and to do this, he often responds in anger. Which parenting style did you iden-

tify with most? Would they have been more effective had they presented a united front? How does Leah drive a wedge between her parents?

8. Will's job situation becomes uncertain during the course of the novel. How does this difficulty play into the plot? How does it affect his character? Would he have been more level-headed in dealing with Leah and Todd had he not been under this added stress?

9. In the beginning of the novel, Zoe is a strong and capable woman. She leads self-improvement seminars and works as a therapist. As the story progresses, she slowly unravels finally developing an addition to Oxycotin. What drove her to this point? Do you believe she will be able to recover the life she lived before Leah's rebellion?

10. What role does Jerry play in the story? How does he help bring the family back together? Does he truly love Zoe, or is he just overwhelmed by being a new father? Does Zoe love him back? Is she truthful with Will about not having an affair?

11. Todd, Hope, and Lupo undeniably are negative influences on Leah, but at times the author discusses each of these characters with compassion and understanding. Were these three really "bad" people, or did they just come from bad circumstances? Did you find yourself going back and forth between distaste and affinity for these characters?

12. Discuss the significance of the bracelet Zoe buys for Leah, Stormy. Does the birthstone ring she presents to Leah at Christmas hold an added significance; what is it? Are there any other important symbols in the story? What about the rope swing? Justine's science project? The strangled hamster? Zoe's flashbacks of a young Leah?

13. Music plays a huge role in the story. From Zoe and Will's affinity for older tunes (such as those by the Beatles, Tom Petty, and Van Morrison) to Leah's obsession with Ani diFranco, and Justine's attempts to understand rap. How did these musical allusions add to the plot and help us to better understand the characters?

14. Thematically, what struck you most about this novel? Did it lead you to contemplate any deeper questions about family, responsibility, and life?

15. How much control should parents exert over a child's life? Do Zoe and Will push Leah too hard? Is it necessary for parents to push their children in order for them to succeed? How do Zoe and Will's actions protect and in what ways do they fail their children? Does their intervention help or does it back-fire? How might Zoe and Will have better handled Leah's rebellion? How do micro-managed children fare later in life?

16. What might cause a seemingly "perfect" child to rebel? Is Leah's anxiety caused by her parents' expectations or is it genetic, part of her personality? Is there such a thing as a perfect child? If so, how would you define the perfect child?

17. Do zero-tolerance policies work? Why or Why not? Are they necessary? Should schools ban adolescents from activities that could keep them out of trouble? Did Coach Thomas respond properly to Leah's outburst? Should Will and Zoe have exercised greater tolerance? Or were they too lax?

18. How do parents prevent children from falling under the influence of the wrong people? How might Zoe and Will have prevented Leah's relationship with Todd from getting serious? Should they have banned Todd from their home? Why or why not?

19. Are a child's personality and conduct influenced primarily by nature? Nurture? Both? How are Justine and Leah's personalities a result of their parents' influence? Might parts of Justine and Leah's personalities be inherent? If so, which?

20. Hillary Clinton said it takes a community to raise a child. What role does a community play in the lives of its children? Is the community responsible for the actions of an ostracized child? Why or why not? How do gossip and judgment affect adolescents? Are the effects always negative?

Continue reading to preview the psychological thriller
Nowhere to Run
by Terri Giuliano Long

Nowhere to Run

Where do you run when you have no place left to hide?

Prologue

1851

They found the Chase girl in late spring, when the black flies
were spawning.

After a long, violent winter, the snow had finally melted and
the Earth thawed, the sodden New Hampshire spring turning the
roads to sludge. The Chase House, an elegant Queen Anne
Gambrel, sat at the foot of Mount Washington, on a knoll
overlooking the town of New Madbury. Three hundred rods
behind the house, runoff from the mountain cascaded over a
granite ledge, forming the head of the Indian River. In spring, the
bloated river ran swift and hard across the meadow and arced
west, skirting the town.

In the kitchen of the Chase house, the colored servant, Mag,
was bent over a wooden trough, kneading dough for the week's
bread, her large hands turning, folding, pressing the satiny disc. A
cool breeze blew through the open window, rustling the lace
curtains, the perfume of blossoming lilacs masking the gamy odor
of yesterday's mutton.

In a cramped garret above the rear ell, Mag's sons lay sleeping, a hunk of lamb for their breakfast tucked in the pocket of her
apron. This morning, their wait would be long. While the dough
proofed, after she'd skimmed and churned the milk, and hauled
water in from the well, a sack of coffee beans had to be roasted
and ground. Mag sang quietly as she worked—*swing low, sweet*

chariot, coming for to carry me home—her rich contralto voice accompanied by the distant drum of the swollen Indian River.

Outside, a horse whinnied and a farmhand dismounted noisily, babbling.

Curious, she wiped her aching hands on her apron, and strode to the window.

A dozen men had gathered by the open door at the front of the barn.

As the boy's words registered on the faces of the elders, a terrible urgency penetrated their hushed voices—"girl" and "nigger-boy" the only words Mag could make out.

The sun rose over the mountain, swaddling the earth in amethyst shadow.

Mag and Willis, her eldest, rode at a safe distance behind the search party, Mag, seated behind her son, on the crupper of the chestnut mare Mr. Chase had given her the spring before last, when he moved his wife and children up here from Portsmouth.

Her son rode proudly, his back erect, his legs loosely draped.

Terrified, she'd woken him from a deep slumber.

The baby had stirred as she entered their tiny moonlit room. Mag nursed him briefly, stroking his cheek, rocked him back to his dreams, and laid him on her pallet, under the window. Seven-year-old Emmett, her sweet, blue-eyed boy, slept beside Willis, his skinny brown back tucked in the hollow between his big brother's knees and chest.

She lowered herself to the floor by her eldest, pressed her lips to his ear. Willis?

He opened one eye. Mama? Sat, blinking. Mama, what is it?

Wha'choo know bout a girl, Willis? Tell me, boy. Choo been doin' all night?

Nothin. I been here, Mama. You seen me. Don't know nothin bout no girl.

I looked over Jordan and what did I see, Coming for to carry me home?

The nag trekked dutifully over the rocky field and across the hilly south meadow.

As they rode, Mag's arms and legs turned to granite and crumbled. Fear begged her to turn back, and fear urged her on. Her mama, the daughter of a preacher, had taught her early to open her eyes, always be on the lookout—no good ever came of not knowing.

If thou shalt not watch, sayeth the Lord, I will come on thee as a thief.

At the fringe of the woods, Willis slowed the horse to a walk and they slipped in to the forest. The river surged, and small white Mourning doves swooped and took wing.

The search party, to the fore, progressed slowly along the bank of the river, the riders swatting fruitlessly at the swarming black flies, the horses switching back and forth, twenty rods east, twenty west, the boggy terrain like quicksand under their hoofs.

Across the river, an enormous gray moose tracked their progress.

Confused, the young farmhand had difficulty locating the tree. "It's in close neighborhood with the river," the bewildered boy cried. "Close neighborhood." *Close.*

Light beaconed through the eye of a needle. The boy pointed, nodding furiously, and reined his horse sideways, giving way to his elders. As the lead horse entered the clearing, the rider pulled up short. His shoulders sagged. Stiffening, he raised his rifle, signaling the others, an agitated drone buzzing down the line as the party closed ranks.

Willis halted the nag by a cluster of white pines, at the outer edge of the clearing.

Squinting, Mag watched through a breach in the cavalry wall, her heart heavy.

The child's slight body swayed in a soft vernal wind, her skirt fused indecently to her legs, revealing the contours of her slender thighs. Her left foot was bare. Her tiny black boot lay in the dirt, the heel buried in muck, the narrow toe box pointing to Heaven.

Her name was Cornelia. She was thirteen years old, a year younger than Willis. Mag covered her mouth, her nipples tightening with the memory of suckling this child.

Crickets chirred.

At last, one of the men unsheathed his knife, and began sawing the rope.

In the morning light, the girl's flaxen hair shimmered like silk.

Black fly bites had raised angry red pustules on her flesh. Pale blue eyes bulged from a grotesquely swollen face, and her mouth was contorted, her rosebud lips frozen in a silent plea—

"Nigger," a voiced hissed. "Goddamn nigger boy."

Mag's heart rang in her ears. "Willis—" Gently, so as not to startle him, she touched her son's wrist, and he steered the nag back, and away from the clearing.

A band of angels. Coming for to carry me home.

One

Simulacrum

The heat was stifling.

The Saab's air conditioner had been rumbling for ten minutes, warm, dusty air blasting from the vents. I flipped the vents, restricting the airflow, and opened the moon roof. We were two hours from our destination, the Chase House Inn, in New Madbury, New Hampshire. Seeing as the kids and I planned to stay at the inn for the month of July, I saw no point in stopping for roadside service along the way. Once we were settled, I figured I'd ask around, find a reputable mechanic, one I could trust to do the job right.

Sweltering, I fanned the scoop neck of my tank.

Callie sighed, tucking her knees, curling like a kitten in the passenger seat. My daughter was small for twelve, barely four-ten, a late bloomer like me. She'd dozed off holding her journal—a hot pink notebook with sparkly white butterflies on the cover.

With my fingers, I combed her damp bangs back, out of her eyes.

My son was sprawled across the backseat, playing with his PS2, his head bopping to a tune on his iPod. Jack and I had given him the PS2 for his birthday last year—my husband's bright idea, not mine. I lost on the Venus-Mars rule. "All the guys have them," Jack had argued. "What's the big deal?" Let's see: gaming is a waste of time. The games the boys his age liked were violent; they glorified sick, sadistic behavior. We bought him Dance Revolution, DJ Hero, Pro Evolution Soccer. With friends—did Jess think we were stupid?—we'd caught him playing Mortal Kombat, Grand Theft Auto. Assassin's Creed.

From my hobo bag, I fished a pack of peppermint gum. "Jess—" I tapped my head, a signal to remove his headphones. "Why don't you put the PS2 away for a while. Read a book." I'd insisted he bring his summer reading. Jesse had been an honor student since the first grade. Last year, his grades had slipped and he'd been placed on academic probation. Jack, an alumnus, had called in a favor to keep him enrolled at Choate. If Jess hoped to graduate in a year, he'd have to hit the books, pull up his GPA.

Oliver, our eight-year-old Pug, pawed the door of his traveling crate, whimpering. Poor little guy. He detested his crate. I'd set it on top of my suitcase, so he could see us, the cooler wedging it in place. He had to be roasting back there, in the bed of the wagon.

"Jess?" Catching his eye, I said, "Drop a few ice cubes in Oli's water bowl? And tighten your seatbelt. If we have to stop fast, I don't want you flying through the windshield."

The classical station I'd been listening to lost its signal and turned to static. I switched it off, plugged a quiet Copeland suite, *Appalachian Spring,* into the player.

Looking up, I noticed the sign for Dartmouth College, and felt a bittersweet tug.

I'd met Jack and my first husband, Cody, at Dartmouth. The White Mountains had been our sanctuary. Whenever we needed a reprieve, a break from our studies, we'd pile into Jack's Jeep, and drive to Conway, passing through New Madbury on the way. In good weather, we camped; if it was too cold or rainy to sleep outdoors, we rented a room in a lodge. The summer after graduation we worked for the Appalachian Mountain Club, leading volunteer trail maintenance crews. On our days off, we hiked. If we were too tired or hung-over to hike, if we needed space, time away from the rest of the crew, we'd raft on the Indian River. I'd been back only once since then, to spread Cody's ashes.

"Mom?" Jesse rattled my arm. "Can't you do something?" He mopped his sweaty face with his forearm. "I'm dying back here."

Dying? Please. They say girls are drama queens. I'd put my money on kings. "Open the windows back there. A crack, or it'll get too noisy. And damn it, Jesse, tighten that seatbelt. Don't make me say it again."

Heaving a sigh, he yanked theatrically at his belt. "OK?" he snarled, and flopped back down, propping his raunchy teenage feet on his sister's headrest. "Happy?"

"Yes." It took restraint, but I resisted matching his tone. "I am. Thank you."

We needed this time away—badly, I thought.

After Molly, our youngest, died last June I'd gone AWOL, physically present, utterly absent in spirit. I'd stolen a year from Callie and Jess—a year I could never give back—and I wanted badly to make things right. I'm ashamed to admit this: I'd nearly backed out. My anxiety had been building all week. I dreaded leaving home, the only place I felt physically connected to Molly. I kept wandering into her room, opening drawers, folding and refolding the size six clothes I couldn't bear to give away, winding myself into a knot. Yesterday, I called to cancel our reservation. Had the receptionist not put me on hold, forcing me to think and rethink my priorities, I'd have bailed. I was glad I'd forced myself to do this. I vowed to make the most of this trip. Key aspects of my work—interviews, research—would have to be done when people or resources were available. Otherwise, I'd work nights, early mornings, when the kids were in bed. Days, we'd swim, hike, listen to music—simple activities we rarely found time for at home.

Terri Giuliano Long grew up in the company of stories both of her own making and as written by others. Books offer her a zest for life's highs and comfort in its lows. She's all-too-happy to share this love with others as a novelist and as a lecturer at Boston College.

While her passion lies in the written word, Terri's primary inspiration comes from her interest in existential philosophy and her observations of people and human nature. Her stories expand upon the subtle truths and what-ifs of everyday life. No matter where her stories journey, they always tie back to the family— the ways we love yet, in loving, too often hurt one another, the grief, the sorrow, the revelation, and the joy. Terri's goal is to offer lasting hope and deep emotional connection in a compact and entertaining package.

Her life outside of books is devoted to her family. In her spare time, she enjoys walking, traveling to far-flung places, and meeting interesting people. True to her Italian-American heritage, she's an enthusiastic cook and she loves fine wine and good food. In an alternate reality, she could have been very happy as an international food writer.

Terri loves connecting with people who share her passions. To learn more, please visit her website www.tglong.com. Or connect with her by e-mail at terri@tglong.com or on Twitter @tglong.

CPSIA information can be obtained at www.ICGtesting.com
Printed in the USA
LVOW041807211111

255956LV00002B/61/P